"The 'secret' is out—Patti Lacy is easily one of the most gifted authors in Christian fiction today, and her stunning new novel, *The Rhythm of Secrets* is absolute proof. From the delicious jazz-filled streets of New Orleans to the seedy underworld of Bangkok, Thailand, embark on a journey that transcends the mere pages of a book to become a riveting life experience. No longer a "well-kept secret," Patty Lacy is a master storyteller who speaks to the soul with a powerful and unique rhythm all her own, weaving a tale so rich with emotion that story and reader become one."

—**Julie Lessman**, author of *The Daughters of Boston* series and *A Hope Undaunted*

"Patti Lacy weaves together another beautifully written and haunting story in *The Rhythm of Secrets*. I couldn't put it down!"

—**Melanie Dobson**, award-winning author of *The Black Cloister*

"Patti Lacy has written yet another absorbing novel with words as dazzling and rhythmic as the musical world in which her characters live. *The Rhythm of Secrets* is a stirring story of faith and endurance that will keep readers turning the page until every last secret has been revealed."

—**Tina Ann Forkner**, author of *Ruby Among Us* and *Rose House*

"Patti Lacy is known for riveting tales that span continents, decades, and lives. *The Rhythm of Secrets* is another great Patti Lacy story, this time of a woman whose past secret lives have caught up with her. Captivating, heart-rending, and heart-expanding, *The Rhythm of Secrets* is a vibrant journey across time in search of the greatest truth of all: grace."

—**Tosca Lee**, author of *Havah: The Story of Eve* and *Demon: A Memoir*

The Rhythm of Secrets

A Novel

PATTI LACY

Kregel
Publications

The Rhythm of Secrets: A Novel
© 2011 by Patti Lacy

Published by Kregel Publications, a division of Kregel, Inc., P.O. Box 2607, Grand Rapids, MI 49501.

Scripture taken from the King James Version.

Library of Congress Cataloging-in-Publication Data
Lacy, Patti, 1955-
   The rhythm of secrets : a novel / Patti Lacy.
   p. cm.
1. Spouses of clergy—Fiction. 2. Birthmothers—Fiction. 3. Mothers and sons—Fiction. 4. Psychological fiction. I. Title.

PS3612.A3545R59   2011   813'.6—dc22   2010042941

ISBN 978-0-8254-2674-2

Printed in the United States of America
11 12 13 14 15 / 5 4 3 2 1

To my family at Grace Church in Normal
for not only loving this weird writer,
but for liking me

And to my agent, Natasha Kern,
for nudging me toward the precipice
so I can spread my wings and fly

Acknowledgments

The poignant memories of Sandy Sperrazza, featured by *Chicago Tribune* reporter Gail Rosenblum in July of 2007, birthed this story. Blessings to Sandy, who exposed painful memories to help me get this right.

Without the expertise of Vietnam veterans Buddy Anderson and Cary Young and Thai nationals "Winn" and "Pam," I could never have forded the exotic yet treacherous waters of Vietnam-era Thailand. Y'all, thanks for your patience, humor, and generosity.

Fred Hatfield, lifelong New Orleans resident and tour guide, encouraged and educated me from day one of my romp through World War II–era Crescent City. Thank you, Fred, for invaluable suggestions and keen recall. Nonagenarian New Orleans native Henry Schmidt replayed his Quarter memories with such accuracy, I traced his "path" on a map. Michael Williams of New Orleans Fire Museum and Craig Fata, firefighter, walked me through the emotional and physical manifestations of a 1940s four-alarm fire. Oliver Delacroix, Gentilly native, master gardener, and another active nonagenarian, kept his cell phone near his onions and peppers to field calls from a curious writer.

Thank you, Gracia Maria Lopez, who located precious Moody documents, and then made sure I handled them with special gloves. I will long remember Millie Benson, who devoted her lunch hour to helping me "see" Moody with 1950s glasses. Sally Pullen and David Hirst, your treasure trove of musical knowledge enriched this manuscript—and me—in a joyous way. Thanks.

Chapter 1

Rhapsody on a Theme of Paganini

Spring 1969, Chicago, Illinois

Stormy days call for Rachmaninoff. Rain thrummed the window and blended with cantata chords Sheila Franklin coaxed from her piano. Soon she'd be done with the choir piece and could continue her Rachmaninoff affair. Or maybe she'd play jazz, wild and free, though Edward had forbidden it. But Edward wasn't here . . .

"Jesus is love." She sang as she played, but her movements jerked rather than flowed; a second-year music student could do as well. Eager to be done with it, she glanced at the clock. Ten more minutes, that would do it. Ten more minutes, and she'd play the jazz she'd heard when Papa set a needle on a scratched record in their marvelous Esplanade parlor. Or Rachmaninoff. Yes, Rachmaninoff would be better. Safer. Sheila sat up straight, precisely positioned her hands on the keyboard, but her past refused to be disciplined. Her past . . .

Oh, New Orleans! Images of the noisy French Quarter and Maman's heart-shaped face pulled her into a keyboard promenade, slow and sassy, toward the Mississippi. A tugboat sounded . . . or a wrong note. She glanced at her hands, again heard the musical hiccup. She hadn't missed a key. It was that darned phone, threatening to shut down a riotous Mardi Gras parade. Irritation clapped through her. She continued to pound the keys, but the wretched thing buzzed insistently.

When icy resentment froze her hands, she stared at them. Her diamond solitaire dazzled her eye and reminded her of her commitment eighteen years ago. She'd agreed to interruptions like this when she'd married Edward Franklin . . . and his congregation. Life, death, or a dozen things in between waited at the other end of the line; the knowledge propelled her toward his phone. She and Edward had battened down their marriage with the surety, the safety, of Christ. And it was enough, Lord. Yes. It would have to be enough.

As she moved to his study, she kneaded her knuckles but could do nothing for the memories. Beautiful memories. Painful memories. The lonely Russian composer understood—his music affirmed it—but Rachmaninoff would have to wait.

She picked up the phone from its perch on Edward's rolltop desk. "Hello?"

Static answered, and a noise like the wings of a large bird taking flight. She leaned against the desk, reminding herself to be polite, even if it was Mr. O'Leary, ringing up Edward from the pay phone outside the neighborhood pub. Or someone who needed money. "Franklin residence. Can I help you?"

"Is this Sylvia Allen?"

She tried to breathe; nearly choked. Her elbows banged against solid oak. Nobody knew she'd once been Sylvia Allen except . . . What was this? Blackmail?

The room whirled, rows of Bible commentaries reduced to smears of gold and blue against a wash of brown. Only the solidity of Edward's desk kept her from crumbling to the floor.

When Edward found out about Sylvia Allen, her marriage would crumble, like a mansion built on sand. She would crumble, all her secrets exposed. Who would dare do this? She gripped the phone and stumbled into Edward's chair. The telephone cord stretched taut, but the connection held. Her mouth opened. Nothing came out.

"Hello? Are you there?"

This is a man's voice. Could it be?

"Mrs. Allen?"

It's not a blackmailer. It's . . . him. Intuition set a wildfire ablaze in a heart accustomed, with his absence, to a sputtering light. He'd found her, after all these years. Heat raced to her limbs and set off sparks in her fingertips.

"Y-yes. I'm Sylvia Allen," she whispered, though she longed to burst out in song. *He's alive!* As if she'd put on glasses, Edward's study came into brilliant focus. She took in the glorious words on Edward's book spines, the glowing face of a portrait of Jesus. Even the rain let up to gift a window view of scarlet Japanese maples and budding tulips. Alive! Like . . . him.

"This is Samuel."

Yes. I know, baby. An inner symphony began, the chords so dramatically chromatic, her slick hand struggled to hold the phone. "Y-yes," she managed.

"I'd like to see you, if it's possible."

If it's possible? I'd give my life for it. "Of course." Somehow she managed to answer in a controlled way. She cradled the receiver against her shoulder, wanting him to speak again and fill the tinny void. He wanted to see her. Could that mean he'd forgiven her?

"I hoped we could have dinner. Friday night. Do you know a place?"

She closed her eyes to concentrate. He had such a lovely voice!

"Ma'am? A place?"

His business-like tone muffled her music. She'd best gather her wits. "Y-yes." She cleared her throat to stall for time. Somewhere discreet. Out-of-the-way. "Yes," she repeated, "Etienne's." Her voice sounded shivery, distant. Like it belonged to someone else. And *wasn't* she somebody else? *Three* somebodys?

A time was arranged. Forty-eight agonizing hours away. The dial tone sounded, and she fell to her knees, shag carpet cushioning the phone receiver as it plunked next to her. "God," she prayed, "thank You." Whispery words fought their way out. "Make him understand. Make him love me." Her heart thumped the pleas until her chest ached, but she gladly accepted the pain. How long had she prayed for this moment? Twenty-two years, two months, and five days.

The chiming clock reminded her of choir practice, prayer service, and the shirts that needed to be pressed and hung in the clothes bag for Edward's three-day meeting in Dallas. An amazing coincidence, that meeting. A coincidence allowing her to arrange this other meeting with her Samuel.

She rose from the floor, hung up the phone, hobbled to the kitchen. As if she were in a stranger's home, she grazed the chair arm, the counter edge, yet she was ushering in hope, joy, and something else. Something looming, now that she'd had decades to pay the price for what she'd done. With one call, God had sent a precious, dangerous gift her way. Something akin to the explosive power tucked into an atom. As she gathered her things, she prayed that she could harness that power which had been stored up all these years and keep it from destroying them all. Her Edward. His church. Most of all, her Samuel.

◆ ◆ ◆

"Good morning, darling." Edward stepped into the kitchen, his face cleanly shaven, a robe belt cinching his waist. Flushed cheeks and alert eyes evidenced yet another sound night's sleep. Pulling her into the smell of old-fashioned shaving powder and deodorant soap, he pecked a kiss on her forehead and then sat before his cereal bowl and favorite mug. "Come pray with me," he ordered.

Nodding, she sat across from him, clasped his solid, sure hand, and listened. A man who preached twice on Sunday, Wednesday nights, had slots on radio and television, and had been invited to keynote in Dallas had mastered the art of prayer. Even with a traitor as a wife.

"What would I do without my Sheila?" He spooned yogurt and berries onto his cereal and smoothed a napkin into his lap. "I'll miss you."

Though she smiled a dewy morning smile, deception weighted the corners of her mouth. She'd laid out his packed garment bag on the spare bed, like she always did the morning of his flight. But today she couldn't wait for him to leave, couldn't wait to implement her plan.

"Would you mind if Thelma dropped off the bulletin Saturday morning? I'll review it Saturday when I get in."

Sheila nodded past a cringe. Though she generally avoided Edward's busybody secretary, agreeing to his request lightened the concrete slab lodged in her gut. She'd do anything for this husband she was about to betray. Except stop the betrayal.

"Do you really think the blue shirt works?" He rambled on about his suit, the weather, in a manner uncharacteristic for the confidant to senators, a general, ambassadors, even one president.

She nodded, patted his arm in the way he liked, though icy chills ran up her arms. Edward hadn't been worried in years. "Our foundation's okay, isn't it?"

"Never better. We've sat back and let the nation march to the beat of 'Make love, not war.'" Gray eyes settled on her. "High time we're heard here at home. Thank heaven the president and his men aren't wearing tie-dye and smoking weed. With their support, we'll return to the fundamentals that built this country. God in government. On campuses." Edward took her hand. "We're going to the top, Sheila."

Butterflies fluttered in her stomach. "Wh-what do you mean?" she eked out. That lawyer and their Washington friends had wanted a "feminine touch" on the foundation board. Of course she'd agreed. She'd given input when the men shut up long enough so she could be heard, the one soprano in an alto section bent on relegating "different drummers" to the practice room. Sure she'd formed alliances, in her quiet way. Quiet or not, every legal document bore her name. What they *thought* was her name. With her past, she never should have accepted a position. "What do you mean by the top?"

"We're speaking out against draft dodgers. Cowards masquerading as proponents of love and peace." He shrugged toward a rolled-up copy of the *Tribune*. "Stuff we read about every day."

"That's what this Dallas thing's about?" She toyed with a piece of toast, hoping a bite would settle nausea. She'd kept mum on Vietnam even though TV images of lumpy body bags made her question the entire mess. But if Edward made his bed with this so-called Christian Right and reporters started digging, her dirty little secrets might be unearthed and ruin everything. For Edward. The foundation. For the life they'd built. The old familiar grip of anxiety made it impossible for her to eat. She set down the toast. Her napkin. Tried to keep from falling apart.

"It's time for politics and religion to mix. At least on big things." Edward put down his spoon, reached over to brush a curl off her brow. "Don't worry your pretty little head about it. Things will work out fine."

As he set his dishes in the sink and left the room, she stared at toasted crumbs and prayed that he was right.

◆ ◆ ◆

A pastor's wife shouldn't use a valet. To avoid the appearance of a grand entrance, she wheeled past the attendant and maneuvered her car into a parking spot. She checked her face in the rearview mirror, noting half-moons under her eyes that makeup hadn't concealed. Not surprising. She'd barely slept in the two days since he'd called.

Trembling fingers dug through her purse, found a tissue, and dabbed at her lips. Might he see her as presentable? Pretty, even? Unlike Maman, she'd never been pretty. But she'd been strong, hadn't she, thanks to Maman? "You can do anything, little Sheba. With God's help, anything." Maman's words covered her like a shawl. She stashed her keys and the tissue in her purse and got out of her car.

Wind off Lake Michigan plastered her skirt to her legs. She staggered, but that memory of his blue eyes cemented her resolve. All had gone according to plan; she couldn't stop now. She smoothed the crisp linen of her best suit and hurried to a cobblestone path that wound through a dense stand of maples. Lights twinkled from stately branches and created a fairyland for the Gold

Coast clientele who frequented Etienne's. Those disdaining the sixties craze to see and be seen. Those prepared to pay dearly for velvet-covered, mahogany-backed anonymity.

She had joined their rank.

A canopied entrance beckoned her. A uniformed attendant opened massive doors and ushered her into a paneled lobby. Prickles frolicked across her arms. "Ma Vlast," one of the world's greatest musical achievements, burst intoxicatingly from a budget-breaking sound system. Etienne's served only the best food. The best drink. The best privacy, especially at the "quiet table for two" she'd reserved, though Etienne's patrons wouldn't likely include any of the fourteen hundred congregants Edward had pastored for twelve years. Of course one never knew what a person cloaked behind a nice suit and a pleasant Sunday greeting.

"Welcome to Etienne's." With narrowed eyes, the tuxedoed maitre d' appraised her bargain basement suit, simulated leather purse and shoes. "Reservations?" His every gesture shouted, "You don't belong here!"

"Yes." She lowered her head, as if that would stop the ringing in her ears, glanced toward the doors. She could still leave . . . and waste the twenty-two years spent praying for this. Giving the maitre d' her best smile, she pitched forward on rarely worn heels. "The reservation's under the name Sylvia. Sylvia Allen." The old name rolled off her tongue, and she envisioned that frightened young girl . . .

Oboes heralded their appearance in "Ma Vlast," infusing the motif—and Sheila—with new life. Spring had marched through the Midwest and brought the buttery scent of daffodils, as well as a salty smell to the warming lake. Right now, Sheila Franklin, the pastor's wife, didn't care whether this meeting was of God or of man. It was enough to know she would see him again.

"This way, madam." The maitre d' led Sheila toward what she hoped was the out-of-the-way table she'd requested.

Again she smoothed her suit, her heels sinking into plush maroon carpet. Feeling the highbrow stares of the rich and famous pierce her cheap suit, Sheila locked her gaze on the maitre d's slim back. Surely they wondered why she had entered a place like this. She wondered the same thing.

She sat down. A waiter sidled up to their booth. "Would you like something from the bar?" In perfect synchronization, the maitre d' slipped away.

As if to encourage her, glasses clinked at a nearby table. A smartly dressed couple drank deeply from champagne flutes.

Though internal fires had parched her throat, she shook her head and averted her face, hoping her thirst wouldn't be noted by this waiter with questioning eyes. She hadn't taken a drink in over twenty years, but she craved one now.

"Ma'am? Are you all right?" The waiter managed to keep his eyes on her as he lit a votive. His hands were steady. So unlike her own.

Sheila nodded, but of course she wasn't all right. After going to the trouble to find her, would he stand her up? Again she checked her watch, fiddled with her wedding ring. Six fifty. Ten minutes from the time she'd agreed to meet the son she'd given up for adoption. Ten minutes from the time she would set eyes on the baby she visualized first thing every morning, last thing every evening, and countless times between. Eyes . . . his were china blue. *Little boy blue, come blow your horn*, she'd sung to him in that taxi. Little boy blue. Samuel.

She bent her head. Again checked her watch. Six fifty-one. A blur to her left quickened her pulse. The rarified air in Etienne's took on weight, moisture, as if a storm had seeped through the casement windows. Yet this storm bore the scent of citrusy aftershave. Her pulse hammered at her temples. She turned. A gasp slipped from her lips.

Blue eyes pierced into hers, their gaze neither cold nor warm but hovering dangerously in between. A uniform emphasized a tall, slim physique. Shiny medals and colorful ribbons assured her he'd demonstrated courage and perseverance. A tic at his jaw betrayed his otherwise cool demeanor and infused her with hope that he, too, wanted to be here. She pressed her hand to her breast. Surely not as badly as she did!

Two feet from her stood the baby she'd held that one time, a week after his birth on January 8, 1947. Oh, she remembered every clock tick that day! The hospital had discharged her and sent her, clenching the precious blue bundle to her breast, back to the Home. "Go slow, please," she'd begged the cabbie. Eyes heavy with unexpected compassion had met her gaze in the rearview mirror. With a nod and a soft smile, the cabbie had stretched a six-minute ride into twelve glorious hellish eternal split-second minutes. Twelve minutes to give a son a lifetime of love. Before others stole him away.

The room hushed, yet the votive—and her heart—fluttered with abandon. She drank in the curve of lashes against his café au lait skin, again thinking of Maman. Caught the hue and shape of his eyes, inherited from his father, also a soldier, though in quite a different war than the one now splitting the country apart.

God had let her see her baby again. If He took her now, she would die a happy woman.

"Ma'am, are you Sylvia Allen?" The unwavering gaze, the straight back, told her he already knew the answer.

She nodded, but couldn't speak, couldn't move, thanks to the music that engulfed her. But she kept right on looking! Well-manicured hands. A musician's slender hands. Her Papa's hands. High cheekbones, casting shadows on a strong jaw and chin. Maman again. In Samuel, God had melded the grace and refinement of both her parents, the blue eyes of her lover, the piercing gaze, the thick, dark hair of . . . a thrill rippled through. Of *her*.

Her son slid into his seat. "As you surely realize, I'm Samuel Allen." He folded long limbs into his chair with such elegance, tears filled Sheila's eyes.

"He grew in wisdom and stature," she thought she whispered, but not an eyelash moved on her son's face. Perhaps she hadn't voiced it. But the words . . . and her son . . . had captured her heart.

A manila folder appeared on the table, right next to the votive, which sputtered ominous shadows across Samuel's face.

Hope plummeted. What secrets did that folder contain? What would he do with them? "They tell me you're my mother." He eyed her but pointed to the folder.

"Good evening." A waiter, his smile professionally calibrated to show just the right amount of interest, appeared and pulled a leather order book from a back pocket.

Sheila battled a grimace. She didn't want this man—or anyone—to interrupt them. Even if Samuel brought news that would slay her, she would take that over being separated from him again.

"Shall we start with drinks?"

"Mrs. Franklin?" Samuel glanced at her, only courtesy in those eyes.

Mrs. Franklin? Sheila's throat clamped like a vise, yet reason loosed the irrational grip. What would she expect him to call her? To feel for her? She should just be glad he was here.

"Would you like me to order for us?" The eyes got bluer, the voice softer.

She nodded wordlessly, her mind reeling backward in time. Papa would have loved Samuel's way of taking control. And Maman would have positively swooned over him. Maman always liked handsome, well-mannered men.

"Club soda with a twist of lime. For both of us."

"The menus." The waiter thrust one into her hands. Set another by the folder.

"We'll order a bit later, if you don't mind," Samuel said. "I'll let you know."

Nodding, the waiter disappeared.

"Thanks for meeting me." The folder flopped open. A sheet of paper was removed. "If you don't mind, I have a few questions for you."

His inscrutable expression muted her soul's music. She eyed the folder warily.

The paper shook as he shoved it close. "According to . . . my sources, you are both Sheila Franklin and Sylvia Allen." His shoulders grazed the leather booth when he leaned back. Ice glazed his eyes. "If that's true, then who is Sheba Alexander?"

The question tore open a lockbox of memories. A blazing fire. A one-armed prostitute. Maman. Papa. A thirteen-year-old girl who thought she could conquer the world, thanks to her parents' gift of that name she'd had to abandon. A name she just might have to reclaim . . .

"Sheba Alexander was . . ." Words fought to escape her cottony mouth. ". . . a silly girl." *A very foolish teenager.* She swallowed hard. How could she explain things to a man she'd just met, even if he were her son? Again she studied him, and then made up her mind. To show him her love, she would've picked up the steak knife in front of her, stabbed her chest, pulled out her heart, and handed it to him. But he hadn't asked for that. He just wanted the words. The truth. Would she, could she, break her lifelong rhythm of secrets? Perhaps, with God's help. She gave her son a sad smile and began her story.

Chapter 2

Jazz Me Blues

Summer 1942, New Orleans, Louisiana

"Can I go to the Quarter?" Thirteen-year-old Sheba danced across the planked parlor of her Esplanade Street home. The Jackson Square artists, with their scraggly beards and paint-stained fingers, the saxophonist with the soulful eyes, called to her with the sneezes and clangs and wheedles of jazz. Mellow notes fluttered in Sheba, and she twirled about until hair teased her eyes. The French Quarter in early summer was the most exciting place in the world.

Louise, a basket of laundry gripped in her chubby arms, glared at Sheba. "No'm, Miss Full of Youself." Louise's red kerchief flapped and snapped like her tongue. "Got no reason to go in dat Quarter. Ain't no place for a lady. Dey throwin' folks on boats, shippin' 'em all de way to China."

Louise's sour notes interrupted Sheba's secret melody. Why did the maid who cooked her favorites, cheese grits and *etouffe*, who dusted her books, who even let her play in the old slave quarters out back, get ornery when it came to Sheba leaving the house? Why, Louise was twice as strict as Maman and Papa!

Maman floated down the stairs. "*Non, non,* Sheba. Louise is right."

Sheba stomped her foot. How could they trap her inside on a day like this?

Maman pulled a pendant watch from its bosom nest, checked the time, and pointed toward the parlor. "Your piano calls, *chérie.*" She smoothed marcel waves from her heart-shaped face. "The new tutor will expect dedication." She touched Sheba's cheek and then glided toward the stairs.

Victory gleamed in Louise's eyes. Humming a gospel song, she shuffled away.

"But I don't want to play the piano!" Sheba huffed across the room, taffeta skirts and nylon petticoats swishing against her legs. Without jazz, the afternoon loomed bleak. Why didn't Maman, who also loved music, see that she wasn't meant to be a pianist? That it was the clarinet that captured her breath and transformed it into magic when she blew into its ebony tube? Spurning the hard piano bench, she plopped onto a salon chair, folded her arms, and made a face.

Her little tiff was wasted; Louise had sung her way to the courtyard laundry line. Maman had disappeared up the stairs. Sheba and her bad mood were alone.

The walls burst with color and light, thanks to the paintings of Maman's friend, the Impressionist painter. Her last tutor said Impressionists brought the outside in. But they sure didn't take Sheba outside! Splashes of color seeped off the canvases and threatened to drown her. If Louise had kept quiet about the Gallatin disappearances, Maman would have relented.

Strains of "Blue Danube" streamed from Maman's room and trickled downstairs. Sheba sank back into brocaded silk. As she listened, bows shivered across violins to produce just the right tone. The music was wasted on gilded tables, cloisonné vases, a mahogany armoire hiding decanters of sherry, fifths of whiskey, Papa's money bags, and lottery tickets. Sheba harrumphed. On a day like this, classical music congested her soul. Oh, for air cleansed by the strum of the street musician's banjo, the wheedle of Irish flutes! The music beckoned with such insistence, she flew to the window and peeked past drapes, half expecting a spasm band to pass by. She would have followed, despite what Maman or Louise said.

The door banged open. In came Papa, impeccable in a white linen suit.

The closed-in feeling ebbed. Sheba flew across the room and flung her arms about Papa, who was ten times better than a parade.

"How's my girl?" Tickets and green bundles peeked out of the satchel Papa cradled. Sure strides carried him to the armoire, where he stashed their rent money, their music money . . . their life. Business done, he turned to Sheba and swooped her off the rug and into his arms.

She didn't speak but buried her face in a jacket smelling of imported cigars. Just by the bent of her head, the intensity of her hug, Papa would understand how confinement on such a lovely day choked her spirits.

As she expected, Papa patted her head. "What is it, my sweet?" He gently pried her away and studied her face.

"It's Maman."

Thick brows furrowed. Papa glanced toward the stairs. "Has she been taken ill?"

Sheba pursed her lips. With Maman, she could never be sure. Vials of pills, bottles of absinthe, even voodoo powders had been stashed in the oddest places, just in case headaches took hold of Maman's pretty head. Louise said constitutions like Maman's "wasn't made for no heat." Maybe Louise was right. Or maybe Sheba's headstrongness drove Maman into her bedroom refuge. "No, Papa," she finally said.

"Then what, *ma chère?*"

She daren't mention Maman's insistence on her practicing the piano, for Papa lived to please Maman. And Louise had ruled out a Quarter visit. "Would you give me a clarinet lesson? Please?" If only she could explain with the clarinet, Papa would understand.

Frowning, Papa stepped to the window, shoved back the drapes, and peered outside. "I'm not sure we have time," came out squeaky. Very unPapa-like.

Callers never arrived until after supper, which Maman insisted was for the three of them—four, if she counted Louise. So what, or who, had placed furrows in Papa's brow?

Papa smoothed the drapes in place, put on his company smile—one that didn't touch his eyes—and moved toward the chest where he kept his instruments, his sheet music, his stand. Nimble fingers unwrapped his clarinet from the blue velvet that shielded against humidity. Freed it for music. For her soul.

The reed's tweedle stilled Sheba's nerves. Papa, one of New Orleans' best musicians, was giving her a beginner's lesson! She whirled her skirts about and tapped her feet against wood planks. Like Sheba, Papa was at his best with music around.

His real smile in place, Papa unfolded his stand and waltzed across the floor with the funny-looking metal dance partner. After a deep bow, he set the stand by the piano and offered Sheba his hand.

Sheba beamed. Papa was the handsomest man in the world!

Someone banged on the door, rattling Maman's vases. Rattling Papa, too, from the look on his face. Sheba gripped his hand.

"Upstairs, Sheba." Papa broke from her grasp, his tone cutting off pleading. The clarinet disappeared into its case. Sheba moved to the stairs, her eyes fixed on the door.

"Who is it?" Papa strode forward. "Who calls?"

Sheba froze on the staircase, straining to hear. To see.

A man growled an answer, but she didn't understand a single word.

Bolts clicked open. The door creaked. One, two, three men barreled into the room.

Sheba crouched down, peered through banister rails, cringed when the stair creaked. Surely Maman's music would trump her sneaking-around sounds. Even if it was eavesdropping, she had to see this!

The uninvited guests hunched up padded suit shoulders and ringed around Papa.

Sheba's arms prickled. *Ring around the rosy, pocket full of posies* played in her head as she watched the circle formed by the men and Papa. But this was not a nursery rhyme. She itched to rub her skin but daren't move. Over the strains of Maman's music, flowing from upstairs, she *had* to hear every syllable.

"We need to talk, Thomas."

Papa laughed his company laugh, cocked his head so she glimpsed his company smile. Things Papa did to pretend all was well. Lies. "Surely not here in my home."

"Ah, home, sweet home. Bought by the boss's money."

A man pulled out a gun and stroked it as if it were a lap cat.

Violent waves rocked Sheba's stomach. Guns meant trouble. Police. Danger. She doubled over but kept her eyes glued to the deadly metal.

"Let's step outside, gentlemen." Bowing low, Papa swept his hand toward the courtyard doors. "The slave quarters will lend privacy to—"

A stocky man shoved Papa with his meaty arm. "Ain't no time for privacy. The boss wants to see you. Now."

Papa smoothed his coattails, which still had the perfect creases Louise and her iron had steamed into them. Her papa was a perfect gentleman, unlike these men with tight suits and scuffed shoes. Sheba darted glances about the parlor. The men had muted the colors of Maman's paintings, the shine of Papa's piano, the glow of their safe home. She glared at the men, trying to match their ugly expressions.

"That's not possible, with the run behind schedule." Papa made a show of pulling out his pocket watch and studying it. His gaze fixed on the men, he stepped back, opened the armoire, pulled out the satchel.

Sheba opened her mouth. Clamped it shut. The contents of the satchel proved Papa had made the first run, picking up bought tickets, selling new ones. They never made the second run until after lunch, when the bordellos and bars yawned awake. Papa's lie coiled about her throat. With the lie, things had gone from bad to worse.

The stocky man thumped toward Papa and shoved him.

Sheba's nails dug into the rail.

The satchel thudded to the floor. Lottery tickets and bundles of money swirled browns and greens onto the rug's crimsons and golds. "The run will wait." One man scooped up the cash, leaving ticket bundles on the floor. The stocky man stepped over the tickets and stuck his gun into Papa's side. "The boss won't."

Sheba cupped her hand over her mouth. Papa had gone too far! And so had these men!

"The run can't wait," Papa insisted, his voice unwavering.

"You can do it later. Least you better do it later, you or one of your colored flunkies. Or Johnny, that drunken Irishman."

"Drunken Irishman?" sneered another of the men. "What a waste of a word. For a waste of a man."

"I happen to like Johnny," the first man said. "But only when he's sober."

"You mean never." Laughter swelled to shake the room. Needles jabbed Sheba's skin. Now they had attacked Johnny, Papa's right-hand man. Her friend. She hated these nasty men.

"Ledger gets opened tonight, Tommy boy. Better hope your books ain't cooked."

Again Papa smoothed his lapels. "I assure you, everything will add up."

"Ain't that fine and dandy? You tell that to the boss, you'll be back here for tea."

So . . . Papa would be okay? Then why hadn't that prickly feeling gone away?

One man opened the front door. The other two sandwiched Papa with their shoulders and hips. As they dragged him forward, Papa somehow got his watch back into his pocket. He brushed his suit as if these men were no more irritating than the mosquitoes plaguing the city. "At least let me inform Madame," he said.

"Madame? You mean the two-bit tramp?"

A lightning bolt skittered down Sheba's spine. How dare that rat slander Maman? Why, she'd pound that ugly face, kick those cheap pants. Her fists clenched.

Catcalls engulfed the room and threatened to drown out the final codetta of Maman's record. Had the music shielded Maman's delicate ears from such ugliness? Sheba squeezed her eyes shut. *I hope so.*

"Don't worry, Thomas. We'll bring you back to the lovely Valerie Ann."

"You cough up the rest of the dough, Tommy boy, and you and the missus'll be dining in that nice, safe courtyard with Miss Priss, just like usual."

Sheba relaxed her death grip on the balustrade, felt her lip pooch. So she was Miss Priss? Then she straightened. The neighbors had called her worse things. Besides, it didn't matter what they called her. They said Papa would be all right, so he would. But dirty rats would lie, and apparently spied as well.

Shoes slapped the front porch steps. Then the noise faded. Papa, and the men, had disappeared.

Silence rang through the house. A rare silence, in a house usually drunk on music. Sheba pricked her ears, hoping for Maman's soothing voice, the scratch and hum signaling the start of another of Maman's records, but silence reigned.

Sheba huffed as she climbed the stairs. The second run had to be made. But who would do it? Not Maman, who surely napped behind her closed door. Their hoity-toity neighbors would not lift a finger to help. They had sucked in Creole cheekbones as Maman's antiques had been uncrated in the front yard, had hurled a *lagniappe* of curse words when Papa's colored friends hefted their piano inside. Louise, who was just a maid, could not do anything, either. But Sheba could do something. *Would* do something. Wasn't that why Maman had named her after the daring African queen?

Suddenly notes from a ragtime ditty seeped under Maman's door, whirled Sheba about, and pushed her downstairs. Gritted teeth and a new beat pumped resolve through her. For Papa, for their family, *she* would make the second run! Her imagination sprinted ahead as she gathered up ticket bundles, straightening those whose corners had been bent. Hadn't she helped Papa a hundred times? Why, her nose would pied-piper her past fruit and flower vendors, coffee shops, the macaroni factory, the bakery. Her ears would prick for saloon guffaws and drunken roars. Every ticket would find its proper home. When Papa returned, he'd beam. Maman, stuporous from her headache, her music, or both, would never know she had been gone. Fire would blaze from Louise's big eyes, but Maman and Papa would be so proud, they would pooh-pooh Louise's tiff. Besides, Louise was just a maid.

She would complete Papa's task, for all of them, and he would simply *have* to reward her with a music lesson! Humming the last notes of the ditty, Sheba paused from her work to peek out the courtyard doors.

Louise, bending and stretching in her laundry dance, filled the air with her

"Amen" choruses, which seemed to take Louise's mind off everything . . . *thank goodness for that!*

While a rare breeze fluttered the drapes and stirred gumbo-thick air, Sheba scooped up the last of Papa's scattered bundles and stuffed them in the satchel. She'd start with Johnny's bar. Distribute the tickets. Collect the money. Save Papa. Now that she had a plan, the tight feeling in her belly disappeared. She grabbed the satchel, her pink straw hat, and hurried outside.

Handsome homes, their yards lush with oleander, clematis, honeysuckle, and hibiscus, rose from both sides of Esplanade to greet her. In spite of Papa's mess, the hope of a New Orleans summer day unfolded like delicate moonflowers and released a heavenly-sweet smell. With each step past latticed porches, wrought iron balconies, her confidence grew until it crowded out the men's nasty smiles. Bells rang out from the city's steepled churches, affirming her plan. With the surge in kidnappings, the war rumors from exotic-sounding places like El Alamein and Guadalcanal, she had been confined too long inside their courtyard, which hid old slave quarters, deep wells, dark secrets. Today she had gotten out. To help Papa, she could do this. After all, her name was Sheba.

Chapter 3

All That Meat and No Potatoes

The breeze, and Sheba's determination, pushed her down Esplanade and over the ridge. As she waited for the policeman to whistle-stop rattling trucks and chugging cars, the breeze vanished. Sweat beaded her forehead and trickled down her back. She wiped her brow and leaned against a live oak to catch her breath.

The metallic odor of the river, with its cargo of oyster loggers, barges, and steamboats, joined the sizzling-tar smell of hot pavement and blared news of exotic ports, just steps away. Dangerous. Exciting. She gripped the satchel and tapped her toes against the pavement. Just like this day. Never had she dreamed she would deliver the tickets herself!

After the policeman motioned her across the street, Sheba sidestepped broken bottles, old gray men reeking of stale cigarettes, and women dressed in nighttime colors of scarlet and blue. Near the Mint, a man stood, glaring at her like he knew about her secret mission. *Did a city need dirty rats to survive?* She broke into a run and sprinted past the barrelhouse, the final landmark en route to Johnny's saloon, as if the rats were chasing her. Then she stopped and composed herself.

She had never been in Johnny's without Papa, yet she shoved open double doors like a regular. Her skirt swished and lent her a march tempo. She had to convince Johnny she was a businesswoman.

Johnny's curly head disappeared behind a bar scarred with cigarette burns and beer mug rings.

Sheba checked the back door before approaching the bar. Police, with their potbellies and bulging shoulder holsters, stood out like masked revelers.

Though the boss man managed them with bribes, it wasn't a foolproof system. Sometimes people landed in jail. Papa had taught her to exercise caution. Her eyes and ears informed there were no police, just a snoring old man who had made the back table his bed.

Sheba climbed onto a stool, heaved her satchel onto the bar, opened it, and found an order form. "Hey, Johnny. You can come out. It's only me."

Jack-in-the-box-style, Johnny popped up. "Sheba, whatever are you doing here without your pa?" He grabbed a rag near the cash register and set to scrubbing the bar.

Sheba drummed on the pocked wood. If she told Johnny the truth, he would never give her the money. But she hated to lie, especially to an old riverboat captain. "Papa is . . . tied up," she said, then grimaced at the thought. "So I am helping." She forced a smile. "After all, I'm nearly fourteen."

"Yer Papa okay?" Bleary eyes met hers. Then Johnny grabbed a bottle, sloshed liquor into a shot glass, and tossed it down. He guzzled another, then slammed down the glass.

No river talk? No Irish yarns? What does Johnny know? Sheba checked both exits, but no one was there. "Why wouldn't Papa be okay?" She hooked her feet around the stool rungs to keep them from trembling.

"Well, he ain't here, is he?"

Sheba crossed her fingers so the lie wouldn't count. "He's running an errand, Johnny. That's why I'm here. He asked me to help."

"That ain't what I heard." Johnny opened his mouth, as if to say more. Shut it. Slopped more liquor into his glass.

Sheba leaned across the bar, ordering her hand to quit shaking as she reached for his freckled fingers. What had jittered happy-go-lucky Johnny? "Tell me what you heard." She tried to purr like Maman did when she coaxed things from men.

"Boss man came 'round." The quaver in Johnny's voice seemed to call for another drink. "Asking questions none but yer Papa knows the answers to."

"Qu-questions about what?"

"What does the boss always ask about?" Johnny nodded toward the register. "Collections ain't addin' up. Like someone'll be havin' their hand in the till." He leaned so close, she saw gold in his prickly red whiskers. "Tell yer Papa I won't be a middleman anymore." He licked his lips, as if tasting more drink. "Now, you'd best leave."

Her veins throbbed at the harsh words. Johnny had been Papa's right-hand man and their friend. But shaky movements and strange answers signaled change. Why would he quit a good business like gambling? Because of police? A rival boss? It didn't matter; she couldn't trust him. She slid off the stool. "You'd better give me the money." She sandpapered her voice. "Now, or your name is mud." She ducked so he couldn't see her face, which surely burned red. She hated lying, but it was the only way to collect for Papa.

Johnny laughed, but it wasn't the rollicking sound that usually shook his shoulders. "Just last week, a grown man got robbed, not five feet from the Absinthe. I'm done with this, ye hear? I won't be involving a child in this mess."

She jutted her jaw, folded her arms. "I'm not a child. I'm almost fourteen. Unless you want Papa breathing down your neck, you'd best hand it over. Now." She stood still as Andrew Jackson's statue and mimicked the hero's steely gaze though she longed to collapse on the bar floor like a payday drunk. Having to do her father's work was awful.

Johnny ducked behind the bar, reemerging with bundles of money. "Whatever am I doin', throwin' ye to the mob? Aye, more skeletons in my cupboard." He slapped the loot on the bar. May ye help me, Blessed Mary." He crossed himself, then emptied his glass.

Pressure released from Sheba so she could breathe—and smile. The rest of the pick-ups should flow like the lazy Mississippi.

The door swung open, allowing raucous laughter, men, and the smell of the sea to stumble into the room.

With Papa there, Sheba would twirl about on a barstool and let the men's stories carry her to exotic ports. Oh, to sail to India, to China, to an unnamed island. But Papa wasn't here. And there was the run . . .

Bar doors again accordioned, letting in more laughter. More men. Too many men, without the security of Papa. Sheba's lips trembled. She thanked Johnny, forced a smile on her face, and shoved open the saloon doors. It was only when the sailors' guffaws dimmed that she allowed her shoulders to slump. Everything would be okay with her Papa. Wouldn't it?

◆ ◆ ◆

"I'm here for Papa."

"Where ya been? Where's your pa?" asked the lottery dealers. None but Johnny hinted that something was amiss. Still, Sheba pasted on Papa's company smile to greet the bar and alehouse men. She couldn't be too careful when she held Papa's reputation, Papa's livelihood—that satchel—in her hands.

The satchel popped open. Tickets flew out. Money bundles plopped in. Success made her bold; she cajoled peanuts from a lottery agent and a hunk of Heavenly Hash from the *Maison Blanche* counter clerk. Quarter sights and sounds had boosted her spirits and filled her tummy.

The sun sauntered away from the river, finished with its daily work. After gathering tickets from the last alleyway box, Sheba set down her satchel, fished out and shelled peanuts, then massaged sore calves. Toting money and filled-out tickets was harder than she had ever dreamed. She licked salt off her lips and picked up the satchel. Surely Papa had returned. Though her legs ached, she kept envisioning Papa's smile when she brought home the lovely green money bundles.

She meandered through back streets and alleys, past the stench of too-ripe bananas, moonflowers, and urine. Battling the weight of the satchel, she tried to walk faster, eager to see Papa. Maman, too. She turned onto Decatur.

An old woman stood like a gnarled oak in her path. Sheba shuddered and nearly tripped.

A bony hand reached out, brought a fishy smell. "Sugar pie, got a dime?" Pale lips circled toothless gums. A filthy black shawl covered humped shoulders.

The hairs on her arms stood up. "No—no, ma'am." She swallowed hard. She had told lies today. Despite all the treats she'd eaten, they left a bitter taste in her mouth.

"Liar! May you be cursed!" The woman crooked her finger, hunched her back, turned and poked through garbage, all the while mumbling to herself.

The words trembled Sheba's lips. Beggars plagued the city, along with rats and stray dogs. Sheba paid them no mind. But this voodoo woman, with her bulging-eyed, haintlike glare, her raspy voice, grabbed her good mood and shook it hard.

Exuberance gone, she pushed past men wearing top hats, overalls, sailor suits, delivery uniforms. In two hours, men had swarmed the Quarter. Their laughter buzzed from doorways and muffled the iceman's cry, even seagull screams. Without Papa, too many men.

Energy ebbed from Sheba, who longed to sit on the dirty curb and hang her head. She'd seen too many sights. Heard too many sounds. She would hand over the money and the burdens that went with it. For months, she'd longed for summer, and her fourteenth birthday. Sheba set down the weighty satchel and swiped sweat from her face. Right now, thirteen was complicated enough. Too complicated. She scuffed home, the witchy woman's curse echoing in her ears.

◆ ◆ ◆

So I'm an Alexander, whatever that means. Somehow also an Allen.

Nearby, glasses tinkled. Giggles cascaded, surely in proportion to the number of shots knocked down. Inane people having inane conversations while he sat here with this woman—his mother—who controlled his future. He clenched his jaw. He'd do whatever it took to rescue Mali. He'd listen . . . then decide.

"So they named you after a biblical character?" He dangled conversational bait, buying time to dig past her middle-class façade. The Marines had trained him to read character, motives, *lies*, with one soul-piercing look. Nam had honed that skill into an art. How many times had a dozen lives hung on his take of the slant of a peasant's eyes? The movement of a pretty girl's hand either to smooth silky *ao-dai* folds . . . or to pull a grenade pin that would blow them all to Cambodia if he didn't spot her tense knuckles, fingers tightened into claws by stress?

"Some might debate that Sheba's a Bible character, but yes."

He continued to size her up. Thick black hair had been pulled back and twisted in a way that showed off a face full of angles and contours. Yeah, she was a looker, especially with those eyes. Deep and soulful. Like . . . Mali's. Yet webbed lines and dark circles spoke of sorrow, and threatened to penetrate the bulletproof vest that shielded his emotions.

He studied his drink, avoided those eyes. He had to say something about her papa. His *grandfather*. The thought grated. He set down the glass, focused on water drops beading its surface in case he was broadcasting disgust. His grandfather mixed with the mob and hid lies behind dapper suits. How about Maman? His *grandmother*. A woman for whom headaches were an excuse for slugging booze and pills. A woman whose eyes were rumored to act as an aphrodisiac to men, just like—his mouth went dry—Mali's.

He looked across the table. Instead of seeing his mother, he saw Mali's innocent smile when he'd bought her a scarf. Taken her on countryside rides. Innocent despite the fact . . . He blinked, Mali's image gone. This woman—his mother, he reminded himself—needed TLC. He'd better dish it up if he expected her to reciprocate.

"Sir? Madam?"

Samuel's insides knotted. Vision pinpricked. He jerked his head. Took in the waiter's priggish smile and arched brows. He breathed deep. Slow. This was no jungle ambush. Just a waiter praying against all odds that teetotalers would tip big.

"Are you ready to order your entrees?"

"Not quite." Samuel grabbed the menu and selected expensive enough appetizers to bring a smile to the man's thin lips.

"Yes, sir. They'll be right out."

Funny what money can do. *Sure hope this works . . .*

The waiter scurried away. Samuel eyeballed his mother. Silence hung heavy. She must have felt it too, as she made a hobby of twisting her ring. "I'm sorry that . . . I never looked for you. It wasn't because I didn't want to." Again the bent of her head muted her voice; Samuel had to lean forward to catch the words. "It's just that . . . you see, I've put myself in an awful position."

His eyes narrowed. He studied scraped knuckles. *Yeah. In a marriage with that husband, whose bank account's as big as his ego.*

"I wouldn't blame you for hating me," she continued.

Surprise made him raise his head. Dim lighting didn't hide her wet face. His throat tightened at the thought of another beauty who shed tears. This woman bled inside. Like Mali.

"No, no," he stammered. She'd made him veer from the direct route; if he didn't watch it, she'd burst into tears and scoot out of here. Something he couldn't afford. "I'm sure you have your reasons." *Just like I do.*

She pressed her palms together. "I wish I could explain it."

He leaned back. Forced a smile. He wished she could, too, because unanswered questions stuck in his craw. Like where he got his skin color. From the looks of it, not her. He lined up his silverware, thinking of the orphanage jobs. He'd been the only black dishwasher. The only black boy. His knife clinked against his spoon, setting his teeth on edge.

"Well, why don't you try?" He commanded his shoulders to relax. He *should* hear her story. It was *his* story, too. Eventually he'd build the bridge that would take him to Thailand. Mali. Even if it meant . . . blackmail.

The waiter smoothed in with the appetizers. Samuel took in Etienne's dark paneling and flickering candles, inhaled lemon butter, felt his hands shake as he unfolded his napkin. Money, money, everywhere. In her purse as well. *Go slow, be gentle* trumped the other thoughts.

A faraway look softened her eyes. Softened him. *Face it, Bub. You need this story as much as she needs to tell it.* He speared prosciutto-wrapped crudités and fried shrimp, set them on a plate, slid it toward her, then helped himself. He felt a gaping emptiness. The nuns' discipline, Uncle Sam's regimen, kept him from gobbling the food like a marine returning from recon. But it wasn't food for which he most hungered. He was starving for the truth.

"Should—do you mind if I pray?" she asked him, in that same soft yet sure voice.

Great, Bub. Ignore God. Why had he forgotten? A guilt trip over what God would think of his plan? He set down his fork, bowed his head, and listened to her earnest, whispery blessing.

After she said "amen," he looked her in the eyes. "Tell me more of your story. Please."

Chapter 4

Solace

Lies. More lies. One to Maman, one to Louise. Had she told four today or five? Sheba tossed her hat on her bed and hurried into the powder room, splashed water on her skin, made a face at the mirror. The sun had blushed her cheeks, perhaps added a freckle. Thank goodness, the lies were nowhere to be seen.

Footfalls jittered on the porch. The door squeaked open. Clicked shut.

Sheba tore down the hall. It was Papa, she knew by those musical steps! Without bothering to dry her hands, she flew to the landing and down the stairs, desperate to see his pressed pants and calm brow. "Papa!" She streaked into the parlor.

Papa sat on the piano bench, a record player sitting close by, like a best friend. A strange mix of ragtime and blues poured from the funny grid on its front. Sheba grinned so hard, her jaw ached. Music had returned to Esplanade. Not a moment too soon.

With one hand, Papa plunked ivory keys. The other hand patted the beat on his trousers. A smile spread across his face as his head bobbed and his foot tapped.

Music and the sight of Papa's white linen coat, free from even a trace of those ratty men, made Sheba hurry close to Papa and plant a kiss on his clean-shaven cheek.

Though Papa kept smiling, worry lines bunched at the corners of his mouth and eyes. Sheba slid next to Papa on the bench. "You—you are all right, Papa?"

"Of course, *ma chérie.*"

"But those men . . ."

"A necessary evil." Papa's dark hair shone, not just from the sunlight pouring through the window, but from the brilliantine he so carefully applied. Just as shiny were the oxfords that Papa tapped. But the shiniest part of Papa lay buried deep within; only the clarinet could coax it out. After her day, she needed all of his music.

As if he understood, Papa uncased the clarinet. "Our lesson, *chérie?*" He wet the reed, put the mouthpiece to his lips, fluttered fingers along silver keys. Squeaks gave way to growls, then a hollow sound.

A music lesson this close to supper? And not a word about work or those men? Her nose twitched. "Papa, the collections—"

"The boss took care of it. That is part of the business, *chérie.*" Papa set down his clarinet and turned up the volume on the phonograph. Jazz poured into the room. "Listen, so you can play along."

"No, Papa." Battling the loud, lazy notes, and Papa's lie, she jumped off the bench. "*I* made the run. First Johnny's. Then . . ." Words tumbled out. Words that should have earned smiles and a head pat. Yet Papa's eyes narrowed as she shared her adventures.

"Thank you, *ma chère,*" he finally said, when the banjo and trumpet and clarinet on the record gave way to the soft, deep bass. "Papa's little helper." His voice shrilled, like when he scolded Louise for not starching his shirts cardboard stiff.

Papa hadn't fathomed the depths she'd plunged to do his work! She longed to stomp upstairs but consoled herself with the fact that Papa *had* returned safely. Her manners forced a brittle smile.

The music lesson resumed, yet Sheba failed to mimic Papa's careful fingering, his rhythmic puffs. How could she, when he kept glancing at the door?

A jarring note, strummed by an out-of-tune banjo player on Papa's record, crept up her back. She set the clarinet in her lap, unable to manage a single note. As she listened to Papa play, she tried to focus on the beautiful objects Maman had so carefully arranged in the parlor. Instead, the face of that voodoo woman captured her mind. Something sinister had taken root in their lives. Though she was nearly fourteen, she could do nothing to dig it up and hack it to death.

◆ ◆ ◆

Forks clattered. Maman chattered. Carrying steaming platters, Louise bustled from the kitchen to the courtyard. Papa and Maman drank wine and laughed. As usual, Maman drank more than she ate. Sheba devoured red beans and rice and buttermilk corn bread. The day's unpleasantness melted away now that routine had returned.

Sunset painted the sky pink. Flowering vines latticed their weathered courtyard wall. A wall so high, so strong, intruders wouldn't dare come in. Or would they? Spasms seized her belly. Hunger, and fear.

"You want some more, honey chile?"

Sheba nodded. Louise's meal would surely quiet her silly nerves. If she weren't careful, she'd be as finicky as Maman about food.

Louise scraped the last bit of beans and rice onto Sheba's plate, then set her hand on her hip. Her dark eyes rolled about, searching for something out in the flower beds. "May I have a word with you, suh?" she finally asked Papa.

Papa clunked his glass onto the table. "Can it not wait until after supper?"

"Well, suh, I needs to git home."

Maman, her silk gown sighing, excused herself. Her face buried in her wine glass, she hurried across the courtyard and into the house. Sheba's curiosity glued her to her seat, until Papa's raised eyebrows signaled business talk. Young ladies mustn't be present at such times. Sheba curtsied, walked to the fountain, and let water bubbling from a fish-shaped spigot spill over her hands. Despite the polite distance, her ears pricked to catch every word.

"De ice and produce mens came by axin' for pay."

Memories of the day's troubles rolled in like a Gulf storm. Here came another.

"Surely they can wait until next week."

Louise shook her head. "I don't know, Massa Tom. They sho' do look mad."

"Is that all, Louise?"

"Nah, suh. Madame Alexander, she come by today."

"My mother came here?"

Sheba whirled around, droplets splattering off her fingertips and onto her dress. She hadn't seen her grandmother since Papa started his band, since—

"She ax me to give you this." Louise's hand disappeared into her apron pocket. She pulled out a letter and handed it to Papa. Then she gathered glasses and plates and set them on a tray. "In dem great by n' by." As she carried things to the kitchen, Louise sang of the Lord God, whose power would reign forever. A strange emptiness took hold of Sheba, though her belly was full. When she was happy, Louise turned to God. When troubles struck, Louise turned to God. What kind of God could help smooth the day's highs and lows to a nice, even consistency?

Papa dug for a pocketknife, slit open the letter, unfolded a single page. He studied it for a long time. Then he set it down and shoveled in food like a hog. So unlike Papa, Sheba hugged her arms. The letter *was* bad news.

The bell at the service gate rang.

Papa's fork clanged as it hit his china plate.

Sheba opened her mouth, swallowed hot, heavy air, ran to Papa, and grabbed his sleeve. "What should we do?" she cried.

Papa stood trancelike, his company smile in place.

The bell clanged and banged and battered her insides.

"Papa!" She gripped him until he winced. If he didn't do something, who would?

Finally Papa removed her arm, stuck the letter in the envelope, folded his napkin, and laid both things by his plate. With strides that signaled a return of his composure, he swept across the patio, past the old slave quarters and carriage house, to the gate.

Sheba ignored her gurgling stomach and tiptoed across moss-covered bricks to follow him. No banister would shield her this time. No, she'd face the ugly rats head-on.

"Who is it?" asked Papa.

"Jes' us, Tom."

Sheba's breath caught. It sounded like Negroes. But it could be a trick.

The gate creaked open. Men sauntered inside, natty-looking men who wore dark suits, white shirts, and narrow black ties. Negroes with tight kinky hair. Never had they looked so fine! They carried cases that hid gleaming saxophones and oboes and, best of all, clarinets.

Sheba relaxed. No dirty rats! And music! Tonight she had wanted Papa and Maman to herself, but having the musicians appear was swell!

Louise pattered across the courtyard. Her meaty hand grabbed Sheba's. "What he lettin' dose fools in here fo'?"

Sheba's mouth fell open as she stared at a puffed-up, crowing Louise, who usually reserved her feelings about the musicians to glares and snorts. Why would she disdain her own kind? New Orleans—especially its Negroes—simmered with mysteries.

"Givin' dem more ammunition to have yo' papa arrested." Louise swatted at the musicians. "Y'all get on, now, heya?"

If they saw Louise, nothing about their slouched posture or lazy smiles gave it away. Sheba huffed. If only *she* could ignore Louise so easily.

The courtyard rang with laughter and foot tapping. Even pigeons cooed for the musicians' prelude. Apparently forgetting the letter, Papa helped the men carry their things inside.

But Sheba hadn't forgotten the letter, which called her to the table. "I'll stack the rest of those plates," she told Louise, making sure to flutter her lashes, widen her eyes.

"Honey chile, if you don't beat all!" As she gathered glasses, Louise threw back her head and laughed.

The instant Louise turned her back, Sheba snatched up the envelope and pulled out the embossed sheet. She ran lickety-split toward the carriage house, away from prying eyes so *she* could pry. A glance backward told her she was safe.

She slowed her step. Evening had fallen on the shaded part of the yard. Dew slicked mossy bricks. Ready for their night light, moonflowers opened wide, dotting the back wall with fragile white blooms. The scent of jasmine and mint hung in the air. The branches of an oleander bush drooped to touch lush green grass. Nature held its breath, waiting, waiting. But Sheba wasn't waiting another second. Blood throbbing at her temples, she unfolded the letter.

> June 16, 1942
> Gabet, Toulong and Steiner, Solicitors
> 162 Canal Street
> New Orleans, Louisiana
> Dear Mr. Alexander:
>   Our client, Clara Alexander, has requested that we
> notify you of recent revisions to her Last Will & Testament.
> Due to your present circumstances, she regrets that she
> must remove you as sole beneficiary to the holdings of
> the business known as Alexander & Company, Cotton
> Merchants. Also effective immediately, you will no longer
> receive a monthly allowance.
>   With kindest regards,
>   Emile Toulong, Attorney for Madame Alexander

Mimi had been giving them money? Sheba rubbed the letter's embossed seal and studied the looping signature. How long had it been since Mimi stood in the parlor, her bosom heaving as she declared Maman unfit to raise a child,

Papa drunk on music? Three years? Four? She pushed back a curl. Reread the letter. How could Papa's mother do this to him?

Sheba jammed the paper back into the envelope. Though laughs filtered into the courtyard, she longed to cry. Why would her grandmother have an attorney write such things? If only she could throw her arms around Papa and say she was sorry. But then he'd know what she'd done. Her chin quivered. Conniving led to this. She had to keep quiet.

The last ray of sun fell behind the wall, removing light and warmth from the yard. Birds fluttered to safer nighttime roosts. Talk of money—and how to make more of it—was the greasy black crow always flapping about their house. Sure, they'd lived in style, thanks to the last-minute flip of a black ace, a well-timed tip in the day's last race. Or so she had thought. But she had been wrong. If Mimi's money had brought expensive antiques and custom suits to their house, what would happen when the pretty things disappeared? Would smooth-tongued Papa, with his knack for seeing and seizing opportunity, find a way to keep their lives sunny and gay? Sheba shivered. She just didn't know.

◆ ◆ ◆

She stood outside the parlor near the landing, her hand resting on velvety wallpaper. Contrary to her earlier thoughts, she didn't need or want the musicians. They should leave so her family could be alone.

Her ears rang from guffaws, giggles, and boasts pouring from the parlor. And the sound of her name. She tiptoed closer.

"Too bad she ain't got your eyes, Madame." Maman's answering laugh was rich as clotted cream.

Sheba plopped onto the bottom step. She didn't mind that men thought Maman beautiful, herself plain. She had Papa's ear for music, Maman's love of culture. As Maman had told her countless times, God had picked and chosen her traits, then sprinkled in spunk for seasoning. She'd come out just right, or so Maman said.

"You hear what that little dickens did?"

"Say what?"

"Took it on herself to run the lottery!"

"There'll be heck to pay for that, don't ya know?"

Heat rushed to Sheba's face. Her parents must have wandered into the dining room for those musicians to say such guff.

Glasses clinked. Spoons stirred. The more Papa's friends drank, the less they played music, and music was what this house needed. Now. When had Papa last flicked the radio dial, blared Jimmy Dorsey into the room, and started a *real* party, with her parents dancing, Sheba laughing? Real fun. Not party fun.

Strums rose from a banjo, then were drowned out by more laughter, more clinking of glasses . . . more nothing. Cigarette smoke and too much nothing tightened her throat. Sheba pattered to the French doors and stepped outside.

Fog had shrouded the moon, the stars, even the treetops. Under the misty canopy, stepping-stones became grave markers; trellised vines, tattered goblins. Shivering, Sheba remembered the voodoo woman's curse, skittered inside, and bounded the steps that led to her library. Music had not worked its magic; perhaps her books would.

Shelves lined two walls and bordered an arched fireplace. Sheba moved to the balcony and breathed deep. Instead of perfumed moonflowers, an oily smell filled her nostrils. Perhaps a breeze had carried river stench across the Ridge. She closed the balcony doors and stretched on her tiptoes, past *Tom Sawyer* and *The Canterbury Tales*, to reach Maman's old Bible. Just touching its worn binding soothed her like Maman's hugs. She hurried to her seat. The book in her lap, she curled into a velvet chaise and found the tattered ribbon that marked the story. Her story. *And she came to Jerusalem with a very great train, with camels that bore spices, and very much gold, and precious stones . . .*

She skimmed through verses about servants and rich food. Long before she could read, Maman had told her about the queen whose daring had inspired her name. "You can do anything, my Sheba," Maman said. "Just like *this* Sheba, who traveled through a desert to find wisdom."

Sheba smoothed down the precious page, remembering her little-girl struggles to roll the strange words of this story against the roof of her mouth and conquer them, one by one. Seeing the love in Maman's eyes, reading about the riches of the great queen, she'd believed she could conquer anything.

After today, she wasn't so sure.

Her eyes fell down the column of fancy letters decorating the onionskin page until she found what she wanted to read.

Happy are thy men, happy are these thy servants, which stand continually before thee, and that hear thy wisdom. Blessed by the Lord thy God, which delighted in thee, to set thee on the throne of Israel . . .

The words of Louise's spirituals came to Sheba in snippets. Did Louise praise the God searched for by the great Queen Sheba? How did this queen's—and this God's—power compare to that of the voodoo woman's curse?

Sheba closed the Bible and ran her finger across the worn black grain cover. She had so many questions . . . and no answers. Could this book tell her about the Lord God? She opened it again, stared at the first page.

Holman Home Bible
The Holy Bible
This Bible Belongs to *Hattie Pearl Carver*
Houma, Louisiana, 1905

"Ah, here you are." Elegant in a green silk dress, Maman floated into the library on a cloud of perfume. She nudged Sheba's legs out of the way, smoothed her dress, sat on the edge of the chaise longue. "*Comment ça va?*"

Sheba ignored the question, instead pointing to the Bible. "Who is Hattie Pearl?"

Maman's face whitened until her rouge stood out like red ovals. Her fingers fluttered to twist heavy gold rings.

Questions danced in Sheba, questions she didn't want Maman to dance around. "Did she give you this? Is she my *grand-mère*? Was France your home? Or Houma?"

A sigh rose from Maman. "It isn't polite to ask such questions, *chérie*." Lamplight caught her gleaming, twisting rings. "Tell me, what are you looking for in that musty old book?"

Maman fanned emotions that had risen and fallen inside Sheba all day. Now she was at high tide, wanting answers, not more questions. But it wouldn't do to sass Maman. "I'm looking for the Lord God." She loosed the words slowly to avoid a torrent that might overwhelm Maman. "I want to know about Him."

Maman slumped forward. Tears brimmed in the eyes that men swooned over. Maman was so beautiful, even when she was sad.

"He is your maker," Maman whispered. She caressed Sheba's cheek. "He sent His Son to die for you; a Son Who loves you more than I, if that is possible."

Someone knocked at the door.

No! Sheba snuggled into Maman's curves. *Go away!*

The door opened. A man who had appeared after the musicians strode in. He wore a seersucker suit and flowery tie. His smell of strong drink and aftershave overwhelmed Maman's perfume and ruined their sweet sanctuary. "There you are, Valerie Ann." The man gave Maman a narrow-eyed smile.

Sheba longed to push him from the room and lock him out. Why did men look at Maman like she was a piece of fruit, ready to pick and devour?

Maman's smile did not touch her eyes, did not travel across that perfect heart-shaped face. Still, Maman smiled.

It tore at Sheba to see, by Maman's smile, that Maman wanted to be picked and eaten. She grabbed the Bible and settled into the seat as if Maman had already left the room. And with a rustle of silk and a silly little laugh, Maman did.

The Bible lay heavy in Sheba's lap as she curled into a ball. Maman said the Lord God loved her more than anyone else. How could that be? Again she opened the book. Scanned the page. Turned back. Forward. Passages had been underlined. By Maman? Or Hattie Pearl? Pages crinkled while Sheba noted the words someone had felt important.

The Lord is my rock, and my fortress, and my deliverer.

Why standest thou afar off, O Lord? Why hidest thou thyself in times of trouble?

God is jealous, and the LORD revengeth . . .

Sheba thumbed through more pages, rubbed her eyes, and set the Bible down. Surely this book spoke of different gods. One God couldn't be all those things. She longed to understand, but God was a mystery, like Maman's illnesses, Papa's business. Perhaps Louise would explain. Or perhaps the sad-eyed priest who waved to her from the cathedral steps and tossed birdseed to the pigeons. She sank into the chaise and rubbed her thumb against her cheek, soothing herself like she had when she was a little girl.

A saxophone sounded. Low and rich notes from the lips of an unknown musician filtered upstairs and made their way into the room. Her thumb slowed, and on the waves of the music, she drifted to sleep.

Chapter 5

Nobody Knows the Trouble I've Seen

"I am the Lord God." The voice boomed from a heaven sizzling lightning and raining fire. Strangled, moaning voices answered. The angry God thundered closer.

Sheba writhed about. Then her hand brushed comforting velvet and brought back the cushiony feel of her chaise longue. Her library refuge. Her home. She ran her hand through damp curls, felt her breathing slow. She'd had a bad dream.

Someone screamed. Dream fragments shattered her moment of peace. Something crashed. Her brain clanged an alarm. What had happened to the musicians? To Maman and Papa? Sheba jumped up, ran to the door, and yanked it open.

Thick gray smoke billowed into the room. A hot-dust smell engulfed her and singed her eyes. Tears streamed down her face. She choked, coughed, and slammed the door. Fire!

Steps pattered on the second-floor landing. "Sheba!" Maman rasped. "The ... balcony ... *ma chère!*" A crackling, like burning green wood, tried to drown out Maman's cries.

"Maman!" Her sweat-slicked hand wrenched the knob, but this time the door stuck. She wrestled with slippery brass, beat her fists against the door, yet it didn't budge. They fought an awful tug of war, Sheba and the door. Or was it Maman, pulling on the outside knob, entrapping her? Maman would never do that!

"Ju-m-p, *ch*—" Coughing rendered Maman's voice nearly unrecognizable. "The bal-cony."

Had Maman lost her mind? "No!" Sheba screamed. "Let me out!" Again she kicked the door, but it didn't budge. Curls of smoke seeped around the doorframe.

"Sheba . . . listen." Spasms of coughing continued to plague Maman's voice. "I'll . . . g-get Papa. Jump off the b-balcony. Now. We'll meet you—"

Something tinkled. Glass shattering? Then a thud. Maman would get Papa, who would rescue her. Soon.

Sheba backed into the corner behind the door and wrung her hands while the house played a dreadful symphony of cracks, pops, and sizzles. Blood roared into her ears but failed to mute the fire's notes. Was the voodoo woman's curse coming true?

Smoke streamed in now, finding every crack. Sheba slapped her hand across her mouth to keep it out. Her head swiveled to the French doors, the only avenue of escape. Surely she didn't need to jump, as Maman had ordered. But what *should* she do?

Snaps and crackles singed her every fiber. She zigzagged about. Wild breathing crescendoed to yelps. Then she thought of Maman, who always knew best where her welfare was concerned. She ran to the French doors, shoved them open, and stepped onto the balcony.

Night's black fingers clutched her throat and acted as a dropcloth for the day's strange occurrences. She longed to scurry back to her refuge, but smoke was having its way with the room, choking out the chairs, the bookshelves. It would choke her if she returned. Now coughing as Maman had, Sheba slammed the balcony doors. Maman, Papa, were they trapped inside? She pressed her palms, her face, against the glass, peered into the room she'd left. Smoke had snuffed out all the light. Her old refuge was now a dark hole.

Something crashed; closer, louder. Dancing crazily to the tune of pops and crackles, fire leapt through the floorboards and heat registers in her beloved room. Oranges and yellows cast shadows so dreadful, Sheba longed for the dark to return. But it didn't.

A scream pierced the air as she kept staring into the room, so hypnotized by the ghastly sight that she barely recognized her own voice. Part of the floor collapsed, dumping a bookshelf into a glowing orange pit. A fireball exploded. Smoky arms seeped through the French doors, tracking her down, sizzle by sizzle. Every nerve ending begged her to revolt, yet her limbs were paralyzed. She couldn't leave. She couldn't stay.

Red and orange imps leapt with delight, swallowed another bookshelf, and vomited out red embers, orange flames.

"Help!" she yelled. Nobody answered but the flames, which licked the paneling, the ceiling, birthing smaller flames that grew devil heads and horns. Energy gushed into her hands and feet. If she didn't move, fire would gobble her up.

She crept to the railing, peered over, drew back, shuddered at the dark grassy carpet, the gaping void of night. She ground her teeth. The fire left her no choice.

The doors rattled, then blew open and shut and fanned the study into a hideous abstract of oranges and yellows. Her shoulders shook. Tears streamed. She couldn't do this. She couldn't—

Sheba.

Who called? Maman? Sheba waited, desperate to hear more.

You can do it. The tree, Sheba. Jump to the tree.

Was the swirling hot wind whispering the words? Or was it Maman, down below, coaxing her into soft arms?

Sheba squeezed her eyes shut. With the wrought iron rail as a guide, she groped her way to the balcony edge.

Wind stirred cape jasmine and magnolia, their perfume combating smoke stench. The heady scent opened her eyes, spurred her forward. She could, she would, do this.

Fire flickered across the leaves of Maman's beloved trees, the trees that must grab her tight and keep her from falling. "Please," Sheba cried, "hold me. Hold me, do you hear? Till Maman can!" She clenched the railing and flung her right leg over. Wrought iron bit into her groin, but the crackling sounds, the heat radiating from the study, made the pain easy to ignore.

Something crashed in the study. Sheba bowed her head. She wouldn't look. She gritted her teeth and threw her left leg over the rail. Tears streamed from her face, mucous from her nose.

She had no more time to think. She had to jump. Now. She crouched low. Tensed her back, her calves, and her feet. Her hands ached as she gripped the iron lifeline of the railing. "One, two, three," she counted, and then let go.

Breath caught in her throat as she fell, but tree leaves formed a safety net. She whimpered as branches groaned, bent, but did not break. She had an ally in this hideous war! Half clawing, half climbing, she got down the tree and collapsed onto the ground. Blood throbbed in every part of her body. The grass was cool and damp under her fingertips. She was safe . . .

As she lay there panting, rustles and moans continued. She arched her neck, peered into the tree canopy, but the leaves were still. She turned her head. That awful sound was the house, surrendering to the terrible insult. The house—their house—was coming apart. Maman had said they would meet here. Where were they?

"Maman, Papa!" She scrambled across the yard, onto the patio. Bricks bit her knees and elbows. She had to find Maman. Papa.

A siren screeched like a hundred crazed alley cats. An air horn bellowed.

The house shuddered, shifted. Beams disintegrated and burst into orange fireballs. "Maman. Papa . . ." Her ability to say more had vanished, along with their home. She fell flat against bricks.

Embers glittered in the night air and then fluttered to the ground. She tried to grab remnants of her books, her chair, her life, but the collapse of her home had sucked every ounce of energy from her. "Maman," she wailed. "Papa."

Red beams flashed from the alley. More sirens screamed through the night, pierced her ears, penetrated her skull. If police were after Papa, he must be alive! She belly-crawled past the fountain, ducked under a clump of azaleas, then peered through forked branches.

Men burst through the gate, dragging hoses, carrying hatchets. She hunkered into damp soil, recalling that old hag's curse, the boss's dirty rats. Until her parents came to get her or she knew more, she would hide. Besides, smoke had scalded her lungs. Her limbs had turned to stone.

"I need Alpha. Beta. Find Charlie, you hear?" Boots clambered onto the brick patio. "You hear? How we lookin' back there?"

The yard came alive as men darted about, illuminated by flashing lights and the fire. They had on thick rubber suits, black boots, and helmets. One man wore business clothes.

Water spurted from a thick hose and pummeled the house. Her house. She sighted the top line, where the roof had been. Gray-white smoke billowed, conquering even the orange flames. A burnt praline smell wafted through the air.

White-hot stabs charred tender spots. "Papa, Maman," she whispered, still hoping that this was a bad dream. Branches scratched her as she leaned back, burying her face in her hands.

"Give us a master."

"Charlie, do you read? This way."

"Turn it off, ya hear?"

Sheba watched the firemen, listened to their chatter, but she said nothing. Thought nothing.

"Signal 29, Chief."

"How many?"

"A couple of 'em."

"Cut off the master stream!"

"Command to alarm. We need an investigator."

"We've got a neighbor here, Chief, who claims she saw a little girl up there."

Sheba peered under a branch, saw house shoes, the hem of a housecoat. Which neighbor? She'd seen no one except the imps of fire. Since they were not human, they did not count.

A cursing fireman waved his arms and propelled others into action. Awkward in their bulky uniforms, they clomped across the patio. One headed toward the street side of the house, the other toward the neighbor side.

Sheba bit her lip. What was all the commotion? Had Maman and Papa returned? She craned her neck for a better view. Branches poked her arms, blossoms tickled her nose. She sneezed.

"Well, I'll be. That neighbor was right." Black boots stomped two men near. Rough-gloved hands seized her shoulders, pulled her out, and hoisted her in the air.

Her skin crawled at the strangers' touches.

"She's in shock!"

"Get ahold of that driver. Now!" A scratchy blanket, reeking of gasoline and smoke, was draped about her. She coughed, desperate to rid her lungs of the noxious smells.

Other hands, gentle now, placed her on what felt like a cot, soft and cottony-cool. Another siren split the night.

Images amassed like thunder clouds. The rats who grabbed Papa. The voodoo woman, her hairy chin jutting, cursing Sheba. Cackling her victory. Cackling . . .

Sheba's eyes closed from the burden of so many dreams, so much night, so much fire. She drifted into darkness, this one comforting. This one shutting out everything.

Chapter 6

Sometimes I Feel Like a Motherless Child

M "ay the Lord have mercy on the poor little dear."

"Just scratches, can you believe it?"

"And everything else up in smoke."

Sheba's heavy lids fought their way open. She wore an unfamiliar cotton gown. She struggled to sit up, pushing back a sheet and a thin blanket. Where was she? Where were her parents?

"No, dear." Women swathed in black moved close. Nuns? "Settle in." A sleeve brushed Sheba's cheek. "Go to sleep." The nuns smelled of liniment and hand soap. Strong. Clean. Sure. She wanted to obey. But she *needed* her parents. Again she tried to rise.

The women coaxed her back into the cool, cool sheets. Maybe she had stumbled into another dream, this one with nuns and a soft bed. A good dream, instead of one with cackling imps and flickering fire. To shut out the images, Sheba closed her eyes and drifted away.

◆ ◆ ◆

Skirts rustled. A door clicked shut. Her eyelids fluttered, revealing a table laden with a cloth and a basin of water. She shut her eyes and rolled on her side, but questions troubled her rest. Something crashed. She again flipped over. Her gaze fell on a crucifix that hung over a door. She heard soft but rapid steps, then whispers. Creaks. Another rustle. She jerked upright; the questions pushing so hard, her body ached. And the dreams—she shivered, wanting Maman's arms about her. She had to get answers. Stop the dreams. Now.

"*Ma chère.*" Black and flesh and the scent of roses whirled toward the bed.

A billowy warmth settled over Sheba. The voice was not Maman's but spoke Maman's French. She sniffed. Not Maman's Eau de Joy, but roses nonetheless. "Who—who are you?" she asked, her lip trembling.

"Just call me Honey. I'm an old friend of your Maman's." An arm extended as if to pull her close. Honey's lips had been painted blood red. Streaks of blue and black had made a mess of her eyelids. The tracks of tears gouged thick makeup.

Sheba tried not to stare but lost the battle. Maman had no lady friends . . . or did she? Curious glances, whispered comments, swirled about Maman. And then there was the mysterious inscription in that Bible. What *did* she know of Maman?

As Honey rustled closer, her black drape slipped off and fell to the floor, revealing a fleshy nub where her other arm should have been.

The room seemed to whirl. Honey had lost an arm! She rubbed her eyes, sure that this was another nightmare. She could not abide another nightmare. "What—" came out as a screech.

"Shh," Honey whispered. "They mustn't know I'm here, or they'll throw me out."

This was the voodoo woman's hex! Sheba leapt from the bed and stepped back until she slammed into the room's cold, damp wall. "Why are you here?" Her lips began to tremble, her insides began to crumble, just like the roof. Or had that been a nightmare too? "Where are my parents?" She darted about the room, desperate to gather clues.

Bandages and a tube of ointment were laid on the table. Medicine. Why, she was in a hospital! Charity Hospital! She bit her lip to stop its trembling. Perhaps her parents were here as well.

"Sit down, Sheba," the woman commanded. "Now."

This woman named Honey had taken the reins, like Maman always did. She needed someone to take the reins. Obeying, she sat on the edge of the bed and hugged her arms.

Again Honey moved close. Put her hand on Sheba's shoulder. Her eyelids drooped to show that riot of blue. "I'm sorry we had to meet like this. But I'd promised your Maman, if anything ever happened . . ."

Tears clouded Sheba's gaze. This poor one-armed woman, beautiful as Maman, was clothed in sorrow. Her soft voice and graceful movements pulled at Sheba's tender places. Honey seemed to love Maman, so Sheba had to trust her. Now. She leaned close. "Please tell me what happened."

Honey turned her head. "Joe told me you escaped . . . by jumping."

"Joe?" Sheba batted about the words coming from that too red mouth. So this Honey, Maman's friend, was saying the fire, the jump, was real.

"Joe is a fireman. One of my . . . regulars." Honey grabbed Sheba's hand and squeezed hard. "He told me what happened. Oh, Sheba . . ."

The soft, soft words from that red, red mouth scattered the fog shrouding Sheba's mind. "Maman," she managed through chattering teeth. She imagined orange and red imps pulling at Maman's hair. "No!" she whispered. The imps grabbing Papa's long, slender fingers. "Papa! No, not Papa!" Sheba's composure began to melt, as if the imps had caught her too. And hadn't they, if her parents had burned up? Hadn't her whole life been destroyed?

Desperate to see a different answer, she sought Honey's gaze, then began to drown in bottomless pools of sadness. She bowed her head, tried to shut out memories of awful sizzles and crackling sounds. But she couldn't. No, she couldn't!

Honey stroked her back. Such soft, smooth strokes.

Cool misty fog rolled in. It wasn't true. The ugly images that had seized her brain were lies. If she kept her head bowed, her eyes closed, she could shut away the horrid things. She could not, would not accept them.

"Joe told me they brought you here," Honey continued.

Soundless sobs racked Sheba. She *was* here. But Maman wasn't. Papa wasn't.

"Your Maman, your Papa"—tears shredded her words—"they didn't make it, Sheba." A moan reverberated through Honey and shook her thin shoulders. Her trembling arm pulled Sheba off the bed. Then she buckled, as if the heaviness of her words, the heaviness of the *truth*, dragged both of them to the floor.

Desperate to escape the images crawling through her mind, Sheba burrowed into the bosom of this woman she had just met. Flames leapt to burn her voice, char her soul. Everything she cared about had gone up in smoke. She opened her mouth. Nothing came out. With one terrible blaze, her family had been incinerated, and she couldn't do a thing.

"Sweet Jesus, carry us through this. Sweet Jesus." Honey buried her face in Sheba's hair. Wet it with her tears.

It did not matter that until now, Honey had been a stranger. Honey knew Maman, loved Maman. She also seemed to know Louise's God, sometimes called Jesus. That was enough.

Sheba poured her sobs into Honey's bosom. Let Honey hold her in a death grip with her one hand. What would she do without her parents, who had given her love and light and life and music? Oh, what would she do?

For what seemed an eternity, they lay on the floor, bound together by death. No matter how tightly Maman's friend held her, no matter how many tears she rained, no matter how their cries split the silent air, the dreadful fire images refused to disappear.

"We can't go on, Jesus." Honey wailed with such agony, Sheba flinched. She stared at the floor, ran her hand over cold tile. An image of Maman's steady gaze hovered near. Ever so slowly, the dreadful burned faces evaporated. *My Sheba.* Maman's bell-tone voice overpowered Sheba's sobs and gave her the strength to prop her elbow against the floor. What would Maman say and do? Of course she knew. *Never give up, no matter what. Darling, pull yourself up. Don't stay down.*

Sheba removed herself from Honey, gently, for Honey had come to get her. Honey cared. Her gaze on the sad nubby arm, she smoothed Honey's hair, patted her head. Honey needed her, and it felt good to be needed. It also felt good to think. Maman would want her to think.

It was as if Sheba weren't there, the way Honey continued to mourn. A way Maman would never have mourned in front of others. From the tremble of her mouth, the swollen sadness of her eyes, Honey showed love for her family. For her. To save her parents' memories, she would keep Honey near. They would talk of what happened. Talk of what must be done. And, being only thirteen, she needed someone. She grabbed Honey and pulled her up.

The motion brought Honey out of a grief trance. She cupped Sheba's face with her one hand. "I'd best leave, *chérie.*" Though she had regained composure, tears continued to streak Honey's cheeks.

Sheba stepped forward and gripped Honey's shoulders. She could not lose this one connection to her past. "Take me with you." Though she stood tall, tried to talk strong, her words came out whispery.

"Wha-what?" Honey sniffed, then found a tissue and blew her nose. "You don't understand, child. Where I live, you cannot come."

Sheba can do anything. Be anything. "Why not? You are . . . were Maman's friend, were you not?"

Honey nodded. "The very best of friends. But my home . . . is not a place for a girl."

The door banged open. A woman dressed in a beige shirtwaist clattered inside on matching beige heels.

Sweat popped out on Sheba's forehead. It was Mimi, her eyes glittering in a way that Sheba did not remember. Sheba felt her limbs stiffen. Though Mimi was her grandmother, her longtime absence and the look on her face made Mimi seem the stranger in this room, not Honey. Sheba again found herself edging backward until she brushed against the wall.

"Dear Sheba." A beige turban hid all but a wisp of Mimi's iron gray hair. The Alexander cheekbones shaped a face hardened by thin lips and those eyes. "Let's get you packed." Mimi tugged off beige gloves and snapped her fingers. "You're coming with me. Now."

What blazed that fire in Mimi's eyes? Loss, or something else? Where were the tracks of Mimi's tears? Sheba flattened herself against the smooth, cool wall to keep from melting onto the floor. Her mouth opened, but no sound emerged. She begged Maman to appear and tell her if she should obey Mimi or leave with Honey.

"Now, Sheba."

A gossamer-thin shadow floated through her mind. Maman wouldn't want her with Mimi; neither would Papa. *She* didn't want to go with Mimi, especially with her loveless tone, the words of that letter etched in her mind. She stood tall and raised her chin. "But I'm going with Honey."

Mimi crossed her arms, tapped her toes. "Over my dead body."

Sheba begged more words to come, but they had died. She cast glances about, searching for an escape from those glittering eyes. With her back against the wall, there was nowhere to go.

"Spit spot." Again Mimi snapped her fingers and thrust a bundle of clothes at Sheba. "Here. Change. Now." She lifted her chin, let her gaze fall on Honey. "You? Get out." The refined Southern drawl Sheba remembered had vanished, in its place, cold steel.

Honey collected her shawl. Stepped forward. "But she's coming with me. I'll—"

A slap split the air.

Sheba's cheeks flamed. She watched helplessly as Honey, weeping, slipped to the floor. If Maman and Papa were here, they would take control. But Papa was gone. So was Maman. If they were here, there wouldn't *be* a problem.

"I'm her family, you hussy." A ringed finger was thrust at the trembling pile that was Honey. "What were you thinking, walking in here like a civilized woman? Why, you are nothing but a Gallatin whore."

A whore? She'd heard such whisperings in alleys and on the waterfront but never by a lady. Maman's friend would not do such things with men. The bundle of clothes a shield from such ugliness, Sheba huddled against the wall. Oh, to have Maman here to explain things! Except for an uncle in Mississippi, she had no one but this grandmother, who had cut off their money and slapped Maman's best friend.

Weeping seeped from underneath Honey's shawl, which she had draped over her face, as if to ward off another blow.

Tears welled. Another slap might crumble poor Honey into ashes. Like Maman and Papa. Sheba dropped the clothes bundle and shuffled forward to console Honey.

Mimi wedged between Sheba and Honey. "No, you don't." She tilted her head until her chin pointed at Honey. "I'd rather see her in hell than with you." Her voice remained steady. "Of course, that's where you would both be, over on Gallatin. Now get."

Sheba's hands flew to her face. She could not fight a grown-up who wielded such horrid words. Why did this have to happen?

"Sheba . . ." Honey extended a limp hand and shook her bowed head, helpless to fight Mimi.

"Sheba." Mimi spat out. "The name of a foreigner seduced by riches. Ridiculous!" She adjusted her turban as if *she* were a queen.

The room whirled; Sheba grabbed hold of a bedpost to steady herself. Honey seemed to drift away, like the apparitions of ash and smoke. The fire had engulfed more than just their house, and it wasn't finished yet. "Now." Mimi picked up the bundle and untied it. "Let's get dressed."

Sheba accepted the clothes Mimi thrust forward. Numbly she put on a high-necked dress that pinched her waist. She pulled on gloves that swallowed her hands. Let Mimi pull her hair into a bun so tight, her head ached. She stepped to a mirror that hung over the basin, touched a familiar cowlick, yet it wasn't her old self she was seeing. The fire had destroyed her parents, and now it was destroying her.

Mimi's cold hand led her from the hospital room. Sheba thought of nothing. Felt nothing. Life as she knew it had ended. And things would never be the same again.

◆ ◆ ◆

Samuel stared numbly at the flickering votive, then let his eyes travel to his mother's profile, which was splashed with orange and yellow. Like that buddy whose body the enemy had doused with gas and set afire. To shake off Nam, he zeroed in on his mother. Time travel had deepened the lines about her eyes. Those eyes . . .

"Sir?" There stood the waiter, pad in hand.

"Yes?" Samuel battled a desire to tell him off, but the man had no clue what he was interrupting. The crowd's laughs and boozy giggles seconded the hunch that big spenders came here to escape trouble, not face it. Camouflaging real feelings. He should know . . .

"Your entrées, sir?"

"I'll order for both of us," he managed hoarsely after a glance at her ashen face. He fired out an order for steaks, medium, potatoes with the works, salads, vinaigrette, and then waved the man away. People had died, and he needed to hear about them. Her people. *His* people . . .

The waiter disappeared.

Samuel hesitated before reaching across the table, taking her hand. What would be worse, to lose both parents or to dream about what might have been? His heart drummed the answer. She'd suffered more, he'd bet his paycheck on it.

His touch seemed to loose tears, which streamed down her face. Her emotions didn't surprise him. What did surprise him was the tear sliding down his own cheek. When a VC blew out his best friend's brains, he'd never shed a tear. So why couldn't he get a grip now? "I'm sorry," he said, and then winced. He couldn't risk more emotion.

She raised her head and pierced him with a haunted look. "I've missed them every day of my life. Just like I missed you."

He begged an image of Mali to grab hold of his emotions, which were slipping out of control. Instead an image of that brave little girl in New Orleans danced across his mind. To think he'd come here planning to blackmail her if he had to . . .

"Sheba—I'm sorry. Sheila." He swallowed hard and vowed to get her name straight. "Did you ever find out what happened?"

"Arson." She fumbled for a tissue in her purse and dabbed at ruined makeup. "Or so they said." A swipe at her eyes removed mascara and exposed her vulnerability.

Again he thought of beautiful Mali, forced to do things . . . "Surely you don't think a lottery run set off the mob."

"They were all about *machismo*. Brotherhood. Papa broke the rules." She gripped his hand until it ached. "And I think he did dip his hand into the till. That alone warranted a hit."

What could a woman like her know about the mafia? Despite his doubts, he nodded. Such a small thing to keep shadows out of her eyes. Such a small thing to do for his mother. *Mother.* How long had he waited to say that word? Peace engulfed him, like when the nuns sang to him. When Mali looked at him.

"We left the hospital," she continued. "Met an investigator at the scene. I helped him fill out the report." The tissue became a wad in her hands. "Rumor mongers had seeped out of the sewer drains and were milling about our house. Or what was left of it. They all wanted a chance to be seen, to be heard, by the esteemed Mrs. Alexander. My grandmother." Bitter lines tugged at the corners of her mouth. "At least get her to listen to them. And she obliged."

"And they said?"

A faraway look entered her eyes. "To have a mere child tromp through the Quarter with bundles of money was the last straw. The boss had to get rid of Papa. Send a message. While Mimi talked with neighbors and the law, I stared at my old home and prayed for a gowned Maman, a suited Papa, to emerge unscathed. Yet there was nothing but chimneys, a cast-iron stove, music stands bent like cheap umbrella spokes, and charred beams sticking up like human ribs." Her voice broke. "A rack of crystal goblets begging you to fill them with wine. So they could shatter and let Chateau Latour Bordeaux stain the rugs blood red." Her high pitch warranted stares of nearby diners. "My parents were reduced to ashes, yet those goblets remained intact." Though Samuel sat across from a grown woman, what he saw was a sassy little girl, giving a mock bow to a drunk Irishman; a petrified child, jumping off a balcony, thick hair streaming through the night.

He took her hands, which were ice cold, but not from lack of love, like those of Mimi, his great-grandmother. No, hers burned like dry ice, as if retelling the story had drained away her warmth yet enflamed her soul. He caressed her hands until they warmed to his touch and she resumed her story.

Chapter 7

Backwater Blues

N*o true Frenchman would set foot in Gentilly, even with that name.*
Sheba clutched the door handle of Mimi's black Packard and tried to forget Maman's words. Had Maman hated Gentilly because Mimi lived here or because Gentilly, with its barns and cattle, was a world away from their Quarter? Even with the windows rolled up, a manure smell seeped into the car. Though the sun shone brightly, grass shimmered with dew, and majestic oaks stood tall and proud, life without Maman and Papa was colorless, lifeless.

"Here, James." The leather seat creaked as Mimi leaned forward and handed her driver a list. "Make a market run after you drop us off. We've an extra mouth to feed."

Who cared about food? What Sheba hungered for wasn't a chauffeured car or pretty scenery. Her eyes stung. Why had Maman sent Honey to her? Had the voodoo woman's curse killed her parents? Sheba blinked away tears. No one could tell her why her parents had to die except the Lord God. Where could she find Him?

James set down the list Mimi had given him and again gripped the steering wheel with thick-knuckled hands. He slowed for a railroad crossing and veered right. A wooded land, swelling slightly into a gentle hill, loomed ahead. The car strained and leveled out as they rounded a curve. Sunlight cast diamonds on a huge expanse of water.

Drawn from grief by the dazzle, Sheba pressed her face against glass. "What's that?"

"Lake Pontchartrain," James said. "De mix of salt and fresh water breeds shrimps and crabs so thick, you kin whistle and dey'll come. You kin swim those troubles away." A Dixieland hum swayed James' shoulders and head. Jazz, she realized, then leaned back and let his low, slow bass notes probe at the death fog surrounding her. Perhaps she'd found a friend in James. Someone who understood music. Someone who understood her old life . . .

"Just a germ-infested bog," Mimi harrumphed. "I wouldn't set my toe in there."

Sheba sat up straight. *I would!* The daily run had taken her and Papa by the river, which brought Indian curry, Brazilian coffee, and heaps of fine things into the Quarter. No lake could compete with her Mississippi, and yet the waters might nourish her soul. The lowest and slowest of notes sounded deep within. Perhaps she would find answers—and hope—here.

James maneuvered around a curve and left the lake behind. They drove past a block of brick homes, identical as pralines on the tin sheets at Leon's. Shingled roofs pitched tents over picture windows. Square garages had been tacked on as if afterthoughts. No wonder Maman turned up her nose at Gentilly. Still, if there was music, and a water's lifeblood, there was hope.

A sign boasted: *Welcome to a Better Living Home. Where Living Is Fun.* Maman had criticized the building boom that had hung on despite the war. Entire neighborhoods filled land once swamped by bogs. But Maman was gone. Sheba's head drooped. Why, *why* did her parents have to die?

"Here 'tis, Miss Sheba."

She closed her eyes. Tensed her shoulders. Dared she look? What if she hated it?

"We're home," announced James.

The words fluttered open her eyes. She raised her head. If only this could be a home. Or something like one.

Stubby stilts lifted a stucco house off the ground. A lush green lawn, shaded by banana, mulberry, and peach trees, stretched on forever, unlike the assembly-line houses on the previous block. Why, this lot could accommodate half a dozen Quarter homes! Esplanade, with its gables and grillwork and flagstone walks. Esplanade, ashes and rubble.

"4949 Music Street," James announced, as if he owned the house himself.

Sheba sat up and studied the house more closely. Music Street? Mimi, who called jazz the devil's handmaiden, lived on Music Street? Now Sheba studied her grandmother. Despite those tight lips and crossed arms, a love of song might be buried inside.

The hum that had started with the lake swelled into a waltz. Music Street had to possess a spirit of music. Papa's spirit. She tapped Mimi's shoulder in a hopeful way. "How did Music Street get its name?"

"Heaven only knows," Mimi said.

James cleared his throat. Caught Sheba's gaze in the rearview mirror. "All's I know is what dis ole man up on the Ridge say. A Gentilly dairyman had a son who couldn't see hisself shoveling manure. He took off fo' de Quarter, got lost in music and womens. Only ways his papa got him back to Gentilly was by namin' this street Music. Brung de Quarter here fo' him."

"A likely story." Mimi brushed at her jacket. "Quite unsuitable for a young girl."

James chuckled. "Well, now, Miz Alexander, de best stories got enough pretend to make things interestin'. All good N'Awlins folk keep ties to de Quarter."

"How far is it?" Though she sat in a car parked in a Gentilly drive, Sheba envisioned the Cathedral spires shadowing Jackson Square. She could catch the streetcar and find Honey, Maman's old friend. Ask Honey questions about Maman and the Lord God. She could survive here if the Quarter occasionally nourished her soul.

"A hair under six mile, Miss Sheba." James shifted until his face was no longer visible in the mirror. "'Bout one light year."

"What's a light year?"

A shaft of sun pierced the dense shade and spotlighted the back of James's head. "It's how far light travels through space in a year."

As James went on, Sheba envisioned sunbeams pouring through their Esplanade parlor windows, setting dust motes to waltzing, along with Papa and Maman. Sorrow drooped her head. She could see the light, imagine the light, but would she ever again *feel* the light?

"Don't addle her brain, James," Mimi huffed. "And we *really* need to get busy."

James got out and opened the door for them. A door to a new world. Sheba's emotions felt pulpy, exposed. Would there be a place for her on Music Street?

Giant oaks canopied the house. A small porch sheltered the front door. Five narrow windows broke the pattern of the long, straight wall. Sheba clasped her hands. Oh, that music would flow here! With Maman and Papa gone, she wanted, she needed music to live.

"Miz Sheba!" A Negro woman bounced down porch steps. She wore a starched apron over a dark dress and a kerchief over her head. She twirled a broom as if it were a baton. With her smile, this woman could lead the biggest Mardi Gras parade of them all.

"Now, now, Camille." Mimi laid a gloved hand on the crook of James's elbow and let him maneuver her up the stairs. "Let's don't get Miss Alexander all riled up."

Not Miss Alexander! My name is Sheba, she wanted to scream. When Mimi signed the hospital discharge papers, scratching out *Sheba* and writing *Miss Alexander* on the dotted line, a whisper had started in Sheba that had grown when Mimi introduced her to the fire investigator as Miss Alexander. She longed to toss down her bag and stomp S-h-e-b-a into the green, green grass of this Gentilly yard. But Mimi's glare informed Sheba that *she* was the stranger here. Her mouth crumpling, she headed to the porch steps.

Camille leaned the broom against a porch rail and pattered forward. "Well, Miss Whoever You Is, I's glad to have you. A chile what dis house needs." Camille's pepper-and-lemon smell birthed waves of comfort. "'Specially one named Sheba."

Camille understood! Her gap-toothed smile helped Sheba climb the stairs.

Two rooms flanked the entryway. To her right, floor-length drapes shut out all but a hint of light. The room was a study in beiges and browns, from the couch to matched cane chairs. A drop cloth covered a piano, which beckoned Sheba to fling off its cover, bang the keys, and punish it for what had happened. But this was not her house. In a hundred ways, this was not her house.

If she could only be in their parlor, where Maman's baby grand gleamed with dark mahogany pride, its curved case lifted proudly by a spindly hold, as if to say, "Look at me." Like everything else, it had been reduced to a charred pile. A sob caught in Sheba's throat. She hurried after Camille so Mimi wouldn't hear her cry. Every time she'd shown emotion, Mimi had told her to shush. She couldn't abide a reprimand. Not now.

They passed through the kitchen, veered down a dark hall, zigzagged into another dark hall. The only sound was the rub of Camille's skirt against her calves, the clomp of Camille's worn shoes against the wood floor. Dizzy from so much darkness, Sheba leaned against the wall, her hand resting near a framed picture. She squinted, felt her eyes widen, then lost herself in the dancing eyes of a round-faced little boy. Her papa.

A tidal wave crashed against her. Fingernails raked the wall. She clenched her teeth, not only at the screechy sound made by her nails, but to squelch sadness. Her Papa, dead.

Camille pulled her close, as Louise had often done, and massaged her head with warm, sturdy fingers. It was enough to make Sheba want to wail, as Louise had done just hours ago, when the fire chief interviewed them both. Hot tears burned Sheba's eyes. Louise had begged to help care for her. She'd begged too. Mimi had curled her lips and said, not just no, but "Never." Sheba again leaned against the wall, sure that she would crumble into nothingness.

"Lord Jesus, you gotta help dis chile carry on," Camille cried.

The Lord Jesus? Was that Hattie Pearl's Lord Jesus? Maman's Jesus? She opened her mouth to ask Camille and found she had lost not only her family, but her voice.

"Come on, chile." Sturdy arms tugged her into a room.

A lacy white spread stretched over a double bed. She blinked at so much whiteness, dazzling after the dark halls. Her stomach churned. In this house, dark and light were at war.

"I cut you some roses from my garden at home. But I ain't brung 'em in." Camille shuffled close. "Missus said they'd set off her allergies."

"Let's get you settled." Mimi strode into the room, bringing the smell of strong soap. Sheba ached for the scent of roses, the perfume favored by Maman and her mystery friend, Honey.

"How . . . did Maman know Honey? Tell me about her."

Mimi's face contorted like a House of Mirrors reflection. She pointed her finger at Sheba. "Don't you ever again mention her name in this house. You hear?" Heat crackled from every syllable. Mimi was on fire.

Sheba hugged her arms. Darted glances about the room. But she could not escape the flames this time . . . or her emotions. A choking sound rose from her throat.

"There is a balm in Gilead," Camille sang. She crossed the room, dug in a chest drawer, then gently closed it. Sheba shut her eyes, comforted by the words Louise had loved to belt out.

"You'd best rest for a bit." Mimi took Sheba by the arm as if she owned her and led her to the bed. "We've much to do."

The covers spread back, the pillows fluffed up, obedient to Camille's dark hands, which softened Mimi's harsh pronouncements. Sheba eyed the downy whiteness, which beckoned her to sink in and disappear. If only she could disappear from life . . .

"Forty winks, that's all you'll need. It'll do wonders." Mimi laid a hand on Sheba's shoulder and drew away. Her mouth opened again, but then closed as if she didn't know what else to say or how to say it. She turned and left the room.

"Here." Camille handed her a gown, then turned her back. "Hold your light," she crooned, "on Canaan's shore."

A pretty song, but it didn't brighten the drab gown that swallowed Sheba. Another unfamiliar thing. She got in bed, craving sleep, yet closed eyes brought smoldering images. Tears slipped soundlessly down her face.

"It gwine be all right, Miss. The Lord Jesus gwine get you through." Camille settled the cover about her. "He done know our troubles . . ."

Bathed in lemon-pepper spiciness, Sheba let Camille's voice wash over her. Later she'd ask about the Lord Jesus. For now, she let the voice of her first friend on Music Street rock her to sleep.

◆

Black as the coffin drapes. As her funeral clothes. Sheba tossed a lumpy black jacket onto a dressing room settee in New Orleans' finest department store. She'd worn black to the service that showed nothing of Maman and Papa, the service Mimi declared off-limits to Papa's music friends, the service in that dank funeral home parlor. Why must she wear black during the hot southern summer, and even worse, to a public school? Why must she even go to public school? She'd always been tutored at home. Another change fit as poorly as these stiff, scratchy clothes.

"She needs black stockings. A hat." Mimi's voice echoed down the corridor.

"Yes, ma'am," answered Godchaux's sales lady.

"Black shoes."

"Yes, ma'am."

The door to her dressing room opened. A manicured hand held out more black. "Here you go, dear." The sales lady chirped like a bird greeting the dawn. "Try this one."

Sheba slumped against a flowery wall. *You've dark hair, dark eyes. Quite enough darkness without wearing it, ma chère.* Thanks to Maman's eye for fashion, her wardrobe had overflowed with pink sweater-and-skirt sets, blue and orchid dresses. That wardrobe was now ashes. As was her old life. She had to build a new life with Mimi. Even if it meant wearing black.

Sighing, she slipped off her clothes, put on the dress, pouted at the tri-fold mirror. If Mimi had her way, black would fill her wardrobe and drain color from her already pale skin. Another peek showed dark circles ringing puffy eyes. She longed to sink into the dressing room's plush pink carpet and shut out black. But when she closed her eyes, flames moved in and made black a preferred choice. "Hurry up, now." Mimi's voice boomed from the hall. "We're to get you tested at two. Let's see. We'll need black gloves. A black purse. Black slip." She ticked off items as if she had a list. Perhaps she did.

Sheba let go of the dress, which dropped about her ankles. The sales woman slipped into the room and gathered padded hangers and discarded dresses. "I'll be right back," she told Sheba, who'd wrapped her arms about her body, averted her head. She wasn't used to strangers seeing her half-dressed. The fire had exposed her to many unfamiliar things.

"We must be quick about this." The door creaked open and Mimi entered.

Sheba kept hugging herself, not wanting Mimi to see her budding breasts, her rounded tummy. A span wider than the Mississippi separated her from her closest kin, Papa's mother. Sheba glanced at Mimi's reflection in the mirror, hoping to see some resemblance to Papa. Perhaps the angle of her jaw . . .

"Do you want me to choose for you, *dear?*" Steely eyes studied Sheba. Eyes that Sheba hadn't seen cry a single tear, even through the funeral.

No. I want you to grieve. Like me. Sheba snapped her jaws to stop the nasty retort but let resentment push back her shoulders. "I can manage." She sorted through clothes mounded on the dressing room chair, laid aside the black suit, the black skirt, the black Eisenhower jacket, seized the black dress from the floor. "This one." She held it over her slip, more to shield herself from those hard eyes than to model the dress for Mimi.

Mimi's eyes narrowed. "Hmm. In a pinch, it'll have to do."

The little victory gave Sheba strength to move toward the dressing room door and open it. She gestured for Mimi to leave; to her surprise, Mimi did. She waited until the door shut and she heard Mimi click down the hall. Then she collapsed onto a bench, her legs trembling, the dress clutched in her hands. She folded back its skirt and ran her finger along a pink binding some fanciful seamstress had used on the hem. Out of sight, where Mimi couldn't see it. Pink as Maman's favorite cocktail dress. Hot tears burned her achy eyes. In small, secret ways, she'd hang on to Maman, Papa, and the life they'd had. After all, her name was Sheba.

◆ ◆ ◆

Servers unloaded platters of steaming food, and it was a good thing, or Samuel might have cursed at his great-grandmother's stingy, loveless spirit. No wonder defeat tugged at his mother's eyes.

Aged beef, proclaimed on the menu as the Stockyards' finest, potatoes, rolls, and drink refills covered their table. But a little girl, hungry for love, drew his attention.

"How long did you live with her?" he asked as he split and buttered a roll.

"Four long years."

"Light years?"

His stab at humor was successful. Did she ever have a smile!

"There were meteor showers here and there." She rubbed the tablecloth, as if scouring an unseen stain. "Mostly we lived in a black hole. My grandfather's dark secrets, my father's lifestyle, had sucked the air out of Mimi, and she filled the void with rules." A sigh shook her shoulders. "She determined that I live in the same way."

"Did her scheme work?"

Again she gave him that sad smile and continued her story.

Chapter 8

Nothing but the Blood of Jesus

What would Maman say about me going to church? She bit her lip. What Maman said didn't matter anymore. But what Mimi said did matter. And Sunday meant church.

On the outskirts of Gentilly, James stopped at a light. Dark-skinned girls with braided, bow-tied hair crossed the street with a strut that made their skirts bob like fishing lures and showed lace petticoats. Once across, they dashed into a clapboard building topped with a steepled cross. On its steps, women in sherbet-colored dresses hugged like long-lost friends. Men in vested suits clapped each others' backs. Sheba pressed her palms against the window. "Is this the church?"

A chuckle came from James.

"Of course not!" Mimi plunked her pocketbook into her lap. "What would possess you to say such a thing? White folk setting foot in a Negro church? The very idea!"

Would it be so bad? She belonged there, she could feel it in the rhythm of their movements. Maman and Papa had never cared about skin color. But Mimi did. *So that's that.*

James veered onto the highway and crossed Canal, flooding Sheba with memories. Just a few turns, and they would be on Esplanade. She leaned back, closed her eyes. If only she were home! "Mimi," she cried, suddenly afraid of another change, "must I go?"

Mimi crossed her gloved hands and laid them atop her pocketbook. "Of course. It'll do you good to get out."

A trolley car clanged a warning, bore down on them, and chugged away as they turned onto St. Charles. Great oaks with scraggly moss loomed over a grassy boulevard. Cricket chirps and cicada buzzes split the silence that hung heavy over shuttered homes. The Garden District awoke Sunday memories of strolling through Audubon Park till the heat brought on Maman's thirst, which she quenched in a café. No church; Maman couldn't abide it, except when Papa insisted they go on Easter. Uncertainty crowded into the back seat with Sheba. Could *she* abide church?

"There." Mimi pointed to a colossal limestone building with a blocky bell tower, classical arches and columns. Solid, sure gongs announced the hour.

The weight of death lightened, as always, when music spoke. Sheba scooped up her new Bible and waited for James to open the door. She could study the slopes and slants of this grand place. Listen to a piano. A choir. Perhaps Mimi was right about church.

James pulled under a porte cochere shading double doors. He bowed before helping them out. "I'll be back at noon," he mumbled, and left.

"Is that her? Is that the girl whose house burned down?" A woman with a wide-brimmed hat broke stride to whisper and stare, as if Sheba were a circus freak—*the Daughter of the Dead Musician!*

Churchgoers streamed toward the doors. Toward her. Had they heard the woman?

Sheba longed to run after James, crying, "Take me home." But Music Street wasn't home. She hunched her shoulders and shadowed Mimi into the building.

A balding man with a "Greeter" badge hurried forward. "Well, well, who have you brought today?" he asked Mimi. He had a circus barker's bow tie, rosy cheeks, and chuckle.

"This is my granddaughter." Mimi smoothed a curl from Sheba's face. "Thomas's daughter."

"I see," the man said knowingly.

So they have all heard about the fire. About me. Despite a desire to lash out, she resolved to show manners. "I'm Sheba," she said, before Mimi could butt in with her "Miss Alexander" routine.

"Hello, Sheba. I'm Mr. Robertson." The man found a pen and tilted his head birdlike to study her. "Is that S—?"

"S-h-e-b-a. Like the queen." She sighed, thinking how Maman loved her name, how it really was quite simple to spell.

"Yes. Well . . ."

"We need to find her class." Mimi cut off further explanation. "She's thirteen."

"Fourteen. Almost, anyway."

Mimi's eyebrows arched to meet the felt edge of her turban. "Excuse me?"

"By the time I start school, I'll be fourteen."

"The teachers will figure it out." Mr. Robertson pinned a name tag onto Sheba, pricking her in the process. It hung lopsided, which matched her off-kilter feeling.

They were led into a low-slung, modern wing. Classrooms lined a broad hall. Mr. Robertson asked Mimi if there'd been "developments." More fire talk. Unending. She lagged behind so as not to hear their whispers, nearly positive that the fresh start she needed wouldn't begin in church.

"Here you go." An open door bore a sign that said *Junior High Girls*.

Sheba fiddled with her name tag, tempted to rip it off. Even without the silly thing, she would be the odd duck. Nothing would change that fact.

"Good morning." A woman with stiff blonde hair met her at the door.

"This is Mrs. Baxter." Mr. Robertson did an about-face and disappeared.

"Hello, dear." Unblinking blue eyes squinted. Mrs. Baxter was nearsighted, curious, or both. "Sheba, is it? Did I say that right?"

Sheba nodded and scooted closer to Mimi.

"I'll be back soon." Mimi turned to leave.

Sheba clutched her grandmother's sleeve. She'd rather stay with predictable Mimi than with strangers. But Mimi pulled away and was swallowed by a chattering crowd.

"It'll be fine, once you get settled." Mrs. Baxter nudged her into the classroom, where a dozen girls sat in a circle of folding chairs. *Girls who look much younger than me.* Sheba couldn't stop the voice whispering *Odd duck, odd duck.*

A man in a blue suit sat by a small table at the back of the room. When he smiled, Sheba ducked her head. Why did she tear up at the most unexpected things? Like kindness?

"Let's get you registered." Mrs. Baxter led her past whispers and giggles.

Sheba tensed at each girlish sound. They knew about her parents, too.

"Can you get us a visitor's form?" Mrs. Baxter asked the man.

"She's not a visitor." Though low-toned, his voice had authority. "She's Mrs. Alexander's granddaughter. We'll use a member form."

Mrs. Baxter motioned for her to sit in the circle's only vacant chair. "Where did y'all go to church, dear?"

A heavy silence made Sheba long for the chatter to return. "St. Louis Cathedral." She swallowed. It wasn't really a lie. They did go, on Easter. Tucked-away images unfolded. Maman kneeling. The priest, with rhythmic swings of an incensor, perfuming the air. Papa, dipping his hands in holy water. Tears threatened but she willed them away.

"You mean you're *Catholic?* Surely Mrs. Alexander didn't—"

"Why, it's a fine church, Mrs. Baxter. I've been there myself." The man stepped near, took the form from Mrs. Baxter, and led Sheba to his back-room table, which had posters of bearded and robed men tacked above it. They both sat down.

"She's *Catholic?*"

"I heard they didn't go to church."

"And her mother was a . . ."

Sheba gripped the chair seat. She forced her gaze on a poster of a blue-eyed man riding a donkey through crowds of people waving palm branches. Despite his plain robe, he had a king's posture. She stared at his soft eyes, hoping such a king would order the girls to hush.

"Perhaps y'all could practice the opening song. We'll do the form."

The girls' chatter continued as Mrs. Baxter just stared and soaked up the scene.

Sheba's knuckles tightened. Mrs. Baxter should do her job and make them stop talking.

"The piano, Mrs. Baxter." The man's voice muffled the noise. "Girls. Quiet."

Mrs. Baxter hurried to a weathered-looking piano and with a thud sat down. The girls pulled hymnals from under their chairs. Sheba exhaled. Finally someone was in charge.

"I'm Mr. Young, Sheba," the man said. "We'll do this together." He gave her a hearty smile. "Sheba Alexander. Same address as Mrs. Alexander? Gentilly, I believe." Neat cursive filled the page. "Age? Thirteen, I'd guess." His smile made Sheba nod.

"Bible brought?" He checked the first box on the form and moved to the next. "I'm sure Mrs. Alexander has your offering." Another check. Another. Sheba wiped her forehead. What she didn't know about Sunday school would fill a hundred boxes.

A set of chords, played with a heavy hand and little style, rose from the out-of-tune piano. Hardly music, but it shut out a chance for chatter to return. *Keep playing,* she begged. *No matter how bad, it's better than listening to those girls.*

"What a friend we have in Jesus . . ." Over the twangy chords rose a pure alto voice. Sheba's head swiveled. *That* came from Mrs. Baxter?

". . . All our sins and griefs to bear," the girls sang.

Sheba watched them all, especially Mrs. Baxter, whose face shone with a light she could not understand. How she wanted to, for it might help her belong here at church!

Fingers roamed the keyboard, pressing C instead of B, A instead of G. It didn't matter, for Mrs. Baxter had left this world and entered music land, which softened the blows from hateful whispers, harsh glares. Music changed things. Sheba was ready for change.

They sang three hymns, each more lovely than the one before. During the chorus of a song about grace, Mr. Young led Sheba to the circle.

When the last note sounded, chatter resumed. So did the knowledge that she was an outsider.

"Let us pray." Bible in hand, Mr. Young stepped to a podium. "Father in heaven . . ."

Sheba squeezed her fists tight. She couldn't pray to the God of these other people, a God she didn't know.

"I thank You, Lord, for those You have brought here today. May we learn about Your holy love, the peace You offer."

If it's about peace and love, I do want to learn. Sheba glanced at Mr. Young's furrowed forehead, his rapt expression. Was her thought a prayer like his? Could she learn to talk to the God of Louise, Camille, Sunday school folks? And learn from Him why her parents had to die?

"We ask it in the name of Your Son, who died for our sins. Amen."

Mrs. Baxter settled into the seat next to Sheba. She smoothed her skirt, opened her Bible, and marked her place with a quarterly. Away from the piano, her jittery motions and bug-eyed glances had returned. Sheba glued her eyes on the podium, ready for something to happen to get the attention off her.

"Good morning, class. Put down your quarterlies. We're doing something different today."

A murmur spread about the circle.

"We don't talk enough about love." Mr. Young cleared his throat, as if his words bore huge import. "God loved us enough to let His Son, Jesus, die for us."

Somehow Sheba knew the donkey-riding man on the poster was Jesus, whom Louise had said was God's son. How could God have a son? She had never asked Louise, had never thought of it until now. What God would let his son die? She tried to keep from biting her lip at the confusion of it all. Did God also let her parents die?

"No matter what you've done, where you've been, Jesus will never forsake you." Mr. Young gripped the lectern, which seemed to totter with his fervor.

Bibles opened, yet Sheba kept hers in her lap. As Mr. Young spoke about God's love, her soul fluttered, like doves alighting under cathedral eaves. She needed this Jesus. But was Jesus part of God? Different from God? It made no sense. Yet the flutter spread through Sheba like the notes of a favorite song, lightening the burden she had carried since the fire.

"He loved even the woman at the well, the thief who mocked Him . . ." Besides Mr. Young's voice, the only sound was crinkling pages. She sat straight, desperate to snag every syllable this man uttered.

"He loves all of you girls. I thank You for every one of them . . ."

Sheba cast sideways glances at bowed heads. Somehow the lesson had gone into a prayer without her knowing it. A sigh escaped. She had much to learn about church.

After Mr. Young said "amen," she rose from her chair, clutching her Bible as if it were a treasure map with clues to find the Lord God.

The classroom door opened. There stood Mimi, her cheeks flushed. "How did you do?" she asked, her voice squeaky.

Sheba stopped short. It was as if Mimi hoped something would happen but was scared of what that something might be. *Scared. Unsure. Like me.*

Sheba nodded, drawn to Mimi as never before. "The lesson, the music, it all—"

Breath released from Mimi. "I'm glad you fit in, dear." Before she could tell Mimi about her conflicted feelings, Mimi took her arm and led her into the hall. "Come, now. We must find our seats." With nods and murmurs, they weaved past chatty folk who came at them in waves.

Like the others, Sheba longed to flow in this church river, which might be how Mimi escaped Papa's death with so few tears. She thought of the family Bible on Mimi's dresser, the Lottie Moon newsletters in the parlor. Mimi could answer questions about the Lord God.

Retracing their earlier steps, they moved into the atrium. Great rumbles vibrated crystal chandeliers. Sheba's pulse raced. What was that sound?

A man nodded at them, gave them a program, and led them to the sanctuary.

Sheba followed Mimi down a scarlet carpet runner. Pealing bells joined the strange thunderous sound to energize the air . . . and Sheba, whose eyes roved the room. Sunlight pierced stained glass windows and glittered off mammoth musical pipes. She peered to her left. Spotted an organ. So that was the instrument making the sound that managed to be both fearsome and majestic! Once Maman had blown across a wine bottle to imitate an organ's sound. But that had been like tapping a shoe to mimic a timpani. With a spring in her step, she followed Mimi into a pew.

People around them chatted; she longed to shush those who dared interrupt the musical feast.

A chord boomed from the pipes, bounced off the ceiling, and tingled her skin. She fought the urge to hum.

Choir members wearing satin robes and holding hymnals poured into a loft and added song to the rumbles and the roars.

Sheba hadn't fathomed the depths of her need for music—for church—for God—until Mrs. Baxter's playing, Mr. Young's words, settled in to crowd out sorrow. Mimi had been right about church.

The choir director signaled for them to stand. Mimi pulled a hymnal from a rack, found the page, and held it out so they could share. The music, the smiles, drew Sheba up, up, until she became part of the choir, as did Mimi, who let off notes so pure, so clear, they eclipsed even Maman's angel voice. Sheba's voice swelled with the finale. Besides the Alexander name, she and Mimi shared music. This fact made it worth suffering rude comments and embarrassing stares. Sheba sidestepped closer to Mimi and inhaled her powdery scent. Perhaps there was a place for her on Music Street . . .

They sang "The Doxology." Prayed for soldiers fighting the Japanese and Germans. After they settled in the pews, the choir sang in G major uplifted by an eight-note cadence. Sheba longed to clap at the glorious sounds, but a man to her right yawned, as did a little boy. Sheba stared at them curiously. How could they not be touched?

When the choir members settled in their loft seats, a stern-faced man rose from a bench and moved to the lectern. He opened a Bible, set it down, and speared Sheba with eyes that blazed under bushy brows. "Moreover the Lord saith, 'Because the daughters of Zion are haughty, and walk with stretched forth necks and wanton eyes, walking and mincing as they go, and making a tinkling with their feet'"—the man pulled out a handkerchief and mopped his forehead—"'therefore the Lord will smite with a scab the crown of the head of the daughters of Zion, and the Lord will discover their secret parts.'" The Bible thudded shut.

Sheba rubbed eyes aflame from the man's stare, the man's words. Scabs. Secret parts. How awful!

The man bowed his head. "May God bless the reading of His holy Scripture, amen."

Sheba kept her head bowed, fearful to again meet the man's gaze. Something horrible was about to happen, she was sure of it.

"Heavenly Father, we ask that You rain fire and brimstone upon this wanton city, if that is what it takes to return it to holiness."

She raised her head, gripped her Bible, moistened her lips. This man wanted God to set fire to New Orleans. This Father couldn't be related to Mr. Young's Jesus.

"With a holy lightning bolt, strike down the houses of gambling." Waving his arms, the man paced to the left, to the right. "The houses of ill repute, of drinking."

The chandelier lights seemed to dim at the fury in his voice. "Open up the fiery bowels of hell for those who flagrantly disregard Your law."

Papa gambled. Johnny guzzled. The mysterious Honey, was she a "daughter of Zion"? Sheba laced writhing fingers. Would God cast the Quarter folk into a burning dungeon, where demons cackled and fires burned forever? She swallowed hard. Glanced to her right, where the man had nodded off. Sheba made fists of sweaty hands. How could he sleep while people were being cast into hell?

"Be forewarned, all of you!"

The preacher pointed his finger straight at her.

Sheba jostled about. Her Bible plunked to the floor. Every instinct said leave. But she had nowhere to go.

Mimi leaned close. "This means you, too. Now be still." She retrieved Sheba's Bible and slapped it into her lap.

As the preacher ranted, heat rose from the podium, traveled in a wave, and surrounded Sheba. She was back in the study, orange and yellow imps leaping about her in glee. She wiped sweat from slick hands. If God condemned her parents to a fiery pit, did she want to know Him?

Desperate to escape the preacher's fiery gaze, she glanced down the pew. The little boy, his slicked-back hair clownish, grinned, crossed his eyes, and stuck out his tongue.

She made a funny face, too, then watched the man, whose jowls shook with wheezy snores. If the boy could cut up, the man could sleep through such a warning, maybe it wasn't true.

"Their lewd behavior has brought about this very war for which thousands of our young men are shedding their blood." Sweat poured off the pacing preacher's face.

Sheba drew in a breath and blew out a sigh. Hitler had started this war, not Quarter people. The pastor's lie hardened the place that had been softened by the Sunday school lesson and the music. She set the Bible between her and Mimi and smiled at the boy, who continued his antics. An offering was taken, more songs were sung. Sheba watched, heard, but let nothing penetrate the shell encasing her heart.

◆

"So they turned you away from God?"

She bowed her head. "I attended Sunday school for years, even GAs—Girls Auxiliary—but only because Mimi made me." She pressed her hands to her face. "Did that . . . that happen to you?"

A smile morphed into a laugh. *At least you can comfort her on this one, Bub.* "No way. Chapel was cool. I mean, for church," he added. Best not to get sappy. "Good thing, too, or the nuns would'a boxed my ears."

Her eyes fluttered, as did a sigh. "I've prayed every day of my life that you would know Jesus. And that He would know you."

Their server appeared. *Thank You, God.* He was melting down. Fast.

"Are you finished, sir?"

"Yes. Thank you." He set down his napkin, stared at his empty plate, yet saw her face. So she wasn't a phony hiding behind her husband's title. He hadn't prepared himself for someone like this . . .

"Madam? Shall I take your plate?"

She nodded, though she'd barely eaten a bite.

"Was . . . everything satisfactory?"

"Satisfactory?" Her eyes widened, the concern in the waiter's voice seeming to startle her. "It was delicious. It's just . . . I guess I was too excited to eat."

The waiter grinned, as if he too was moved by her glowing face. "Could I bring coffee? Perhaps a nightcap?"

Samuel dropped his hand to his lap, pushed up his jacket sleeve, discreetly checked the time. Ten? Late, and he'd just begun. Good thing he was on leave. "We're fine, thanks. I just need the check."

At a snap of the waiter's fingers, busboys moved in and cleared the dishes.

Samuel pulled out his wallet and laid crisp bills on the tray.

"Oh, no. I don't expect you to pay." A blush spread across her cheeks.

"But I want to. Then I'll call you a cab."

"I brought my car." She brushed crumbs off the table, her sleeve dangerously close to the votive. "Where . . . where are you staying?"

"A buddy set up billeting out at Fort Sheridan."

Wrinkles creased her smooth forehead. "That's practically in Wisconsin."

"It's no trouble, ma'am," he said, then winced at the cloud that passed over her face. He shouldn't be so formal with her. He should treat her like . . . a mother. And soon, if he wanted her to meet with him again.

"Of course it is." For the first time this evening, a lilt entered her voice and he heard the music that was part of his heritage. No wonder he'd loved mass, with its ancient liturgies and songs of prayer. Just listening to her, he could practically smell the incense. If she kept talking like that, she might soften the places made rock-hard by Nam.

"Stay with me. I'd like to hear *your* story." She thrust her hand across the table as if to grab his, then stared at it and made a fist. "Edward's out of town. We've got lots of room and we live so close . . ."

Her plea stirred memories he'd suppressed for years. *Mid sorrows and trials to know, that the love of their mother hath ever a solace for woe.* A wrinkled old nun, singing words that blanketed him during cold St. Paul nights. His first grade teacher, pasting a row of stars on his story. In spite of his mother's inability to be there for him, others sure had. Only a jerk would say no to her now. Especially when their business had just started.

He shut out knowledge of what he must do and took her hand. "On one condition . . . Mother."

Tears rimmed her eyes. She nodded.

He looked toward the lobby—no sign of the waiter . . . or his change. "You keep telling me this story." Though he battled with them, questions kept rising from the folder, still lying between them on the table. He let one question rise to the top. "When . . . how . . . did they change your name?"

Chapter 9

Come Rain or Come Shine

Though she'd never set foot in a school, there couldn't be a prettier one. Paved steps led to a dramatic arch. Corniced windows dotted a brick façade. Maman would fancy this place despite her belief that the best schooling happened at home. For what seemed like the hundredth time, Sheba lectured herself. What Maman said did not matter anymore.

Despite her pain, Maman and Papa would have her move on, especially as it related to her education.

Mimi wrestled with the school's heavy door and managed to get it open. They walked together down the hall, Mimi cooing, "There, there," as if she understood Sheba's nervousness. "They have a good reputation." Mimi smiled brightly. "A few remedial classes, and they will have you at grade level in no time."

Sheba tightened her lips. Last week she'd taken the exam to determine her grade placement. She daren't tell Mimi that she'd thought the test easy, that unless she had lost her mind as well as her parents, she'd done quite well.

"Finished already?" the secretary had asked, setting down her magazine and peering over reading glasses at Sheba. "You'd best check them, dear." Sheba nodded but kept to herself the fact that she had skimmed it twice and daydreamed a good ten minutes before handing it in. Perhaps she had misjudged. Since the fire, everything had turned topsy-turvy.

As Mimi chattered, they trod a gleaming tile floor. Granite pedestals held marble busts of aristocratic-looking gentlemen. The school's founding fathers? Sunbeams penetrated casement windows and dazzled silver plates and bronze trophies in display cases. Even Mimi hushed, only her clattering heels breaking the silence as they followed signs to the office. Trembles cascaded through Sheba. What if she were "remedial"?

"Mrs. Alexander? Sheba?" A man stepped from behind a counter and offered Mimi his hand. Dapper in a black suit, his dark hair and moustache slick with pomade, he looked like a Bourbon Street barker. Trying to sell them on this school?

"I'm Mr. Delacroix." The principal led them into a conference room lined with bookshelves and motioned for them to sit. "Coffee?"

Mimi shook her head, opened her purse, and withdrew a handkerchief. She dabbed at her temples and then twisted the handkerchief into a cloth croissant. "No. Thank you."

The tension in Mimi squeezed Sheba's throat. Maybe she *had* misjudged her efforts. She fidgeted until she felt Mr. Delacroix's eyes on her, then copied the posture she'd seen in a *Ladies Home Journal* article about first impressions. Straight back. Toes together. Hands crisscrossed in her lap. Trying to ignore the lump in her throat.

"Miss Alexander, let me say how pleased we are that you have chosen to enroll here." With short, chubby fingers, Mr. Delacroix stroked an onyx ring, a gaudy gold watch.

Sheba forced a company smile on her face. Only with James, with Camille, could she grin, or frown, or laugh. Be Sheba.

Mr. Delacroix pulled papers from a folder and shuffled through what looked like her test booklet. He ran his finger down a page, punctuating his movements with "Hmm" and "I see."

Mimi again dabbed at her temples.

Sheba's legs went numb. She had done poorly. This was awful!

"Sorry." Mr. Delacroix snapped out of his conversation with the scores. "These marks warranted a double check."

Sheba rubbed feeling into her legs. Mimi had been right. She was ignorant and hadn't even known it.

Mimi's cheeks splotched with red. "Surely with time, with tutors—"

Mr. Delacroix's smile revealed small, pointed teeth. "Quite the contrary, Mrs. Alexander. Your granddaughter shows uncommon potential. I recommend that she be enrolled in high school."

"Surely you don't mean *senior* high?" Mimi's hankie became a cleaning rag to polish her chair arm.

"That's exactly what I mean." The gleam in Mr. Delacroix's eyes matched the shine in his ring. "There's really no debate." He beamed at Sheba as if she were his protégé. "Miss Alexander has mastered math, reading, and grammar at a tenth grade level. Due to her ... unusual background, I recommend starting her at ninth grade, though no doubt she would excel even as a sophomore." He smoothed down the folder. "She may take electives. Foreign language and orchestra."

Sheba imagined the quiver of bow against strings, tuxedoed musicians, and a make-believe audience. Again music soothed her hurt places. Barely fourteen, and she'd be in an orchestra!

"How can it be?" The words exploded from Mimi. "She did nothing but traipse about the Quarter. Tutors shuffled in and out of that house like lazy maids."

"Aha." Mr. Delacroix's eyes narrowed. "Perhaps she is naturally gifted. Assuredly she comes from a line of privileged, intelligent individuals." As heat rose to Sheba's cheeks, the principal continued to flatter Mimi, then thankfully checked his watch, rose, and offered Mimi his hand. "You have until September first to fill out the requisite paperwork. Call between eight and three, and we'll set up an appointment with the counselor. If ninth grade proves too simple, she can transition into tenth."

Mr. Delacroix led them out of the building and into the achingly bright sunlight of a June afternoon. With a click of the door, they left the educator and tiled atrium behind. Sheba remained with a frowning Mimi and the unsettled feeling she'd done something wrong. Mockingbirds rasped. Robins chirped. Traffic roared by, like it did on busy New Orleans streets. *She doesn't think I can do this*, Sheba realized as James helped them into the car. *Maybe she's right.*

◆

This doesn't look like a lawyer's office. Plush oriental rugs blanketed all but a thin strip of parquet. Thanks to hours spent with Maman in dusty antique shops, Sheba noted a passable replica Louis XV table clock. Gilt bronze lamps. A baby blue settee canapé, uncomfortable, with its tiny seat, spindly legs, but easy on the eyes. Unlike Miss Scowl Face, the receptionist who ruled from a mahogany desk. Definitely *not* easy on the eyes. Sheba sighed. Who would be, dealing with legal matters day in and day out? Dealing with just this one legal matter had kept Sheba tossing for nights.

A buzzing phone, and Mimi's flipping of magazine pages, broke the silence.

"Gabet, Toulong, and Steiner," the receptionist monotoned as she filed her nails. Sheba battled an urge to scream. Her identity walked a tightrope between her old life and the new one with Mimi. Yet the world yawned about its daily chores. It was maddening!

About the time Sheba thought she would rush to the window and pull back the brocaded drapes, a recessed door opened. In came a woman clad in a double-breasted suit with bulky shoulder pads and a tight skirt. "Mrs. Alexander," the woman drawled. "Nice to see you again."

Mimi strode forward, as if she knew exactly where she was going. The women chattered about Monday's flood, commonplace in the low-lying Quarter, but still newsworthy. Changes were gathering, like those rain clouds had earlier this week. Sheba lagged behind, desperate to stop the latest storm in her life.

Mimi disappeared into an office. The legal secretary turned and smiled at Sheba as if a grand surprise awaited. But Sheba had overheard enough phone conversations to know the truth: she was about to lose the last vestige of her former life.

She longed to about-face, fly past the receptionist, head for Canal Street. With a river breeze at her back, she'd skip along the square, let a mime pretend to take a coin from her ear—do all the things she'd done as Sheba, daughter of Thomas and Valerie Ann. She paused, stared down at the tile floor. Without Thomas and Valerie Ann, could she even do those things? Could she be Sheba?

As if Mimi read her thoughts, she poked her head back into the hall. Her eyebrows peaked like coned hats. "Come, now, Sheila."

Sheila. Now she realized that the tug-of-war over her name had begun the night of the fire, though at the time, Mimi's comments blurred into the whirl of emotions brought about by her parents' death. "How about Clarissa?" Mimi had asked, as Sheba prepared for her first night on Music Street. "Regina?" as Sheba sat for the first time at the piano. It had gone on and on until last week, when she'd heard, "How about Sheila?" as she ate breakfast. Her nod of surrender had set into motion a frenzied concerto whose finale was this appointment.

"Sheila?" Mimi called out. "Come on. Now, dear."

"I'm not Sheila, I'm Sheba," she mumbled. For seven days, she'd wavered about what to do, and decided she must protect the name Maman had given her. But how? If she ran down this paneled hall of barristers, poked her head into each office, and searched for sympathetic eyes, could she find one who would represent *her*? And if she did, could she tell her story in a way that would break through fancy French legal terms and a stubborn grandmother?

"We've gone over this, dear." Mimi's voice banged off the walls and slapped Sheba's resolve. Still, she clenched her fists. Tried to fight.

A young man popped across a threshold not three feet from where she stood. He stared at her, then tripped in his haste to scurry back into his office and avoid a scene. The walls—and the truth—pushed in. No one would understand. Even if they did, Mimi would have her way. Besides, it did not matter. Whatever her name, she'd never again be Sheba of the Quarter. Sheba had died in the fire, along with her parents.

"Come on, Sheila," Mimi whined.

"Sheila." The word reverberated down the hall. "Sheila."

She flinched at the sound of the name Mimi had chosen. Her knees locked and refused to carry her forward. This was wrong. All wrong.

"Now, dear." Mimi stood with her hands on her hips. "You promised."

I did no such thing, she started to say, but could not bear to hear another voice echo down the hall. She bit her lip, slumped after Mimi, and followed her into an office.

"Miss Alexander." A bald man rose from a captain's chair and limped, as if one leg were shorter than the other, to meet her. From behind the man, light poured through sparkling picture windows and illuminated built-in shelves. A musty old-book smell mingled with the aroma of tobacco. Sheba scanned the rolltop desk. Sure enough, an ashtray held the butt of a cigar, from which curled wisps of smoke. Mimi's lawyer loved books and cigars, like Papa had. He might have enough of Papa in him to understand why she loved her name.

"Please. Call me Sheba," she begged. She leaned forward, willing him to see through her, as if she were a glass figurine in Manheim's display window.

Creases appeared at the corners of wrinkly eyes. "All right, Sheba. Call me Mr. Toulong. Or Jack, if you'd like." He gestured toward stiff-backed chairs. She and Mimi sat down. The secretary hesitated, but left the room after a nod from Mr. Toulong.

Sheba let his surname roll off her tongue and settle on the roof of her mouth. "Toulong, is that French?" she asked, breaking a vow to keep quiet. This cigar-smoking attorney—and his name—intrigued her. She loved the language as beautiful, as complex, as Maman . . .

"Partially." Mr. Toulong rolled his chair across the planked floor until it was even with hers. He seemed to be staring out the window as he sat down.

"Around the turn of the century, my father, Jacques de Toulouse, disembarked at Ellis Island with nothing but hopes and dreams." The smell of tobacco wafted near. Sheba settled in her chair. "He spoke no English, other than *bathroom*, *work*, and phrases best not repeated in front of ladies."

Sheba breathed deep and tried to hold the blessed dried-leaf aroma in her lungs. Mr. Toulong could spin a tale like Johnny and Papa. She had missed Papa's stories . . .

"Somehow in the immigration process, my father's papers were lost. When everything got sorted out, Jacques de Toulouse had become Jack Long." He fixed her with a green-eyed gaze and raised a strong chin to display an aquiline nose like she'd seen in court portraits of Charles V, Maman's favorite. No wonder Jack had such a fancy office.

"When I became a partner here, I had my name legally changed. Toulong seemed a compromise between the old and new worlds. A balance, if you will."

She clung to his words. He understood how it felt to lose everything and have to start again.

"A nice story," Mimi huffed. "But we've papers to sign. A busy day ahead."

When Jack turned toward his desk and retrieved a thin folder, Sheba took in the high cheekbones that kept him, with his bald head, from looking like an egg. A character, Papa would've called him. Characters understood things. Maybe even her grandmother.

With a sweep of his arm, Jack opened the folder, pulled out papers.

"It's just a formality," he explained with a smooth, rich voice. Part French, part Louisiana. "Do you understand that, Sheba?" Either something made him blink, or he winked.

Sheba. He'd used her real name! Deep down, she could keep her old identity. Legal papers wouldn't alter the fact that her name was Sheba.

"I do understand, yes." It was hard not to wink back and call him Jack. She'd sign his documents, if for no other reason than to make life with Mimi bearable. Mr. Toulong, with his fine French spirit, had shown her a way to keep Sheba alive, disguised as a girl named Sheila. She sat straight. Looked him in the eye. She was signing a peace treaty so she and Mimi could coexist.

Papers were handed over for her perusal; she barely glanced at them. A fine French quill pen was dipped into an inkwell. As she wrote *Sheila Alexander* on a score of papers, she imagined Papa, singing Maman's favorite love song. Only *je t'aime* had become *My name is Sheba.*

◆

So this is how a mother drives. Samuel braked to keep from banging the bumper of his mother's Electra. In case he lost her, she'd scribbled out directions for him, but he'd never need to check them, thanks to her snail's pace. They exited at Lakeshore and headed west. Downtown lights splashed neon across the windshield of his rented car. The same garish streaks that seeped through the thin drapes in Mali's cell of a room. But it wasn't what came in through Mali's window that chilled his blood. It was the creeps who entered through her door.

He gripped the steering wheel to keep from cursing. Each neon-lit night burned another hole in her soul. If he didn't get her out, she'd crumble like the cigarette ash the men flung about her sheets after they'd . . . used her.

To escape brothel nightmares, he turned on the radio. "Down on the corner . . ." He fiddled with the station. "Gimmie gimmie good lovin' . . ." His palm slammed the power button, silencing the blasted thing. Mali and what she did to survive had infiltrated the airwaves to drive him berserk. Desperate for a distraction, he stared at his mother's car. *Focus, Bub.*

When they both stopped for a light, he checked the directions. Two more blocks, if he'd figured this right, and they'd reach the home he might have had, if she'd kept him.

The Electra's blinker splashed a red glow on an intersection eerily lit by dim streetlights. He veered right to follow his mother into the middle-class world of Chase Street. Cozy digs, with screened porches and shuttered windows. A world he'd longed for as he'd stared out frosty orphanage panes into bleak Minnesota nights.

Moths and fireflies, drunk on the glow of porch lights, swooped from house to house, clueless to the fact that if they got too close, they'd singe their wings and flutter to the cold hard ground. Dangerous, so much light. Illuminating memories he really didn't want to think about. He swiped at his face. *Bub, not the time to go soft.*

She arced into a driveway, parked in a detached garage, and motioned for him to pull in behind her.

He reached across the seat for his duffel. To keep from venting pent-up emotions, he fumbled with keys, brushed at the seat—anything to keep his eyes off her. The last thing he wanted was for her to learn about the grade school taunts. The racial slurs. His gut tightened. *She'd* done this to him; why did he care about *her* pain?

"Welcome." She extended her hand like it was a scepter and she was offering him her kingdom. When he ignored her, she deflated, went to the garage door, pulled it down. Then she plodded along stepping-stones, turned, waited for him.

He strode to the door of 1851 West Chase, taking in every detail. Mali's life might depend on it. Edged flower beds. All-brick exterior. Nice, but his mother and her preacher husband weren't flaunting the wealth the PI's report had bulleted. With the church footing the mortgage and car payments, there'd be plenty of money available for—he slapped a hand against his thigh.

No. He wouldn't do it. She loved him, and he . . . wanted a mother, family. He took captive the grenade of blackmail and flung it as far as he could. Now that he knew her, blackmail was no more of an option than slitting her throat.

"Please. Make it . . . make it your home, too." She crossed the threshold and turned to him, tears saturating her eyes, slipping down her cheek. She ran her tongue over trembling lips.

He breathed easier, now that the deadly explosive had been neutralized. She'd given birth to him, had suffered in ways he was just beginning to get. He'd hear her out and then determine how to save Mali. Include his mother in the plan, if he could work it that way. He bowed his head. *If he* could work it? How this came down had nothing to do with him. The sooner he gave this to God and blew off resentment and pride, the sooner God would grant peace. Wholeness. *Lord willing, Mali.*

He strode inside, set his duffel down. Met her gaze with a conscience washed of his dastardly scheme.

She smiled at him, and he glimpsed vestiges of that naïve little girl who'd thought she could be two persons at once.

Three steps, and she was in his arms.

The fresh, clean scent of her hair washed over him and continued the purge of sinful emotions. How often had he dreamed of holding his mother, of his mother holding him?

A sob came from her. Her shoulders shook.

He winced as if stabbed. Pulled away. He wasn't ready for this much emotion.

"I'm sorry." She stepped back. Dabbed at her eyes. "Let's get you settled." She looked so helpless, like Mali, that last time in Bangkok.

"No hurry," he said, eager to console her. "We'll get to that." Could it be possible—would God will it—that he could free his mother from guilt, from secrets, as he freed his Mali? He bowed his head, prayed, *Oh, Lord, please,* then glanced past his mother.

A baby grand piano angled nicely into the corner of a room. Next to the piano was a pink brocade love seat. The pink theme continued, velvety wallpaper patterned with pink roses. He thought of Maman's parlor, the color of Sheba's hat, and smiled. Her story had taken hold of him and refused to let go. Hey, it was his story, too. "But remember your part of the deal?"

"First things first." Her smile transformed her face, like a rainbow after a storm. She nodded toward a hall. "Your room's down there. First door on your right. The bathroom's on your left." As if his touch and his words had energized her, she bounced toward another hall, then glanced back at him. "Do you like tea?"

"You know us GIs." Her desire to please shook him but he responded casually. "We'll drink anything."

A shadow dimmed her girlish glow. She studied her hands. "I'll put on the water, then finish my story. Like I promised." She continued forward, then whirled. "I've always remembered you, Samuel. Cared." She clasped her hands together like Sister Bridget used to do when she prayed over him. "You have to believe that I wanted what was best for you."

They locked eyes. He was the first to look away.

"I do believe that," he said, and meant it.

Chapter 10

Invention No. 4

*A*h. *Freedom.* Sheila hurried toward room 212, having gained ten precious minutes when her mathematics instructor dismissed them early. Her insides fluttered with expectancy. Sixth period brought peace. Joy. Music.

"In that black, she's as out of place as a nun on Gallatin."

"Isn't that Mrs. Alexander's daughter? The one who . . ."

Girls wearing bobby socks, saddle shoes, and cinched-waist dresses lounged about lockers and smacked gum and gossip in equal measure. To drown them out, she hummed the codetta to the Bach piece that troubled her fingers but soothed her soul. Through room 212's music, Sheba stayed alive, if only in the quiver of strings across her rented violin, the racks of instruments. Not the clarinet, the instrument she'd longed for, an instrument Mimi would not abide, but still an instrument. For fifty-five blissful minutes, she would not only survive, but thrive.

She rushed into her sanctuary and breathed in the wood soap and varnish smell, strong despite a breeze that ruffled sheet music on the piano rack. Her strides carried her past the cellos, which, even in their black cases, boomed boisterous, manly hellos. Bent on fingering through the hard passages, she slid her violin from the rack and hummed the difficult notes as she hurried to her chair.

She dug in her case for her rosin box.

A blur of white caught her eye. She sat straight. Watched sheet music sail from the piano rack, float past yellowed keys.

Her rosin box thudded to the floor. Though it was against orchestra instructor Mr. Bouchet's rules to so much as touch the piano, she made her way to the bench, as if the ebony and ivory had cast a spell on her. What a temptation to tickle keys not controlled by Mrs. Johnson, the piano instructor Mimi had hired to teach her! To toss out the window Mrs. Johnson's adherence to the doctrines of classical beat!

She sat on the piano bench. Let her fingers trace the gold Kimball lettering and tickle the chipped keys, which pulled on the part of her that loved to skip down the street, loved to clap with spasm bands, loved hearing Papa's crazy music.

The breeze, saucy in its victory over the redbud leaves, kept sauntering through the window. It captured Sheila's emotions and twirled them into a madcap tune. Sheet music fluttered, frolicked, teasing Sheba, who unleashed her tentative fingers, at first begging them to stop, and then giving in to ostentatious display. Her soul cried, *Let them strut and dance! Let them shout!*

Sheila bobbed her head. She was free! Any minute, Papa would walk in, unsheathe his clarinet—

"Miss . . . Alexander!"

It was her orchestra instructor! Limber fingers stiffened into claws. She hadn't heard Mr. Bouchet enter the room. Or anyone else, for that matter.

"Miss Alexander, find your seat. Students, check the board for rehearsal pieces."

"Who does she think she is?"

"Just like her no-good father."

Whispers and hisses stabbed her in the back.

Stiff legs lifted her from the bench. She bent to retrieve the sheet music, replaced it, and then fixed her eyes on her chair. Her case. She daren't allow an arched eyebrow or a sneer in her line of sight. Not if she wanted to avoid collapsing in front of everyone.

Sheila slumped down her row and slid into her fourth chair. She picked her rosin off the floor and applied it to her bow, sawing harder, harder. She choked back tears as she punished the innocent rosin cake for the barbs of the students, the loss of her sanctuary.

Finally, the horse hair could take no more of the powdery stuff and released it to the air. Rosin dust fluttered useless into her lap.

"Have your pencils on the music stand. We'll start with the D major scale, in eighth notes, two octaves, slurring two."

A bow shivered across strings. Another. Sounds—music—washed over Sheila and helped her find a rhythm that would let her breathe. She gripped the rosin between her fingers. Let the pine smell cleanse resentment.

"Um, Miss? Sheila?"

The rosin cake fell to the floor and shattered.

Sheila set her violin in her lap and buried her face in her hands.

"Miss?" repeated someone. A boy.

She peeked through the spiderweb of her fingers. Saw a pale, freckled hand scooping up the amber shards. They were musician's fingers. Like Papa's.

"What you played was nice," continued the boy. "I mean . . . not nice. It was amazing."

Her hands slid to her lap and gripped her violin. "Thank you," she whispered . . . then dared to meet the blue-eyed gaze of the third chair violinist with curly hair. And a nice smile.

"You're welcome."

His words—and that smile—empowered her to pick up her violin and decipher the lift-droop-loop, lift-droop language of Mr. Bouchet's conductor hands. Soon music's rhythms loosed memory of the unpleasant incident from her fingers, her mind, her heart. She shut her eyes, listened to the language of the violas, basses, the cellos, and let the strings of her violin speak for her.

As the orchestra pulled music from their instruments, the breeze cooled Sheila's sweaty brow. She cut her eyes at the boy who sat in the third chair, each time seeing a bit more: a button nose, earnest eyes, sandy-colored hair. He held his violin as if it were . . . a fragile dance partner. Like Papa held his clarinet. Maman . . .

For the rest of the hour, Sheila studied both her violin and the boy. Did he truly think she had played well, or did he just feel her pain?

When the bell rang, Sheila lingered in her seat, carefully stowing her violin in its case, delaying the end of the school day . . . and the start of the piano lesson at Mimi's.

Soon only memories of music remained.

"Miss Alexander? Could I have a word with you?" came from the back of the room. Mr. Bouchet. Again.

Sheila's cheeks flamed. Mr. Bouchet's career in the symphony had students— and their parents—clamoring for the free instruction accorded by school orchestra. Supposedly there was a waiting list, just to be in here. Because of her earlier impertinence, would she be asked to withdraw? Gathering her thoughts, desperate to save the highlight of her day, she hurried to the lectern, where Mr. Bouchet was now standing.

"I'm so sorry." The words flew out of her. "I know what I did was wrong."

Kind eyes peeked over wire-rimmed glasses. Rosin dust—or dandruff—speckled a dark pin-striped suit. "Not at all, Miss. I rather liked your composition."

Sheila gripped her book satchel and the handle of her case. The former conductor of the symphony "rather liked" her ramblings?

"However, sixth hour is neither the time nor the place for such exploration. I find creative juices flow best in the early morning. And this room gets quite lonely with an old man transposing pieces." Mr. Bouchet tottered to a desk, retrieved his hat, and plopped it onto his silvery hair. "You're welcome to play then, Miss Alexander, until the others arrive."

The orchestra room? All to herself—well, almost? She murmured thanks as she floated out of the school and into the car chauffeured by James. For the first time in weeks, when James called her Sheba, as if he were aiding and abetting the life of that other girl, the girl she had once been, she didn't bother to correct him. With the hope of music to start—and end—the day, Sheba seemed to stir back to life, if only for a bit. Right now, that was enough.

◆ ◆ ◆

"Keep your back straight." Mrs. Johnson reset the metronome, which ticked time on the console. Baton in hand, she marked the beat of yet another set of sonata scales.

Metronome ticks and repetitive chord exercises threatened to drive stakes into her skull. Her fingers moved over the keys, but her eyes studied the clock on the wall. Ten more minutes, and she could escape to a slab of Camille's buttermilk pound cake. Camille's belly laugh. Camille's warm hug. Camille's smile. Camille.

"You've missed it again, dear." Steel rollers bit into the wood floor as Mrs. Johnson arose from the padded stool and paced. "I cannot fathom what is wrong." For what seemed like the hundredth time, she reset the metronome. "I cannot let you stop till you get it right."

Sheila tensed until every part of her ached. All day, all week, all month, she'd tried to get it right. High school, piano lessons, Sunday school, church. That lawyer of Mimi's—what was his name?—had it wrong. She couldn't live in two worlds. She couldn't be Sheba and Sheila. Until her spirit felt the tempi of this new life, she could not play.

Wooden fingers traced the keys, but she felt nothing. Doing her best to keep her face from crumpling, she nodded at Mrs. Johnson and tried, yet failed, to make music.

◆ ◆ ◆

Thank goodness Camille didn't think caffeine stunted growth like Mimi did. The smell of chicory and coffee and cinnamon washed over Sheila as she sipped café au lait and slouched in the kitchen chair. Camille didn't study on posture. Sheila tried to breathe easy. Uncrossed her legs.

As her Sunday school teacher had taught, she counted her blessings. Chitlins and greens simmered on the stove—a cornucopia during wartime. The day's final sunbeams poured in the window. She did thank heaven for that.

She forced a hum, but it died in her throat. Time had stuck on a sandbar in a sluggish river of homework and piano practice.

Camille brushed floury hands on her apron, shuffled to the table, and laid a calloused hand on Sheila's arm. "What you doin', just sittin' dere?"

"Waiting." She set down her cup, surprised at how the word spewed. She'd been holding her breath, expecting another blow to strike, like Camille ripping off her apron and stomping away from Mimi's exacting standards. Like Germany somehow gaining the upper hand in the war. She dragged from school to home to church, expecting something bad to happen.

Camille eased into a chair. "We gotta do something to wake you up." She turned to the window, then glanced back at Sheila, her face glowing with its usual sheen of sweat. "I know! We gwine start us a vict'ry garden dis spring, you and me."

Sheila stared out the window. *Why bother?* Time ticked so slowly here in Gentilly. She knew she should be grateful she had enough to eat and didn't have to huddle in a bomb shelter like the brave English. She again picked up her cup, took a sip, but the coffee was cold.

"You ain't listnin', chile!" Camille shook her fist like she was fixing to swat her.

"I'm sorry," she stammered. "Really, I am. I don't know what's got into me. What will we plant?"

Camille bustled to the stove. "Collards and peas." A rich hum competed with the rattle of dishes. "Onions and garlics, mebbe even marigolds. Dey keep off de bugs." Pot covers banged into place. "Mirliton and—"

Sheila took her cup to the sink, rested her head on Camille's shelf of a shoulder, and snuggled into meaty arms. How she loved the softness of this hardworking woman, who made her feel safe like a child. "What's mirliton?"

"Girl, you ain't know nothin'!" Camille pulled from Sheila's embrace, but not before tousling her hair, then planting a kiss in her part line. "Mama called it winter pear, but it sho' ain't no fruit. More like a vegetable." She swiveled to the counter, picked up a spoon, and began to beat the dickens out of cake batter. "James say dat soil out dere's jes' right." Somehow Camille hummed, drawled, and cooked. "Got us some river silt, some sand, some good ole swamp gumbo." She added a wink to her act.

Sheila laughed. "You belong on vaudeville."

"Ain't know nothin' 'bout no Vanderbilt." Camille huffed.

Sheila stifled a giggle. Vanderbilt, vaudeville—Camille had a way of smoothing the wrinkles of everyday life into something pleasant, even humorous.

"I do knows sometin' 'bout dem plants," Camille continued. "We gwine do it?"

Sheila hurried to the window. "Yes, let's!" Flowers and herbs and . . ." She pressed her face against the glass and imagined the expanse of grass as a courtyard shaded with magnolia and primrose. Would she ever stop missing Esplanade?

Camille nodded. "Gotta have herbs. And chives. The missus loves dem chives."

Mimi. "She'll never let us do it. Not in a million years." *She couldn't stand for us to actually have fun.*

A hand touched Sheila's back. "I don't know 'bout that. If she think it gwine save her some money, I reckon ole Camille can talk her into it."

Maybe, just maybe, they could grow roses, Maman's favorite. Bridal wreath and lilies and lilac . . . Sheila whirled about and threw herself into Camille's spicy smell. Maybe spring would arrive without bypassing Music Street.

Chapter 11

Stars and Stripes Forever

A sassy mockingbird confirmed spring's arrival, just as it had two years ago, when they'd started the garden. Busy weeding, Sheila tamped down her straw hat, knelt in the garden bed, and inhaled the smell of mud, rain, and decayed matter. How could life and death combine here in the soil in such a strange but wonderful way? She ripped off her gloves, plunged her hands into the thick gumbo dirt, and dug until her fingernails scraped against a fleshy dandelion root. She pulled but couldn't uproot it. Just like her problems at school and church. Algebra. Cliques. Yet the afternoon sun warmed her back, let spring play a French love song, and brought to mind the lanky strings player who hovered near her locker after every class. If only Mimi would let her hear the tune he played.

"Lawd have mercy!" Camille swiped sweat from her brow. "Hand me that hoe." Her bandana slipped off her head, revealing gray kinks glistening with sweat.

Sheila obediently rose, but Mimi, cool in pressed beige slacks and a button-down blouse, reached the hoe first and handed it to Camille, then got a spade and joined her maid in punishing tough clods of dirt. The women dipped and groaned, dipped and groaned, as if they were yoked. It made Sheila wonder if Negroes and whites would be joined in heaven, like Camille said. Sheila didn't dare ask Mimi's opinion for fear both she and Camille would get a tongue lashing. Besides she knew Mimi's answer: there would be a separate heaven for Negroes; in Mimi's world, it couldn't be otherwise.

"Morning, Mrs. Alexander." Mrs. Pence, their eighty-year-old neighbor, sported a bonnet twice the size of her head. Her bony elbows rested on a fence rail.

"Morning, Mrs. Pence," Mimi answered.

"Whatcha cookin' up this year?"

"Beans. Peas. Maybe radishes."

"Them awful birds got my beans. Radishes, too."

"She ain't plant no marigolds," Camille whispered to Sheila, who had been thinking the same thing. At least Mimi had allowed marigolds. Next year, maybe roses.

"Come over later. James'll fix you up." Mimi humored the old woman with more chat, then grabbed a bucket when Mrs. Pence drifted away. Sheila knocked dirt from her tingling hands. The garden softened Mimi's hard places as she chatted with neighbors, worked with Camille. Mimi just might be ready . . .

"Y'all finish weeding. I'll mix the fertilizer." A spring in her step, Mimi moved to the shed. Sheila perked her ears. Mimi hummed an old Broadway tune!

Sheila pulled on her gloves. If only it could always be like this, she and Mimi, side-by-side, producing life. With the sun's rays beating on her back and the smell of life rising from the rich soil, the idea planted by that junior boy continued to germinate.

"James, bring me that box." Mimi heaped chalky powder into a bucket. In charge, as Mimi always was, but part of a team that included her servants and her granddaughter.

Sheila eased her spade under the dandelion, hit the root point, and worked to soften the dirt around the weed. She'd broach the subject that had been niggling at her during class, during church—constantly. That strings player had invited her on a date, and she wanted to go.

"I goin' cross over. Over. Over." Camille hit the high notes of a gospel song. Mimi continued to hum that show tune. James whistled like a dock worker as he pushed a wheelbarrow filled with burlap bags toward Mimi.

Sheila sat up, dusted off. The wheelbarrow held new plants. New life. New hope.

A robin chirped. Bees swooped in, buzzing a chorus. Sheila had gauged Mimi's mood for weeks. The singing, the warm sun. It was time. Fighting shaky legs, she approached Mimi, stopping here and there to pull weeds and toss them into an old milk bucket she gripped with clammy hands. *Careful, now. Not too fast . . .*

"Just set them over yonder, James." The sun blushed Mimi's cheeks, making her look much younger than sixty. Sheila fought the urge to skip.

James nodded and began unloading the wheelbarrow.

Sheila set down her bucket. Stood tall. "There's something I want to ask you."

"And there's something I want to show *you*." Mimi slapped dirt off her hands, moved toward the wheelbarrow.

Sheila envisioned the flushed face of that boy, who'd interrupted her early morning practice time, stepped close to the piano bench, nudged her in the ribs, and stammered out an invitation. *Ask her. Now*, he whispered, leaning close in her imagination.

She lurched forward. "Could I go to the spring dance?"

Camille's song stopped. So did James's whistle. And Mimi's tune. Mimi wiped her brow, the motion freeing a steely gray curl from her wide-brimmed sunbonnet.

"Everyone's going." Sheila rushed into the spiel she had practiced earlier on the bean sprouts. "You know the Parkers' daughter from church? She's going. Mr. Delacroix's chaperoning, as is his wife. And—"

"Everyone may be going. But not my granddaughter," Mimi thundered over birdsong and the buzzing bees.

Sheila clutched her chest, as if to protect the seedling of hope. "Mimi, please. I-I need to do this," she stammered. "I need . . . to get out."

Mimi stepped close, her garden shoes thudding against the damp earth.

Thump. Thump. Her heart echoed Mimi's footsteps.

"Absolutely not!" Mimi spit out.

The words froze Sheila in place.

"Miz Alexander, she ain't but a girl." A bee landed on Camille's red-checkered kerchief, but she flicked it away and settled her dark eyes on Mimi.

Mimi whirled. "I'll hear nothing from a nigger maid, you hear me?"

Tears welled up in Sheila's eyes at the word Maman had *never* allowed. When she grew up, had her own home, she would never allow it.

"I ain't jes' a maid, *Miz* Alexander." Camille locked her jaw, squared her face. "I been a sister to you through things we ain't never gwine forget." She barricaded her body with folded arms. "I's tryin' to be an auntie to this young'un. If you'll jes' let me."

Sheila scuffed her sneaker toe in dirt. Camille did not make a habit of challenging Mimi. *Only for me.* What would Mimi do now?

Camille and Mimi eyed each other. Hands slapped onto hips.

The birds resumed their chirps. Bees buzzed. Sweat dripped from her brow into her eyes and stung, like Mimi's words. Sheila picked up her bucket.

Suffered the agony of waiting for what Mimi would do. Mimi had to be in control. Always.

Time seemed to press down on Sheila. She tensed her knees, afraid of collapsing right here and burying her face in the dirt. Why did Mimi have to act so awful?

A tight smile finally cracked Mimi's pale lips. "You know I can't allow Sheila to attend something like a dance." Mimi stepped toward the wheelbarrow. "The Bible doesn't allow it. Neither does the church." She picked up one of the plants James had unloaded. "Why, look at what Salome did to the Baptist. Though I hardly need explain it to the likes of you." She cast Camille a triumphant look. "But I do have an alternative."

She ripped hunks of burlap off a root ball, cradled a plant, and hoisted it into the air. Stray root tendrils brushed her arms, soil speckled her pants, yet she seemed oblivious to the mess. "Seven Sisters." A breezy tone had diffused her earlier storm. "The best-growing, sweetest-smelling hybrid around. James got them. For you. For us."

Lightning bolts sizzled through Sheila. "Roses?" She bit her lip to stem ugly words. Roses instead of a warmhearted, music-loving boy. Sure, roses would be swell. But compared to that boy? She squeezed back hot tears. The last thing she wanted to do was bawl like a baby.

"I've ordered a dozen more." As if she'd forgotten the earlier scuffle, Mimi traipsed about like a child. "We'll make a hedge. Around the yard, the garden." She thrust pink blossoms under Sheila's nose.

An apple-wine smell wafted from the flowers, teased her nostrils, massaged her sizzles into rolling waves. She breathed deep, let out a sigh. Roses. Maman's favorite. Maman didn't consider herself dressed until she had dabbed her pulse points with her Joy Parfum. Pure attar of roses. Maman filled sachet bags with dried petals and tucked them in her drawers, her clothes, even her pillow. Tears trickled down Sheila's face. *Oh, Maman. How I miss you! You would understand about the boy. You would understand everything.*

"We can do it together." The rose bush Mimi held brushed against Sheila. A thorn pricked her skin, but she ignored it. She was used to pricks of pain. These funny-looking roses would have to suffice. For now. "Could I go next year?" She yearned to tuck in hope with the sachets she'd already determined to make from Seven Sisters petals.

A shadow flickered across Mimi's face. "We'll see. Now let's get busy."

"Miz Alexander! Camille! Sheila!" Mrs. Pence tottered to the fence. Her bonnet had been knocked askew. Snowy wisps escaped a flat bun. "It's over! They surrendered!"

"The Germans? You mean . . . the war?"

"It's over!"

Sheila froze. Then adrenaline deluged her like a spring shower. She ripped off her gloves, tossed them in the air, hopped about. It was over! The earlier disappointment dimmed in light of the joyous news. The boys could come home!

"Thank You, Lawd Jesus!"

"Lawd, You done answered our prayers!"

A whooping Camille grabbed James and they whirled about in the muddy soil. Mimi threw back her head and laughed. She sashayed to Sheila, pulled her close, and then stepped back, as if she'd surprised herself.

The spindly rose plants seemed to blossom magically and perfume the air with joy. Wasn't it grand! The war that would destroy the world had ended. Sheila joined Camille and James in their dance while Mimi just stood with her mouth open and stared.

◆ ◆ ◆

Samuel yawned—for her sake. Circles under his mother's hooded lids testified that time traveling had done her in. He plunked his empty mug onto the coffee table. "Don't know about you, but I'm whipped."

She rose from the love seat, that thick dark hair falling into her eyes. "I'm so sorry. Here I've gone on and on and—"

"It's cool . . . but late." What he longed to say was, "It's early, Mother. We have the rest of our lives—" Marine training—and a vestige of self-protection—halted the words.

"If there's anything you need . . ." She wrung her hands. "I've set out towels. Soap. Toiletries are in the cabinet."

Somehow his hands found their way to her shoulders, and he gripped them. "There is one last thing you could do."

Her eyes widened, and at that moment he knew that she would die for him. Would he be willing to die for her as well?

He shook off the question he wasn't ready to answer and pointed to the piano. "Would you play for me?" A need to lighten things made him chuckle. "I need a nightcap of music."

Her face softened and took on the glow of moonlight. With a nod, she glided to the piano bench. Her head bowed, as if in prayer. Again he thought of his favorite nun. Then she ran her hands across the keys, exploring piano notes. Samuel stumbled backward and found himself on the love seat. A rapt audience of one.

Her fingers plucked, tiptoed, frolicked, tripping up and down the keys. A meandering tune slowed his pulse. He shut his eyes, taken away . . .

She stood before him, a sweet smile on her face.

He startled upright, knocking off a tufted pillow, then set it back on the love seat. Had she played an hour? All night? He glanced at his watch, felt his mouth form an "O." In fifteen minutes, she'd taken him to the heavens, lulled him to sleep, then brought him back. "What's the name of that? It's—" He shrugged. There was no way to describe it, this side of paradise.

"Chopin's *Berceuse*." She rubbed her fingers as if they ached. "*The Cradle Song*. What they play for babies." She raised her head enough to look into his eyes. "I played it for mine. Just twenty years too late."

Chapter 12

I Feel Like Goin' Home

First he heard strange birdsong. Sensed sunlight. Danger . . .

Samuel groped for his M-16 while frisking the room with his eyes. He kicked back a blanket and sat up. It was her guest room. Not the jungle. Adrenaline kept pumping as he absorbed the pink hue through an eastern window, the gleam of an antique desk cluttered with ivory busts of wigged men. His breathing found a groove.

He checked his watch. Seven hours, and no nightmare. He made the bed, dug through his duffel, pulled out fatigues . . . grimaced. He might as well paint "war" on his forehead. He should have brought a golf shirt, khakis. She needed to see something beside a jaded GI as he went into the deal about Mali. He slipped on the clothes that had been splashed with blood and mud and worse, then sanitized by those giant commercial washers, and let his mother's story seep in. To play it safe, he'd hear more from her before trusting her with Mali's secrets.

The smell of frying meat and baking bread pulled him to the kitchen, as did memories of the way she'd caressed the piano keys. Her music uncovered places even Mali had not touched. He understood his mother, perhaps better than anyone, judging from what he knew about her self-righteous husband. The PI that had cost two months' salary reckoned she'd kept her little secret—him—from the esteemed reverend. Now that he'd experienced a slice of her safe little suburban life, he could imagine the aftershocks from the explosives he was detonating.

"Good morning." She wore a checkered bibbed apron with a kangaroo pocket. There was a spring in her step as she turned from the oven to give him a hug. "Go ahead. Sit. Over there."

"Wow," came out of his mouth before he could stop it. Here he was, at a real table, not a bench packed with orphans or GIs, both groups ravenous dogs. In more ways than one. Dizzied at the surrealism of it all, he mumbled something about the good smells.

She rewarded him with a schoolgirl giggle. She looked a decade younger than she had last night. "I didn't know what you liked, so I made . . . this." She swept her arm toward a counter cluttered with casserole dishes, cookie sheets, and platters. "Grits, sausage, egg casserole, blueberry muffins . . ."

"I'll take some of everything." The fresh flowers on the table, carefully creased linens, and gleaming sterling trumped Etienne's class because her signature was stamped on everything. If he hadn't known better, he'd have thought she planned for this. A hunger was filled, seeing that she'd gone to so much trouble. For him.

She bustled about, a spoon in one hand, a spatula in the other, hitting an aria's high notes. *I didn't get my pipes from her.* He chuckled and then frowned. In one day he'd gone from despising to caring about this woman. Caring about people exacted a price.

She hummed as she served a steaming plate of food and glass of juice. Then she slid into the seat across from him. "Did you sleep well?" she asked.

"Like a baby." He stabbed a sausage; let it hover midair. *Bad choice of words.* Her face glowed back at him. He cleared his throat. "I never sleep past dawn." *If that.* "It was cool." He smiled at her, surprised at the strange tensing of his muscles. Not embarrassment. Not nerves. Bashfulness. He hadn't felt this way since he'd met Mali.

She talked of gardening as he polished off a hunk of casserole and attacked the muffin, the meat. Yet his appetite grew. He was hungry for the kind of love she offered. Hungry for more answers. More history. "Could you tell me more of your story?"

She smiled like Mona Lisa, as if she knew this was coming.

"Especially about him."

Color drained from her face. Her lips parted, an asthmatic squeak coming out. Apparently she hadn't expected this.

"My father," he added, like an imbecile. Of course she would know what he meant. Still, he hated to cause her pain. But he had a right to know. Didn't he?

◆ ◆ ◆

Spring 1946, Waveland, Mississippi

So much white. Blue. Nothing but sand and sea. An adventuresome spirit coursed through her, echoing the slap of water against land. She had escaped Gentilly, but it had not been easy. After phone calls and last-minute arrangements, Mimi, who had just made up with Uncle Bob after yet another money spat, agreed to let her spend spring break in Mississippi. A wide-eyed James, who had never crossed a Louisiana border, loaded up the car and drove her the sixty-six miles to Waveland, then U-turned home. The comfort of seeing his fuzzy old head from her backseat perch was counterbalanced by a chance to escape Mimi and Music Street, if only for a week.

Last night, she had caught fireflies with Jenna; at 1:00 a.m. had shushed the chatty nine-year-old, who insisted on sleeping with "big cousin." Jenna's antics continued during breakfast as she had fidgeted with her food and clamored to go to the beach. Thankfully, Uncle Bob had relented. Sheila squeezed Jenna's hand as she helped her from the car. Though Jenna whined and bossed anyone who breathed, Sheila loved her spunky smile, turned-up nose, and freckles. Jenna turned the house upside down—what a tonic to Mimi's ways!

From Uncle Bob's car, the beach had resembled a cotton field. Now that they had left the parking lot and tripped along the seawall down concrete steps to the waterfront, she saw that the white color had been an illusion. She let go of Jenna's grimy hand, knelt and scooped up grains so glittery gold, they hurt her eyes. Her heart turned heavenward, opening to let the sunshine, the salty mist, the stinging spray, soothe old hurts.

The waves crashed like cymbals, banged like drums, hissed like brushes against a snare, producing a symphony. It felt good to let the sea take hold and command the last few years to disappear. It felt good—no, wonderful—to be alive.

"Come on, Sheila. Now!" A squealing Jenna plunged into the surf. Blue blurred with the pink of Jenna's swimsuit.

Sheila tore through the water as if running from a madman. And wasn't it mad? Wasn't it gloriously, insanely mad? Liquid diamonds splashed about her legs, her waist. With every movement, years of holding things back melted into shimmering Gulf water. The Gulf brought back Maman, Papa, Sheba, and their free and easy life, which had greeted her with sand dollar and starfish surprises at every dawn. She had a week here. To be free. To be . . . Sheba.

"What d'ya think?" Jenna, a rubber inner tube about her chubby middle, huffed and puffed and paddled forward.

Sheila threw back her head and laughed, then grabbed Jenna, kissed her salty freckled cheek, and twirled her round and round. The tide ripped off a layer of loneliness and caressed her with salty kisses. She wasn't seventeen anymore but nine . . . seven . . . she was a baby again, thanks to the Gulf. She squealed and wiggled her toes at the wonder of it all.

"Why you actin' so funny?" Jenna's saucer eyes matched her moon-shaped face.

"Because it's the grandest thing in the world!" She tweaked Jenna's nose. Again laughed. Proud waves slapped Sheila's thighs and broke into rivulets that surged to lap the shore.

"Not too deep, Princess!" Uncle Bob's voice boomed over crashing water. Out of place with wrinkled trousers and a button-down shirt, he waved and whistled. "Jenna Leigh! Get up here."

"Come on, Jenna." Sheila grabbed a wet hand. "He's calling us."

Jenna tried to wriggle out of Sheila's grasp. "I don't *wanna* go," she shrieked.

Sheila pushed stringy blonde hair off her cousin's frown. "Maybe we won't have to leave. But I *know* we will if we don't mind."

When Jenna's pudgy body went limp, Sheila picked her up and battled toward Uncle Bob. A nasty current yanked them sideways. She scanned the shore, fear lapping her like the waves. A pink-blue blob—ah, *that* was a jellyfish—floated by. So did bleached driftwood. But Uncle Bob was nowhere in sight. She tightened her grip on Jenna, fought forward, backward. Zig. Zag. Shudders pulsed through her body.

"Over here! Over here!"

Sheila pivoted, craned her neck, saw Uncle Bob's waving arms. But the water refused to let go, clamping on her feet in a strange way, threatening to pull her under. She locked her fingers about Jenna. "Hang on!" she yelled. She gritted her teeth and plowed forward.

With a sucking sound, the water surrendered them to the shore. Panting, she set Jenna down and relaxed taut muscles. The Gulf had taught her a lesson. If Uncle allowed them to stay, she would glue her eyes on the unpredictable waves—and Jenna.

"Y'all pushin' your luck out there." Uncle Bob pulled a lighter and cigarette from his shirt pocket, turned sideways, lit his cigarette, inhaled deep, and blew smoke. "That riptide'll pull y'all to Mexico, Jenna. And what would a princess do down there?"

"Daddy, don't make us leave!"

Sheila licked lips coated with salt and sand. Would being pulled to Mexico be so bad? She fluffed her wet curls. Thanks to Uncle Bob's invitation, there would be a week of this.

Uncle Bob inhaled again, blew smoke in her face. Squinty eyes studied her, then turned seaward, as if a ship had caught has gaze. "Looks like you know what you're doin' out there." He managed to hold his cigarette and pull out a pocket watch. "Thanks to Patton, I got a business to run." He patted Jenna. Turned to Sheila. "Keep an eye on my baby, now, ya hear?"

Sheila nodded. The Audubon Park instructors had taught her how to swim, but a city pool with lifeguards and a shallow end was a bath compared to the wild Gulf. She daren't let go of precocious Jenna for an instant.

"She'll take care of me, Papa." Jenna's sure smile and nod provided final ingredients for freedom. Sheila mimicked the surety displayed by her cousin's bobbing head. She could do it . . . as long as Jenna wore that float.

"All right, Princess." Uncle Bob shoved the watch into his pocket and blew air kisses at Jenna. "Maud'll have lunch for y'all back at the house. No foolin' around, ya hear?"

◆

The tide carried time to a faraway place. When ebbing water left a beach glistening with shells, they found a rusted bucket and gathered treasures. When Jenna begged to play teacher, Sheila built her a sand school for crabs. The sun's rays blushed, then burned Jenna's cheeks, and surely her own, judging from the heat radiating off her face. Salt and sand chapped her legs, but it was a small price to pay for the briny sea smell, the gritty feel of sand between her toes. For freedom.

When the sun sapped their energy, she and Jenna crashed into foamy waves that put bounce in their legs, zip in their arms. Sheila waded into waist-deep water, submerged, and managed to squat and pull Jenna onto her shoulders. Jenna squealed with delight as her feet drummed Sheila's ribs. Wobbling like a clay-feet statue, Sheila fought her way to a stand. She'd never had a sister or a cousin to piggyback. This was the life!

The girls bobbed up and down, Jenna's giggles coursing through Sheila along with the wave music, the seagull rasps, the—

"Sheila!" Jenna's heels dug into Sheila's stomach. "What's that?"

Fighting a tremble in her legs, she stared across the blue-gray horizon. A shark might be zeroing in on them, right . . . this . . . minute. Her pulse hammered as she scanned the water surface. "What? Where?" she hissed, seeing nothing.

"Over there."

Sheila turned her head. Spied something golden. Her muscles stiffened. She'd promised Uncle they would be careful.

The surf roared, a haughty reminder of its power.

Her hold tightened on Jenna's thighs. What was out there? She shaded her eyes. Squinted.

A boy floated toward them, his body spread-eagled across the water as if he were weightless. Burnished gold skin matched the color of cropped hair. A wave picked him up and thrust him forward. He raised his head, arched his neck, and she got a good look at him.

Eyes bluer than the ocean, bluer than the sky, found hers. Before she could look away, their intensity ripped through her, reached a sensitive place, and threatened to pull it open.

"Ow! You're hurting me!" Jenna pounded Sheila's belly with her feet.

She steadied herself to keep Jenna from tumbling off her shoulders and glanced at Jenna's thighs. Her nails had gouged crescents into Jenna's pink skin. "Oops. Sorry."

Jenna jostled about until Sheila relinquished her hold and let her cousin plop into the water. The float kept her bobbing—and feisty—as she slapped away Sheila's hand.

"Who *are* you?" Jenna demanded of the boy. She struggled forward, her plump body churning through the waves like a paddleboat wheel.

Sheila's hand flew to her mouth. "Jenna!" She lunged for the pink bow on the back of her cousin's bathing suit. Missed. Propriety made her glance toward the shore. Jenna shouldn't be talking to a strange boy. What would people think?

"Hey, Peanut!" The boy arched his back and rose from the water. Liquid silver cascaded off his sleek body. With the same effortless motion, he took hold of Jenna, lifted her above his head, and tossed her to the clouds.

The hair on the back of Sheila's neck bristled. He might hurt Jenna! Who was *he* to horse around with her cousin? She churned through the water, intent on snagging Jenna from those powerful-looking hands.

Sunburned legs thrashed and splashed. Laughter poured from Jenna, who kicked free from the boy, collapsed into the waves, and then, spluttering and spewing, came up for air.

"Easy, miss." The boy pounded Jenna's back; with a shove, sent her floating toward Sheila.

Though her breathing slowed, Sheila clung to Jenna with one hand and ran her other hand through her hair. Really, he meant Jenna no harm. And Jenna seemed to like him.

"Let's play ring-around-the-rosy," Jenna managed, when her giggles dried up.

"Right here?" Sheila tensed at the shrill edge to her voice. She sounded like Mimi.

"Sure. Why not?" The boy grinned, ducked his head, and splashed his way around Jenna like a shark circling its prey.

Another glance proved the shore deserted except for droopy umbrellas attempting to shield folks from the merciless sun. Sheila shivered, one minute clammy, the next, chilly. They should get out. She might catch a summer cold.

"Come on!" Jenna ducked and then surfaced. Wet hair slapped her cheeks.

The boy reached for and found Sheila's hand. "You heard her." The blue eyes commanded Sheila, as did the firm grip. "Let's go."

Her fingers tingled.

The three of them joined hands and made a circle.

"Ring around the rosy . . ."

Sheila laughed. Too bad Jenna hadn't a lick of singing talent.

"Pocket full of posies."

"What's your name?" the boy managed, after Jenna screeched the next chorus.

Sheba hovered on the tip of her tongue. "Sh—" She bit it back. "Sheila."

"That's a pretty name." He squeezed her hand. "Like you."

They kept stumbling about, their lazy, crazy circle churning the water. Only Jenna sang, seemingly oblivious to anything but being nine years old and having the ocean, her older cousin, and this boy to herself. But Sheila felt those blue eyes searching her body. Or was she imagining things?

"Where are you from?" the boy yelled, over another of Jenna's silly rhymes.

"New Orleans." She thought about adding *Gentilly* but let the waves carry away the idea. Though she lived with Mimi, her soul remained in the Quarter. "How about you?" She raised her voice, hoping he could hear.

"Over at Keesler." He lifted his chin, as if standing at attention. "I'm an airman."

"I thought the war was over."

The boy locked eyes with her. "The war's never over. Especially not in Berlin."

"Were you there?" He looked too young to have seen fighting, but the *Picayune* reported that boys younger than this one had fought. And died.

He nodded, then turned his head. The horizon garnered his notice, or perhaps strange, distant Germany. "What was it like?" she asked.

He didn't answer but gripped her hand.

Her fingers tingled. She obeyed a sensation rising from her loins and squeezed back.

He rubbed his fingers across hers. Sparks shot up her arms. She longed to pull away, longed to squeeze tighter. A war raged within, and she had no idea which emotion was her ally, which emotion was her enemy.

"Ashes, ashes, we all fall down." Jenna sang, so childishly, so off-key. Who cared, with this boy holding her hand?

"Wha-what's your name?" she managed.

He let go of them both and saluted. "Private First Class Clifton Savage from Richmond, Virginia, reporting for duty, ma'am." Again he shivered her with dancing eyes. "Cliff to my buddies. I suppose I'd let a girl like you call me Cliffie."

Cliffie was a name for an old lady's dog. She didn't want to giggle, but "Cliffie" didn't fit this man with broad shoulders, a narrow waist—the laugh stuck in her throat. She thought of him as a *man*.

"What's the matter?" He moved close and filled the air with a scent both spicy and sweet, like Papa's pomade. It mixed with the sharp odor of salt and fish. She sneezed.

"Gesundheit."

"Thanks. I just . . . I swallowed some water." Another giggle came out as a gurgle.

He again reached for her hand. Kissed her fingers. "Better be careful," he growled. "No tellin' what's out here."

She jerked away her hand . . . but didn't want to. She stepped back . . . but didn't want to. Her head swiveled, searching for an escape. She might not want to, but she had to. Jenna was her charge. She shaded her eyes. Pivoted. No Jenna. Her stomach churned like the Gulf. *Jenna!* She tried to scream, but fear had paralyzed her vocal chords.

Cliff noticed her alarm, also panned the waves, as if searching for Jenna, then dove into the water, murky after their stupid game. As she gasped and shivered and craned her neck, he surfaced and shoved through boiling foam. "Peanut!"

Fear shredded her. Jenna had to be okay. She was a baby, really, against this raging—

"Hey, Peanut!" He tilted his head, as if listening to the sea, and again tore forward. "Hold on! I'm coming!" He swam wildly, the water churning, churning . . .

She followed his wake, beside herself to spot a precious bobbing head amid the foam. There was nothing but water. Water. More blasted water.

A brown blur caught her eye. She spotted a mass of jellyfish tentacles . . . dirty blonde tentacles . . . Jenna's . . . hair.

"Please, God! No!" She zigzagged through weighty water, its spray obscuring a view of everything but Cliff and Jenna's hair. She winced when she stepped on something sharp and pumped her legs harder in a vain attempt to lift her knees out of the water. *No, no, no! God, no!* She tried to pray, but couldn't find any words. She was to babysit her only cousin. If anything happened—

Gasping, she caught up to Cliff. And . . . Jenna, whose eyes were open. Who was breathing.

Waves of relief loosed tension knots. Tears stung her eyes. "Thank God, Jenna. You—you're all right." She gulped down sobs and salt water. Jenna was safe!

"It . . . scared . . . me!" Jenna cried, between coughs.

"Now, now. You're gonna be okay." Cliff pounded on her lobster-red back.

Sobs and coughs consumed Jenna's voice.

"Nasty old current." The pounds became caresses as Cliff kept cooing and talking. His nimble fingers explored Jenna's shriveled float and found the valve. The open valve.

She's okay. Cliff saved her. Sheila clutched her stomach, gurgling from too much salt water, too much fear. In the span of one conversation, Jenna had nearly drowned. What would she have done if . . . her fingernails dug into the nylon of her bathing suit until she winced. It was over. She mustn't think of it. Still panting, she waded toward Jenna, her arms extended.

"You're all right," Cliff kept saying. "See? You're all right."

"Give me a hug." Sheila held out her arms for Jenna, who was scowling. Fussy. Safe.

"No." Jenna pouted. "I want Cliffie."

So Jenna had heard their silly "Cliffie" talk, which had happened . . . an eternity ago. "You had better come here." Sheila tried to sound bossy but relief made her purr. "Or I will tell Uncle you ran off." She waggled her finger but couldn't stop smiling.

"Then I will tell him you have a boyfriend." Jenna bobbed up and down, apparently unscathed from her trauma. "Sheila has a boyfriend. Sheila has a boyfriend."

Cliff pulled Jenna close, then whirled like a top. "You both have a boyfriend."

A giggle started deep in Jenna. As Cliff spun her, she slung water all over them. Her laughs escalated into shrieks. Cliff tossed her over his shoulder like a gunnysack.

Sheila exhaled. Tension crashed in the shallow water and disintegrated.

Cliff took her hand.

Her mind flip-flopped as they moved toward the shore. She tried to understand the strange sensation, but what she didn't know about the opposite sex would fill this ocean.

When they reached shallow water, Cliff let go of her and set down Jenna, who wailed like a crab had pinched her. "Pick me up, Cliffie! Now."

"Hush," Sheila blurted out, "or I will tell!"

The wails stopped. Jenna thrust her hands on her hips. "I won't tell Daddy about *Cliffie* if you don't tell Daddy about me."

Sheila glanced at the beach. A lone sunbather sprawled on her towel, an enormous hat shielding her face. Only the sea and its magnetic tides knew about the near miss. About Cliff.

She eyed the slender waist, the broad shoulders. Cliff was a handsome man. Sure, she had demurely smiled at a church pew partner, let school chums carry her books, been infatuated with the strings player, whom she had never been allowed to date. She tried to sort through the muddle of her mind. Maybe Mimi had been right. Maybe she wasn't ready for this. Cliff made her feel reckless. Free. Flirting with danger, as she had with those waves.

"Did you hear what I said?" Jenna broke the rhythm of their steps. "I won't tell if you won't."

Cliff found her hand. "Sounds like a deal to me." He squeezed tight. "Tomorrow? Will I see you here tomorrow?"

You . . . not y'all. It sounded like a deal to her as well.

Chapter 13

Be Careful, It's My Heart

Come on, Jenna. Don't make me call you again." Aunt Audrey scoured the kitchen counter. A curl played hooky from her teased bouffant, oddly enhancing her chic style. Ever since Mimi had made a Depression loan to Uncle, she had harped about Audrey's extravagance. But Sheila admired her aunt's scalloped suit sleeves, thin-as-a-pencil belt. Aunt Audrey brought Joan Crawford's glamour to a Mississippi town. Sheila took in Aunt's new venetian blinds and just-installed metal cabinets. Stylish, modern, fun—everything Mimi's house—and Mimi—was not. In just days, this seemed more like home than Music Street. Was that because of Aunt Audrey and Uncle Bob . . . or Cliff? Sheila knew the answer was in the bluest eyes, the softest touch . . .

Jenna stomped into the kitchen. "But I want to go with Sheila."

Sheila stabbed at scrambled eggs and jabbed them into her mouth. Jenna just might doom her and her soldier's plans for solitude. One glance at Jenna's freckled nose made Sheila bow her head with regret. *This cute cousin adds laughs and light to a place. Like . . . Cliff.*

Aunt Audrey again fussed with her hair. "Sheila's practically a young lady. And just look at your freckles. Enough sun for you. Besides, Satterfield's has a sale."

Emotions warred in Sheila. Yesterday, Cliff had kissed her amid the foaming surf, a lone pelican the only witness. The day before, she and Cliff had played chase along the beach with Jenna like they were best chums. Was it wrong to want Cliff to herself? She set down her fork. Stared at greasy bacon strips. This was a mess!

Only months ago, she had rolled her eyes at schoolgirl whisperings of first kisses. Look at her now! When her lips had first met his, the world had tilted and blurred the sky and sand and sea into a canvas of blue and white. She had clung to him to keep from falling . . . and to be closer to her first love.

As they'd splashed their way to shore, she had steadied to match him stride for stride. He talked of the great ship that took him away, brought him back, and would soon take him again. They had three more days to be in love. Surely she could juggle time with Jenna and Cliff. When Cliff came home for good, they'd be together for the rest of their lives. He had as much as told her so.

Their secret place was far from a beach crowded with pasty—or blistered—vacationers, away from the keen-eyed lifeguard on his solid, safe tower. She didn't need saving. Did she? Questions pummeled her quivery soul. Was she old enough to get involved with a soldier? With anyone? Of course Mimi's answer was no, but what was *her* answer? Again she poked at her eggs, consumed by thoughts of Cliff. She was so inexperienced when it came to men . . .

Dared she confide in her aunt? No, Aunt Audrey would sniff her turned-up nose at an affair with a soldier. She shoved away guilt as she tossed down her napkin, set down her fork. Begged her aunt and uncle and cousin to leave. So she could go to Cliff . . .

"Audrey, I'll see you at dinner. Don't go overboard." Uncle Bob planted a smooch on Aunt's forehead, grabbed his hat, and headed for the lumberyard. With Aunt Audrey's new Danish furniture and parquet floors, he'd best be ramping up the saw cutters.

One down and two to go. Sheila squirmed, hoping to push her aunt into motion. She had agreed to meet Cliff ten minutes from now, if the weather held. And not a cloud marred the blissfully blue sky.

Blue like his eyes.

"Come on, sweetie pie." Aunt Audrey tugged Jenna's arm, then rested her other hand on Sheila's shoulder. "Sure you won't go with us?"

"No, no," Sheila said, much too quickly.

Jenna glared at her with such malice, Sheila feared she would spill the truth about Cliff. But Jenna clamped her lips and miraculously let her mom lead her outside.

"All right, then." Aunt blew a kiss. "Have a nice day." With Jenna in tow, Aunt left the house.

The car was barely rumbling down the street when Sheila tripped down the porch steps, swung open the gate, and flew past picket fences to the sandy path.

He was waiting for her, she was sure of it. The "nice day" Aunt referred to would start when she saw his face.

◆ ◆ ◆

So much sand on this beach. So much heat. Though her heart crashed against her chest, she slowed, wary of curious eyes. She had always loved places that pulsated with people. Not now. Every man, woman, and child was a potential busybody who might tattle to Aunt and Uncle. A backward look told her she needn't worry. Morning bathers had become dots of red, splashes of flesh, no more harmful than sand fleas. Her secret was safe. In minutes she would be in his arms.

As she walked east, the familiar khaki swim trunks materialized from a backdrop of wavy sun rays. Cliff stopped at the water's edge and looked seaward, then surveyed the beach.

She smiled. Like her, Cliff feared prying eyes. Cliff knew her concerns, *shared* her concerns. No one had done that, except Maman and Papa, and they were dead. But every inch of Cliff was alive.

Her sandals sank into hot sand; she bent and slipped them off, and it was then that he rushed close and grabbed her hand. Tremors wracked her body. She tensed every muscle, trying to fight the desire welling inside. Desire led to trouble . . . didn't it?

They whirled and walked east together. The journey away from humanity continued, only now they were side-by-side, welded together by his grip. Silence reigned, silence that allowed the wind to whirl about her and whip up the fire started by the hand holding. Desperate now to keep her quivering self under control, she made a game of trodding in the very footprints he had made earlier as he'd walked to meet her, but she had to lengthen her stride to do so. He seemed not to notice, walking with strength, surety. Like Papa had done.

They went on for what seemed like miles, still tethered by their hands. When the beach curved, she looked over her shoulder. Only a beady-eyed gull looked back. She exhaled the last tightness and inhaled delicious salty air. She was herself again. Was that self Sheila, who obeyed Mimi's rules, or Sheba, who lived for music and let life twirl her about? Or had she changed into somebody else, someone that she didn't yet know?

He let go of her hand. Turned away. Strides smoothed into a lope that rippled his back and led him to a series of dunes, separated by sloping grassy areas.

She followed, stopping only to shove hair out of her eyes. She had to see every inch of him.

His swim trunks flapped against his legs as he darted between two golden mounds of sand. The only sounds were a faint whoosh of the surf and the clicking of sea oat shafts as they rubbed against one another.

She slipped as she pounded up the steep incline, only to slide backward in the powdery sand. He reached out and pulled her up and over the crest of the dunes. Gritty fingers covered her eyes, led her through a sea of sand.

"I've got a surprise, sugarplum." A ground clove smell blended with pungent salty sea spray to intoxicate her. She staggered into his arms. He spun her around.

"Okay," he announced.

She opened her eyes, struggling to see past the white-hot glare.

An army blanket lay across a carpet of sand. He'd scattered primrose blossoms across the coarse wool, adding pinks to dull olive green. She bit her trembling lip. He had remembered her fancy for primroses. Not since Maman and Papa had anyone cherished her like this.

A bottle dewy with condensation had been laid on a crumpled towel next to tin cups. Burning from the sun, she sank onto the blanket and ran her hand across the cool bottle. Yet it did nothing to abate the fire within.

He sat next to her, poured, and made a toast. They clinked the cups as if they were imported goblets. Desperate to slake her thirst, she gulped the wine. Drank more.

Suddenly she heard the hum of cicadas, the drone of bees. The fruity smell of the wine made her feel heady, brave. Even the landscape shifted in intensity. Dunes loomed over the scene like fortresses; the waving sea grasses, shaky sentinels guarding their love.

Was that what this was: love? Or was it seduction? Woozy, she wobbled to her feet, atremble at the thought of what he wanted. What she wanted. She stepped toward the gap in the reeds, desperate to find the sea, as if the sea would explain what she should do.

"Sheila." With a husky voice, he called to her. "Sheila, please."

Never had the name she hadn't wanted sounded so lovely. So right. Just like being here. Her loins ached as she struggled through the shifting sand toward him.

His hand found her chin and turned her head to meet his gaze. She stared into his eyes, seeing all the blue. She wanted to see more of him. Know more of him. And he understood.

As one, they sank onto the blanket. Wind whipped the sea oats, the wild grasses, into a concert of thuds and moans. The surf met the shore with pounding thrusts. It wasn't until he kissed her forehead, her lips, then worked his way down that she realized that the thuds came from her heart. The moans came from her lips.

Uninvited images glided in, trying to interrupt. Mimi's frowning face. The poster of Jesus in her Sunday school room. She blinked, not knowing whether to accept them or shut them out.

While she tried to decide, the heat and his whispers combined to perform a symphony so frenzied it overpowered everything else. When the music stopped, she fell into his arms. And slept.

◆ ◆ ◆

"So I was a love child." Staring across her table, he bit back swear words his GI buddies spit out like gristly meat. Thank God *he'd* resisted the clingy arms and painted eyes of bar girls selling quick fixes to shell-shocked troops. Quick fixes that camouflaged sick souls and bodies and led to things like VD. He'd even resisted Mali's delights. Miraculous, considering she'd shed her clothes the first time he'd seen her. Chastity was possible. All it took was willpower. Principles. Things his parents hadn't had.

As if to cover her shame, she bowed her head. Dark curls gleamed like a glorious crown. "I'm sorry," she whispered. "I was so lonely, so naïve."

"Did you ever see him again?" He itched to know more about his father. What passions—other than the obvious—consumed him? Could he risk what he might say if she admitted she knew nothing about him except for those darned blue eyes?

Tears slid down her cheeks. "I thought I loved him. Of course I didn't know what love was."

"Please." He pinned her with a look. "Answer my question."

"I never saw him again," she finally said, and buried her face in her hands. Though her shoulders shook, she didn't make a sound. He should console her, but he couldn't, now that he knew he'd been the product of a cheap seduction. For years, he'd imagined, because of the nun's gift, that his parents had been love-struck, godly teenagers, stirred by passion into a sinful act. *Oh, the pretty lies we believe* . . . He opened his mouth to say something, anything, to keep her heart from breaking. His own crushed hopes . . . like those primroses

. . . kept him from uttering what she surely longed to hear: *It's okay, Mother. I understand.*

Her sob changed everything.

He extended a hand. Touched her arm. She deserved something for protecting this jerk. His father. "You were only seventeen. He was, what, twenty? Twenty-one?"

She sat up, as if reciting facts would salve her pain. "Twenty-one, yes."

There was such a longing in her eyes, he found her hand. Clasped it with fervor, hoping it made up for the things he couldn't yet say.

"I'm sorry for your sake that it couldn't have been different." A whimper escaped. Then she dabbed her eyes, took a deep breath, and gave him a glazed look, as if awaiting a bullet from a firing squad of one.

The fact that she was a victim in the sordid mess kept him from grinding his teeth and pacing the floor. He could imagine what kind of lies she'd been spoon fed by the soldier. He'd heard them all—in the latrine, on watch, in the mess hall. He fidgeted with his hands, trying to flush disappointment. To refocus, he returned to the questions he'd formulated for over a decade. "I'm confused," he finally said. "He had blue eyes?"

Her trademark sad smile made another appearance.

"How can it be?" He kneaded his hands. "I mean . . . where do I get my dark skin?"

She seemed to wilt, like a picked orchid. "That's another story, Son. A long one."

The doorbell rang.

His skin crawled. He blinked, expecting a bayonet flash. Listened for thuds against soggy ground. Another blink and Nam disappeared. He sprang from his chair. Someone had invaded their peace. The Reverend Franklin?

"Yoo-hoo. Yoo-hoo." A nasally female voice pierced the windows and echoed off the hardwood floors. He rubbed his knuckles together. *At least it's not her husband.*

At the sight of his mother's ashen face, he tiptoed toward the hall.

She slammed her palm on the table. "Hold it! Right there."

He obeyed, secretly pleased. So she wouldn't stash him in the back room after all.

"I'm sick to death of secrets." Steel hardened her voice. She'd be a formidable opponent in love . . . and war. "Get back over here and sit down," she commanded. And he did.

Chapter 14

Downhearted Blues

"Yoo-hoo. Sheila? Mrs. Franklin? Yoo-hoo."

Thelma wouldn't drop by without calling. Would she? Sheila smoothed her apron to cover her pajamas, padded in her slippers to the music room, and flattened herself against the wall near the window so she could see the driveway. A glance past burning bushes revealed a car behind Samuel's. Drat. Double drat. It was the blasted Chevy that hogged two spaces in the church lot five days a week. Sundays, too.

"Yoo-hoo." The doorbell rang again.

Sheila bit back, "We don't want any." Of course, a pastor's wife couldn't say that. Especially to the pastor's secretary.

Even on ordinary days, Thelma Morris's whine scratched Sheila's eardrums. "Yoo-hoo!"

Sheila threw back the bolt, cracked open the door. Thelma Morris would not go away; her perseverance was one reason Edward hired her when June retired. Sheila resented Thelma's curious stares and probing comments but never doubted her loyalty to Edward. Hadn't she'd signed up for intrusions into her safe little home when she'd married a pastor?

Just let her in, see what she wants, end it. Putting on the best smile she could muster, she opened the door wide enough to view white orthopedic shoes planted on their welcome mat.

"Good morning, Sheila." With a shove, Thelma and her eau de hairspray swept into the entryway. Snug as a sock hat was her shingled bob, a perfect complement to a pleated skirt, high-necked blouse, a cardigan looped about her shoulders. "Here's those bulletin notes. And I'm afraid I have some bad news," she chirped, her tone devoid of sorrow. Choppy steps carried her toward the hall. Her head swiveled, as if scoping out the layout here.

How had she forgotten her promise to do this for Edward? Samuel, that's how. Sheila felt her muscles tighten. *What's the bad news? Has Edward been—* she leaned against the wall to summon her wits. No. If catastrophe had hit Edward, Thelma would be sobbing. Still . . . "Is Edward OK?"

"Oh, I haven't heard from Edward. He didn't leave a number." The morning sun blared through the window to magnify the foundation line along her jaw. "I hope I'm not interrupting anything." She sniffed her way into the living room. All she needed was a hound's-tooth cap and a magnifying glass to uncover . . . Samuel.

A geyser erupted within. She brushed past Thelma. How dared she act like a realtor previewing a home? She whirled. Pasted on a smile. "You said you have bad news, Thelma. What is it?"

Thelma knotted bony arms across her chest, leaned forward, and peeked into the breakfast nook. "Is your . . . family staying over while Edward—Mr. Franklin is gone?"

Sheila debated several tacks. Demand that Thelma answer her question. Shove Thelma outside. Scream, "None of your business." All impossible choices for a pastor's wife. If she leaned back, stretched just so, surely she'd block a view of the kitchen. Of Samuel.

"I couldn't help but notice the rental car," Thelma continued.

Of course. There'd be the rental sticker on the car window. Sheila begged logic to organize mushy thoughts. Being Edward's secretary didn't merit Thelma an open house. "Yes, family's here." She sought a polite yet disinterested tone, yet sweat streamed down her back. "I'm sorry, Thelma." Now her *voice* was mush. "I'm in the middle of something. What has happened, and how can I help?"

"Well." A frown creased Thelma's brow. "John Paul died last night."

John Paul? A former pope? Sheila's head throbbed. What did the pope have to do with this?

"You know. From church?"

Sheila envisioned the pictorial directory she'd studied, for Edward's sake. John Paul . . . Mr. and Mrs. John—She shook her head, focusing on a mole on Thelma's cheek to avoid her glittery eyes. This was getting worse by the second.

"Chair of the building committee. *Former* chair." Thelma puffed exasperation. "The funeral director needs answers. First Jean wants to talk to Edward." Caterpillar brows twitched. "He didn't leave me a number. I thought surely you'd have his lodging information, an emergency contact . . ." She stepped onto kitchen tile.

Hope of concealing Samuel evaporated. She'd grab Edward's itinerary, which lay on the kitchen counter not three feet from her son, show it to Thelma, then show Thelma the door. If Thelma saw Samuel, so be it. "I do have that number," she said. "Let me get it for you." Silk clung to sweaty legs as she swished into the kitchen. She passed Samuel without a glance, set down the bulletin notes, and picked up the paper. *Just get it, get her out of here.*

"Good morning," Thelma chirped. "And you are . . . ?" The words slammed into Sheila's back. Whirled her about. The memo fluttered like a crude paper airplane. She caught it, smashed it into a wad.

Samuel's chair scraped. He stood. "Good morning," he said, ignoring that second question. The one that would change her life. To help Samuel, perhaps her life needed to be changed.

Sheila eyed her son. Thanked God only a tic at his jaw worried his precious face. The wad clutched to her chest, she inched forward. She'd tried to crumple up and hide her past . . . for years. It hadn't worked. The time had come for her to answer questions. *Oh, God, help me!*

"I'm Thelma Morris. Mr. Franklin's secretary." Thelma long-necked the mess of pots and pans, the flowers on the table, every freckle on Samuel. Her ample bust expanded to become all the pious members of Edward's congregation with their do-and-don't lists, their raised-eyebrow judgments. *Edward's* congregation. Not hers.

A decade of memories gushed; she did nothing to stem them.

"Pastor, too bad your wife can't stay for the meeting."

"What denomination did you say you were raised in, Mrs. Franklin?"

"Reverend Franklin, perhaps you could persuade your wife to lead our sewing circle. Your lovely mother always found the time."

She knotted her fists, just thinking of Edward's congregation and how she really wasn't one of them. She'd tried grafting onto the vine, but it hadn't taken. Now it never would. Holy pruners would snip her and toss her into a pile of chaff, to be bundled and burned. A sinner. Like her parents.

Samuel stepped toward Thelma. "Nice to meet you." Her son's voice cut into Sheila's stupor. "I'm Samuel Allen. Here on business."

"Oh. I'd understood that you were family. Aren't you?" Her eyes blazed with questions. All of them nosy. "There's a slight resemblance, especially about the eyes."

Samuel snapped to attention. "Military business. Hush-hush. I'm sure you understand."

Sheila battled hot tears. Her son, cleaning up her mess. Doing what she should've done. Well, she would finish things up. "Here it is." Sheila infused finality into her tone. To busy her hands, she smoothed out the itinerary and thrust it at Thelma. "If that's all you need . . ." She tore down the hall. Opened the door. Heard her son and Thelma say good-bye, but barely listened. By the end of tomorrow's services, half the church would know a pajama-clad Sheila had housed a handsome and mysterious young soldier while Pastor Franklin was at a conference. Word would trickle into Edward's ear. At the door, Thelma's final glare amended Sheila's thoughts. No trickle. The word would be blasted at Edward via amplifier.

Though the aromas from the festive breakfast hung heavy in the hall, her gaiety had evaporated, as had her anger. What remained was the grim reality that Edward must be told the truth. By her. Sooner rather than later. She dragged into the kitchen, did her best to smile. It wasn't Samuel's fault. This must not ruin their time together.

"You'll have to tell him now." Samuel's crisp, businesslike tone had disappeared.

She shrugged, as if her gut weren't burning, her throat weren't parched. "Oh, well. It's long overdue. A lot of things are overdue. Things I never dealt with."

"Like your grandmother?" With precise movements he stacked dishes, took them to the sink. "What did she say—and do—when you told her about me?" Samuel took her arm. Led her to the table. They sat as they had earlier, before being interrupted. But the sun had vanished behind a steely wall of clouds and robbed them of a perfect Saturday. Though it hurt to remember this, her son deserved to hear the black and white of it. She would tell him.

"Lawd, it's only eight, and I's about to die. Heat's taxin' my lungs sometin' awful." Camille leaned against her hoe and mopped her brow with a kerchief. "N'Awlins ain't had no August like dis since I was a chile."

Sheila picked up a trowel and knelt, anxious to get her hands in the soil and break a strange lethargy that had settled over her. When she bent close to the ground, the oily earthworm smell brought waves of nausea. One hand covered her mouth; she slapped the other on the ground to keep from toppling.

All summer, she'd nodded and mumbled with the old-timers who let weather rule their lives. She'd risen early to avoid heat that scalded sidewalks and birthed wavy air currents. Still, her stomach twisted from summer's onslaught. The only buffer was to disappear into a dream of Cliff and the cool Gulf breeze. His touch and the salty water. His kiss and the grainy sand. She swallowed a bitter taste, halfheartedly stabbed a dirt clod. Oh, for just a minute with Cliff!

He had pulled from her embrace that last day of her vacation—the day he would leave with his unit. Kissing tears off her cheeks, he had promised a mail pouch of letters. Letters she vowed to intercept. Letters that would lay out their future. Letters yet to be received.

Sweat dripped into her eyes as she attacked clumps of weeds. Doubts mushroomed. Had Cliff's love talk been lies? Had she meant nothing to him? She pounded her frustration into the soil, the questions throbbing pain into her temples.

"Dese crops gotta have water. Soon." Camille moved sluglike among the bushy plants. "Least the heat's heck on de bugs."

Images of creepy things made Sheila gag. She tossed down the trowel. Clutching her stomach, she stumbled across the yard.

"Girl? What you—"

The heaving worsened as she reached the back stoop, doubled over, and vomited bitter, churning liquid onto an azalea bush.

A calloused hand caressed her back. "Lawd, what's got into you?"

Still gagging, she shook her head. Camille led her inside and guided her into a kitchen chair. Sheila cradled her head in her arms and slumped onto the cool enamel-topped table. Her eyes closed, she lay still until the nausea subsided. It felt so good to cool off. To rest.

"You didn't eat no breakfast."

She gave Camille a nod.

"You didn't eat much last night, neither. And I's made chicken and dumplins' jes' for you."

Another nod. The strange heat *had* sapped her appetite. She hadn't hungered for anything since she'd come back from Mississippi. Except him.

Camille sighed heavy and long. She gripped Sheila's skull and massaged, deep and soothing. A sob escaped Sheila.

The soothing massage stopped cold. "Have yo' lady come to visit?"

Sheila sat up. Stared into Camille's wide eyes. "Lady? Visit?" She fidgeted like she'd been caught in a lie. But she had done nothing, except . . . the outside heat seeped in and bore down on her face. Camille couldn't know what she'd done with Cliff.

"Yo' monthly time, chile. Have you had yo' monthly?" Her eyes stretched until they bulged. "You ain't had yo' monthly!"

May, June—she hadn't connected her body rhythms with that day on the beach. Roiling waves again churned her stomach. Her mouth opened. Closed. Fingers raked her hair. *Slut. Whore.* Words boys spat at "those type of girls." She buried her head in her hands and cried. Now *she* was one of "those type of girls."

"Lawd, Lawd." From Camille came a sob, thick as molasses set in the fridge. "Oh, Lawd, how we gonna tell the missus? What we gwine do?"

Sheila broke out in a sweat. If Camille, who had managed four white households as well as her own, didn't know what to do, no one did.

Chapter 15

Piano Concerto No. 2 Adagio Sostenuto

This heat's a killer." Mimi set her handbag on the counter and dabbed a handkerchief at her temples. "Camille, a lemonade. Crushed ice with plenty of mint."

"Yes'm." Camille moved toward the refrigerator as if in a trance. She'd been that way for the last half hour, ever since she'd led Sheila to the awful truth.

"Daddy always said cotton couldn't have too much heat. Well, Daddy was wrong." The steamy climate that had drained Sheila and Camille had energized Mimi, who flitted about, adjusting a china knickknack, a table runner tassel. She chattered about a broker appointment, a gloomy crop forecast failing to dim an eerie gleam in her eye.

"You want some, Miss Sheila?" Camille asked dully.

Sheila shook her head. Just the thought of a lemon . . . She swallowed bile.

"I'll tell you, I thought I'd die in that back seat. Something is wrong with the blower, and not a place in town knows how to work on 'em."

It took everything in Sheila to remain seated. She'd planned to be safe—and alone—in her bedroom before Mimi's return. Then Camille had brewed peppermint tea and sweetened it with honeycomb, claiming it helped nausea. She'd pulled Sheila close and hummed cello-tone notes. With Camille around, sun rays pierced her dread and lent hope. But Mimi, who ferreted out hidden things and heard unuttered mutters, shadowed the light with her presence. Sheila must guard her thoughts, her actions.

Nausea gathered, then crested, from fear of what Mimi would do. She wasn't ready to face Mimi with the truth. She must leave this room. Now. She pushed back her chair. Rose.

"Sheila, dear."

Mimi's ringing falsetto froze Sheila in place.

"I need to talk to you."

"I-I'm feeling . . . peaked." She wheeled so Mimi could not see her face. Mimi was good at deciphering expressions, too. She had to be careful.

Heels clicked across the floor. "It will just take a minute."

Sheila slid into her seat by the window. Turned to catch sight of a sparrow, fluttering to a tree. Escaping a hawk's talons? How she longed to escape. If she fled to her room, Mimi would follow. Mimi wanted to chat. Now. And Mimi got what she wanted.

"I spoke to Mr. Toulong today." She heard the thud of Mimi sitting down, felt the piercing gaze. "You remember him, don't you, dear?"

Sheila dipped her head, hoping curls would shield her face and hide her shame. She fought the urge to lay her head on the table, as she had earlier. The cool, cool table.

A clap split the air. "This is serious, dear."

You don't know how serious. She focused on Mimi's gray suit jacket, unwilling to give Mimi her soul's portals, which surely proclaimed: *I'm having a baby.*

"He thinks—we both think, actually . . ." A gray sleeve lifted as Mimi talked with her hands like a conductor. *As usual, trying to orchestrate my life.* "Now that you've graduated, it would be good for you to work with him. Type. Learn Gregg."

"Greg?" Her stomach roiled at the thought of another man.

Lacquered nails tapped the tabletop. "Shorthand, dear."

"I been 'buked and I been scorned," Camille sang as she scoured a pot with such vigor, soapy water splashed onto the countertop. Tears dotted that beloved old face.

Sheila fought the urge to scurry to Camille, who had caressed away aches, sang away blues. Camille—and James—made this house a home. They really loved her. Not Mimi. A sob caught in her throat. Not Cliff.

"Mercy, what's all that wailing about?" Mimi fanned herself, color rising in her face, now that Sheila dared to look.

Another glance at Camille's tortured expression tightened Sheila's fists. She would not allow this to go on. "It's . . . about me." The words stuttered from her mouth and hovered over the table, along with a white-hot light that blurred her vision.

"Chile, no!" Camille tore across the kitchen, grabbed her by the shoulders, jerked her out of the chair, and pulled her into her bosom. "Don't let it come out like dis."

Sheila gripped the waistband of Camille's housedress until her fingers ached and hugged Camille, as if that would contain labored huffs and puffs.

"What on earth is going on? Camille, let go of her." Something—Mimi's palm?—smacked the table.

Camille pulled Sheila close. "Ain't gwine let go of her," rang in Sheila's ears.

"Oh, yes, you will."

Sheila let out a breath. Though Camille called on the Lawd Jesus, a maid did not possess the weapons to fight Mimi. Besides, this was her battle, not Camille's.

She mustered the strength to pull away from Camille, cross her arms, and pivot to face Mimi, who would surely win this tug-of-war of wills. *But I can stop Camille from losing.* Camille, whose husband had a gimp leg. Camille, whose son had a shattered mind. Camille, whose cooking and scrubbing kept food in her family's pantry. Camille needed this job. Sheila would ensure that she kept it.

"I need to talk to you." Sheila's voice sounded distant. She tossed damp curls out of her eyes and sat back down. She could do this, for Camille *and* for herself.

Mimi started to speak, then shut her jaw tight. Her gaze flitted from Sheila to something out in the yard. That poor sparrow?

"When I was at Uncle's, I met a boy." She hadn't practiced this, had never planned to tell until after her engagement. There would be no engagement. What a fool she'd been to imagine one!

"Oh, Lawd!" Camille wrung her hands as she padded about the kitchen.

Every movement wrenched Sheila's heart.

Mimi narrowed her eyes; otherwise, she didn't move, didn't speak.

"I . . ." How could she describe the wonder of Cliff's smile, Cliff's kiss, so Mimi would understand? Did *she* even understand, now that wonder had been clouded by steely gray truth? "I—we fell in love," she stammered. "I'm going to have a baby."

Mimi rose. Slammed her fist on the table. "Fell in love? *A baby?* . . . Who is he? Tell me that."

Sheila bowed her head against the hate Mimi broadcast with her glare. Hate that cheapened what she had had with Cliff. Had it been cheap from the start? "A soldier," she finally said. *With the bluest eyes, the softest lips. Eyes and lips that promised the moon. But gave a black sky.*

"*A soldier?*"

Camille's raspy breathing and the smell of sweat filled the room.

Regret pummeled Sheila. How could she do this to Camille? To Mimi? Despite their differences, Mimi had sheltered and fed her. Both Camille and Mimi deserved better. Sheila cupped her hands. Dug fingernails into her palms.

"I suppose he wants to marry you." A sneer deepened lines about Mimi's lips as she sat back down. "That's just fine. But y'all won't get Father's money. You'll have to provide for your little brat." Her handkerchief dabbed beads of sweat, wiped off saliva.

Sheila bit her lip. Tried to pray. *If only Mimi could see inside me. Perhaps she could love me.* Adrenaline surged. She raised her head, desperate for a miracle to warm the Alexander eyes. She leaned across the table. "Please, Mimi. Please . . ."

"Did you hear me?" Mimi screamed. "Not a cent!"

Sheila leapt to her feet. "He doesn't want to marry me," she shouted. "And I don't want your money. If you could just . . ." *Love me?* Again she bit her lip and raked fingernails across sunburned arms. To be loved! To belong! What she'd wanted from Cliff. Dark truth shook her soul. It wasn't to be had.

Mimi leaned back, her face gray. "Of course you want my money. You're just like your mother, the harlot."

A gust of wind rippled the back door screen, swirled through Sheila, and impelled her to lean across the table. Her fists knotted. "How dare you say that about Maman!"

"Because it's true."

Camille rumbled to the door. "Ain't gwine stand here and listen to this, huh-uh." She jerked the door open and stiff-backed her way to the garden.

Restraint melted, now that Camille had gone. "Don't you dare . . ." came out as a snarl. The table edge knifed into her middle as she stretched toward Mimi until she could see every pore on her grandmother's ashen face. "Don't you dare say that about my mother."

Mimi's spine became a rod. "Why? It's time you knew the truth." Her mouth twisted into a sneer. "Your mother worked at a flophouse called Birdie's. She was nothing but a two-bit—"

"No!" Flashes of light dazzled the room. "I don't believe it!" Sheila grabbed at Mimi's sleeve, Mimi's hand—anything to stop this. Maman had refinement. Poise. Culture. Mimi lied!

"You will when I get through." Mimi's lips stretched taut against lined cheeks.

Sheila gritted her teeth. Shoved away from the table. Straightened. Why, Mimi enjoyed this!

"Where do you think she met that one-armed woman?" Mimi continued.

Again Sheila's vision blurred.

"The one at the hospital. *Remember?*"

The smell of roses flooded her senses. A black cloak. A scarred nub of an arm. Sheila's hand flew to her throat. She did remember. But that had been so long ago. What did that woman—Honey—have to do with Maman? Have to do with her?

"Sit down," ordered Mimi. "Now."

Her world tilting, her sight unreliable, she had no choice but to obey.

A tight smile distorted Mimi's face. "Back in the '20s, your mother blew in from Houma, rags on her back, her hands blistered from picking cotton." Mimi's enormous glittery solitaire caught the room's light and beamed luxury and power.

The sensation of insects crawling down her spine shivered Sheila. Mimi wore the face of revenge. But was it the face of truth? God, was it the face of truth?

Her eyes closed. Maman, with her silks and satins and ropes of pearls, had been tattered? Torn? No! Yet the inscription in that Bible flamed her soul and burned away lies. *Hattie Pearl, Houma, Louisiana*. Not France. Maman had lied about her origins. Wasn't it possible—probable—she'd lied about other things? Sheila opened her eyes. She must listen—and try to discern truth.

"Though she was just a tramp," Mimi continued, "she had assets men couldn't resist. And she knew how to use them." Glistening sweat lent an eerie sheen to Mimi's skin. "She started in burlesque, ascended to the dubious heights of Birdie's, where she met your father."

Sheila thought of Papa's lips at Maman's cheek, his courtly bow when Maman swept into a room. "But they loved each other," she managed. She begged clarity to revive her mind. Perhaps Maman had been starving. Alone. Who could blame a person for trying to survive?

"Love?" Veins throbbed in Mimi's neck. "She loved my son's money. Nothing more, nothing less."

"My mother wouldn't do that," Sheila insisted, yet her voice rang hollow. Mystery had always cloaked Maman . . . as had silks and satins and fur. She'd attributed it to Maman's foreign blood. Had she been wrong? Her lip quivered. Had she lived a lie?

"Your mother would do anything to get money. Anything. And the smell of her quadroon blood made men swoon."

Quadroon blood? Sheila's own blood boiled. "My mother was not like that."

Childhood scenes rallied to Maman's defense. Rocking chair times. Front porch times. Maman had taught her to read, to love. Sheila shoved back her chair, stumbling as she rose. "I don't believe it. You're lying." She would silence Mimi before she destroyed the memories.

A cackle rose from Mimi as she thrust a finger forward. "I haven't even told you the worst of it."

Sheila fell into her seat. Clapped hands over her ears. "I won't listen."

"Oh, yes, you will." The words spewed from Mimi, as if bottled up for years. Sheila pressed her lips together, desperate to avoid the poisonous air. A strangling noise died in her throat. She tried to rise but she was cemented to the chair. As if mesmerized by an awful news report, she froze to await every word despite an inner voice screaming, "No! No!"

"That harlot serviced my husband," Mimi continued. "Your grandfather." Her voice took on a cold metallic sound, like a cracked bell.

Sheila shivered. Mimi was describing something horrible. Something . . . beyond words.

"Thomas knew and still married her." Mimi jumped to her feet, as if the chair could no longer contain her story. "Iniquities of the fathers, visited on the children."

Despite closed eyes, Sheila heard the swish of Mimi's skirt, the tat-tat of her shoes pacing the kitchen. If only she could be somewhere, anywhere, but here! Blood rushed into her ears. Would another word kill her? Would she die, right in this kitchen?

"I did my best to stop it." Footsteps pattered near. Mimi yanked her to her feet, grabbed her jaw, turned her head until they were eye to eye. "God help me," she snarled, "I did my best. But my husband had been caught in your mother's web. Thomas knew that, but she trapped him, too. That witch! It was her fault they burned. God had to judge her sin." Mimi's hands fell to her side. Her shoulders slumped, yet her eyes held their mad glitter. "You are their seed. God will judge you, too."

Their seed. Sheila's face flamed. Yes, she was. They were her parents, and had been loving. Kind. She stared at Mimi, whom hate had transformed into a wrinkled hag. She shivered to remember that awful voodoo woman's curse, then shook her head to get rid of old memories . . . and new ones, none of which could be true. Mimi had always hated Maman. If she didn't get out of here now, Mimi would poison all she had believed in. Mimi would destroy *her.*

"Don't you look at me like that!" Mimi's breath pummeled Sheila. "I kept you from that one-armed woman, took you to church, did all I could to save you." Words sizzled the air. "The seed couldn't be saved."

Mimi grabbed a vase of roses, raised it as if in a toast, then hurled it to the floor.

Glass shattered, as did hope. Her relationship with Mimi could never be repaired.

"You and your child"—hate hoarsened Mimi's voice—"will mire in the muck and the blood of Gallatin! You and that one-armed woman, peas in a pod!"

Sheila tore toward her bedroom. *Honey.* Once Maman's best friend. Honey, who once wanted to be *her* friend. Dared she hope one thing remained the same? Remained *sane*? Honey would tell the truth and tell her what to do. She would find Honey. Everything depended on it.

She heard the rattle-slam of the kitchen door. Then blessed silence. She tossed things into a knapsack. "Get out of here," she kept whispering. James, as the long-standing family driver, would know the way to Gallatin. A thought slithered into her mind. Had James driven her grandfather to that place called Birdie's? Had James conspired in this debacle? She knotted her knapsack ties, strode back to the kitchen, her jaw set. It was time to talk to James.

She glanced out the window, hoping to see James huddled under the elm where he ate his lunch. No James. She crept closer. Cast her eyes toward a stand of trees where James liked to sit and whittle.

Still no sign of James.

She let her eyes rove the yard.

There was Mimi. In the garden.

Buzz. Snip. Buzz. Snip.

A shiver ran through Sheila. It was the cicadas, screeching their love—or hate?—of the heat. Sweat trickled into her eyes. *Snip. Snip.* She stared at Mimi, who bent, straightened, hurled weeds. Gardening, at a time like this?

"Ohhhh," slipped from Sheila, who could not tear her eyes from the dreadful sight. Her nails raked the screen, adding a *scrape, scrape* to the *snip, snip,* the *buzz, buzz.*

Boiling blood surged. She dashed down the hall, out the front door, did not stop running until she reached the bus stop, a mile away. As she climbed onto the rumbling vehicle that would take her to the trolley, she continued to hear, continued to see that horrid image: Mimi clipping off the heads of the pregnant buds of the Seven Sisters, then flinging them to the ground.

Chapter 16

Someone to Watch Over Me

Clangs and honks failed to mute the memory of Mimi's guillotine snips of the roses. Sheila clung to her seat rail, the swaying trolley spiking nausea. She closed her eyes. Recalled childhood images. Had she once marched so boldly down these teeming streets, sure she would save Papa by running the lottery? As her mind raced backward, the trolley careened forward, lurching as always while zigzagging through downtown.

Brakes squealed and bells dinged to signal the Quarter stop. She had failed to save Papa; could she at least preserve his memory? Maman's memory? It depended on a woman named Honey. Did she still live at Birdie's?

Slatted seats became handrails as she weaved to the front of the streetcar. She stepped close to the driver, whose cap shielded his eyes. Dared she ask him about Birdie's? Subject herself to ridicule? She brushed off her skirt. Ran her tongue over parched lips. Ignored the flaming of her cheeks. As a girl "in a bad way," she'd best get used to such things. This driver couldn't treat her worse than Mimi had. "Sir?"

"What'cha doin', holdin' up my run?" The driver gripped the enormous steering wheel while he shooflied her with his free hand.

"Sir, could I trouble you with a question?"

Someone buzzed impatience by pulling the cord. Complaints rang in her ears, as did the snips of Mimi's clippers. "Where would I find a place called . . . Birdie's?" she whispered.

Someone catcalled from a nearby seat. Tears sprang to her eyes. It was horrid to have a trolley of people consider you common . . . or worse.

"Well, now," asked the driver, his voice smooth as cream, "why's a young miss like you goin' to a place like that?"

She gripped her knapsack. "I'm looking for a woman who lives there."

The driver pushed back his hat. Mopped sweat from his brow. Suddenly he seemed unconcerned with the crescendo of groans rising from the passengers. "Birdie's." His eyes misted until they were watery, old, and full of memories. Good . . . or bad? Sheila didn't know.

"Down by da docks," he finally said. "Past da barrelhouse. Got a sign. An old, creaky porch." He leaned close. "Hope you know what you doin', young lady."

She bowed her head, overwhelmed at this gift of kindness, then rushed from the car before she suffocated from heat rising off impatient riders and her flaming face.

◆ ◆ ◆

Yeasty smells rose from the corner bakery, but she had no appetite. The burned nut aroma of chicory failed to revive her. And that pungent, salty reminder that the great river flowed on while her life stagnated intensified the bitter taste in her throat.

With a heavy step, she clutched her stomach and veered past drunks slumped against storefronts. Sweat streaming down her face, she made what should be the final turn, if the driver knew what he was talking about.

Wedged between a saloon and a boarded-up theater stood a three-story house. Neon signs, dull by daylight, informed that she'd found Birdie's. A shudder shook Sheila. Had Maman climbed these rickety porch steps and . . . entertained in those upper rooms? One way or the other, she would find out. She sidestepped rolled, yellowed newspapers. Knocked on a warped door. Tried to ignore the clanging of fear within. Knocked louder.

Hinges creaked. The door opened. An expressionless ebony giant filled the doorway. "Can I help you?" he boomed.

"I-I'm looking for a woman named Honey."

"What is your business?" The man looked past her, at something in the street.

Sheila glanced backward, saw nothing but a mix of today's businessmen, tomorrow's sailors, and last-night's revelers. She gripped her knapsack, refocused on the man. "She was an old friend of my Maman." Urgency empowered her to reach out and touch a huge hand. "Please, Mister. My name is Sheila." The man's glistening skin and steely eyes jumbled up her words yet exposed raw honesty. "I . . . my mother was Valerie Ann. I need to find out about her. There's . . . I need to know some things. Can you help me?"

An eternity passed as the man seemed to scrutinize every inch of her face. Then he stepped back and motioned her inside. "Miss Honey's not up to receiving guests." He spoke like a favored servant guarding entry to an estate. "But for Valerie Ann's daughter, she'll likely make an exception. You wait right here. Winston'll check for you." With nary a floorboard creak, the man climbed a curved staircase and disappeared.

Sheila stepped forward. Somehow she'd convinced him. She couldn't fathom why.

Sunbeams poured through milky windows, exposing dust-coated tables, wine-blotched carpets. The light proved a harsh judge, declaring crimson divans, purple love seats, and gold draperies cheap and garish. Sheila put on youth's rose-colored glasses and tried to see it as it once had been when—if— Maman lived here.

Winston reappeared. "Last door on the left." He slipped past the divans and left the room.

Silence stretched taut her nerves. She padded up the worn runner of the staircase, a need for truth quickening her pace. Puffing, she reached the top stair, marched down a landing lined with closed-off boudoirs, and headed for the room where Honey surely entertained men, slept, laughed, cried. Had Maman once done the same?

She knocked on Honey's door. "Ma'am?" she whispered. "H-Honey?"

A low, deep moan answered.

Her skin crawled. Was the man mistaken? Was Honey . . . entertaining?

She peeked down the hall, relieved it was still deserted. "I need to talk to you," she said, a bit louder.

"Oh-h . . . Ugh . . ."

Sheila startled. "Ma'am? Are you okay?"

Mumbles and moans slid around the doorframe to bristle the hairs on Sheila's arms. Honey needed help. Dispensing with etiquette, Sheila turned the knob and tiptoed into the room.

Shades had been stretched over the windows, yet fingers of light painted shadowy figures on flowery wallpaper. Vials, bottles, and half-empty glasses littered a carved dressing table. Ammonia and menthol failed to mask urine and vomit stench. Gagging, Sheila clapped her hand over her mouth, edged past a huddle on a bed, and hurried into a tiny bathroom. She knelt by the toilet and emptied her stomach's scant contents, then rinsed her face, relieved that the woman hadn't seemed to notice. Her pulse quickened. Why *hadn't* the woman noticed? She patted her face dry, pattered to a massive claw-foot bed.

A woman who wore a scarlet nightgown lay in a sea of satin sheets. Dark hair fanned dry and listless across a wrinkled pillowcase. The woman's complexion matched the color of lake scum. Yet the scarred nub of an arm identified Honey, the woman who had visited her hospital room. Had it only been four years ago? Honey had come to help her then. Now Honey was ill. Sheila steeled her nerves. *It's my turn to help.*

Honey moaned, loud and low.

"What—what's wrong?" She hefted herself onto the bed, felt Honey's forehead. Its heat trembled Sheila's fingers. When acid rose in Sheila's throat, she swallowed, tensed her stomach. This room held enough sickness.

"Honey!" The questions could wait. She had to help Maman's best friend. Before it was too late. "We need to get you to a doctor."

Honey's lashes fluttered. Pus oozed from listless eyes. She flailed about, her arm waving, her legs tangling in the sheets.

Sheila shuddered as the emaciated arm reached for her, then scolded herself. How dared she be sickened by poor Honey's diseased body? With fervor, she grabbed crippled fingers and tried to massage life into them.

"Valerie? Valerie Ann?" Honey moaned.

"I'm . . ." She bit back her words. What would it hurt to let Honey reminisce? Perhaps she'd learn about Maman in a different way than planned.

"Why are you back, Valerie Ann?" Honey thrashed about, as if angry. "Don't let him throw you out. Don't—" A spasm of coughing choked out the words.

"Thomas didn't throw me out." Sheila's teeth chattered with impatience to get Honey help, yet she played along with the charade. "We're still married."

An angelic smile settled onto Honey's wan face. "That's nice." Her eyes tracked, caught Sheila's. She struggled to a sitting position. "You're not Valerie Ann." Her eyes widened, then contracted into slits. "Who are you?"

"Don't you know me?" Sheila moistened her lips, threw up her hands in desperation. "I'm Sheila—Sheba. Remember, you came to me in the hospital. After the fire." If she were to learn about Maman, she had to get through to Honey. Now. "We met at the hospital, Honey. Where you need to go."

"Sheba." Honey feebly patted her hand. She sank back and let the sheets swell up and swallow her. "Oh, I see. You're Valerie Ann's girl. Little Sheba."

"Something's . . . happened." Sheila squeaked, like the bed springs. "I need to ask you something. First we've got to get you to the hospital."

"Hospital . . . no. Don't you think Winston offered to carry me himself?" The sweet smile returned, along with a dreamy gaze, as if Honey peered into a window of the past. Perhaps with Maman. "Talk, yes." Honey giggled. "I always like to talk."

"Honey. Please listen." She found Honey's hand among the damp, satiny sheets and squeezed it. "Look at me."

Honey's eyes seemed to focus. She again struggled to sit up.

"I'll talk if you agree to go to the hospital."

"A talk with Valerie Ann's daughter. That's nice."

"Do you agree?" Her nerves frayed; she bit back a scream. "Honey?"

"Of course." Another dreamy smile. "Now talk."

She interlaced her fingers, stared past Honey. "I met a boy. A soldier. My grandmother, Thomas's mother, threw a fit." Her head bowed. "But not before she—"

Another giggle. "Soldiers are nice. Sergeants, colonels. Especially colonels."

Sheila gritted her teeth against the putrid smell rising from the sheets. "Listen to me, Honey. We're getting you out of here." She rose and began gathering wrinkled gowns and undergarments.

"You're in the family way, aren't you?"

The words punched Sheila in the belly. Honey's clothes slipped to the floor.

Color tinged Honey's cheeks as she propped herself up with her elbow.

"How . . . did you know?" Sheila sidestepped the clothes, climbed back on the bed.

"There's ripeness about your hips, yet dark moons under your eyes." A lock of hair fell over Honey's face. "If that weren't enough, you mentioned a soldier, trouble with your grandmother . . ." Honey shuddered, coughed, struggled to suck in air.

Chills flitted along Sheila's spine as she stared at Honey's ghastly grimace. She leaned close, smoothed back Honey's hair, hurried to the sink, found a glass, filled it with cloudy water, and offered Honey a drink.

Cracked lips parted, managed a sip. Honey swallowed and then winced as if in pain.

Sheila's hand shook so, water slopped onto her, but what did it matter? Honey was dying. "We must get you help," she cried. "The hospital—"

Honey shook her head. "It's too late for that."

Too late. If she had only come sooner! Then she thought of Maman, Papa.

Her shoulders shook. Sobs wracked her body. Her wish was impossible. She, of all people, knew death stopped for no one.

"When it's time, the old priest will handle things."

Chills rippled through Sheila. Would Honey die now? Sheila tried to speak, but her jaw had frozen.

"Let's talk . . . about you," Honey managed, between coughs. "What do you want from me, little Sheba?"

She closed her eyes to envision Maman's secret smile and bow-shaped lips. She could confide in Honey, Maman's best friend. "I've nowhere to go, no one to turn to," she sobbed.

"Your grandmother . . ." A cough spasmed Honey's voice.

Sheila again held the glass to Honey's lips. "Hates me." Tears began to fall. "I cannot abide it there anymore. I cannot!"

"God will help you." Honey's focus shifted away from Sheila. "Unto Thee I lift up my eyes . . . have mercy on me . . ." Prayers hung like mist over tangled sheets.

Sheila bowed her head. God wouldn't help her now. Look what had happened to Maman, Papa, Honey, who'd all flaunted His rules and paid the price. So would she. "It's too late," she whispered, hot tears sliding down her face.

A papery hand stroked her cheek. "It's never too late, baby girl. Not with God."

Sheila slumped against Honey's bosom. Maman had called her "baby girl." "I miss Maman," she cried brokenly. "She'd know what to do. What will happen to me?"

Gentle caresses continued. "Once she didn't know what to do, *ma chère*."

Sheila lay so still against Honey, she could hear her heartbeat, her wheezy breath.

"We met here, you know," Honey continued. "At Birdie's."

So Mimi had spoken truth. A myriad of images interlocked, like a jigsaw puzzle. Even as a girl, she had watched men devour Maman's dark eyes and full lips, women arch their brows and sniff at Maman's French perfume. It all made sense now, had always made sense. But it hurt so to bear the weight of the truth!

"Thomas and your mother met here, too," Honey continued.

Another piece, locking in place. Sheila exhaled, protection against truth that might smother her to death.

"From the first, Valerie Ann sensed your father cared for her, but things between a girl and her john . . . don't often last."

Sheila sat up. Hugged trembling arms. "What about my grandfather? Is it true?"

The bed groaned as if it would splinter into pieces. Perhaps it had borne too much.

"When Valerie Ann realized he was Thomas's daddy, she cut off ties. It drove the old man wild." Honey coughed and wheezed. "Your grandfather threatened to disown Thomas. Close down Birdie's." Honey cackled. "But Madam got her back up. Got Winston to throw him out. Love took over after that."

"Papa didn't mind that she was . . . part Negro?" Sheila ventured.

"Half this town's got colored blood. Some got the brains to admit it and move on. Your papa was one of them."

Sheila buried her face in her hands. So it was all true. "What about my grandmother—the other one, Hattie Pearl?"

A fly pinged against a windowpane, desperate to escape. Sheila battled a revolting stomach. She, too, wanted to escape her past, but it was impossible. Poisonous engraftments had tainted the fruit of her family tree. Would she be poisoned, too?

"Hattie Pearl was a slave, used and abused by her master, one of the cruelest in Houma, Louisiana. Your Maman was a product of that twisted sickness."

The noisy fly—and the truth—pushed Sheila past the point of distraction. If she learned one more thing, she just might explode.

Honey's face took on a grayish cast. "As death rattled in the old master's lungs, God struck fear into him. He tossed a wad of bills at Hattie, who used them to send your mother to New Orleans, where Birdie's—and its men—awaited."

Sheila blanched. "How could she do that to her own flesh and blood?"

A coughing fit seized Honey and strangled her words. She rummaged for a handkerchief, spat red-tinged phlegm into it, then accepted another sip of water from Sheila.

"If the old master were a hog snake, his son was a python," she finally managed. "He would've sucked life from Valerie Ann before she stood up a grown woman." She found Sheila's hand and squeezed it. "Believe me, it was the only way." The soiled handkerchief became a ball and fell into the sheets. "Have her fend for herself or let that viper kill her."

Sheila locked eyes with Honey . . . and saw Maman's soulful gaze. No wonder they had been best friends. Her lip trembled as she latched onto Honey, her one connection to Maman. *How can I lose her now? No, God, no!* She bent over, pulled Honey close, squeezed tight.

Tap. Tap. Tap.

Sheila scuttled behind the drapes. Had a customer come to call? The madam? Again someone knocked.

"Who is it?" Honey managed.

"James."

Blood rushed through Sheila's ears. How in the world had James found her? The door opened.

Sheila peeked from behind the drapes, tried to dart back into hiding, but it was no use. James stepped in, straight and stiff as ever, holding his hat in front of him, and stared right at her. "We needs to go."

"How—how did you find me?"

"Miss Sheba, I been workin' for dis family a long, long time." He bowed his head, as if he were embarrassed. "Could drive here wit' my eyes closed."

Sheila flamed from shame. What must James think of the fine Alexanders?

"Come on, now, Miss," he pleaded. "We gotta go."

She had never disobeyed James and did not want to now. Then she remembered that snip, snip. She stepped back. "I can't go back there."

"You can and you will." It was Honey speaking, her voice clear and strong.

Heat surged in Sheila's breast as she whirled. How many people would tell her what to do?

A disheveled Honey wobbled to her feet.

"Honey!" Sheila leapt forward. Took her hand. "Get back in bed. Or I—"

"You'll what?" Honey wrenched from Sheila's grip. Tottered to the night-stand. Retrieved a Bible. "Here. Take this. It has all you need to know." With surprising force, she thrust it at Sheila. "Now git."

Sheila fell forward, clutched satin and bones and straw hair. "Please, Honey. Let me stay here! Don't send me away." Yet she knew she wasted speech with every word. With life growing inside, she could not live in this decaying mansion.

"Go, little Sheba. Now." Honey's voice floated through a mist of grief. "Take her, James."

"James, please!" Sheila cried. "Don't take me back to Music Street!"

"Miss Sheba, we got places to go and peoples to see."

She clung to Honey. "W-who?"

James put his hat on his head. "We's meetin' yo' grandmother at the doctor."

James gripped her arm and led her toward the door.

The putrid odor, suffocating heat, buzzing fly, and tortured words swirled into a devil duster to melt her resolve. Mimi had been right. God wreaked vengeance on sinners. She would start paying for her sin now. Energy drained from her. She could not fight God and His rules. If she followed Him, followed them, perhaps God would spare her and her baby.

Defeated, she collapsed into James' arms. The old man pushed her head against his crisp starched shirt and patted her hair. He got her down the hall, down the stairs, past the hulking Winston, onto the street.

There was Mimi's Packard, shiny and sleek, in contrast to run-down, defeated Birdie's. Remorse flooded Sheila. Birdie's, where her mother had lived. Where she would rather live if the alternative meant Mimi. Mimi, who had said such things about Maman. "I-I can't do this, James."

"You got to, Miss Sheba." He opened the door.

"But I can't live there anymore."

James looked toward the street, as if someone in the crowds might provide an answer that would calm her . . . or at least get her into the car. Then he lowered his head and studied his outspread hands. "You ain't gwine have to, Miss Sheba."

Sheila gripped those weathered, beloved hands. "Wh-what do you mean, James?" Images of licking flames, singed boards, of Mimi slapping Honey in that sterile hospital room, played havoc with her sanity. What would Mimi do to her now?

"She gwine pack you up and send you nawth." James eyes glistened. "Come mornin', the *City of New Orleans* done be pullin' outta the station. And you gwine be on it."

◆

His senses reeling, Samuel tried to focus on his mother, who sat across from him, her hands on the table. "So your *mother—my grandmother*—was black?"

"She was the daughter of a slave and a French Southerner. A quadroon. Down South they'd call me an octoroon."

Samuel bristled. "Lincoln ended that talk over a hundred years ago."

Her gaze fell on him in that quiet way she had. "Not in Houma, Louisiana, he didn't."

He'd read things like this, in history books, happening to other people. Not his mother. Not him. He slumped into a chair, hung his head, exhausted though it was only 10:00 a.m. He had enough to worry about with Mali's predicament, and now he'd been hung on the branches of this bizarre family tree. Even for someone trained for combat, for stress, it was too much.

"I wish it were different." She twisted her napkin.

But it's not. As if he were in Honey's room, Samuel could smell death. A smell that Nam had branded in his brain. He studied his palms, wishing there was a nice and easy way out of this mess. For his sake, of course, but most of all for Mali's and his mother's sake. Yeah, he now had two women to worry about.

"I'm sorry to have to tell you all this." His mother's eyes brimmed with tears; when he caught her gaze, she ducked her head, as if she feared he'd strike her.

Her words shot him from his seat. *So she thinks I'm turning up my nose at them? Perhaps I did. And I was dead wrong.* He paced about the kitchen, unused to emotional meltdown. He'd better get over it if he wanted to help . . . both of his women. And draw from the Living Water. "It's just—Maman reminds me of someone."

Her head lifted. Exposed her delicate neck, chiseled cheekbones. "Are you in love, Samuel?" There was a catch in her voice.

He nodded, amazed again at her intuition. "I met someone in Thailand, someone who means the world to me."

She rose from the table, got his cup, refilled it with steaming coffee, set it near him, then folded her hands in her lap. "How did you meet her?"

Her thoughtfulness swept through him like a warm wind. She cared, he could see it all over her face. It was time to build that bridge to Mali.

"I'd had . . . an incident." The image arrived in Technicolor. The bodies, calling out to him from the moonlit jungle, begging for a proper burial. The hours spent whittling bamboo and bending it into little crosses. Shovel in hand, crawling past the sentry, thanks to a camouflage cloud of tobacco and reefer smoke around the sentry's head. The rich, dank soil slurping as he shoveled into it and then thrust stiff corpses into the trench. His face, contorted at the sock-your-jaw stench of maggot-covered flesh. The buzzing flies. The—

". . . all right, Samuel? Are you all right?" A blur—her hand—bridged the table.

He closed his eyes until the room quit spinning, then nodded decisively. "My commander ordered me to R&R, in Bangkok." He focused on her face, yet the faint outline of the crude crosses remained. Better than the other stuff. "I met up with some buddies, and we hit the bars." A mother didn't need all the sordid details. "They wanted to go to a brothel. Since I didn't . . . partake, I was the designated babysitter. Anyway, that's where I met Mali." He envisioned the face of an angel, the body of a woman. "I just held her. So many men had used her. Abused her. She knew enough English to tell me her story." Words tumbled out. "We went for walks. Boat rides. Innocent things." He looked square into his mother's face. "I made sure to keep it that way, though Mali didn't think I could love her despite how she makes a living."

"I can imagine." His mother's eyes misted. Her cheeks colored.

"Yes," he continued, emboldened by his mother's understanding. "Her parents sold her when she was fourteen. Somehow she stayed sane in spite of . . ."

"What they make her do?"

Hope surged. "You understand?"

She jostled about in her seat. "Yes, I believe I do, Samuel."

He nodded, then reined in giddiness at her perception. For now he wouldn't speak of the nightly tricks, the attempted escapes, the brutal beatings by that piece-of-dung pimp.

"I love her." *Now finish, Bub.* "I want to marry her. But that's impossible. Unless . . ." He couldn't sit still, not with everything out on the table. He rose and again paced. "I checked around. The Thais won't help."

"You mean their police won't get her out of there?"

Bitterness hardened his laugh. "They're in the pocket of the brothel owners. Uncle Sam won't touch it, either." He cast a sidelong glance. "Unless top brass intervenes. And I do mean the top."

A shadow fell across her face, clouding his earlier exuberance. "The top?" she asked. "What does that mean?"

"An ambassador. A general. Congressmen." He felt her gaze but didn't meet it. He had to tread carefully to get through this without admitting he'd hired a PI to uncover her secrets. "Someone who'd let Mali safe-house at the base. Who would answer an SOS. Only top brass could influence the Thai army." He rapped his knuckles on the table. "That's not in my control," he said. "Maybe it's in yours. I mean, a prominent pastor's wife . . ." No. He would not tell her about his blackmail plan. Not now. Probably not ever. His hand raked his hair. It truly was a mess. He shouldn't be dragging his mother, and her husband, into it.

A glance caught her scrutinizing him. She squirmed in her chair as if she were the nervous one. "I don't know if we can get involved," she finally said.

He struggled to keep his composure. Squeezed his fists until they ached. He longed to say, "I understand," or "It's okay," but with Mali's image filling the room, he only managed a nod.

She rose and walked to the window. With her head tilted back, she looked like an angel, begging God to draw near. He craved God's presence, too. He bowed his head. Tried to pray.

He heard her step close. Slide into her seat. "Maybe I can help," she whispered.

"How?" popped out as he lifted his head.

"Edward has friends. We both do. You see, we—mainly Edward—founded a nonprofit organization. With ties both here and overseas."

And I know that, too, thanks to the report. "Well, I hate to . . ." he began, then felt such pain in his chest that he jumped up, scooted his chair close to hers, and took her hands. "Look." The script had been thrown out; he was going with his gut. "I don't want to hurt you, but we're talking about my future wife. Yet I'm worried about what your husband will say, and do."

"He's coming back today. You let me worry about him, Son."

Son. He recalled the piano music she'd played, just for him. He bowed his head and waited until his vision cleared. This was no time for tears. "Are you sure? I'll phony up some papers. Military mumbo-jumbo. He doesn't have to know about me."

Her jaw tightened like it had when Thelma arrived. Good. She didn't like lies, either. "It's high time Edward and I talked." She took his cup to the sink. "I should have told him before we got married."

"Should I stay with you or go?"

Again she faced the window. "I'd better do this on my own."

"Yes," he agreed, exhaling hard. He rummaged in his pocket and put a card on the counter. "Here's the number at the base. I'll be out there. Waiting. And praying."

With robotic movements, she went to the sink, rinsed the cup. Set it on the counter. "That's what I'll do myself."

The sight of her compelled him to leave her with something. He moved to the sink. Put his arms on her shoulders. "Wait right here."

His stride matched his heartbeat on the trip to the guest room. He dug his most precious possession from his duffel and returned to the kitchen.

It was the book the nuns had given to him. The book he'd lugged to boot camp, stowed in cargo holds, secreted at the bottom of smelly laundry bags. *Honey* had been written in spidery cursive on the inside cover, right above the other thing, perhaps smudged by tears, perhaps smudged by sweaty fingers. Something still legible. Something that had sustained him through soulless dark Vietnam nights. "I have this Bible."

His mother's hands flew to her face. "Thank You, Lord. They did it," she whispered.

"You left it for me, didn't you?" He pointed to the inscription he knew by heart. *To my precious son. Love, your mother.* "Did Honey write it?" he asked, his voice hoarse.

"Her name was in there when she gave it to me. I wrote the rest. Then prayed you'd get it."

He set his Bible on the table. "Thank you." He took her hand, as if he were proposing. The pose he hoped to repeat soon. With Mali. "You'll never know what it meant."

Sunshine streamed through the window and onto her face. "I think I do know, Son. It once meant the world to me."

Chapter 17

Mood Indigo

Hours after Samuel left, Sheila pounded the piano keys until music answered her SOS. Brahms, Tchaikovsky, and of course, Rachmaninoff, doing their utmost to ward off dread.

A gust of wind tore through the room. Sheet music flew. She leapt off the bench, swatting and twirling for the papers. They danced about, taunting her like wild children.

She snatched them up, one by one, her footsteps crushing the pile carpet she'd so carefully vacuumed. Wind twirled the drapes, threatening to wreak more havoc, yet bringing a clean, fresh scent. Her world had been blown upside down in just this way—a glorious, frightening thing.

She opened the piano seat and stashed the music, leaving only Rachmaninoff on the music rack.

The phone ringing in the study set off a thrumming in her heart. Shaky legs carried her to the desk she'd dusted and adorned with a vase of roses. Breathless, she picked up the phone. "Yes, dear?" she said, so sure it was him, reporting in.

"I'm at the airport, Sheila."

Gone was Edward's velvety tone, confirming what she'd suspected when Thelma called earlier to say he'd be home around five. She wrapped the phone cord about her wrist.

"Hi, honey." She forced a bright tone. "Sure you don't want me to pick you up?"

"I'll be home in an hour, if baggage claims goes okay. If I find a cab. If traffic's not too backed up. See you then." A dial tone sounded.

Edward, rude? Her temples pounded as she gripped the phone. He knew. Before she'd had a chance to explain. She hung up. Walked robotlike into the kitchen. Found her to-do list.

Steak. Marinating in lemon juice and cracked pepper, the way he liked it. She checked off items; she was a wife desperate to please her husband. To *keep* her husband. *A bag of charcoal.* Out by the grill. *Potatoes.* Pricked with a fork and wrapped in foil. *Iceberg*, quartered, set on salad plates, topped with her homemade Thousand Island, heavy on the ketchup. *Boiled eggs*, sliced and wrapped and waiting in the ice box.

She tossed the list on the counter. Silver and china gleamed from the table, which she'd dressed up with a starched cloth. Vetoing more roses, she gathered tulips from the garden, stood the firm stems in his mother's antique frog, arranged them in a vase. She'd do her part to make Edward receptive to the idea of *Samuel*. The other things, including the fate of Mali, could be worked out later.

Nervous energy led her to inspect every room, hunting for annoyances to her fastidious husband. Good thing Mimi and the nuns had taught her about dirt. The activity helped lessen the anxiety swirling in her stomach.

Her mission ended in the dining room, where mirrors shone, wood floors gleamed. Everything Edward had provided for her was in its place except her heart, and that was really her own, wasn't it? Pounding in her temples, her wrists, to disrupt the façade of calm she attempted to maintain. She moved to the piano room, replaced Rachmaninoff with a hymnal, begged ebony and ivory to soothe her, as always. Her eyes closed. Fingers tickled the keys. *There, that's it.*

An old spiritual rose from the piano, loosed the windows of her mind. She saw Camille, James, Sister Carline . . .

The door banged open. Bags thudded onto the floor.

Her fingers flailed against the piano keys, which shuddered and groaned, as if they resented the interruption. For a moment, she too resented the interruption. Then she jumped to her feet, hugged her arms to combat a chill, smoothed down her skirt.

"Darling." Her steps tremulous, she met him in the entryway. He turned away, something he'd never done. Desperate to right things, she picked up one of his suitcases.

"I'll get it." He slung a garment bag over his shoulder, hefted a suitcase in each hand, her Edward resembling a lopsided scale. And would he give her justice?

He kicked the door shut in a most un-Edward-like way, muttering something—surely not a curse—when it failed to catch. A scowl distorted his brow. Spots of red mottled his fine English complexion.

Her muscles tensed as she noted other oddities. A twisted tie. Wrinkled trousers. A stranger had burst into the house she and Edward had made a home. She didn't know whether to cry for help, flee the premises, or welcome him with a kiss.

Deciding on the kiss, she scurried close, but he blocked her path. She curved her arms to hug his neck, but he turned, the bags deflecting her, pinball-bumper-style.

"What—what's wrong, Edward?" she asked, knowing full well what had caused the tight lines across his chin, his forehead, clouds in the gray eyes.

"I think you know what's wrong," he confirmed. "As does the whole church."

She stiffened her arms. Pushed away jitters. "Are you going to hear my side of it or rely on your secretary's version?"

"I'm all ears, Sheila. As soon as I unpack. Change."

She bit back a nasty retort. Did he have to toss the clothes in the hamper now? Couldn't he brush his teeth, comb his hair later? He'd rather she pressure-cook while he gathered his thoughts, whispered a prayer. Or just kept his routine intact while she fell apart. Again she hugged her arms as he left the room. She'd give him that much. The whole thing would tidal-wave their safe little lives. Desperate to stay calm, she returned to her bench, employing the only tactic she knew to push away white-silent insanity.

With tense fingers, she thumbed through the hymnal. "Amazing Grace," she whispered, "can it save a wretch like me?" She played—and *prayed*—the song Edward had requested so many Sunday mornings, so many Wednesday evenings, so many—

"Could you stop that?" Stripped to boxers and T-shirt, Edward and his hairy white legs and gaping mouth stomped back into the hall. "Let a man have peace?"

A protest rose in her throat but died as she considered her options. She shut the hymnal. Sat. The wait maddened her thought processes. Still, she waited. She had no choice.

◆

"Now, let me get this straight." Calm reigned now: in his voice, in the perfectly creased khakis, the Oxford white button-down shirt. He had entered her sanctuary and sprawled on the love seat, leaving no room for her. Perhaps it was better that she stay here, on her piano bench, close to her music. The thing she'd always been able to count on. Before Edward. She whirled around to face him, her back to the keys.

"You don't deny that a young soldier stayed *in our house* while I was gone?" Even his ears blushed red. "Who is he?"

"My next of kin," she whispered. "My blood."

"Now, wait a minute. Thelma said he was twentysomething. How—"

She gripped the sides of the piano bench. "I tried once to tell you about him, Edward. But you said it didn't matter. You said—"

He jumped to his feet. "That was then. This is now." Stomped forward. "What were you thinking? Or is that it: you *weren't* thinking? Just playing your dreamy music?" He mopped his splotchy brow. "I don't get it. You said those people of yours were killed in a fire."

Her insides became a boiling cauldron. How dared he call her parents "those people"! When she flung out her arms in protest, her elbows banged on the keyboard and unleashed discordant sounds. Edward was being so hateful, so unfair, both to her and Samuel. She sat up straight. Interlaced her icy fingers. "What question should I answer, Edward?" She fought to modulate her voice yet accept the spirit of Maman, Papa, rising up after decades. *You are an Alexander. You don't have to take this from him.* It had been way too long since she'd acted like herself.

"Who's the soldier boy?" A cross between a smirk and a sneer transformed him into an unattractive, self-righteous prig, like Deacon Snyder, the one who had voted against the halfway house, against the counseling program for unwed mothers. Mothers like *her*, only Snyder didn't know that he'd cast a vote not only against the wife of his beloved pastor, but against *his own daughter.*

"The soldier boy is my son." The words felt like marbles in her mouth, but she was glad she'd said them. Edward needed to understand her pride in Samuel if . . . if their marriage was to survive.

His face paled to a sickly pink. "Your son? When? Who? What?" Hoarseness robbed eloquence from the voice that had mesmerized folks for years. Had mesmerized her, too. "You had . . . the surgery, didn't you, because of female problems? Or was that a lie, too?"

She gritted her teeth against the word "lie" and forced her lungs to inhale, exhale. Which question had he asked first? "It was long before I met you, Edward," she finally said. "I was seventeen. He was a soldier, in a war quite different from this one. I did have the surgery, right after I had my son. Another soldier." She wanted to tell him how lonely she'd been, wanted to tell him about her holier-than-thou grandmother, wanted to tell him why the doctor had done what he did. She yearned to tell him everything!

The jut of his chin padlocked further comment.

"You've got a thing for men in uniform, I see." He smirked and then ogled her, like a dirty old man would. Her Edward, reduced to this.

Pressure built in her temples. She gripped the sides of the bench to keep from picking it up and hurling it, not so much at Edward, but at the judgmental jerk he'd become. The nerve of this man who spouted grace, love, and mercy but dished out sarcasm. Right now, she struggled to love him . . . and certainly didn't like him.

"No, you don't see." She gritted her teeth in an attempt to remain civilized. "You don't see at all. It was a mistake, Edward. The mistake of a very young, very foolish girl."

"Which will be the absolute damnation of all we've tried to build here."

"When did you become a hellfire and damnation preacher?" she spat out.

He looked her up and down, not a hint of compassion—another favorite sermon topic—in those blasted gray eyes. "When I walked in here today."

"Well, you'd better get the bellows—" she pointed toward the den's ceramic fireplace "—and start fanning the flames, because there's more I've got to say."

Every bit of redness encored on his face, as did piglike eyes. He looked mean, old. Her Edward, an old man . . .

Twinges of guilt pricked like bee stings. She closed her eyes, bowed her head. *Lord, he's been good to me. He doesn't deserve this.* Praying, she envisioned Samuel's blue eyes and smooth brow. What did *he* deserve after an orphan's life? She rubbed her arms. "My son—Samuel's his name, Edward—needs my help. Our help." She begged him with her eyes. Received a rock-hard stare. Her gaze fell to her lap. She studied her hands.

"I see." He tapped his toe on the floor. "He wants money, doesn't he? He won't get a cent."

Mimi's face appeared. She blinked it away. "No, not exactly money, Edward."

"Then what?" he shouted.

She bowed her head, sorry to yank Mali across the ocean to a chilly room in Chicago. But she was done with lies. "Nam was hard on Samuel, but he met a girl over there. In a brothel."

"Saigon's full of them," he spat out.

How do you know? she wanted to shout. Instead, she smoothed her skirt, fought the whine that tickled her throat. "She's not in Saigon, she's in Thailand."

"And I suppose he loves her." Something like a laugh came from the love seat.

Words like Mimi had spat at her. She ground her teeth. This had to stop before it *really* got ugly, as it had long ago, down in New Orleans. "I think he does." She jumped off the bench, wrung her hands. "People can change, Edward. Just look at me!" She knelt beside him, desperate to clasp the hands that had touched her, loved her, held her, for eighteen years. She began to sob, her heart crying out, begging him to see behind the mask she'd worn for so long. Before he could see Samuel, he had to first see who she'd once been, who she was, even now. Not just Sheila, but Sheba. And Sylvia—

"Yes, just look at you." He shoved her away with a forearm.

Flames blazed like she'd been doused with gasoline and a lit match flung at her. *I'm an Alexander. Not even my husband touches me like that.* She drew back her arm, as if to slap him, held it steady, then rose and moved backward until she thudded onto her bench. "Yes. Look at me. Look good. You'll see my son's forehead. My son's coloring. He's part black. Like me."

Edward's mouth flew open. He half sat, half laid in that love seat, arms splayed, jaw slack, looking like a dead man.

"Something else to throw in my face. Along with the fact that Maman was a prostitute; Papa, a gambler." Her spit showered the air. "They gave me my spirit, though it's lain dormant too long." She shoved back curls, which were trembling like every inch of her. "Thankfully it's resurfaced." She crossed her arms. "Just in time to help him."

"So help me God, Sheila, if you lift a finger—"

Now he'd involved God in this? If he didn't shut up—"What, Edward?" she shouted. "What are you going to do to me? Don't you understand? I lost my heart, my soul, when they took him away. Now I've got a chance to help. Wild horses and Englishmen—or an Englishman, I should say—aren't going to stop me."

He stood. Inched close. The calm, collected pastor face had returned; any minute he might shake her hand and thank her for attending service. "You've got a choice to make. The foundation—our life, Sheila—is into something big."

She deflated. So it had to do with his career. *Their* career. Isn't that what he'd always said? "What do you mean?"

Passion lit eyes that had begged hundreds to walk the aisle. "Dallas is just the beginning. We plan to change the way Christians are viewed. Could you at least listen?"

Her arms dropped to her side. She owed him that. She slid to the edge of her bench; he sat back down on the love seat. Something had swooped into *his* life as well as hers. She would hear him out. She encouraged him with a nod.

"We've been cut out of Washington, cut out of society, cut out of the arts, the sciences. Looked at as wild-eyed missionaries."

"And what's wrong with that?"

"It's time to reclaim America for the kingdom of God. And not just on Sundays."

She wrapped her feet around the piano bench legs to keep from jumping up. Shaking him. He was classic Edward, totally in control. Had he even *heard* her?

"I need you behind me, Sheila. More than ever."

She wiped her face. Perhaps there was a way. For Samuel. For her. "I'll be there, Edward. Behind you." Was that compromise hovering near, tantalizing her with hope? "First I need to help my son."

"Huh-uh, Sheila." He smiled his little-boy smile she'd always thought cute. Only it wasn't cute now. "Not on this. You've only got so much to give. I come first."

She dug her fingernails into the bench with the illogical thought that if she didn't, she would evaporate. "Edward, I've given to your ministry—our ministry—for years. Out of love." She enunciated carefully. "I've led the choir. Sat in the first pew. I've always been behind you. A hundred and ten percent. I'm asking you for this one thing. Help me reclaim what I've lost with my son."

"I thought you loved doing all those things."

"I do—I did, Edward. But now I have a son. Who needs my help."

"Like I said, Sheila, you have a choice." He gave her a tight-lipped smile. "It needs to be—"

"Either him or you?"

Edward nodded.

The fires had blazed out, leaving smoldering coals. He didn't even know what Samuel needed. Worse, he didn't care. "That's a fine place to put me." Words might continue exiting her mouth, but talking had ended. They weren't settling anything now. Maybe not ever.

"You put *yourself* there." He wiped his hands on his trousers, as if done with the discussion. "It was your sin."

She battled and then gave in to a bitter smile. "Always the rules, isn't it, dear? Well, I've played by them for years, and I'm done with them."

"Then you're done with me."

A knife plunged into her. Twisted. In minutes, they had gone this far? Did he mean divorce? A trial separation? The man she'd vowed to love and cherish, through sickness and health . . . couldn't he love her, in spite of her past? Lord God, *because of* her past? Her jaw clenched in response to his conditional love, yet a quiet Voice rose up in her and urged peace. As the room seemed to cave in, she searched for a compromise to end this impasse. She moved to him, laid a hand on his arm. To her surprise, he didn't jerk away. "I'm not done with you, Edward. We married each other for better or for worse, remember? But I need to do this for him."

"What, exactly, is 'this'?"

So he finally asked. She exhaled. "Help him get that girl out of there."

"The one in the brothel?"

"Her parents sold her into hell when she was fourteen. I'm going to help get her out. If it means going to the ambassador. The general. Whoever, whatever it takes."

"They won't help you. They're my friends."

Another stab. She set her jaw. She'd better get used to this. But with God in charge, it could be done. "That may be, Edward." She smiled in the tender way he liked. "Still, I must try."

His shoulders hunched up, making his head look boxy. He clenched his fists, then dropped them to his side. "Him or me." His face took on a grayish cast, as if he were ill.

She leaned forward, sorry for what she'd put him through, and then sat up straight. What had Samuel, her flesh and blood, endured? And Mali, the girl he loved? She interlaced her fingers. Rested them in her lap. Her top priority? To help Samuel.

"Well, then. That's that." He looked out the window, as if checking the weather.

"Yes. That's that." He did understand at least one thing. She headed for the closet. Grabbed a suitcase. Hurried to their bedroom. Packed. The minute she'd seen her son in Etienne's—no, the minute she'd heard his voice on the phone—her fate had been sealed. Nothing and no one—not even Edward—was going to stop her from helping him.

"Where are you going?" As she walked back into the music room, he followed her and had the audacity to sit on *her* bench.

"I'm not sure, Edward. I won't know until I talk to my son."

"Will you at least keep in touch? Let me know what you're doing?"

She staggered, caught off guard by the pain in his voice. This was the man she'd pledged to have and to hold, forever and ever. The bags under bloodshot eyes, the droop of his shoulders, nearly propelled her into his arms.

"Edward, I can keep in real good touch." Her bag slid to the floor; she used her hands to plead with him. "Together we can do this. For him. For us."

His eyes narrowed.

"Come with me, Edward. At least talk to him."

Though he deflected his gaze from her, his shoulders straightened. "No *him*, Sheila. No *him*."

Then no "us," Edward. At least for now. She squared her shoulders. "I've said my piece. Good-bye." On her way to get her purse, she walked past the welcome-home dinner she would not serve. She pressed her lips tight, because if she opened her mouth again, she might explode.

She paced the shabby room, jumping out of her skin every time a plane roared overhead. In twenty-four hours, she hadn't gotten used to the flight patterns that shook the walls of this cheap hotel. But it wasn't the noise, the blotchy bedspread, the wobbly TV tray table, that raced her pulse. It was waiting for the one loose end—the flight plan—to be knotted up so she and her newfound son could travel to a country eight thousand miles away.

There was a knock at the door, a pause, then three rapid-fire knocks. His knock. She slowed long enough to angle past the bed without banging her hip against the dresser. Shaking fingers slid back the chain and released the dead bolt.

Her son walked in, bringing life and light and a fresh laundry scent into the room.

She moved close, wanting his embrace. In spite of all they'd already said, more needed to be known. More needed to be said.

He stepped away, searched her with those eyes. "How did it go with him?"

She worked to stem tears. "Not so good."

"Figures." Furrows lined his brow, making him look much older than twenty-two.

Samuel's tone irritated already sensitive nerve endings. So he'd checked out Edward. Her as well? Right now she couldn't bear to know more ugly secrets. "How are things working at your end?" she asked, desperate to switch subjects.

"Not so good." He turned away from her. "I can't go through with this."

Her face fell. So he would give up on someone he loved, like Edward had? She battled those hot tears . . . and lost. "Just like that, you're abandoning her?"

He gripped her arms. "Never. It's *you* that's staying here. Where it's safe."

He did know how to love. So did she. That made sense; they were flesh and blood. "I'm going." She snorted as if she were angry. "We settled that when the Old Horseman said they wouldn't refuse a—what do you call it?"

"*Farang.*"

"*Farang.* Especially American. Especially female." With her shoe toe she ground cigarette ash into the carpet, swallowed disgust. This might be a palace compared to her Bangkok digs. "You get her out of the brothel. We'll head for the embassy. Hope that Old Horseman knows his p's and q's."

"A World War II general has clout to talk about."

"We'll need it, huh?"

He didn't change expression, but light from the cheap bedside lamp twinkled in his eyes. "Commercial takes us to Hawaii."

She imagined lush exotic orchids. "I always wanted to go there."

"We're not talking leis and Waikiki."

"I understand," she said. *Just so I'm with you.*

He jingled coins or keys. "After Honolulu," he finally said, "an Air Force buddy will get us on a C-141 to Kadena, then a C-130 on into Bangkok."

"A C-130 . . . ?"

"A transport."

"That's wonderful." She clasped her hands and smiled, but he didn't. "Isn't it?"

"We're talking permanent hearing loss. A cold flying tank reeking of filthy GIs." He winced. "No 'Coffee or tea?' No steaming towels. No glass of Chablis."

"I don't drink, anyway." She added a lilt to her voice. "Besides it'll get us to her, won't it?" She hoped she sounded confident. For him.

Doubt filled his eyes. "I'm not sure. But it's the best I've come up with."

She nodded, understanding how he felt. When she'd called friends for help, they'd politely listened, then insisted on talking to Edward before "committing." Thank God for the one exception. The general, an old Moody friend and one of the revered Four Horsemen, had sent typewriter carriage bells dinging, couriers zipping to procure her papers in twenty-four hours. Amazing what colorful ribbons and shiny medals could do. She'd tucked away the documents, along with money withdrawn from a modest savings account. Her account. "Everything's ready and waiting, including a letter from that general."

"That's great." He laughed hollowly. "Until we get her to the embassy, we're pretty much on our own. Those papers are as useless as cheap insect repellent."

"On our own. Just like that first time."

He moved close and put his arms around her. Tucked her head under his chin. "It's all right, Mother. You gave it your all. I know that now."

Alleluias sprang from her, like they once had from old Miz W, another Moody helpmate, who sang praise in doubt's midst. She whispered a prayer. Rested against her one and only son.

"Um, Mother?" He gently pulled back. Smiled shyly. "What else did you learn?"

"I have an embassy contact, thanks again to the general. He'll pressure the base commander to do what we need."

"I have a contact or two as well. We'll need all of them." As if to change the subject, he slapped his thigh. "Let's grab a bite. Somewhere close. And fast. The flight's before dawn."

"Should we just stay here?"

"We need to eat. Get some air. If you haven't noticed, this ain't the Waldorf." He made a prune face, showing Papa's humor. "We'll go someplace quiet. So you can tell me where Mimi sent you—sent us."

"Etienne's?" she joked, an adventurous spirit taking hold. She grabbed her handbag and swung it about, then took his arm and headed into the night. Her son's presence warded off thoughts of Edward and the inherent danger of travel to a third-world country. She was traveling light, as she had on that first trip with her baby.

Chapter 18

The Train They Call the City of New Orleans

S he jostled about in the Packard to get a better look. Another first . . . and many lasts.

James opened her door. "Come on, Miss. I'll jes git your things." He pulled his cap low, as if to shut out a view of the men still milling about Rampart's bar-rooms at 6:30 a.m.

With bags in hand, James guided her toward the terminal. People waved tickets and shouted orders to loaders. Wide eyes and rosy cheeks bespoke ex-citement and adventure and tamed her frazzled nerves. Still, she clung to James.

"Dere! Dere it is!" James' face glowed. "Da *City of New Orleans!*"

Orange blazed the brown body of a creature that hissed and shot sparks. A green diamond festooned its nose. Whistles split the air. *Clear out, man and beast,* it roared.

Wow! It really *was* something! She let go of James, wove her fingers together. The train's *chug-chug* soothed a lonely place inside and spawned hope for a good change.

James whistled. "Man, would ya look at her?"

She nodded and then tried to exhale fear and worry. The horrid doctor's examination, the silent going-away supper, echoed the whisperings in her soul. She could not stay with Honey and was not welcome with Mimi. The North called. She would do her best to answer.

They went through double doors to a service window. James leaned close and set down money. "One-way ticket for St. Paul via Chicago."

A crimp-haired woman glared at him and slid a green slip under the partition.

James eyed the line that had formed behind them. He nodded toward Sheila. "It ain't for me," he mumbled. "It's for the little missus."

"Well, why didn't you say so?" the woman huffed.

"Yes'm. I's sorry, ma'am." He bowed and mumbled, his eyes on the floor.

Sheila's face flamed. Why did he kowtow to such rudeness? She bit back a desire to tell him, tell all of them, that she too was a Negro, but a public place like a train station was not the place to reveal such things.

The woman dug through a metal box until she found a blue ticket, which she shoved under the glass. "What now?" A sneer wrinkled a flat nose.

James continued to stand at the window. "Where do we board, ma'am?"

The woman nodded toward a set of doors. "Where do you think, coon?" She slammed the box shut. "Next?"

His face pinched like a crab apple, James handed Sheila the boarding pass, then hoisted her trunk on his back.

If people knew her roots soaked up slave blood, would they call her names, too?

When they stepped away, she tugged James' sleeve. "What was she mad about?"

"Dey call y'all first." Words mixed with wheezes. "Den dey put us in Crow cars."

Her brows creased. "Why do they call it a Crow car?"

"'Cause of Jim Crow laws."

"Who's Jim Crow?" she persisted.

"Miss Sheba, I ain't gwine go into it. Jes' a way of pokin' fun. Ain't nuttin' much." A downcast face contradicted his words.

Why would anyone make fun of the South's lifeblood? Sheila had gobbled up servants' kitchen talk, hummed along with hymns that poured from golden voice boxes. Who could live without them? Of course she *was* one of them. Again she tugged James' sleeve. "Can I sit in the Crow car? With the Negroes?"

"Course not." He flashed a rare frown. "What kine foolishness got into you?"

Wild imaginings grabbed her mind as she held onto James' sleeve. She would tell him the truth. Make him change her ticket so she could sit in the Crow car.

"You stick with yo kind." He patted her head. Gave a sad smile. "Like I do."

If James knew she was a Negro, would he fence her off or open the gate to his community? She kneaded her hands at the insanity of it all. Would anything be gained by a last-minute confession?

James whistled, as he sometimes did when nervous. She glanced at the weathered face. Swallowed hard. James, the trusted Alexander driver, likely knew about her past and desired to keep it buried, as things had always been. Bitter tears sprang into her eyes. James had no choice if he wanted to keep his job. She could not risk embarrassing him, or exposing herself to another rejection, at this their last meeting.

The issue decided, she battled tears and followed James and her bags toward the train. She would remain silent about her heritage. With James, anyway.

Cars stretched out like a caravan, waiting for passengers whose arms were piled with luggage. Couples knotted in lusty good-byes. Sheila ached for Cliff to pull her into such an embrace. Then her heart whispered that Cliff's every caress, every kiss, had been a lie.

Porters wearing blue pants and shirts and red caps whisked luggage from carts and handed the bags over to other porters, assembly-line-style. Sheila rubbed feeling into numb hands. Soon she and her bags would speed north and leave everything she'd ever loved. She hurried to James. If only he would go with her!

"Suh! Hey, you! In de red cap!" James called and then whistled.

The porter whipped about. His jaw jutted like a ledge. "What you want?"

To her dismay, James went into his bow. "I got da miss bound nawth. Be much obliged if you'd help." James fumbled in his pocket for money.

Sheila opened the clasp on her purse.

"Let me do it, Miss Sheba."

Last night, nausea—and Mimi's words—had robbed her of an appetite for Camille's last supper of shrimp and corn pones. "I'll cover your ticket. Food. Lodging. Nothing more," Mimi had said as she stabbed shrimp with her fork, Sheila with her words. "I have arranged for your incidentals. Period. Remember, you've chosen this lot."

Her lot indeed. She would take care of herself. "I have money, James."

"I know that, ma'am." James boomed over calls to board. "But me and Camille done put back a little sometin'. Reckoned you'd need it up Nawth." He handed money to the fidgety porter, dug a wad of bills out of his pocket, and pressed them into her palm.

"James, I can't—" Tears sprang into her eyes, creating a green-and-white blur. How many hours did he bend and stoop over that hoe to earn just one dollar?

A brown hand covered hers. Closed her fist. "We want to. You'se family. No matter if we never sees you again or not."

Her heart swelled until it threatened to burst. James did know that they were kin. Camille, too, she would bet this wad of bills on it.

A tear slid down her face, despite her struggle for control. "Oh, James. You . . . you understand . . . everything. Thank you . . . for . . ." Sheila stared at the pavement. *For loving me, despite my family's treatment of you. For all the things they won't let us say but can't stop us from feeling. For truly being my family, James. No matter what they've done to all of us.*

The grizzled old head bowed and then rose to show bloodshot, teary eyes. "Don't know how to tell you dis, Miss, so I'll just spit it out. Miss Honey done passed. Last night."

Her vision swam. The sky darkened. "I . . ." She blinked to see something, anything, but Honey's waxy pallor. Nothing appeared.

James cupped her chin. Turned her face until she met eyes lit like the sun off a tin roof. "You listen up, Miss Sheba. Miss Honey done gone to glory. Dis world ain't brought her nothin' but misery." He warmed her with his gap-toothed smile. "It gwine be all right up dere, Miss Sheba. Up nawth."

"Final call, northbound for Chicago." A red-jowled man wearing a gold badge strode near. His bellows mixed with train whistles and the crowd's buzz. He pulled out a pocket watch and studied it, then directed them into his kingdom of the rails. A crush of red caps and passengers stepped aboard. Ready or not, the journey had begun.

"How—how can I ever thank you?" Sobs she had begged to stay hidden sprang alive. She clung to James like a fearful child.

"Aw, come on, now, little miss." James patted her on the back while steering her to the right car. "It gwine be okay. God gwine take care of you."

She searched his eyes, desperate to find truth. "Do you really think so?" She held her breath, as if the promise hovering in the thick, hot air might blow away.

He bent his knees until his face was level with hers. "I done lost my boy on a beach in France. Lost my wife to de fever."

She curled her arms about his neck. It was maddening, to want to stay, to have to leave!

"De Lord carried me through my grief. He'll carry you, too. Whether up Nawth or down here." He pried away her hands and nudged her toward a stair box. "You gotta go." He patted her arm. "Got dem papers she give you?"

Sheila wiped her eyes, tried to shake off a woozy feeling. Nodded.

"All right. You git on board." His face brightened. "Ain't gwine be no trouble, hear? Ride dat iron horse right on to Chicago and on to St. Paul." He waved like he was seeing off troops. "Ain't nevah gwine forget you, Miss Sheba! Nevah!"

Sheba. To him, she had always been Sheba. It was one reason why she loved him.

They ushered her into a whites-only car. As the train pulled away, images of the sun setting fire to the cathedral bell tower, of Café du Monde umbrella tables, of Honey's face, crowded into the car with her. She might one day return here, but innocent Sheba would never skip through the Quarter again.

The porter led her down the aisle. "Right up there, miss. One seventy-six."

She squinted. Spotted numbers pinned onto aisle seats. Found hers. She sat down, flattened her face against the glass in an inane desire to see James's warm smile.

The landscape had been reduced to gray blurs. No James. No station. Sheila slumped over. Perhaps it was better that she get used to being without James . . . and New Orleans.

Travelers chattered. The train whooshed and hissed. She ground her teeth, commanded her grief to bury itself deep and hide from public view. She'd been banished, but life, like this train, rolled on. To survive, she could not look back.

⋄ ◆ ⋄

They barreled through green hills ribboned with water. Sheila secured her handbag under the seat and dozed through crackly station calls of the familiar—Hazelhurst and Jackson—the unfamiliar—Yazoo City? In the fog of time measured by naps, a porter had taken lunch reservations, but she had demurred, stifling a groan at the thought of even a bite of food.

A noisy bunch boarded at Memphis, their screeches and catcalls echoing down the aisle. She took advantage of the stop and visited the facilities. Sickly sweet deodorizer failed to mask the smell of urine and sweat. She knelt by the toilet. Vomited. Dry heaves continued until cramps eased. She pulled a towel from a dispenser and wiped sweat from her face. Despite Camille's assurance that this sickness was common, she shivered at the thought that something was amiss.

Raps on the door cut off her thoughts. With a glance in the mirror, she smoothed her hair into a semblance of order and opened the door.

A portly woman looked down her nose at Sheila. Was it because only "common" girls traveled alone, or did the woman note her rounded belly? Before

Sheila could move, the woman elbowed her way into the bathroom and slammed the door.

Sheila cupped her palm about her middle. Would the North offer her—and her child—sanctuary from glares and slammed doors? Troubled in mind, she slid into her seat.

"Dinner, Miss?" A cherub-faced porter swayed along with the train. His blue uniform struggled to contain his bowling-ball-shaped body. Stubby fingers grasped an order pad and a pencil. "Gwine be good. Old Mitch done cooked up a feast. Sho' beats the Rainbo sandwiches down in da snack bar."

Dinner? She longed to avoid the judging eyes in the dining car, but a sudden rumbling—and empty—stomach won the battle. She nodded.

"We got seatings at six thirty or seven. What'll it be, miss?"

It was impossible not to smile at such a chubby, happy face. "Six thirty's fine."

He scribbled on his pad and waddled to the next car.

She checked her watch. An hour to fend off images of Honey's face, of Mimi snipping the roses . . . she rummaged in her bag for Honey's Bible. Honey had said everything she needed would be in here.

Ezra, Nehemiah, Esther . . . she thumbed through the pages, searching for underlined passages as in her grandmother's Bible. If only she had something of Hattie Pearl's, something of Maman's, to cling to . . . The word *belly* caught her eye.

"When he is about to fill his belly, God shall cast the fury of his wrath upon him, and shall rain it upon him while he is eating."

What hateful words! She shut the Bible, tired of reconciling this God with the loving God she searched for in Sunday school. With one sin, her efforts had crashed like the waves around the dunes where she'd been loved and then discarded like an empty clamshell.

She drew her arms and legs close to protect herself from another onslaught, this one not by the boy or her grandmother, but by harsh Bible words. Her mind began to shut down, the only way to stop the thoughts that confirmed her isolation from the world.

◆ ◆ ◆

"Now calling . . ."

Her eyes fluttered. She wiped hard sleep from her mouth, her eyes. No dreams. No racing thoughts. A nap had sharpened her appetite.

"I repeat, those with six thirty dinner reservations, make your way to the dining car."

She pulled out a compact. Grimaced. Her looks would ruin everyone's appetite. She pinched wan cheeks. Pinned back unruly tendrils. Not much, but it was the best she could do. Gripping the seat edges to combat the train's rocking, she ambled toward the exit sign—hopefully, the dining car. Funny clipped accents perked her ears; the fiery sinking sun caught her eye. New horizons, new people, lay ahead. And she'd escaped Mimi.

She pushed a button. A metal door whooshed open. She stepped into a portico-like area between the cars, which allowed her to watch the landscape of browns and greens streak by. She wobbled, vertigo attacking as if she were stuck between two worlds.

Wasn't she?

She heaved herself forward. Pushed another button.

The door opened. Her pulse clickety-clacked with the train as she rushed inside another car . . . and safety.

"Dis train is bound for glory, dis train."

"Sho' is."

Altos, mezzos, a soprano, and a half-dozen voices ranging in between rose in a raucous chorus. Someone plucked a banjo.

"Dis train don't pull no jokers, dis train."

"Dis train done spanned de river, dis train."

Jazz notes sauntered through her soul. She'd found the Jim Crow car, crowded with people in overalls, double-breasted suits, calico dresses. What a beautiful car! What beautiful people! Charcoal, au lait, and mahogany faces pulled her close. The Jim Crow car was her car, full of her people. Her heritage of rich voices, strong backs. Her hand touched her throat. Dared she sing along? Forget Crow. Forget—

As if a conductor had waved his baton, the singing stopped.

"Lil' whitey come to spy on us."

"You got that right." Voices rose from both sides of the aisle and silenced her. She clung to a seat bar, her eyes falling on women holding babies. Men holding foil-wrapped bundles. Children holding baskets. How she longed to tell them about Maman. About herself. And learn about them.

Sneering resentment met her longing gaze. Mumbles and mutters fought the train's peaceful rhythm. She hugged her arms, wishing to vanish. She belonged here, but they did not know it. Only a miracle would have them look past her light skin—in this car, more isolating than the bulge in her belly. She gulped down pain. Tried to stand tall. "Can . . . can you tell me where to find the dining car?"

"Ain't got no notion 'bout no dining car."

A man slapped his knee and cackled. "Got that right."

Her face flamed. The dining car was off-limits to colored folk. Her folk. Would they believe her if she told them they were kin? Her stomach cramped—from hunger and the knowledge that the Crow car occupants wanted her gone. She stalked forward, intent on complying with their wish.

"You headed the wrong way, chile," said a woman wearing a red kerchief.

Sheila turned toward the voice, bell tone beautiful, battling the growls of the other passengers—and the grumbles in her soul.

"Dining car's at da front." The woman pointed her toward the way she had come.

More groans and moans rose like a mist off a swamp.

"Don't want us even smelling their food."

"Ain't that the truth?"

She mastered a trembling jaw. She had done nothing wrong and would not give them the satisfaction of seeing her cry.

The woman smiled. "God bless you, young lady."

Sheila returned the smile . . . until she about-faced. How it hurt to be rebuffed by the people whose smells, looks, and sounds she loved! People who couldn't accept her white skin because they had been rejected for their dark skin.

Doors hissed open. Night air moved in, as did dusk's shadowy blurs. A lonesome whistle sounded and rent her soul in two. She gritted her teeth, threw her weight against the door, heard the whoosh that allowed passage into the white car. Her car. For now—perhaps always. She buried the thought of unveiling her heritage on this trip up north. That was the safe way. The sound way. Though it murdered a part of her soul, for now, it was the only choice she had.

◆ ◆ ◆

Waikiki . . . I can't believe it! Wearing the lei Samuel had given her, Sheila looked about the tiny room, used to house R&R soldiers, and checked her watch. *Eighteen hours since I slept . . . really slept.* Unlike Samuel, she hadn't grabbed more than ten winks on the two flights crowded with tipsy passengers, screaming children, and a snoring seatmate. The lure of the Pacific, with its surfer-sized waves, acted as a tonic for her exhausted body . . . and soul.

Yawning, she sat on a twin bed covered by a khaki blanket. Here she was in Hawaii, a place known for luaus and frosty drinks festooned with paper umbrellas and pineapple wedges. Hotels with floating bars, hot tubs, and pools. She stared at concrete block walls, a view not seen on travel brochures. Yet the fact that Samuel wanted her here transformed this Waikiki base housing unit into a thing of beauty.

A pounding surf called her to open blinds and a louvered window. Palm trees swayed a greeting. A blue patch and salty scent spoke of the ocean. So near. Another ocean. So far. She gripped the ledge. What awaited them in Thailand? Would Mali really leave? Though she questioned Samuel's choice of a life mate, intuition told her to trust a man who'd merited formal salutes and admiring glances when they'd checked in here. She bowed her head and thanked God for the chance to be with this son she thought she'd never know. Begged peace for the husband she knew only too well.

A triple knock rattled the door. Samuel. The same thrill coursed through her as when she'd first heard his voice. Would she always feel this way?

"Come in." She picked up a jacket and hurried to meet him.

Hawaiian humidity had made his miliatary cut fuzzy. No sign of arduous flight holdups showed on his clean-shaven face. "Let's stretch our legs before we meet Hank. Or would you rather hang ten?" Chuckling, he offered her his arm, led her outside.

She took it and again thanked God for the miracle of knowing this son.

The surf drummed sugar-white sand. Tiny dates clicked castanet-style against palm fronds. They walked to the beach music she'd first heard with Samuel's father. She rested her hand on his arm, glad that he knew the truth about Cliff. If God took her now, she'd die happy with his face and the sea symphony her last memories here on earth.

"You're fresh as a daisy." He gestured for her to duck under a coconut tree. "Apparently you're quite the traveler." She obliged and then waited for him to catch up to her.

"Only that once." She pulled off her flats, wriggled her toes in powder-fine sand, and remembered massaging Samuel's tiny baby toes.

"Up North, huh? Kind of an odyssey."

"You and me. That was my—our first big trip."

The sand crunched as they walked side-by-side. "Now we're in Hawaii. Next up, Thailand." When he faced her, the tropical sun splashed oranges and reds on his face. "After that, who knows?"

Who knows? Sheila whispered a prayer of thanks for an itinerary out of her safe little world. Yet she couldn't help but think of Edward, over four thousand miles away, and what she'd done to *his* safe little world.

They tread on a glistening shore. Conversation rose and fell like the tides. She kept shaking her head at the hues displayed on the sun-kissed beach, her son's smooth brown cheek.

"How did you find the strength to go up there?" he finally asked.

A fog of gray shivered her soul as she remembered plunging the depths of loneliness during those first days at the Home. How *had* she done it?

"There was no choice, Samuel. God sent me there, but I didn't know that then. I just did what I had to do."

Chapter 19

O, Mio Babbino Caro

No sun. No strolling people. No New Orleans. The taxi screeched to a halt at a stoplight in a residential neighborhood. Sheila gripped the door handle. Though grateful to end the bumpy ride, inside the Home, things might get bumpier. The slant of sunlight across the horizon, rolling hills, thin trees, rustling fall leaves—*in September?*—spoke a language she didn't understand. But Mimi had been quite clear when she slammed shut her life in the South.

The cabbie adjusted a checkered cap and tilted his rearview mirror to lock curious eyes with hers. "Here's your place, ma'am—933 Carroll."

At least he had not called it Catholic Home for Unwed Mothers. For that, she whispered thanks. She lifted her chin. Whatever lay ahead, she had arrived at the Home—if not home—and would face it as best she could.

A three-story mansion with a pitched roof sprawled on a tree-lined lot. Lintels arched tan brick eyebrows. A well-clipped hedge and wrought iron fence mimicked the Garden District back home. But a stiff cold wind confirmed that she was thousands of miles away.

Her imagination swelled to reveal not a Home, but a prison for fallen girls. She tried to quash such thoughts as she picked up her bag and followed the cabbie, who lugged her trunk and suitcase up steep steps. She looked over her shoulder, half expecting to see a smug-faced housewife standing on the porch of one of the neat brick bungalows across the street, shaking a broom at the latest inmate paying for sin. What exactly would she pay?

◆ ◆ ◆

"We've been expecting you, Miss Alexander." A black veil framed a fleshy face marred by a wine-colored birthmark and pocked forehead. Fierce brows met pouched eyes. The nun moved from behind a massive oak desk between two windows in her office. As she swayed, so did a pearly rosary about her neck.

Shudders coursed through Sheila. She backed against a wall, near a crucifix, and nearly tripped over the luggage set down by the cabbie before he had fled the building. Had this woman scared him away?

Another veiled figure crept into the office, her head bent as if she were ashamed to show her face.

Heat rose. *I am the shamed one.*

"Could you get the janitor to help with her things, Sister?" asked the woman who was obviously in charge here.

The sister nodded. Her habit skimming the floor, she left the room and quickly returned with a man who wore a blue uniform. The two—and her things—disappeared, leaving Sheila alone with the imposing—no, downright scary—woman who controlled her future.

Icy fingers crept up Sheila's spine, buckled her knees, and set the room to spinning. Could this Sister be more domineering than Mimi?

The black cloud drifted closer. Closer . . .

A firm hand grabbed her elbow and guided her into a straight-backed chair. "Now, now, dear." The nun sounded like Camille, without her lazy Southern drawl. Yet any resemblance ended with the melodic voice. Parted lips revealed discolored teeth. A coarse black hair curled about a mole, prominent as a bull's-eye in her chin.

Sheila did her best not to shudder. Never had she seen such an ugly woman. Of course appearances could be deceiving. She had learned that from her soldier.

"I suspect you've had quite an ordeal." Though the nun fixed Sheila with an unblinking gaze, her matter-of-fact tone quelled waves of nausea. This nun was not a witch.

"Yes, ma'am. I mean . . ." Sheila stared at her hands. She, who'd been schooled in first impressions, was definitely out to recess. She sat up straighter and tried to smile.

A symphonic laugh came from the gaping mouth. "Forgive me, child. I didn't even introduce myself. I'm Sister Carline of the order of St. Joseph of Carondelet. With the Holy Mother's help—and a staff of angels—I try to run this place."

Sister Carline's velvet palate was enough to remind Sheila of Maman. Sheila envisioned the rustle of her mother's silks, the smell of her Eau de Joy. Memories rose like sea waves, as did tears. What would Maman think to see her in a home like this?

Yards of material rustled when Sister Carline moved to the desk, fetched a lacy handkerchief, and gave it to Sheila. "Now, child." She bent her head, crossed herself. "You've found refuge here. May the Holy Mother and her blessed Son protect you."

After drying her eyes, Sheila tried to peer past a bulbous nose into Sister Carline's soul. Would Jesus really watch over her, care to see into *her* soul?

"In a bit, we'll get you unpacked." Sister moved to her desk and opened a bound journal. "First I need your medical records and birth certificate." She folded her hands. Hard eyes and a pointed chin belied the polite speech. This wasn't a woman to trifle with.

"Y-yes." She dug through her bag. They were here somewhere . . .

A slamming door, giggles, and wails trembled her hands. What awaited her outside of this office? Refocusing, she shoved aside a cap, skirts—there! She pulled out the sealed envelope, waved it, eager to please the one who controlled her future.

Sister clapped her hands. "Don't dillydally. The day is short, and there's no time to waste."

Hurrying forward, Sheila laid it down, as if she were turning in homework.

Sister opened a drawer, pulled out pince-nez, and balanced them on her nose. She removed a folder from the envelope and flipped it open.

Sheila returned to her seat and sat so primly her calves ached. Her life had been reduced to words on pages. Her future depended on Sister's evaluation of those words. All she could do was wait.

The nun's sallow skin took on a gray cast. She turned another page, removed her glasses, rubbed them against her sleeve, again put them on. Read another page. Finally she set the papers down and dizzied Sheila with a holy gaze.

Sweat popped out on Sheila's forehead. What horrible things had Mimi and her doctor said in those reports? She'd sinned with her soldier, but hadn't every girl here sinned?

"Your grandmother, what was she like?" A growl had replaced melodic tones.

What should she say? Desperate to make that good impression, Sheila crossed her ankles, sat even straighter. A Southern upbringing offered one way out of this trap: sweet, safe lies. "Prim and proper." She tried to smile. "A churchgoing woman. A fine—"

Sister Carline's fist slammed against the desk. "A churchgoer would have nothing to do with this." She huffed to the window and tugged on the blind cord. Sunlight dappled her habit and transformed dust motes into glittery fairy powder.

Sheila turned her head, unable to take in the burst of brightness, the strange words. She'd had eighteen hundred miles to consider the options of a church-going woman whose granddaughter had stained the family name. No one would expect such a woman to raise an illegitimate child and support its mother. So why had Sister Carline attacked Mimi? "I'm sure she meant well, ma'am," she managed.

"Meant well?" Sister whirled about. Oomphed into her seat. "Far from it!"

The room closed in. "What . . . do you mean?"

Sister Carline eyed Sheila, the paper, as if struggling to make a decision. Skin tightened about her eyes. "Her doctor declared you feebleminded."

To combat trembling legs, Sheila dug her heels into the floor until her arches ached. "Feebleminded? I-I don't understand."

"They conspired. To render you sterile." The folder flew across the desk; a document fluttered to the floor, landing at her feet.

Sterile? Hospitals and bandages were sterile. She caressed her middle. She was not sterile! She dared not say a word. Trembling, she leaned over and picked up the paper.

I, Vernon LaFourche, a licensed physician in the State of Louisiana, upon examination and evaluation of Sheila Marie Alexander, attest to said child's feeblemindedness and resultant inability to make sound judgments as to her welfare. Thus, it is said doctor's determination and said guardian's concurrence that said child should be sterilized.

A notary seal rimmed the signatures of Mimi and the doctor whose exam she had endured—had it only been two days ago?

Sheila gripped the page. Suffered cold chills as she ran her finger across the embossed letters. "I . . . still . . . don't understand." She met and then escaped blazing eyes. What had so angered this nun?

"Your 'well-meaning grandmother' wanted them to operate on you."

Why? For what? She bobbed. Gripped her chair arms. Pressed her lips together, making it impossible to talk. It didn't matter; words had clogged up her mouth, her brain.

"To fix things so you could never have another child," Sister continued.

A cyclone whirled through Sheila and threatened to suck out life. She opened

159

her mouth. Closed it. Leapt to her feet, tripped, sat back down. She squeezed her fists to keep from tearing at her hair. How could Mimi consider such a thing? Her vision blurred the paper into nasty black blots.

"Dear child . . ."

She hung her head. Mimi had never spoken to her with tenderness, and she had learned to live with that. But to call her feebleminded? Subject her to surgery? She doubled over and began to cry.

Footfalls pattered near. Tears were wiped from her cheeks, damp hair smoothed from her forehead. Like Maman used to do. And Camille. Tears continued to flow. To be with them again! Oh! Oh! To have someone hold her . . .

"Dear, dear child. You can rest assured that we would never allow it."

They would not allow it. She gulped air, grateful. Yet the words of that paper reverberated through her soul and set her limbs atremble.

Sister took the paper and ripped it apart. A waste basket became the perfect place for the horrid thing. "There'll be no more talk of this." She rubbed her hands together, as if ending the matter. "It will never be mentioned outside of this room."

Sheila nodded mutely, "sterile" playing in her mind like a stuck record. She'd viewed Mimi's rigidity as an attempt to raise her "in the Lord's ways," believed Camille's claims that Mimi's heart had been shrunk by lack of love. But the signature on that paper revealed the truth and scratched their relationship beyond repair. Mimi did not love her . . . Mimi just might hate her. No matter what happened at the home, she would not go back to Mimi. No. Matter. What.

Sister rubbed her chin, as if she too were trying to rub out the words *sterile* and *feebleminded*. She cleared her throat. "We have more important things to discuss. Like your name." A tight smile began a charade that nothing had happened.

"My . . . name?" Sheila stammered at the thought of another change, then remembered the little girl who had tried to save her Papa. Could she again be Sheba, named after a queen? Sheba, who had been able to do anything? Perhaps Sheba could survive here.

Sister Carline removed her glasses and studied them. "Dear child, it must seem cruel. But it's for your protection more than anything else."

"Protection?" burst out of her. No one knew her old name save Mimi, the lawyer, the servants . . . the soldier. People out of her life. A sinful Southern girl needed no protection. "I-I don't understand," again seemed to be the only thing she could say.

"We've found it best for our girls to adopt fictitious names during their stay. For their own good." She picked up a pen and what looked like a journal. "We'll call you Sylvia." Pen scratches broke the silence. "Sylvia Allen." Stiff black material draped her head, accentuating her difference. *Separating her from girls like me.*

"Syl-vi-a Al-len." The syllables rolled off her tongue. Dropping Sheila, the name she'd never favored, was one thing. But what did the name Allen say as to her family? Nothing. Desperate to think of something besides Mimi's legacy, another change, she let her eyes rove the room. A massive file cabinet next to the window was the only furniture except for Sister's desk, the chairs. There was nothing to soothe her, nothing to hang on to, nothing—

Her gaze fell on the crucifix, hung by the door. Jesus' head drooped low to meet his bare chest, hiding His face. A skilled artisan had shown the yank of gravity on His body by lengthening taut muscles, stiffening muscular legs. Jesus had suffered horribly for sins such as hers. She clasped her hands together, concern about a name change fading in the face of what He'd gone through, the sorrow she had caused Him. Maybe He would somehow, someday redeem her, if she followed the rules. Stayed safe.

"Sylvia, just sign under my name." The nun handed over a form.

Numbly Sylvia complied. How strange it felt to write this name!

"Sister Aggie will help you unpack. It's high time you settled in your new home. And, dear Sylvia, this *is* your home."

Sylvia nodded at the nun. Gazed at the crucifix. She would try with all her might to get through this. Somehow. Some way. If Sheila and Sheba had to die like Jesus had, so be it.

◆

She's a nun? Sylvia tried to keep from staring at the lovely figure sashaying down the hall.

"Good morning." The same black head covering that yellowed Sister Carline's skin brought out ivory tones in this sister's oval face. Eyes danced under curved brows. "I'm Sister Agnes, but you may call me Aggie." She giggled like a schoolgirl.

So Aggie was a beautiful nun who laughed? Sylvia bent at her knees, bowed her head, then straightened when another giggle told her such formality was not necessary.

"We'd best get started." Aggie twirled about, right in the hall. "That is the nursery." Aggie pointed to a room across from Sister Carline's office.

Wavy glass shielded the room's interior, but mewls and wails confirmed its purpose.

Something punched her stomach. Sylvia inhaled sharply, then cupped her palm over her belly. Was such movement normal? Not knowing what else to do, she massaged the area until the sensation stopped. "So the babies stay here?" she asked, trying to ease anxious waves.

A shadow stilled the dancing eyes. "Only for a bit." Aggie inhaled, averted her face. "We'd best move on. Lunch is at noon sharp. You'll see the doctor before chores."

Again? To will away waves of nausea, Sylvia glued her eyes on her feet. Images of a sneering Dr. LaFourche, a probing, painful exam, streamed on. Her body sagged under the weight of another revelation. Exams such as these came with being pregnant.

As if she understood Sylvia's agitation, Sister patted Sylvia's shoulder. "It's just a checkup. Dr. Carruthers will take good care of you."

Sylvia managed to nod, though she didn't believe a word of it.

They moved toward the stairs and a closed door. "That's the chapel. The priest says mass every day. Eight thirty sharp."

"Every day?" slipped out. Seven times a week, she'd hear about sin's wages, her soul's blackness. And every word would be true.

"Most girls find it a haven from the world's cares."

What else do you expect them to say? Surprised at her venom, Sylvia stared at the wall. *Was* there a haven for fallen girls? If the Catholic God were like Mimi's God, sermons about sin's wages would stab fear into hearts. Memories of her old church blurred the bent image of Christ that had shored her up moments earlier. Her only hope, for her and her baby, was to beg for mercy and try to follow the rules.

Sister rested her hand on a carved newel. "I shouldn't like you to know that the smoking room's down there, but you'll find it, with or without my help." Saucy eyes matched Sister's smile. "The maids purportedly find card decks stashed behind the couch."

You could play cards? Smoke? Her soldier had smoked, claiming it eased the pressures of war. When he had offered her a puff, she'd coughed and then gagged at the noxious taste, the choking cloud. Yet the colorful boxes of cigarettes symbolized freedom, adventure, things she never dreamed she'd find in a charity home.

Aggie gathered her skirts, which brushed the steps like mop cords, and hurried upstairs. Sylvia trailed like an eager pup. What path had Aggie taken to get here? Could they truly be friends? All she knew of religion dismissed the possibility, but on the strength of Aggie's lovely hum, she floated to the second floor. When music was in a place, there was hope.

"Here's your dorm." Aggie switched on a light. "The other's across the hall." She stepped aside, let Sylvia enter first.

Three rows of cots, covered with white blankets and crowned with pancake-flat pillows, filled a long, narrow room. White wooden nightstands were bare except for books and an occasional rosary. A white tiled floor had chipped in places but whiffs of ammonia attested it had been scrubbed clean. Light poured in large windows, adding a haze like that of dawn over the bayou. Peaceful, in spite of its starkness. Holy.

Memories scratched hard. She had to forget New Orleans. Now. "When will the others be back?" Sylvia asked, really wanting to know, *Will Northerners cotton to a Southern intruder?*

"Soon enough." Sister knelt by one of the identical cots. Pointed under the bed. "There's your trunk. I left your books in it. Your clothes are in the closet; your toiletries, in the washroom"—she indicated a door near Sylvia's bed—"which is right in there."

"Lights out at ten," she continued. "Breakfast at eight. Chapel, chores, classes."

"Classes?" Dared she hope they'd allow her to take college credit?

"Job skills." Aggie's smile returned as she clasped her hands. "Enough of that. You need time to settle in." She headed toward the hall, singing, "*O mio babbino caro, mi pace e bello, bello . . .*"

The sound floated through the air to melt Sylvia's stiffness. She curled onto the bed. "*O mio,*" she whispered, seeing Papa in the hazy Louisiana light. Maman, gliding across the planked parlor. She eased her head onto her pillow. "*A comperar . . . Si ci voglio andare . . .*"

Sister Aggie stepped back into the room, a rapturous expression on her face. "You know . . . this?"

"My mother taught it to me before . . ." An image arrived of flames, mangling the instruments, conductor . . . the illusory band. Music had blanketed her pain, yet as it always did, pain roared back. Hands flew to her cheeks but missed a tear. Why had such awful things happened?

"Tell me, child." Sister sat on the bed. Took her hand. "We have time before the others arrive."

"There was . . . a fire."

"Oh, I'm so sorry." A soft smile and warm eyes coaxed her on.

"My grandmother adopted me . . ." She stemmed emotion to share her story. Only when she mentioned the train called *City of New Orleans* did she begin to cry. Yet the tears cleansed the stain on her soul from those awful words *sterile* and *feebleminded*.

"It will be all right," Aggie repeated as she patted her shoulder.

"It will?"

Aggie nodded. "God loves you, Sylvia. Plain and simple. Nothing can change that. Not a fire. Not even a train ride north."

A shiver ran through her. *It gwine be all right up dere,* James had said. Maybe, just maybe, James and Aggie would be right.

Aggie said good-bye. Bangs and squeals drowned her dainty steps.

Sylvia sat up straight, gripped a bedpost. Another change. If only Aggie had stayed to help her through *this*.

A tall, thin woman burst into the room. She wore a Sloppy Joe sweater and baggy trousers. Her hands flew to her hips. "Who are you?" Her toe tapped each syllable.

Sylvia sat up. "I-I'm She— Sylvia." She winced under the onslaught of baleful black eyes.

"Well, Stuttering Sylvia." Miss Sloppy Joe stuck out a bony hip. "Welcome to Watermelon Hill."

Chapter 20

Foolin' Myself

Miss Sloppy Joe Sweater, with tanned skin and a mop of black hair, stomped forward. "What happened to your voice? You sound like a stuck record." Others shuffled inside. "Answer me!"

Optimism ebbed. This was every bit as awful as her worst nightmare.

The group of girls studied her like it was her first day in a new school. Eyes widened with curiosity. Glittered with hate. Sylvia longed to crawl under her bed. Why would they hate her? They didn't *know* her. "I'm Southern. From Loo-" She battled her drawl—"Louisiana."

"How far along are you?" Miss Sloppy Joe Sweater continued the interrogation. The others stood like street mimes. Sylvia didn't know what to say or do. But she'd best figure it out.

"What's the matter, cat got your tongue?"

A round-faced pixie with blonde braids broke from the crowd. "Dee, why you got to be so mean?" The pixie's peasant-style dress billowed like it had been hung out to dry on a windy day. When she plopped onto a bed and scrunched into a ball, her dress hiked up to reveal dingy panties. "Come here, Cat," she clucked, leaned over, and pulled something from under the bed.

A scrawny kitten, its face tufted with fuzzy black fur, mewed its way into the girl's outstretched hands and rubbed its face against her dangling braid. "They let you have pets?" Sylvia asked, then wished she'd kept quiet. She didn't need more attention.

"Of course not." A mime came to life.

"They'll skin us—and Cat—if they find it." Another mime spoke, this one a girl with contoured cheeks and full lips. Her hands perched on broad hips and tightened the material of her dress across a bulging belly. "That means you, too, Julie."

"It's just a matter of time," someone muttered.

Sylvia darted glances at the girls. Someone would hurt a pet? What kind of a place was this?

"Poor Cat," Julie cooed, as if oblivious to a debate about the cat's fate. "Don't you worry your pretty little head. I'll bring you something from lunch."

Gazes riveted to the fluff of fur instead of Sylvia. Thank goodness.

"That cat's gonna ruin us all, but I ain't gonna throw her out," announced Dee. "Or tattle." She eyed Sylvia. "We don't tattle here. Got it?"

Sighs broke the heavy air. Queen Dee had extended her scepter to the cat. Maybe she would do the same for a dumb, drawling Southerner.

"Least not now," Dee added, as if cementing her iron-fisted rule . . . and keeping all of them—or at least Sylvia—on edge.

Girls stripped, chattering all the while. Sylvia averted her eyes from strange tummies and thighs and turned her attention to a girl with nut-brown hair who opened her nightstand drawer and pulled out a framed photograph. The girl collapsed onto her bed and hugged the picture, as if it was a flesh-and-blood boyfriend.

The handsome soldier's face flashed uninvited. Sylvia swallowed down pain and turned her gaze to Julie, who had laid the kitten across her belly and was beaming at it with such utter devotion, Sylvia couldn't help but smile. If only real love were so simple as that. Real love hurt.

"Your turn to mop, Carla," snapped Dee.

"Is not!"

Dee grabbed Carla's picture, stuck out her tongue at it.

"You give me that. Now."

Sylvia ignored the room's rising heat by organizing her things. She would mind her own business. Do her chores. Good thing Camille had trained her well. She unfolded trousers, creased seams, surreptitiously studying Dee, who had to be in her late twenties. How'd she end up here? Hadn't she learned anything in life?

"You gonna make me?" Dee huffed to a window, cranked it open, and dangled Carla's picture out. A nasty sneer showed she relished her cruel prank. "You wouldn't," Carla shrieked.

"Yes, she would." Julie stroked the cat and sang a nursery rhyme off-key.

Sylvia fought an urge to scram from Watermelon Hill before Dee clawed them all to bits.

"Fine." Carla leapt up, ripped off a skirt, pulled on slacks, stuffed her feet into sneakers, shot into the bathroom, and returned with a mop. With a whirl, she left the room.

Most of the girls shuffled after Carla, muttering about chores. Sylvia longed to leave with them and avoid confrontation with Dee. But someone else would seize the chance to torment a slow-talking newcomer. She'd best stay put.

"And you, rookie"—Dee's voice muffled as she tossed the picture onto Carla's bed and struggled to pull off her sweater—"might as well break you in with the pump house. Head out back and down the path." She finished dressing, grabbed a pack of cigarettes, and jabbed it in her pocket. "You can't miss the smell."

"What . . . smell?" Sylvia asked. But did she really want to know?

"Diapers," Dee sneered. "There's three buckets. One sniff, you'll know which is bleach, which is water, which is the dirty stuff." She stomped into the hall. "Scrub hard!" Her laughter—and her contempt—rang in Sylvia's ears.

"And what's *your* job?" Sylvia muttered, after clomping footfalls faded.

"Don't mind Dee." Julie set down the kitten, hop-skipped forward, tilted her head, and stared blankly at a spot behind Sylvia. "She don't mean it."

Sylvia breathed deep. Dared she tiptoe toward a new friend? "What is her story?"

"Boss at the airplane factory knocked her up. When his wife found out, he got knocked—black and blue." Julie giggled and slapped her thigh.

Sylvia fought revulsion. How would a young girl know such horrid things?

"The boss fired Dee, who tole her ole man."

Sylvia's jaw dropped. "Dee had a husband?"

Julie nodded. "Till he kicked her out. Now she's on her own."

"How old is she?"

"She don't like to say, but I'd guess twenty-five if a day. Twenty-five if a day." As Julie hopped about, her braids slapped her face, but she didn't seem to notice. "I'll help you with the diapers, Sylvie—can I call you Sylvie?—after I clean the bathroom."

"Gee, thanks." In spite of her loony ways, Julie touched a place Sylvia had reserved for her cousin Jenna. She envisioned a freckly face. Sunburned arms. Surely one day they could reunite . . . *if Aunt and Uncle allow it after they learn what I've done.* Things might have been different if she'd had a sister to care for, to love. She patted Julie's cute little head. Smiled. "But it's okay. Might as well get used to the smell of diapers." Sylvia forced a laugh as she grabbed dungarees and headed to the bathroom, wanting privacy, even if it were just Julie in the room. After she dressed, she joined Julie on her bed.

"I'm Julie from Jacobson," chanted Julie.

"Julie from Jacobson," Sylvia repeated, liking the ditty. Liking Julie more.

They sang together, Sylvia stretching her drawl like melted caramels. So silly, so fun. They screeched into high notes and doubled over in laughter. Perhaps she *had* found a sister. Someone she could protect. Nurture. It would be good practice for her own little one.

"I'm Julie. Julie from Jacobson. Julie from Jacobson." The song intensified and buzzed at Sylvia like an annoying fly. Something wasn't quite right.

"Julie." She raised her voice to drown out the song. "How old are you?"

Julie scooped up Cat and curled onto her bed. As if Cat sensed pleasure, it rolled over, offered a plump belly. "Thirteen and a half." Julie stroked the cat to the rhythm of her song. "Thirteen and a half." Her head dipped low until fur muffled her voice.

Her bones rubbery, Sylvia wobbled to her own bed. "Thirteen and a half," kept running through her mind though she begged it to stop. How had one so young become pregnant? That nasty phrase, "feebleminded," mocked her. Could the nuns truly provide a haven from the outside world—and from the world of Watermelon Hill? As Sylvia sat on her bed and watched Julie, still rapt in her singsong, she did not know.

◆ ◆ ◆

They sat outside the infirmary like truants waiting on a headmaster. Dee filed her nails, flicked ground-up polish and nails and skin bits onto the floor. Others gossiped. A freckled redhead flipped through a book. The rest dozed or stared at their hands. Only Sylvia jostled about, as if already feeling the chill of the examining table. She might deserve this, but it was still awful.

When she wiped her brow, a sour milk and ammonia smell slammed her in the face. No matter how she had scrubbed her hands, diaper-washing memories clung to her skin. She rubbed her belly to fend off nausea. Sometimes it worked. Not now.

The door opened. A girl with a cantaloupe stomach scuffed from the exam room.

Sylvia cradled her belly. How big would she get? Her insides quivered, as they had earlier. Her mouth went dry. Something was wrong.

"Sylvia Allen." A sour-faced nun motioned Sylvia inside.

Sylvia flinched, feeling a dozen stares. She was as soiled as those diapers. Everyone here knew it; soon the doctor would as well. She longed to bolt from here, but where would she go? She and her smell slogged into the examining room.

The nun found her chart, pointed her to a set of scales. Weighed her, took her height, her vitals. "Strip, then put this on." She handed Sylvia a gown. "It ties in the back."

Numb with embarrassment, Sylvia undressed. Another indignity to suffer. She laid her things over a chair back and stared at a mirror hung by the awful stirrupped table. Her breasts had swelled. Her stomach mounded like an ant-hill. She touched her belly button, surprised that hairs had sprouted around it. She hugged her arms, begged the tears to leave her be. She no longer knew her own body. No longer knew anything.

Someone rapped at the door. It creaked open. A man in a white coat stared at her.

Goldfish swam in her stomach as she skittered toward the table and grabbed the gown. "I-I'm sorry. I'm not quite ready."

"Take your time, ma'am." The door thudded shut.

Ma'am? She had never answered to "ma'am." Certainly it was preferable to the other things people might call her. The doctor's kind tone stilled her shaky hands so she could tie gown strings and climb onto that table.

The cold metal surface bit through the thin cotton gown. "Please, God, get me through this," she whispered through chattering teeth.

The door creaked open. "Are you ready, ma'am?" asked the doctor.

"Yes," Sylvia squeaked, then squeezed her eyes shut, lay back on the table, and stretched her legs until her stiff toes found the stirrups. If she kept her eyes closed, maybe it wouldn't hurt so much. At least she wouldn't endure the knowing glare, the silent smirk.

"Ma'am. You don't need to do that quite yet."

Relieved, she jerked her feet from the stirrups. A respite, however temporary, from a mean voice and painful jabs.

"I'm Dr. Carruthers."

She opened her eyes. He was . . . smiling.

The doctor extended a hand with smooth tapered fingers. Musician's fingers. "It's nice to meet you."

It is? She shook his hand.

He pulled her into a sitting position. "Are you okay?" he asked. Steely brows shaded kindly eyes. A coat belted at his waist. The smell of Ivory soap rose from his skin.

Her stomach calmed. She nodded.

He found a stool, rolled it to the table, sat down.

"Where are you from?" he asked.

"New Orleans," she stuttered. Girls were lined up to see him. Shouldn't he hurry?

The doctor folded his hands in his lap, then rubbed a gold band on his ring finger. "I've heard it's a lovely place." He sighed long and hard. "Maybe some day . . ."

"It *is* a lovely place," rushed out of her.

"What do you miss the most? Its weather? Its flowers?" he asked in a tone that made New Orleans sound like a swell lady. He checked her pulse while she talked about magnolias and jazz. More questions punctuated his move to a black bag. He drew out instruments. Examined her eyes, ears, and throat, listened to her heart, and tested her reflexes. Then he laid the instruments on a counter and returned to her side.

She tried to talk but her stomach resumed its wild lurches. His probes and stares would snap this peace; it was just a matter of time.

"My wife grows a dozen varieties of roses. " Despite the doctor's calm tone, Sylvia shuddered. "Right in our back yard."

Mimi. Cliff. Sylvia squeezed her eyes shut, as if that would stop the horrid *snip, snip*, the image of primroses scattered on that army blanket. One day, surely, she would again love roses.

The doctor put his hands on her shoulders and guided her until she was again lying down. "Just rest your feet in these." She felt a slight pull on her right, then left foot.

"What is your due date?" he asked, as calmly as if they were now discussing the Mighty Mississippi.

"I-I don't know," she managed to get out before tears choked up in her throat. Ignorance had gotten her into this mess. Even Julie knew more than she did about the birds, the bees, and everything in between.

The doctor removed his stethoscope and set it down. "Dear child." Watery gray eyes caught her gaze. "No one has told you a thing, have they?"

His gentle voice, *his* tears, coursed warmth through her body. Her feet sagged out of the stirrups and dangled off the table. This man had shed a tear *for her.*

She didn't deserve it. "I only saw the doctor once," she answered, trying to dam the tears. "He didn't tell me anything." Again she thought of that horrid document. "Now the baby's trying to come out and—" A salty river burst through the floodgates she had erected. "I'm . . . scared. Will . . . it . . . die?"

The door burst open. "Doctor."

Sylvia struggled to sit up, to quit crying, but she was a watery mess.

"Yes, Sister." The doctor kept his gaze on Sylvia, his hand firm on her belly.

"The cooks sent a gal to see what's holding things up."

His brow became a squall line. "Feed them. They can return after lunch."

"But the schedule—" A whine shrilled the sister's voice.

"Can wait."

The door slammed and rattled the instruments. But not the doctor. He kneaded her abdomen as if it were piecrust dough. "My mentor said schedules were made to be broken." He winked. "I don't think Sister had that lesson."

A giggle slipped past a sob. He'd made a disaster . . . almost funny.

"When did you last have intercourse, Sylvia? Can you give me an idea?"

She blinked. They had just been laughing. Now he wanted to know about . . . that?

The doctor's off-key hum gave her time to gather her wits.

"The . . . first week of April. Just the once," she added, wanting him to know that. Did it matter to anyone but her?

He nodded, as if he understood. "The exam will confirm it, but your due date will be mid-January." A smile dimpled his chin. "Born in a new decade; isn't that nice?"

"But it's trying to come out now."

He leaned close enough so she smelled the shaving paste Papa had used. She closed her eyes, wished that when she opened them, Papa would be standing there. But what would Papa think of her now?

"Why do you say that, Sylvia?"

She pointed to her belly. "It's fluttering around and grabbing me down there."

"When did that start?"

"Just today."

"April . . ." He ticked off five months and then patted her arm. "Seems just right. You're feeling your baby move. A glorious thing, once you get over the strangeness." His eyes twinkled with life. "My exam will confirm things. Then you are free to go. Next time I can fill you in on Braxton Hicks, edema—things that sound scary but aren't."

The stool rolled closer. She eased her feet back into the stirrups. Something cold touched her groin. Her muscles tightened, then relaxed. It hadn't hurt *that* much.

He talked about Frank, the gardener, Sister Edith in the nursery. She winced when he inserted something into her private area, but his gentle voice salved the discomfort.

Something clattered onto the counter. The doctor helped her up. "Ma'am, you're a healthy young lady." The respect in his tone straightened her spine. "And there's every indication your baby will be, too."

Things were truly fine? Though her limbs remained numb, the doctor's words released pent-up air. She'd make the best of this for herself . . . and for her baby as well.

The doctor checked his watch, washed his hands. "Expect to gain a pound or two a week. Eat fresh fruits and vegetables. Drink lots of milk. Tell the sisters if you experience a discharge. If you have cramps."

"When you're ready, get dressed." He pointed to a hamper. "Put your gown in there." Though he smiled, the lines on his forehead, the limp in his step, bespoke a laborer who'd performed a difficult job.

He left the room, but his kindly tone lingered to blanket her in warmth. She leaned back, relaxed tense muscles, and imagined a tiny baby floating about in her growing belly. Sleepy jazz notes teased her imagination, as if the baby was composing its own birth song. "Hello, little one," Sylvia whispered, nice and soft. With lazy circles, she stroked her stomach. "I'm Mommy. See you next year."

Chapter 21

Gloria from Mass in G

Sylvia gripped the handrail and made her way downstairs. Five days had dragged like five months. Girls had "frogged" her bed. Peppered her soup. Slopped mud on the floors she'd mopped. Smeared toothpaste in the sinks she'd scrubbed. Except for Julie, who seemed oblivious to it all, the others obeyed, afraid to be blackballed by Dee, who orchestrated everything. She looked over her shoulder. If only she could escape another prank.

She turned down the hall. *Mere steps to chapel. To safety.* Now she was the one elbowing people in her desire to sink into the plush chapel carpet and let the aroma of spicy incense and melting wax soothe frayed nerves.

When she entered her sanctuary, sun rays streamed through stained glass and splashed reds and blues on the pews. From the draped altar, candles flickered and spit. Though she did not dip her knees and cross herself, she bowed her head as she tread the aisle and took her seat. Peace enveloped her weary bones. She'd marveled over the sanctuary's hushed atmosphere and classical architecture, like the New Orleans church. It was the preacher, the judging congregation, that had wrenched her insides.

"*Introibo ad altare Dei.*" The priest clasped his hands, bowed, and stepped to the lectern. "Welcome." Kindly eyes seemed to search—and find—every girl. Even her. She leaned back and let words soak into her parched spirit. A respite had come, just in time!

Girls hushed. Nothing remained but the sweet scents, the blazing, hopeful candles, the foreign but soothing words. She took a hungry breath. Begged the mass to wash away every slight, every stab.

The sun's rays blared onto the halos of angels in a Baroque frieze and set them on fire. Holy light pierced her, not to scorch, but to radiate warmth. She needed warmth here in the North.

Her baby shifted. As Sylvia rubbed her belly to the rhythm of the mass, her eyes grew contentedly heavy. "I love you, little one," she whispered. In this time, in this place, she—and her baby—were at peace.

Prayer benches thudded down. Rustling and squirming girls knelt. She joined them, all the while massaging her stomach. Something good, something reverent, something holy met her here. She bowed her head and gave thanks.

◆

She thrashed about, gasping for breath. "You can't have it. It's mine." She aimed a kick at Dee's shins, but that didn't stop a pack of girls from clawing her. With gaping grins, they edged closer. Her eyes flew open, met darkness, searched for and found the moonbeams that streamed through the window over Julie's bed. Breathing slowed. At least *this* prank had been a dream.

She inched open her nightstand drawer, fumbled for Honey's Bible, comfort on sleepless nights. She didn't dare read about God's vengeance, but to feel the worn binding and run her fingers along the gilded pages brought the best peace she'd found outside of chapel. And reminded her of Honey.

Oh, Honey. She grabbed the Bible, cradled it against her breast, hoping to weight down sobs longing to stream like the moonlight. *Oh, Maman . . .*

Someone issued an awful moan.

She set aside the Bible. Scrambled out of bed. It was Julie.

She padded across the room.

Moonlight dazzled Julie's hair and spotlighted a writhing body.

"Now, now," Sylvia whispered. She glanced about. Heard only snores and the steady breaths of the sleeping dead. She caressed silky hair. "It's okay."

Julie flipped over. Tears matted her eyelashes. Full-moon eyes fixed on her. "No, it ain't." Grief twitched Julie's mouth.

"Shh. I'm here. It'll be okay." Sylvia climbed into the bed and enveloped Julie in her arms. The sobs intensified, yet the girl cuddled in.

Every thud of Julie's heart pulsed strength through Sylvia's veins. She would care for Julie like Julie cared for Cat. And that was awfully good. "What is it, sweetie?" she whispered. "Quiet, now, or you'll wake the others."

"I miss my mommy."

Of course. She, of all people, could relate to a homesick girl. And help her.

"Sweetie, we all miss our mommies. But you will be out of here soon. Then you will see her."

"No, I won't."

"Shh. You don't want to wake Dee, do you?"

"Men took Mommy away. Pete said we ain't gonna see her again."

Sylvia shivered in spite of the strangely balmy air. "What men?"

"The ones in white jackets."

White jackets? What could Julie's mother have done to warrant being snatched from her daughter? And why didn't her father stop the snatching? She patted Julie, confused by the story. "Who is Pete?"

"My big brother." A dreamy expression captured Julie's countenance. "It's his baby, you know." She began to hum in her out-of-kilter way.

Sylvia went numb from head to toe. No. A brother wouldn't do that to a sister.

"He had to become the daddy." Julie's eyes absorbed the moonlight. "'Cause Daddy left." A lopsided smile thinned plump lips into a goblin's grin. "Don't you see, Sylvie? Don't you *see?*"

No, dear Lord, I don't see! Chills raced up and down Sylvia's spine. She longed to leap from Julie's bed, bury herself under her quilt, and cry. But she just sat there and rubbed her hands until she could again feel. Then she stroked that silky, silky hair until sleep closed those strange, strange eyes. When the moon, not quite half, not quite quarter, sank into a bank of clouds, it left Sylvia alone with her cold, dreadful thoughts.

◆ ◆ ◆

Here on Watermelon Hill, she'd inhaled enough smoke for a lifetime. The smoking room was the one place she could escape the nuns' starched-habit reminders of her impurity. She hurried down the stairs to their haven, but the trapped feeling followed.

Lynne and Ethel lounged on a lumpy couch and flipped through outdated magazines. Someone yawned. Four girls sprawled on the floor, managing to smoke without choking. Others sat at a table near the windows and played gin rummy. Except for the *thump, ruffle* as Dee shuffled sticky cards, quiet settled in the room. An unusual quiet, since Dee was playing.

From her perch on the other couch, Sylvia glanced out the window. A pair of legs loomed close, then disappeared.

If I don't get outta here, I'll turn into a smokestack. And go crazy. From this vantage point in the basement, all Sylvia saw were legs. Feet. No faces. No arms. It was as if headless, torsoless aliens walked in. Walked out. Never made contact with them.

An urge to scream clawed at Sylvia. Fenced-in. Fenced-out. Alone . . . except for Julie, who since the bad-dream night clung to her like a Siamese twin. At least she had Julie. Watching over her—and staying away from Dee—was a full-time job.

Julie bulldozed a worked puzzle of the Swiss Alps and raked the pieces into a box. "Sylvie, can we do another?"

"We've done them all," she said with a sigh. "Why don't we read?"

Julie pulled books off the shelf and skipped across the floor, her smile lop-sided, her eyes shiny. If Julie didn't have her and Cat—she fought off an image of Julie's mother, limbs flailing, being tied onto a stretcher by men in white coats.

"This one!" Julie climbed onto the couch next to Sylvia.

Sylvia scooted over. *As long as I'm here, there'll always be room for Julie.*

"Hurry up, you idiot!" Dee cut through the languid mood and set Sylvia's teeth on edge. Why couldn't Dee ever *let things be?*

"Just hold on, will ya?" Delores, a sullen girl, tyrannized the other dorm room yet had settled into an uneasy truce with Dee, perhaps centered on a mutual decision to shun Sylvia. At least both left Julie alone, her blend of innocence and madness rousing pity even in their hard hearts. As long as that continued, she'd try to withstand their attacks.

"Come on, Sylvie!" Julie finally settled. "Read!"

"This one, huh?" Sylvia picked up Julie's favorite book. "'My name is Beautiful Joe,'" she read, "'and I am a brown dog of medium size.'"

"You reneged!" Dee slapped down her cards, ground her cigarette into an ashtray, and glared at Delores. Smoke curled over the girls and gave them wispy halos.

"No, I didn't," Delores retorted, but a smug smile told the truth.

"'I am not called Beautiful Joe because I am a beauty.'" Sylvia gripped the book, hope of peace stretched thin. What had she expected with Delores and Dee around?

"*You* sure ain't a beauty." Dee stared at Sylvia, then stuck out her tongue.

Spines that had slouched with boredom straightened. The girls sniffed a fight. If Dee didn't shut up, they just might have one.

Julie rocketed from the couch. "Dee, why you gotta ruin everything?" Her hands on her hips, she stomped toward the card table.

"You just stay outta this, shrimp."

Sylvia jumped up, knotted her fists. Dee had better leave Julie alone.

A slinky black shadow danced into Sylvia's peripheral vision. She turned her head. Thin slats of light streamed in through the window. She squinted.

Black paws. Furry legs. Stretchy, slinking motions. Cat? She fought a shudder as she crept to the windows. Stretched to her tiptoes to better see. Tense fingers gripped the window ledge. It *was* Cat, and she'd never survive in the real world. If Cat died, what would happen to Julie?

Sylvia wheeled about. Snatched a cracker tin off the end table. Knocked into a table leg.

The ace of spades fluttered to the floor.

"Hey, chump! Whaddya think you're doin'?"

"It's Cat!" Sylvia tore past scraping chairs.

"You can't go out there! You can't—"

A gurgle escaped Julie's throat and tightened Sylvia's resolve. Saving Cat was the right thing to do, no matter what. She punished the stairs. Her lungs. Her legs. She clattered to the front doors. Shoved them open.

Sunlight struck her in the face. She groped for the stair rail, rested the cracker tin in the crook of one arm. "Cat?" She tried to baby talk like Julie. "Here, kitty! Cookie." She leapt off the steps. Darted around bushes, her eyes peeled for black fur. "Kitty!"

She heard a mew. A rumble. A terrible, awful sound. An engine. A car.

Her heart in a crazy beat, she sprinted toward the sounds.

Cat ambled to the curb. Sat. Held out a paw, as if waving. Absorbed in the sights and sounds of the other world. Ignorant of the awful, horrible roar.

"N—!" She swallowed a scream, which might propel Cat forward and into the path of that car. Panting, Sylvia dashed ahead, her eyes on a black blur. She had to do this. For Julie.

Cat strolled into the street like a lady of leisure. Her tail swayed to match her gait as the car barreled closer, closer . . .

God, no! Sylvia's field of vision bouncing crazily, she flew into the road, her hands outstretched to grab that twitching tail . . .

Brakes squealed. A horn honked. Sylvia turned her head. Froze.

A car loomed so large, so close, she saw a cigarette dangling from the driver's mouth. But she could no more move than a statue could climb off its pedestal.

As she watched widemouthed, the wheel veered toward the curb. Thudded. A drawn-out honk ripped the quiet. Cat was perched in the middle of the street, licking her paws as if to say, "So what?" Blood rushed to Sylvia's limbs. She ripped open the cracker tin. "Bad Cat." She sugar-coated her words though she longed to grab Cat's scruffy neck and ream her out.

A man poked his bald head out the window. "Whaddya tryin' to do?"

"I'm sorry, sir. She's our pet." Huffing, Sylvia dangled a cracker as bait. "Here, Cat," she begged. She—and Cat—needed to get out of this world where they didn't belong and get back into the safety of Watermelon Hill.

Whiskers twitched. So did a nose. Cat crept toward her, oh so slowly. It was all Sylvia needed. The tin clattered to the pavement as she swept the cat into her arms.

Claws dug into her skin. She winced but held on tight.

"Jiminy, gal." The man's tone had mellowed. "Cat's got nine lives. But you only got one."

Nodding her apology, and clinging to the precious fur ball, she clambered breathless into the Home and to the basement. Girls huddled about the smoking room door, their mouths opening and closing, like air-starved carp. Julie broke from the gang, grabbed Cat, and hurried her to the couch. "Bad, bad Cat," she said, though her tone, her lavish strokes, flowed with relief.

Shaking her head, Dee stepped forward. "Why'd you go and do that?" she asked, in her usual gruff tone. "You wanna get killed?"

Sylvia took her first deep breath since the cat adventure. Only Dee would turn this into a battle. She stood straight, adrenaline pumping for a face-off, this one of the human kind. She had lived under Dee's thumb for long enough. "No, I don't."

Dee leaned close, as if to box her ears. Nicotine breath invaded Sylvia's lungs. "We both know if that cat dies, Julie goes with her. And we jes' can't let that happen." To Sylvia's surprise, Dee's hand was offered. To her surprise, she shook it.

◆

"Captain Allen?" A baby-faced young man interrupted their beach stroll. Saluted. "Private Daniels, sir."

"At ease."

Private Daniels let his arms fall to his side, spread his feet apart. "Sorry to interrupt, sir, ma'am. Hank—Captain Henderson said he's working on things."

"Thank you, private."

"He'll get back to you when he can. Sir."

Private Daniels snapped into another salute, whirled about, and marched down the beach.

Sheila stifled a giggle. Surely he'd slouch when he escaped their line of sight.

Samuel scooped a shell off the beach and handed it to her. "This leaves time for a show. Maybe a luau. You're dressed for it." They both laughed at her plastic lei, dyed a purple no natural flower could achieve.

She wiped grit from the speckled cone shell. Another soldier had given her a shell . . . Samuel's father. Her gaze shifted to the waves. What had become of him? "We didn't come here to watch the hula. We came here for . . ." Words escaped a tight throat.

"Mali," they whispered at the same time. Like mother and son.

He laughed and took her hand. "Mother, you're right on, you know it? About everything. Including your past. I'd like to hear the rest of the story. So forget the luau."

She cupped the shell in her hand, a first memento of her son. With God's help, she would soon have more.

Chapter 22

I Got a Right to Sing the Blues

Hey, Sylv, wanna pway?" The cigarette dangling from Carla's mouth got in the way of her words. "We need a fourth."

"Sylvie's readin' with *me*." Julie wobbled to the bookcase, her huge belly making her list like an overloaded ship.

"Maybe later, Carla." Sylvia yawned and slouched against the couch back. Since she had rescued Cat a month ago, the others not only quit snubbing her, they actually considered her one of them. Watermelon Hill was no longer impossible to climb.

"Here." Julie held out a faded blue book.

A groan escaped. "Again?" Sylvia ran her hand over the cover of *The Real Mother Goose*. Julie just might believe a gigantic goose would deliver her baby.

"I like it." Light streamed through the basement windows and gave Julie's face a cherubic glow. A cherub who couldn't read but who could have a baby with her brother.

"Okay, Julie. But just for a bit."

Julie flopped down next to Sylvia, who read, "Bye, baby bunting. Daddy's gone a' hunting." The creepy rhyme made Sylvia shift about uneasily. This was for children?

The door burst open, Dee all smiles. "Hey, you guys." She rapped on the table. "I've got a surprise."

"Tell me! What is it, Dee?" Julie asked.

"Sister said we could go to the store."

Delores pulled her nose out of a magazine and glared at Dee. "No, we can't."

"Yes, we can. It's St. Paul Day, the president's here, and the nuns wanna see him ride in some ole car. I even got the rings." She stuck her hand in her sweater pocket and pulled out gold bands. Sylvia's mind whirled. *Rings? President? Parade? Who could think of a parade with this wind?* "Why is President Truman here?" Sylvia asked.

"Gee, Sylvie, I don't know. Why do presidents do anything?" Dee slapped two rings into her palm. "Here. These are so's everybody thinks we're hitched. Course everybody knows. One look at our watermelons and they know." Dee showed her crooked-teeth grin. "Now get to it, gals."

Magazines were hurled, cushions tossed on the floor, by a yipping pack of girls. For too long they had been fenced off from the real world and its adventures. Hungering for news, Sylvia scoured newspapers left in the smoking room. There was plenty of it: a draft recall, unrest in a place called Korea. The entertainment section, bursting with reviews of Hollywood's latest films, made her long for Quarter theaters and their blazing marquees, buzzing crowds. What she wouldn't give to see *She Wore a Yellow Ribbon*. In color!

"No ring for you, Barb." Dee gripped the band between her thumb and forefinger as if it were pure gold. "You owe me ten cents."

"I can't pay *you* until Carla pays *me*."

Girls bickered and bobbed about. Except Julie, who slumped in a chair.

Sylvia knelt by her friend. "What's the matter, sweetie?"

Her face flushed, Julie pouted. "Ain't gonna go."

Sylvia felt Julie's forehead. "You're not sick, are you?"

"Sick 'bout havin' no money."

"Is that all? I'll lend you some." Sylvia unclenched Julie's fingers and slipped on a gold band, then put the other ring on her own finger.

"If you're giving it out, I'm all hands!"

"No, me!"

Palms extended, girls clamored about Sylvia. Laughter filled the air, along with a chill that seeped about the window casings. Outside, it was colder than a deep freeze, but cozy in here since the cat rescue. Buoyed by another positive event, she hurried upstairs and into their room. *Hat. Gloves . . .* this was her first outing since she had come to Watermelon Hill.

"Isn't this swell?" came from behind her. Suddenly wherever she went, half a dozen girls followed. Though grateful for friends, their burdens weighed on her increasingly achy back. *Soon she'd be responsible for a baby.*

"Hey, Sylvie?" Julie tugged on her sweater sleeve.

Speaking of children . . .

"Thanks for the dough." Though her face was still flushed, Julie's eyes sparkled. "Can we get pop? Maybe a comic book?"

"Sure." She hugged Julie until she wriggled free. As long as she could, she would put on blinders to the future and be a sister to Julie. "Scoot down to the smoking room and get your coat. It's on the couch."

While girls grabbed their things and hurried to the foyer, Sylvia donned her hat and scarf. Wouldn't Camille just cackle to see her dressed like a snowman? A money pouch fit snugly in her pocket. Such headiness hadn't seized her since she'd slipped into the Quarter for *Krewe du Vieux*. St. Paul . . . or New Orleans? Mardi Gras beads and *beignets* . . . or pop and comic books? She giggled at what Quarter folk would say about good times up here. So what? She was getting out, if only for the cheapest of thrills.

"Ah. Here you are."

Her breath caught. She startled, then exhaled. It was Aggie.

"It's good to hear you laugh, Sylvia. And smile. So good."

"Aggie . . . aren't you going to the parade?" She smiled to cover a sinking feeling. The trip was not off, was it?

Sister Aggie shook her head.

"Don't you want to see the president?"

Aggie's eyes glowed like the chapel candles. "The quiet will be good for me."

Sylvia bowed her head. *She is so holy, so reverent—everything I am not.* Her mind was on rags like *Archie* and *Jughead* when she should be on her knees praying.

"I didn't mean to throw a wet blanket on your fun." Aggie adjusted her habit. "Go on, dear. You'll have a grand time. In fact . . ." She scrounged through her pocket and pulled out a handful of coins. "Here. Get a candy bar. Three Musketeers were my favorite."

"You ate candy?"

"Of course. We were just country kids who rode a swaybacked pinto to school—even in winter—and threw apples at each other until the teacher yanked us inside."

"Did you get in trouble?"

"Most certainly! We had to chop wood for the stove."

"What changed you?" *Put the glow on your face?* "What brought you here?"

Sister sat on a bed. "As I grew older, I realized that world was not to be my world. How I loved it. But it wasn't for me."

"You were too good for it," Sylvia said flatly.

Dark eyebrows arched. Bow lips parted. "Quite the opposite. He called me here." She grasped Sylvia's hand. "Just a pitiful offering, but all I had. For Him."

Of course *Aggie* could say that. She had never done wrong. With a nod, Sylvia turned from starched-habit righteousness. "I have money of my own." She stopped near the door. Cast a glance back. "But . . . thanks anyway." She could barely breathe in here.

A shadow passed over Sister's face. "You're welcome, Sylvia."

Her hand tensed on the knob. How could she make Aggie understand that they could never be close? With a shameful hour on the beach, she had ruined everything. She fingered the phony wedding band on her finger, a reminder of their difference.

"What's wrong, dear girl?" she heard Aggie ask.

Sylvia swallowed hard. Pivoted. "Do we really have to wear the rings?"

Aggie twisted her hands. "It's for your own good. People will think they've recalled your husband or he works the third shift." Her words tumbled like acrobats. "The ring buys respect. Keeps men from staring, women from sneering. 'Tis a pity, but that's how it is."

"I see." And she did see, all too clearly, in the eyes of the repairmen who showed up occasionally to tinker with the Home's coughing old heating plant. "Damaged goods," a cook had whispered just last week, none too softly. Those without watermelons didn't understand. After a nod, she plodded downstairs, her excitement dimmed. A fake ring, giddy girls, candy, and what these girls called "pop" wouldn't do a thing to change it.

"Whew. We made it!" Giggles whooshed into the corner drugstore along with the girls. Mittens and caps were jammed into pockets. A stiff wind—and pent-up energy—had propelled them past ice-frosted yards, past bare-limbed oaks and elms. They might have been schoolgirls, except for bulging bellies, glittering bands. Sylvia flaked away her ring's bright coating to expose a dull gray patch. Their rings were made of fool's gold or something like it. Wasn't that fitting? They *were* fools, to have gotten knocked up.

Julie broke from Sylvia and tottered to a candy counter planted in the middle of the brightly lit store. Shelves burst with Bit-O-Honeys, Hershey's—treats wrapped in shiny paper. Cases displayed Whitman's chocolates and nuts, which begged to be scooped and sold. Years fell away to cotton candy and praline memories. Sylvia fished out a dime and joined Julie, who had propped her elbows on the counter and pressed her nose against the glass. Could creamy chocolate soothe her aches?

A clerk in a belted shirtwaist folded her arms. Bobby pins anchored a hairnet to a pie-shaped face. "No samples today," she muttered.

Julie didn't seem to hear the rebuke. But the words incinerated the remnant of Sylvia's carefree mood. Heat crept up her neck. "We have money," she said evenly, her hand on Julie's shoulder.

"Looka this!" An arm-waving Carla led others past the candy. Dazzling lights framed a Hollywood-style dressing room mirror. Shelves showcased enough bottles and compacts and lipsticks for a hundred actresses.

Sylvia tightened her grip on Julie. Girls like them weren't wanted here.

A crazy grin on her face, Carla picked up a lipstick tube, uncapped it, and whistled at the siren red color. Others clattered across checkerboard Formica to pull makeup off the display.

"Ain't that swell?" With a powder puff in her hand, Bridgette hopped about. Knee-high wool socks wadded at her ankles.

Sylvia stepped away from the bright lights, the mesmerizing sweets, to separate herself from trouble. She brushed lint off her skirt, determined to be a proper customer.

With the push of a swing door, the clerk left candy land and stalked past the wannabe starlets on her way to the pharmacy. More doors swung open.

Before they called the authorities, someone had to take control. Now. Sylvia yanked a glazed-eyed Julie from the candy aisle and pulled her close. "What do you think you're doin'?" she asked Dee, who had slathered on lipstick and puckered up.

"Aw, take a powder, Sylvie."

"Here!" Bridgette shook the puff. Face powder filled the air. "Want some?"

"A girl's gotta have fun."

"They're gonna throw us out." Sylvia tightened her grip on wiggly Julie.

A man who wore a white coat and brown trousers stomped close. "Vat's the meaning of this?" Round glasses magnified weary eyes. His frown spelled trouble, as did his pharmacist name tag.

Sylvia eyed the door. Should they all run for it?

"We didn't mean no harm, sir," Dee said, her red lips pinched and tight.

"You have, vhether you meant to or not. My store is for decent womens. Now scram."

Dee set her shoulders. Tightened those red lips. "My money's good as the next dame's."

Sylvia stepped back to escape the hot wind swirling around the man and Dee.

Julie yanked on Sylvia's hand. "I gotta go, Sylvie. Now!"

The man shooed at Julie. "Yes, go, you vixen. I'll not have you dirty up my facilities!"

Energy surged through Sylvia and landed her just short of the man's pug nose. "She isn't dirty! Don't you talk to her like that!"

"Sylvie. Sylvie!" Julie heaved, then fell, convulsing, onto the floor.

"Holy mackerel!" Dee shouted. "What's with her?"

"Ve von't have that in here," the man bellowed.

Doors banged. The clerk, a broom in her hand, approached. "Out! Out!" She wielded the broom like a patrolman's nightstick.

"Jeez, Louise. Get off our backs." Though Dee radiated her trademark glare, she ripped lipstick tubes out of the others' hands and tidied the display cases. One tube pinged off the case, plunked to the floor, and rolled into Julie.

The pharmacist scrambled onto hands and knees, as if recovering jewels instead of a lousy tube of lipstick.

Julie's wail split Sylvia's ears. Why would she throw a fit over candy and makeup?

"Shut her up!" Dee yelled.

Sylvia tried to get Julie off the floor, but all she got for her effort was more screams. "Hey." Sylvia pointed at Dee. "You get her legs."

Dee complied, but even with Dee's help, Julie did not budge.

Sylvia ground her teeth. They had a problem. If Julie didn't cooperate, they'd have a bigger one. "Be still." She squeezed Julie's wrists. "*Now.*"

Julie arched her back and her head and clenched her teeth. "Oooh." Moans escaped pale lips as Julie kicked up her skirt and exposed flushed and swollen legs. As Sylvia smoothed her skirt, Julie went limp.

A puddle seeped out from under her body.

Dee's face paled to the color of putty. "Her water broke," Dee cried. "If we don't get a move on, she'll have that baby. Right here on the floor."

Chapter 23

Why Was I Born?

*J*ulie is dead weight. Sylvia shuddered at the thought.

"Help us out, Julie!" Dee cried.

The two of them battled to get Julie to her feet.

"Stop it, youse guys!" Julie's groans crescendoed to wails.

Sylvia patted Julie. "Come on, now. It'll be okay."

"No!" Julie kicked Sylvia in the shins, then went limp.

The drugstore employees disappeared behind the pharmacy's swinging doors. Avoiding trouble, or calling the police. Heavens, now they were in for it. Sylvia looked to Dee and raised her eyebrows, silently questioning.

"What're ya lookin' at me for?" Dee groused.

Sylvia battled a sinking sensation. Should they ask for an ambulance or somehow lug Julie back to the Home and let Aggie decide what to do?

"Get her out! Now!"

Sylvia cringed at the hate in the pharmacist's voice, at the wet-straw smell wafting from Julie. The decision had been made.

"Listen, Julie." Sylvia mopped Julie's brow. "We're gonna get a good hold on you, then carry you out before they call the cops." *If they haven't already.* "You have got to calm down."

Julie didn't nod, but she didn't shake her head or kick, either.

"Okay." Sylvia and Dee gripped Julie's wrists. Barb and Bev took her feet. The others clustered about, ready to lift her off the ground.

Sylvia took a deep breath. "One . . . two . . . three, lift!"

They shuffled forward with their load. Paused helplessly before the closed door. Bev freed one hand to open it wide enough to get them started again. The bell over the door jingled merrily as the group maneuvered onto the sidewalk. If only the gaiety could return.

"Two blocks to go." It was classic Dee, spurring them on. And to think she'd once hated Dee.

Sylvia kept whispering, "It's all right," though Julie, with her waxy-pale skin and trancelike expression, reminded Sylvia of a mannequin. She pushed away such thoughts and tried to ignore the feel of Julie's clammy hand. The staring eyes of passersby.

"Carla, run on ahead," Dee ordered when they neared the Home gate. "Ring the bell!"

"Who, me?" Carla asked.

Sylvia felt a twinge in her side. A bell? Had they been locked out?

"Yes, you." As if fearful, Dee darted half-dollar eyes her way. "Ring it now!"

Dee, scared? Though she was shivering, sweat trickled down Sylvia's back. Would she and Dee have to deliver . . . a baby? She bowed her head as they carried Julie up the steps. Tried to pray.

"But it ain't quite time," Carla whined.

What in tarnation was this bell for? Pain shot through Sylvia's arms, calves, and lower back. Her hands begged to go slack. There might be two labors, here on the Home steps. She gripped Julie's arm with all her might.

"Just looka her, Carla." Dee tossed her head. "For Pete's sake, do *you* wanna cut her cord?" Dee stomped her feet. "Go ring that bell. Now," she ordered. "Let's get her inside."

With every step, stabs assaulted Sylvia. Though her hands were numb, she managed to hold on, as did the others. They made it up the last stair, entered the Home, and laid Julie on the floor of the front hall.

Sylvia heard a bell clang. Heard footfalls. Oddly, she thought of Paul Revere's midnight ride, hooves pounding, alarm sounding. *A rescue. And about time.*

As footfalls clomped closer, her world darkened and began to spin out of balance. Sylvia groped for someone's shoulder. She was falling, falling . . .

"Catch her."

"There! Grab her there!"

Sylvia clawed at air. Battled dizziness.

Someone—Aggie?—glided down the stairs.

Sylvia tried to scream, but blackness snuffed out her voice.

*   ◆   *

"The poor dear's overwrought."

"But Doc said she was okay."

Sylvia struggled to lift weights from her eyes.

Fluorescent lights brightened a ceiling blotched with stains. These voices, this ceiling, were familiar . . . She tried to sit up, but firm hands halted her movement. Finally a cabinet lined with trays of instruments came into focus.

"Now, now."

She craned her neck, squinted. The infirmary. But she was not ill. Julie—what had happened to Julie? Her baby? Sylvia struggled to sit up. Stared at Sister Carline. The recognition slowed spiraling panic. Sister knew how to take care of things. Sister would help her Julie.

"You did a fine job, dear girl."

Sylvia shivered . . . and was back in the cold with Julie, who was writhing in pain. Julie, gasping for breath. A bell, tolling, tolling.

"Just lay back, dear," Aggie whispered. "You need to rest."

Lay back? She kicked off a blanket. "Where's Julie? How is she? Why was that bell ringing? And why am I here?"

Swathed faces stared at each other, then at her.

Her stomach flip-flopped. What had upset the nuns?

"The bell lets us know when it's time," Aggie mumbled.

Sylvia crossed her arms. "Time for what?"

Sister Carline stared at her aged, swollen hands. "To call a cab."

"You mean y'all ride with her to the hospital?"

"The cabbie does."

Her breath quickened. "Y'all sent her alone with a cabbie?" She telescoped a look at Carline, then Aggie. "What if she . . . has it . . . in the back seat?"

Quiet pressed in harder than Julie's dead weight had. Gingerly, she slid off the table, smoothed her skirt, slipped on her shoes.

"Sylvia . . ."

She paused, her hand near the doorknob. What they said would not change the fact that they'd sent a pregnant, feebleminded girl alone to the hospital.

"It's . . . better this way," Aggie whispered. "Trust me."

A battle raged in her soul. The sisters had lavished love on her, had lavished love on all of them, but deserted Julie in her time of need. The same thing would happen to her. Fighting dizziness, she gripped the doorknob. Nothing made sense right now. She wanted to talk to Dee, who, being older and more experienced, could explain things.

"Lie down. You're overwrought, but not in labor." As usual, Sister Carline regained a grip on things. But Sylvia had had enough of the cramped room, the wan faces in a sea of white. So much white. While Julie lay alone, red-faced and heaving, in a hospital room.

"I've got to find the others," Sylvia said, and left the room. No one tried to stop her.

◆ ◆ ◆

A rare quietness shrouded the dorm. No giggling over the gardener's baggy pants, the postman's love-letter eyes. Sylvia adjusted the pillow that buffered against her iron headboard. Surely the sisters had heard about Julie by now. But no one had said a word. She dug for her Bible, opened it, but fixed her gaze on the bed by the window.

Blackness seeped into the room and further darkened her mood. No giggly little girl. No Cat, who had been cajoled with dinner scraps to move across the hall. Nothing.

Girls moped about nighttime rituals, surely thinking as she was: How is Julie?

Someone rapped at the door.

"Come in!" Dee said.

Aggie, a sticklike object in her hand, stood at the threshold. Her eyes danced. She tapped her foot.

Sylvia scooted to the edge of her bed. Set aside her Bible. How she longed for good news!

"What—what is it?" Dee reached for Aggie, then let her arm fall, perhaps surprised by her eagerness. Her eyelids fluttered awkwardly.

"Girls, I have something to tell you—and a surprise."

"What?" Magazines fell to the floor. Lamps rattled. In spite of the protection of a faded hook rug, the floor got pounded as girls swarmed Aggie. "Please. Tell us. *Now.*" They gaggled like hungry geese.

Sylvia's heart began to bloom, though she clenched her fists in case intuition failed her. But Sister wouldn't be smiling if the news were bad.

"Our Julie," Sister beamed, "came through fine. So did a beautiful baby girl."

A girl! Sylvia leapt up and then doubled over. With moves like that, *she'd* have a baby, right here and now.

The room exploded with New Year's gaiety, bras and panties instead of streamers and confetti. A pillow smacked Sylvia in the head. Tears streamed from Dee's eyes, softening her angular face. Julie's girl belonged to them all.

Sister Aggie held the stick—a flute!—to her lips and tweedled pure glee. Then she handed a harmonica to Sylvia. "The way you sing, surely you can play."

Time fluttered back to her father's musician friends, sitting in the parlor, harmonicas to their mouths, banjos in their laps. Squeezing her eyes tight to recall every detail, she licked her lips, then blew on the instrument, softly at first, searching for C. She found it, blew again, then winced. A frog had just croaked!

"What's that?" asked Carla.

"A harmonica."

"Hey, I wanna try."

Girls crowded around, but Sylvia paid them no mind. C-E-E-E-D-E-F-E. She took a breath, then repeated the segue.

Sister Aggie added her crinoline habit to the circle of flannel, wool, and brushed cotton. She drew the flute to her lips and echoed Sylvia's little ditty.

"For she's a jolly good fellow . . ." Penelope, the newest resident, was the first to catch hold of the old song and make it her own.

Music swirled about the room as Sylvia flirted with the harmonica, handed it to another, played, sang, played, and sang. Dee pounded an overnight case with her knuckles. Another girl tapped on the windowpane. What fun it was to celebrate new life!

"For she's a jolly good fellow, which nobody can deny."

They sang the chorus—again, again. Slights and disappointments rolled away. Even as she celebrated, Sylvia longed to distill the off-key voices, the laughter, the shining faces, and bottle them for the pain that she knew lay ahead. Then she pushed away the hovering sense of doom and plopped onto Dee's bed.

"Listen to this!" Dee sat beside her. "For she's a jolly good mother!"

They all joined in, the craziest choir in the world. Anita found a ring of keys and shook them. A Quarter band couldn't have been more energized than this ragtag group. Finally they collapsed around Sylvia's bed, some on pillows, some leaning against a footboard. Gasps and the hissing radiator took over. Sweat added its musty-sweet smell to the air. Sylvia leaned back so Penelope could nestle in. Another one to comfort, to reassure. Again she thought of Julie. How *was* she, really?

"Her baby's beautiful." Aggie sat at the end of Sylvia's bed, as if she understood. "Perfect tiny toes, the pinkest bow mouth—"

"How do you know?" Dee rumbled to her feet, her eyes suddenly stormy. "Did you see her?"

Dee's words echoed off the room's tile floor and drowned out the merry music. As quickly as the celebration had begun, it halted. Doom slipped into the quiet and sent a shiver up Sylvia's spine.

Aggie bowed her head, as if offering penance—to whom, Sylvia wasn't sure. "I did . . . this one time," she mumbled. "With yesterday's hustle and bustle, I slipped out." A tremble parted her lips. "Of course they let me in the nursery. I'm one of them." Her shoulders fell, as if burdened by the weight of her words.

"But did they let *Julie* see her? Tell me that. Could she tweak even one tiny toe?" Dee shrieked so loud, Penelope cupped her hands over her ears.

Remorse fled Aggie's eyes, leaving them glittery hard. "You know the answer, Dee. There's only so much one can do." She gathered her skirts, her flute, and exited, leaving her harmonica and stunned girls behind.

Mumbles replaced the music. Sylvia got ready for bed, stashed the harmonica in her trunk, then had second thoughts and laid it on her table. After her nerves settled, after moon rays beamed through the slatted blinds over Julie's bed, music might return to her soul, and she could rejoice for Julie. The reality of what had happened to Julie, what would happen to all of them, halted her attempt to even think of a middle C. She crawled into bed and tried to sleep.

◆

It is not the same and never will be. Sunshine poured through the dorm room windows and spotlighted Julie's old bed, stripped of sheets. Sylvia sat down, massaged swollen ankles. She had to get moving or she would be late . . . again.

Saying bye to Julie had cast a pall on all who loved the girl with the blank smile, the girl too young to have a baby. But seeing Julie give up that baby, without so much as a good-bye kiss, snuffed out a light Sylvia had tried to keep burning. Even helping Penelope adjust to the Home failed to rekindle the spark. She hung her head, rubbed her aching neck. Yet her rational side argued that Julie couldn't care for herself, much less a baby. What a horrible mess!

She pulled on her clothes, patted her hair, not caring what she looked like anymore. Even the nightly concerts had lost their glitter. Some girls lay face-down on their beds, their hands muffling their ears, as if even a note of music would make them explode. And maybe it would.

The door squeaked open. Aggie padded into the room. "Mrs. Stanz is here."

"Do I have to, Sister?" Sylvia dreaded the social worker meetings more than the monthly exams. At least Dr. Carruthers considered her human.

"Yes." Sister stepped close. "But first you must know something."

Sylvia braced for bad news but dismissed the thought with a glance at Sister's smile. "What? Tell me," she intoned. She grabbed a cardigan, Delores's hand-me-down, stuffed her arms into the sleeves, tried to button it, and gave up. Soon she'd be reduced to wearing sheets.

"The Lindquists—"

Sylvia scratched at itchy wool. Everything irritated her now. "Who are they?"

"The nice family that adopted Julie's baby. You know, they came several weeks ago and got her." Words tumbled from Sister. "They're so happy."

Sylvia nodded dully. Sure they were happy. Who wouldn't want a baby? But how about Julie; how did she feel?

Aggie's eyes danced with light. "They're so happy, they're adopting Julie as well!"

"Adopting—" She tried to get up, but Aggie's words froze her in place. "You mean—"

"She's free of that brother!" Aggie's hands steepled. "And they took Cat, too."

Sylvia's breath caught. So Aggie knew about the brother and sent Julie back there? She pushed away everything but the news that Julie was free . . . and with her baby. She struggled to her feet, feebly mimicking Sister's spins. Strange as it sounded, Julie could be a sister to her daughter. Maybe, just maybe, the Lindquists would love them both.

Laughter mixed with Aggie's words and fluttered at the dark portals of Sylvia's soul. Could there be hope for all of them, even her?

The door banged open, rattled against the jamb, bounced back. Carla stalked into the room, freckles standing out like sores on a face white as Sister's habit. "Dee's gone."

Sylvia's field of vision narrowed until all she saw was Carla's face. No. Not Dee. She bit her trembling lip. Though she was crusty as old bread, she could be counted on to take care of things. With Dee gone, who would help her with these girls?

"Gone? I saw her at breakfast." A trace of gaiety remained in Aggie's eyes, but she began wringing her hands as she did when she was nervous.

"She was at breakfast for sure." Carla yanked a note from her pocket. "Right after a meeting with Mrs. Stanz." Carla's face twisted, as did Sylvia's. The caseworker, with her made-up face and fancy airs, considered them unsuitable to be mothers. Unsuitable to be anything.

"Well, what does it say?"

Carla bowed her head. "It's—it's private."

"Nothing's private here, I tell you. Give me that!" As Carla stood there, her eyes saucer-wide, Sister grabbed Carla's fist, bent back her fingers, and extracted the wadded-up note. Her brow wrinkled in concentration as she smoothed the paper. Her lips formed a thin, tight line.

Sylvia edged close to Aggie. If she stood on her tiptoes, she might learn what Dee had done now. She stretched just enough for her eyes to capture the words.

I've had enough of Mrs. Stanz. Enough of all of this. No stranger's takin' my baby. I'm leaving. And don't try to find me.

P.S. Say good-bye to the girls. I'll miss them. Diane Esther Harris

"You're already late, Sylvia. Shoo." A glare completed Aggie's transformation into someone older. Someone mean. Someone Sylvia didn't care for.

Sylvia bowed her head, acting contrite. "Yes, Sister." As she slumped toward the bathroom, the words in that letter burned in her soul. Soon she would have a decision to make. Just like Dee's.

Chapter 24

Slow Blues

*W*ill this *ever be over?* Teeth chattering, Sylvia tossed about in bed, searching for a position that eased her cramping back, aching legs, and swollen belly. New Year's had dumped record amounts of snow on St. Paul, creating a magical winter wonderland such as a Southern girl had never known. Yet the Christmas card beauty brought winds that snaked through cracks in the windows and doors, crept up her body, and chilled her to the bone.

It wasn't just the weather that raged against her. Her body rebelled against so many foods, she hardly knew what to eat. Life blurred into a kaleidoscope of chores, aches, chapel, pain, school. Worry was the only constant that bound everything together. How could she, an unwed mother, support her child? For despite what the nuns thought, that was her plan: to leave here with her baby.

Yesterday, as she lay on the examining table in the infirmary, Dr. Carruthers had pressed his stethoscope to her belly. "Best guess is another week, Sylvia. Maybe two. January 10?" He smiled. "My wife's birthday. She'd like that." He patted her, as always, guided her into a sitting position, as always, had the teary look, as always. Did worry cause his tears? Or did he understand her hopeless position? When he left the room, she turned to face the wall. "God, help me," she whispered. As usual, God didn't say a word.

◆ ◆ ◆

"Get up!" Carla hissed. "Sylvie! Sister's gonna ream you out."

Sylvia covered her ears to block out the screech that interrupted Maman's song. Maman—she closed her eyes to recapture the vision. Nothing materialized.

She sat up straight, a sob in her throat. Maman's image had vanished from Sylvia's memory.

"Gee, whiz! You look awful!" Wide-eyed Carla, her hair a mass of bobby-pinned curls, leaned close, as if inspecting an exotic but ugly bug.

"Gee, thanks." Sylvia grabbed her blanket and pulled it over her head.

"Hey, are you okay?" Carla plopped down, her hip crushing Sylvia's arm.

Pain shot along her shoulder. She shoved off her blanket and sat up.

"I'm sorry." Carla touched her pajama sleeve. "Why don't ya hide out in here? After breakfast, I'll slop your end of the hall."

The words coaxed a smile. She had no family but had found friends, like this hog farmer's daughter. "Thanks." She playfully punched Carla. "I'll slop my own sty."

Carla hurried off. To avoid the nuns' *tut-tuts*, so should she. Heavy feet hit the floor. Got her to the bathroom. As she brushed her teeth, she rubbed a cramping stomach. The thought of food brought bile to her mouth. A stab of eggs, a scrap of toast, and she'd dump the rest, get on with chores. *If Doctor was right, it'll just be a few more days.* Then what? She shut off the haze of despair that was her future. Hunched over to ease the cramps, she waddled downstairs. *Chapel.* Vowing to survive, one step at a time, she ticked off landmarks. *Dining room*—

"Hey, Sylvie! Over here!"

With effort, she slogged forward, her feet heavy as cinder blocks. *Thump, cramp, thump.* A counter loomed closer. Another step, and she'd be there.

"Morning, Miss Sylvia."

Smile. Pick up your tray. She told her arms to move, but they didn't. Neither did her feet. *Ahh*—someone had drawn a belt about her waist and yanked hard. "Ahh—" She lurched forward, a last-ditch effort to get breakfast.

Something crashed. Bells tinkled—or was it sleet pinging against the window? Her knees crumbled from the nonsense of it all. Falling, falling . . . Her hand hit something sharp, something mushy and hot. *Crawl*, she told her paralyzed limbs. *Crawl!* But she didn't move.

"Ring the bell!"

"Her water hasn't broken. It's not time."

"Have you lost your mind? For the love of Pete, do it now!"

Every word hammered into her skull, but pain swallowed her comprehension of them. She lay in a fetal position to ease the onslaught. *Hold on*, she told herself. *Hold on!*

Sylvia snatched words from the stuffy air. Carla, telling someone to shush.

Sister Angela, calling for help. She struggled for her bearings. Why was she on the floor? As the pain began to melt away, she let the linoleum cool her flaming cheeks. *It feels so good to be still, to be cool . . .*

"Come on, Sylvia. Let's get you up before the next one."

Next one? Memories of spattered food flooded back. Something stabbed her belly, her legs, and her lungs. She flipped over. *Just let me be. Just a minute, now. Just—*

Black-swathed figures gripped her arms, her waist, hauled her to her feet. Her belly flip-flopped, then squeezed so hard, her breath strangled.

When the pain eased, she let out a breath. *So this is it. I'm . . . in labor.*

Warm hands cupped her cheeks. Palms braced her chin, turned her head. She opened her eyes. The nuns had formed a circle around her. She leaned into starched black habits that covered strong bones. Breathed in the sweet powdery smell of chapel incense. She was safe here . . . with . . . these sisters.

"Sylvia, listen to me."

It was Carline; she didn't dare disobey. Somehow she nodded.

"It's your time, Sylvia. I've called a cabbie. He'll take you to St. Vincent's. You will be in good hands."

Good hands? She gripped a habit sleeve.

"God will take care of you, Sylvia."

"In the name of the Father, and of the Son, and of the Holy Ghost—"

"I don't want to leave. Don't make me!" Her words faded into a swish of fabric and prayers. Usually soothing, but not today. Though she had known it was coming, had seen it happen to Julie, nothing could soothe the fact that those who claimed to love her were sending her—and her baby—away.

They draped her coat about her shoulders. Pulled a wool cap so low, it tickled her eyelashes. Led her out the door and into a world of swirling white.

"Careful, now. Careful." They gripped her shoulders, her elbows. Her boots found the next step, the next. A bitter wind bit at her nose and tore through her coat. Sylvia convulsed with shivers. It had to be forty below.

Flakes frosted the nuns' eyelashes and cheeks to create an abstract of white. Like someone stricken blind, she let herself be pulled along, though she wanted to scream, "No! No!"

She heard but didn't see a rumbling engine, heard but didn't see the gate creak open. Harsh smoke drew a cough from her exhausted lungs. She forced open watering eyes.

A thin man in a blue suit and gray wool hat slouched against a taxi splotched with snow. Smoke trailed from a cigarette clamped between two fingers. Looking full into her face, he tossed his cigarette into gray slush, stamped with his boot, spat contemptuously.

She flamed as if he had stubbed her with his cigarette butt. She tried to pivot toward the Home's safe walls. It was awful out here in the cold, cruel world!

Someone opened the cab's back door.

"May the blessed Mother watch over you." The same firm arms that had led her outside guided her onto a seat that reeked of cheap hair oil and smoke. She swallowed, desperate to keep from vomiting. The cabbie would *really* hate her then.

He got in the car, rolled down his window.

The nasty wind iced her face. Her stomach tightened; she gripped it, as if that would stop the pain.

"How 'bout my fare?"

"Sir, we don't have change. Just bill the diocese."

He cursed, apparently displeased with the financial arrangements. Perhaps he was new at this job, like she was new at giving birth.

She panted, hissed, desperate to fend off the strangling grip of another contraction. But it assaulted, heedless of her efforts.

As the cabbie rolled up the window, the wind made a final sucking sound, then was gone. But not the choking pain. She clutched the seat, unable to keep from gagging.

Still cursing, the cabbie revved the engine. Thin shoulders tensed. Tires screeched as they tackled the snowy road. Silently she begged the cabbie to go faster, sure she was near death. "How . . . much . . . farther?"

"Fifteen minutes, on these roads."

Fifteen minutes? A lifetime. She doubled over and arched her head until it thumped against the seat. *God, help me.* She clutched her belly. *Please, God.*

The car's acceleration blurred snow-covered trees into white streaks. Her heartbeat increased, as if somehow tied to the cabbie's press of the accelerator.

One thousand one, one thousand two . . . Desperate to slow spiraling anxiety, she counted until another assault grabbed hold and strangled her. She gripped the seat front, not caring that her hand grazed the cabbie's head. Thoughts faded in the face of grinding, constant pain.

The next thing she knew, snowflakes tickled her face. The time that she had both thrilled for and dreaded had arrived. She began to shiver. Could not stop.

Gloved hands guided her into a wheelchair.

The taxi gunned, shrieked, was silent. Doors flew open. She was pushed into a world of gray walls, red lights, more white faces, white uniforms. Billowing warmth melted the snow on her face, mixed it with her tears. "God help me," she kept whispering.

"Up to OB. Stat."

"Sisters Carol, Peggy, you two can handle it from here."

Two nuns. That should be a good thing.

As she was rolled toward an elevator, a cacophony of bells and buzzes sent orderlies rushing about the halls. Sylvia trembled. Could the baby feel her fear?

"Relax, dear. We're about to take you up."

She craned her neck, hoping to put a face with the soprano voice.

"You poor dear." A hand touched her head. "It'll be all right."

The gentle touch made her eyes heavy. If only she could claim those words as truth!

After a dinging sound, the elevator doors flew open. They rolled her in. Doors clanked shut. Another contraction strangled. "Ohh," whooshed out; then silence reigned. And pain.

A hand extended from a white habit and pushed a button. The car, reeking of ammonia and antiseptic, lurched off the ground. As suddenly as it had come, the contraction released its grip. She breathed deep, raised her head, and searched for the face that belonged with the soprano voice. Met sullen green eyes. "How long did it last?" the woman rasped. Not the soprano.

"Wha-what?"

"The contraction," hissed Sullen Eyes. "How long?"

The other sister, who stood by the control panel, averted her face.

Sylvia opened her mouth but could not speak. A second? An hour? It was horrid to know so little about birthing! Her tenuous hold on her emotions began to slip. She whimpered.

"This is no time for hysteria," Sullen Eyes snapped. "Answer me. Now!"

The elevator whirred. Sylvia bit her lip. Begged her woozy brain to work, but her inner clock had gone haywire. She shook her head, sorry she couldn't help this sister. Couldn't help herself. She shook her head. Closed her eyes.

"Peggy, the dear doesn't know." The soprano voice soothed her pain. "Let it be."

The bell dinged. Another lurch. Doors opened. Miss Sullen Eyes wrestled with her wheelchair. Miss Soprano stayed in the elevator.

As she was rolled out, lava-hot pain returned. "Ooh!" She arched her back. "Please!" rattled from her throat. "Can you help?" she asked Sullen Eyes.

"Doctor said not to call until you're complete. No use wasting staff."

The elevator closed. There went the soprano—and any chance for kindness. Thankfully the contractions released their hold. Sylvia gorged on air, now that she could breathe.

She was pushed past doors adorned with pink and blue ribbons. Pink, pink, blue—

When the chair jerked to a stop, her head smacked against the chair back. Her hands flew to her belly. How much would she—and her little one—have to endure?

"Four forty-two." The nurse stepped around her, opened the door, and motioned her forward. "Here's your room. Step to it."

"You mean . . . walk?"

"What do you think I mean?"

Sylvia wobbled inside.

On the long wall, a window displayed a winter-white wonder.

The nurse strutted to the window. Yanked on a cord. Blinds tumbled down to obliterate her view. Sylvia winced, as if they'd slammed on her face. Would one mistake forever separate her from those who were pure as that snow?

"Get in that bed and don't call us"—the nurse pointed to a buzzer looped about a bed rail—"until the baby's falling out." A glare distorted her big green eyes, a slender nose.

This nurse, who didn't even know her, hated her and hated her baby as well. A sob slipped out.

"Don't even *think* about asking for pain medicine." The nurse jabbed a finger at her. "Next time someone tempts you to spread your legs, remember how this feels." With a sniff and a huff, she and her hate stalked out of the room.

Tears flowed freely, now that the room held just her and her baby. She struggled out of her coat, draped it across the room's lone chair, knelt, and lifted her eyes to a crucifix that hung over the bed. "If you will protect my baby," she prayed, her teeth chattering so hard she could barely speak, "I will never again get in this fix." She tried to remember Sunday school verses, GA principles, but her mind had been vacuumed of any words of hope. "Please, Jesus, please." She begged Him to hear the only prayer she could manage. Having done all she could do, she gripped the bedpost and raised her bulky body from the floor.

As she got up, liquid trickled down her thighs. She gritted her teeth and squeezed, desperate to stop another humiliation. It was too late. A stream dribbled down her skirt, soiled her socks, her shoes, put a gruesome shine on the green tiled floor. Hot tears pooled in her eyes. She had lost control of everything.

She waddled to the bathroom, jerked a towel from a rack, and shuffled to her mess. Near the bedpost, she slipped, fell, and was tempted to lie there until the baby came.

An image of Maman drifted into her brain. She focused on Maman's dewy skin and sure, sweet smile. Maman, who had named her Sheba. Maman, who had said she could do anything.

When the image faded, she breathed deep, scrabbled onto her hands and knees, wadded up the towel, and scrubbed. "I may be a tramp, but I am not a pig." Words whistled through clenched teeth. "I am not a pig. Not a pig. Not—"

"Of course you're not."

Startled, she looked up. The soprano had eased into the room. Someone kind? Someone who would not treat her like filth?

Sylvia's face contorted with a mixture of relief and disgust as she plopped the sopping towel over the mess. It was bad enough to lose control in private; awful when someone else saw.

"I got back in here as soon as I could. When *she* went on break." The sister pitter-pattered closer. "It's not your fault, you know."

Nine months of shame and pain had sucked her dry. Sylvia took in the sister's soothing voice, then hung her head. "I could not . . . keep . . . from wetting myself." She tried to rise and crumpled into a sitting position.

"You poor dear. Is that what you think?" The sister stroked Sylvia's hair.

Sylvia leaned into each caress, each kindness. Closed her eyes . . .

"Dear, your water's broken. You've got to get up." With the strength of a much larger woman, the sister pulled her from the floor.

Recognition dawned. How could she have forgotten what happened to Julie at the drugstore?

"I wouldn't be a bit surprised if you are crowning."

"Crowning?"

"It's the baby, peeking out." The sister wrapped her arms around Sylvia, helped her up, and guided her to the bed. "I'll fetch a wheelchair and be right back."

"Where—where are you taking me?"

"To the delivery room. If I know the first thing about childbirth, you will have a little angel before the night is done." She hurried out the door.

Little angel. Sylvia considered the beautiful words. Would her baby truly be blessed, or did her affair with the soldier doom it for life? Sylvia seized the nun's hope and struggled to express it. "Father," she finally begged, biting her lip, "don't punish the baby for my sin. Let me suffer, Lord . . . if You must," she added, trying to speak the truth to the God whose countenance surely darkened at her cowardice. "But please, God, please. Keep my baby safe."

Chapter 25

Solitude

Pain sliced her in half. She twisted to escape. Couldn't move. She bit her lip, tasted blood. Opened her eyes to a dazzling light. Stared at the ceiling.

A pale-faced girl with wild, dark hair and bloody lips met her gaze. The girl lay on a metal table.

Three figures hovered about the girl. White caps floated on seas of wavy hair.

Recognition brought a gasp. It was an overhead mirror, reflecting her pain. The ugliness of her sin. Showing what happened when a girl lost control. She felt tears on her face, yet the overhead mirror was too distant to reflect them. She tried to meet the gaze of the uniformed staff. Could they see her tears? Did anyone understand?

"I tell you, she's complete. She needs something for that pain."

"She doesn't deserve anything."

"She's just a girl."

Words hovered over her head; she grabbed one she'd heard earlier. Complete, what did it mean?

"Doc's gonna have your hide if she gets in trouble."

Knives stabbed her stomach. She writhed about. *I'm laying on a delivery table, and there's no doctor.*

Someone entered the room.

The others murmured greetings.

"Why wasn't I called?" asked a man in a terse, low tone.

Silence, and a chill wind, shivered her spine. If this man were a doctor, he could stop the knife-wielding assassin.

"Put her out. The mask, for God's sake! Why wasn't she shaved?" Booming words smothered out whines. "Why didn't you drape that mirror? You know the rules."

A rubbery mask was clamped over her face. Gasping, she tried to wrench it off. Someone pinned her arms. She rolled on her side. Flailed her legs.

"Hold her down, do you hear? Watch those feet!"

She struggled against the mask until a heady alcohol smell summoned her to a cloudy place. Energy seeped from her limbs. A green fog dimmed the lights, muffled the moans and murmurs. Then the fog took over and shut everything down.

◆ ◆ ◆

A noise split dark silence. Sylvia pricked her ears. Stirred. Something mewed, like a hungry kitten, so pitiful sounding, a whimper caught in her throat.

"Would ya look at those baby blues?"

"Fit for a freak show."

She tried to sit up so she could help the kitten, but pain kept her down. A dark fog crept near. Groaning, she fought to stay conscious. What had they meant by baby blues? Had her soldier come at last?

"You mustn't say that, Jean. Not where she can hear."

They are talking about me. She tried to open her eyes. Failed.

"What difference does it make if she hears? Can you imagine . . . ?"

The harsh voice upset the kitten, which shrieked like an angry gull. The noise wrenched her insides. Poor little thing. Someone needed to help it.

"Get him out of here before she sees him. You know the rules."

"But Jean—"

Him? The hush set off gongs in her groggy mind. She'd been in labor. The sound was surely her baby! Wild to see him, she battled heavy eyes.

The crying ceased; she heard nothing but measured breathing. Was it her own breath, or was someone still here? With all her might, she wrestled the fog—until searing pain struck her abdomen and set off a boiling river that spread fire from her groin to her toes. She struggled to draw sticky-wet legs close. Every bend of joints, every stretch of muscles, intensified the heat.

Someone—or something—probed at the fire between her legs. She gasped, moaned, anything to release the pain. Nothing helped.

"Jean? Jean!"

Bells clanged. Something faraway banged. The banging grew louder, louder.

A wasp, two wasps—a dozen maddened wasps pierced her groin, her abdomen.

"Severe postpartum hemorrhage."

"She's almost unresponsive."

"Get two units . . ."

"Stat . . . hand me that scalpel."

"We can't sterilize an eighteen-year-old—"

"Hand it over *now* or you'll have a dead girl."

Voices stung like the wasps. Burned like the fiery river. A thousand chains rattled in her skull. Muted everything. Eerie peace descended, as if her struggle was over, yet the river flowed deeper. Faster. She released exhausted muscles. Closed her eyes. "God, I'm sorry," escaped her lips. Her body sagged. An enemy had won the battle. But who *was* the enemy?

◆

"It's all over, dear." A soft hand smoothed damp hair from her face.

She struggled to sit up, to open her eyes, but failed. Pain radiated from her very core; she inched her fingers toward it. Though every touch brought a grimace, she couldn't stop rubbing her palm against the soft, flabby skin of her belly, which was no longer taut.

Something catastrophic had happened . . . to her belly. What had happened to her *baby?*

Again she fought to sit up, clenching her teeth against the pain.

"Keep still." The voice seemed to come from a cave. "You've had a rough go."

She turned her head, hoping to find someone who could tell her what had happened. The movement birthed such pain, she lay back. Opened her eyes. Stared at the ceiling. No mirror here. Her hand felt damp sheets and not the cold metal table. Memory dawned. She had been in delivery . . . with her baby. Panic froze her limbs. "Where am I?" she cried. "Where's my baby?"

"You're in recovery," answered the voice. "We had to operate."

Memories of bright lights, the patter of steps, strained voices, pushed her upright despite the pain. She had to find her baby. Now.

A woman dressed in the white uniform of a certified nurse hovered nearby.

She swallowed, then doubled over at the raw, throbbing pain in her throat. A fraction of the inferno in her soul. "Where's my baby?" she rasped. Surely her baby had survived. God, surely . . .

"Your baby's in the nursery," came from the woman in white.

My baby's alive! She rubbed prickly skin. Felt something on her right arm. Tried to focus.

A thin plastic bracelet encircled her wrist. She squinted. *S.A. Baby Boy.*

A heavenly humming filled her. *I have a boy! Hallelujah. Oh, Jesus, Jesus loves me . . .* Beloved lyrics salved pain. She swayed back and forth, despite the stabs. "A boy!" she said, with such wonder, she barely recognized her own voice. "My boy. Can I see him?"

"Hey, stop!" Hands gripped her wrists. Forced her to lay back. "You'll rip those stitches and bleed to death."

"Stitches?" The music dimmed. She wiped her eyes until she saw the nurse clearly. "Is he . . . all right?"

"He's fine. Probably blasting out eardrums down the hall." The nurse bustled about, opening blinds, stacking towels. Avoiding her.

Sylvia straightened. Stifled a groan. Tracked the nurse's movements. "Ma'am?" A cough shook her voice but not her resolve. He was her baby. "I want to see him."

"Dear, it's not allowed." The nurse pulled a thermometer from a glass jar and stuck it in Sylvia's mouth. "Besides, you're in no condition to take care of him."

You sound like Mrs. Stanz. But I don't believe it. She fought dry heaves at the thermometer's metallic alcohol taste. Somehow, she *would* take care of . . . Samuel. She would give him the name of the prophet she'd learned about in Sunday school and GAs. How could her son stumble, with that name? A smile pulled at cracked lips. She would give him to God. Though God had forsaken her, He would not forsake a child dedicated to Him at birth. Surely God would help her take care of Samuel. Surely—

"Dear, would you like a drink?" A pitcher beaded with condensation sat on a nightstand. "It's been long enough."

Long enough? "What surgery did I have?"

"Hysterectomy." A solitary diamond on the nurse's ring finger sparkled as she poured water from the pitcher, making Sylvia think of her soldier. "Mandatory. You were bleeding to death." As she handed Sylvia the cup, her flowery perfume anointed the air with the fragrance of life.

Memories roiled up and smothered the sweet smell. Sylvia opened her mouth, but a hovering dark thing—death?—seized her voice. The gamey smell of blood filled her nostrils. So death had been the enemy, had won a partial victory by stopping her ability to have more children. Despite what Sister Carline had done to stop her, Mimi claimed victory as well. God had exacted a price for her sin. But she had claimed a son. Samuel, whom she needed to hold. Now.

"Ma'am?" She leaned forward, as if to grab hold of the nurse. Pain pushed her back into the sheets. "Ma'am?" escaped her throat. "My baby . . . can I see him?"

The nurse's pretty face darkened, as if she too sensed that death had flitted about the room. "I told you, it's not allowed," she said, and then left.

◆ ◆ ◆

What time is it? What day is it? Where is my baby?

A bowl of porridge and a dish of brown, gummy banana slices sat on the bedside table. Sharp pains had dulled into aches . . . except for that knife in her heart. She needed her son. "Please, God," she cried. "If You'll just let me see him, hold him, I'll obey You. I promise."

She ran her tongue over cracked lips. Battled relentless fatigue. Faded. Woke. Slept. Aides, orderlies, RNs, doctors, created a human turnstile through her room. She knew days muted into nights only when incandescent street-lights glowed through slatted blinds. Day brought giggly flirtations between the orderlies, barked orders, gossipy news. Night brought muffled clangs, distant cries. Time melted under the pressure of unanswered questions. Nurses changed dressings, applied salves. But no one answered the one question that consumed her thoughts: Where's my baby? She clenched her teeth until they ached like the rest of her. Whatever she must do or say, she would find him. Somehow.

She eased into sheets that smelled of sweat and her unwashed body. To get him, she had to regain strength. Yet the thought of them being separated tortured her day and night. Her eyes closed. Opened. How could she sleep when the memory of that pitiful cry pulled at her heart?

A knock jolted her from another nap cycle.

"Come in," she managed.

A doctor bustled forward, shadowed by an aide in her blue cap and belted uniform. "Well, well, you're looking better," the doctor said. "Good. Good."

She ran fingers through tangled hair and tried to smile. Hesitantly, she sat up, arched forward, her hand anchored against the small of her back. No pain. She sat up straighter. Soon she could get her son—and herself—out of here.

"Let's take a look." The doctor flipped through her chart, then laid the file on her bed. "We'll have you out of here in no time."

And I'll have my son in no time.

A cold stethoscope pressed against her chest. The doctor narrowed his eyes, as if concentrating. "Hmm," he finally said. "Much better. The lungs are finally clear."

The aide handed him a pen. He scribbled onto her chart. With practiced movements, he checked her eyes and ears, and laid his hands on her abdomen. She gasped at the sudden stab, sharp as the knife piercing her every time she thought of Samuel. She would not heal until she could see him. Hold him.

The doctor gave instructions to the aide, nodded good-bye, and left the room.

"It's time to get you up. After I clean the bathroom." The aide picked up the chart, emulating the others who'd padded in and out of here for—

She clenched her fists. "How long have I been like this?"

The aide glanced at the chart. "Five days."

She gripped her bed rails. She'd lost nearly a week of her baby's life? "When was I admitted?"

The chart rustled open. "January 8."

"So he was born that day?"

"That night."

January. A month for new beginnings . . . with Samuel. "When can I see him?"

The aide's lips tightened. "How many ways do we have to say it?" She picked up a bucket and a mop and made her way to the bathroom. "It's not allowed."

If looks could ignite, the aide would disintegrate into ash. An image of Sheba, who had survived a different conflagration, hardened her jaw and her resolve but softened her approach. "Ma'am?" Sylvia cooed. The aide would like being called ma'am.

The girl whirled about, sloshing water onto the floor. Her eyebrows lifted, as if to say, "What business do you have bothering me?"

Sylvia yawned, then covered her mouth. "I'm really tired," she mumbled as she rolled onto her side. "Could you do that later?"

The aide's eyes brightened. Would she seize a chance for a coffee break? "I don't see why not." She stashed the mop in a corner and sashayed from the room.

Step one had worked. Sylvia eased from bed. Step two? Find the nursery . . . and a blue-eyed boy. "Little boy blue," she whispered. Soon she would gaze into his face! Hold him!

Anticipation gave her the strength to thrust stiff arms into her robe. She looped the belt, surprised at the loose fit. Her body had changed. So would other things. She put on slippers, scuffed to the door. Listened for footfalls.

Silence blanketed the ward.

She opened the door. A glance showed the wing empty. She tiptoed into the hallway like a truant. Her nostrils flared. Imagine, sneaking after her own son! She turned to shut the door.

A blue card hung from a metal clip. Powdery blue, like Cliff's eyes. Her pulse beat a message into her thighs, abdomen, and wrists. She again read the card.

Baby boy. Sylvia Allen. Six pounds, five ounces.

Drums rolled, cymbals crashed, in a heart hungry for music. Soon *Samuel* would replace *baby boy* on the hospital records. And he'd have a middle name—Thomas—after Papa. She imagined Papa's crinkly blue eyes, his tapered fingers tamping a pipe, then setting it aside to take her—and her baby—in his arms. Fantasy, but she needed it now.

A door creaked behind her.

Her hand banged the card, which fluttered to the floor. She whirled, lies on her tongue. She would say the call button was stuck. She had suddenly taken ill—

"Isn't it swell?" A rosy-cheeked girl peeked out of a room across the hall.

Relief flooded her. It was just another mother, radiating joy in her plump cheeks and bright eyes. Sylvia felt her soul blossom after days of blight. She nodded. It *was* swell.

"What did you have?" the girl asked Sylvia.

"A boy." A desire to share her joy bubbled from deep within. "Samuel."

"That's a nice name." The girl pulled her door shut. Stepped near.

Sylvia swelled with pride. Samuel *was* a lovely name. "How about you?" she asked, her gaze shifting to pink roses hanging from the girl's door. If things had been different—if *she'd* been different—she'd have blue ribbons announcing the news to everyone who walked by.

"Sophie. She's perfect." The girl rubbed her eyes, as if she couldn't believe the miracle of it all. Sylvia needed to see that miracle, touch that miracle.

The girl's door opened. A man stepped out and wrapped his arms about the girl. The doorway framed the couple and made a lovely Impressionist painting. *The way I wish life could be.*

Sylvia thought of her soldier, tall and handsome in his uniform. Oh, to share this with one who cared!

The couple kissed and then the man peered down the hall. "Where's our girl?" he asked.

"Honey, she's down there. In the nursery."

"Well, what are we waitin' for? Let's go see her!"

The girl grabbed her pink card and, with her husband's help, ambled, along with their giggles and hugs, down the hall. The couple's intimacy gnawed at her joy. How she yearned for the comfort of Cliff's arms. Perhaps one day. She closed her eyes. Floated on sand-castle images.

Fading giggles dissolved Sylvia's daydream and snapped open her eyes. Pink petals drifted to the floor, a reminder of the family celebration in room 441. A celebration Room 442 would not have. Reality was a door with no ribbons. No flowers. Reality was a baby and no husband.

She tightened trembling lips. Focused on the task ahead. She would lavish the love of two people on Samuel. She bent over gingerly. Retrieved the card that had fallen. *If a card can get her baby, it can get mine.*

Unused to being on her feet, she wobbled, yet clutched the blue ticket that would redeem her Samuel. Did he really have the soldier's eyes? Would his chin jut out, Alexander-style?

Clunks and rattles announced an orderly before he appeared, pushing a meal cart.

Sylvia froze and then tried to walk naturally. Why act skittish? She'd done nothing wrong. In fact, she was doing right. Samuel needed his mother. Now.

◆ ◆ ◆

"Isn't she adorable?"

"Ooh, look!" Gurgles swelled into a bubbling brook of voices. Laughter, chuckles, togetherness, happiness. *Happiness not meant for me, until I find him.*

A cast-out feeling slowed Sylvia at the bend in the hall. Dared she turn the corner, join the chorus? She imagined her son's downy skin. *Yes.* She surged ahead, her heart pounding its desperation. She had to see him, hold him, and tell him his name.

New mommies and daddies clogged the hall. Proper people. She swallowed. Kept her distance. Would Samuel, though an infant, intuit her sin?

"She smiled, I just know she did!"

"Now, Martha . . ."

Mothers wore bathrobes or hospital gowns. Fathers wore wrinkled shirts and trousers. Older women—new grandmothers?—wore matronly suits. They all huddled around a nursery window, cooing like birds. One gray-haired woman tapped the glass, then drew back when a nursery attendant raised a finger to her lips.

Sylvia glued her eyes to the window.

Lights illuminated cribs of swathed babies. Clenched fists nestled on flannel blankets. Knit caps framed red faces. Sylvia leaned close, her breath condensing on the window. Mere glass separated her from a world of life and light and love, streaming from those precious bundles. She narrowed her gaze to find blue caps, one of which surely covered Samuel's little head.

Nurses handled the babies as if oblivious to the adoring throng. One pinned a tiny diaper onto a squirming body. Another rocked a swaddled form. One strode from crib to crib, monitoring her charges. Sylvia dared not blink and miss one second of glory. Oh, to be in such a place!

"Dot! Where's our little doll?" An older woman flung a chubby arm around a younger version of herself.

"Don't know, Mum, but we'll find her." Dot dug into her robe pocket, pulled out a pink card, held it up to the window.

So that's it. Sylvia fumbled for her card. Quickly, lest her heart explode.

A nurse wheeled one crib from a drum line of infant beds until it fronted the window. Sylvia's forehead touched the warm plate glass. She would see him. Soon!

The nurse pulled a swathed bundle from the crib and held it up as if for display. A bundle wearing a pink hat. Not hers. Still, she feasted on a button nose. A cherry chin.

"Look!" Dot's mother clutched Dot's arm. "She's got your eyes!"

Sylvia bobbed glances at the baby, then the mother, seeing no resemblance at all, yet she couldn't help but smile. Samuel might look like Papa, or Maman. She found her card. Waved it at the nurse. Perhaps Samuel would be the one to play the clarinet. She envisioned piano duets, impromptu concerts.

The nurse tapped on the window. Mouthed words Sylvia could not understand.

Chattering and cooing ceased. Eyes fell on Sylvia, who stepped back but locked her gaze on the nurse's white cap. That nurse was the gatekeeper. Sylvia would get in. Or get him out.

The gatekeeper moved to the door. Opened it. Light from the room haloed auburn hair as she stood under the threshold of the heavenly world that held Samuel.

"Nurse. Can I just hold her for—?"

"Nurse? Nurse! We'll just be a minute."

Women babbled. Shrieked. Flapped their hands. And Sylvia was one of them.

"Time's up!" The gatekeeper raised her palm. "We'll bring them around at noon. After their feedings. Then there's the evening viewing . . ."

A collective moan rose from the hall.

Sylvia raised her hand. She had to see him. Now. "What about my baby?" Words surged from a molten lava core to scald her mouth. She didn't care.

"Your card?" The nurse's gaze tried to burn a hole in her. So what? She was already on fire.

She held out the crumpled blue paper—"damaged goods," like her. That didn't matter. "I want to see *my* baby." Her voice cracked from pent-up emotion. "My *boy*."

The nurse's pencil-thin eyebrows shot up. "It's not allowed."

"Why?"

"It's your . . . circumstances. We don't allow it."

Her jaw clenched. Not allowed? "Give him to me!" she screamed as she lunged forward and grabbed the edge of the door. "He's my baby! Mine, you hear?"

Lamb mewls seeped through the crack. Her hands became claws. Was that Samuel? What did he need? Had someone hurt him? She froze. Strained to hear.

The nurse shoved her away, slammed the door, shut out the glorious, awful music.

Slam. It reverberated through her. Rent her in two. Empowered her more than any hate—or love—ever had. She grabbed the doorknob. Twisted until her knuckles burned.

It didn't budge.

How dared they lock her out? She dug her fingers into the door. Chipped white paint from wood. "He's mine!" Her cry echoed down the hall and shivered a body feverish with rage. "You've no right. No right at all." She knotted her hands. Pounded the door.

Murmurs rose like steam. Feet clopped, skittered, scuffed, faded, and left her without a baby. Without a husband. And where was God?

She pounded more, needing to keep the lava boiling through her. She flew to the window, rested her forehead against the glass as before to see the display, but the cribs had been moved against a far wall. Though she craned her neck to find a blue cap, she saw nothing but blurs. Ice-cold silence grabbed hold. Chilled the fire raging inside her. To fan it, she banged the windows. Heard a yelp rise from her throat. They had to let her see him, or she'd go mad!

A nurse approached the window. Her eyes were crinkled with age. Wisps of white hair softened a shrunken face. A face that had felt pain. Known grief. Someone who'd perhaps raised a little one, perhaps lost him in the Great War.

Sylvia flailed her arms and then cupped her hands to her mouth. "Please," she begged, "let me see him. Hold him . . ."

Blinds tumbled over the glass.

An icy river rose from the floor and numbed her feet and legs. Cold seeped into her jaw and her eyes. Tears froze. She brought a stiff hand to her mouth. Bit her nails. Moved her hand to a swollen but useless breast. Stared up at white ceiling tiles. Ground her teeth together. She hated all of them. *But not as much as they hated her.*

The knowledge propelled her away from the heavenly nursery gates . . . or were they hellish, since they would not admit her? Trying to ignore the blur of pink and blue ribbons, she staggered down the hall. She would die without him, but not here, where the nasty gatekeeper, the nasty white walls, would see. An eternity passed before she came to the bare white door of room 442.

She wrenched it open. Squeezed out the memory of white, cold blinds, tumbling to shut out her light. Her life. Rage festered as she plopped onto her bed. "Take me now, God," she shouted, not caring how many happy couples she disturbed. "End it. I dare You."

White-cold silence filled every corner of the room. Sylvia dug her fingers into her pillow, waiting. God, as usual, did not answer. The white-hot anger trickled away, leaving her alone, with regret and despair.

"My baby," she cried as she huddled under her blanket. Her teeth chattered. Her legs shivered. "My baby," she sobbed, until hoarseness captured her voice. Then tears moved in, helpful tears. She handed the reins to them and let them flow from her eyes, her nose, her mouth, until darkness came and shut everything out.

Chapter 26

Something to Live For

They said she'd been here seven days. It seemed more like seven years. She completed her toilette, checked herself in the mirror. Sorrow curtained her eyes. If Samuel was given to another family, her view would forever remain cloudy and gray.

"Miss Allen?" The morning shift nurse walked into the bathroom.

"Yes, ma'am?" She adjusted her collar and tried to smile.

"Doc said we could discharge you." She thrust a clipboard at Sylvia. "If you'll sign this, we'll get that baby."

The words scalded her face. *That baby? Does she mean my son?* She stepped back. Her skirt grazed a towel rack. She slumped, letting it support her. Seven days, and she could finally see him. She seized the clipboard, the pen. Scanned the release agreement. Found the dotted line. *Sign,* her brain screamed. The pen scratched the paper, tore a hole, and wrote nothing. She shook it, hoping to ink the nib. *Hurry! They may change their minds!* Again she put pen to paper and had a crazy notion to write her real name, but then they wouldn't let her have him. She'd sign. It was her first step to getting . . . and keeping . . . Samuel.

"Hurry, now. The cabbie is waiting. The nuns will be waiting, too."

She, who had waited nine months to touch him, needed to hear of waiting? She snatched up a skirt pleat. Wiped the clogged nib across coarse gray wool. Ink pooled on the fabric and bled into its fibers. She didn't care. She'd ruin a thousand skirts to hold him for one second. Ink flowed. She signed as Sylvia, the name they'd given her. Pen again met paper. *Samuel's mother* she printed, as if that could convince them that she loved him, that she wanted him. Then she thrust the clipboard toward the nurse with such force, the woman drew back in surprise.

"I've done what you want." Sylvia crossed her arms. "Now bring me my son."

◆ ◆ ◆

"Samuel," she kept whispering. She placed a steadying hand on the cold vinyl seat as she climbed in, clutching the precious bundle. Her heart beat a crazy, original solo. *My son. My baby.*

Blue eyes captured her gaze. She sank into the most mysterious, most glorious wells of color and depth. "Little boy blue," she whispered. A perfect nickname for a baby.

She focused on squeaks and grunts purer than notes drawn across the strings of a Stradivarius. She cradled his body and let his breath puffs warm her skin. She had never imagined such bliss!

Her hand held the downy head, so perfectly round, crowned with fuzzy dark curls. When he shivered, she arranged the flannel receiving blanket around his ears.

"Ma'am."

She sat up straight, adjusted her blouse, her coat, her scarf. This was her time, his time . . . perhaps their only time. "Could you wait, sir?" A sob caught in her throat. "Just for a while?"

"Ma'am," repeated the cabbie. "We need to be getting on, ma'am. They ain't gonna pay no surcharge."

Her gaze traveled to gnarled hands gripping the steering wheel, then honed in on the rearview mirror, which framed eyes too bloodshot to tell their color. Did they know enough of life to offer a tincture of mercy? Had they experienced enough love to grant a mother's desperate plea?

"Mister," Sylvia began. A sob escaped. "Mister?" She clutched Samuel tighter, as if that would somehow help convince him of her plight.

The cabbie's eyes softened . . . and infused her with the energy to continue.

"Could you drive really, really slowly?" She took a ragged breath. "You see . . . I have this one ride . . . to give my son . . . a lifetime of love."

◆ ◆ ◆

"Did they let you feed him?"

"Does he look like you or his daddy?"

The bed groaned from the weight of five pregnant girls. *And their constant questions.* Sylvia longed to burrow under her covers to avoid them—and the memory of Samuel's wail when the Home's nursery worker had taken him from her. That memory had chilled her soul for two nights and morphed into imaginary wails that squeezed under the nursery doors, slid down the halls, crawled upstairs, and seeped into her room. Of course the solid walls of this old building soundproofed the dorm from any first floor nursery noises. For all she knew, her Samuel was crying, and they wouldn't let her comfort him. Wouldn't let her see him. Imagine, not being able to see her very own baby!

Milk flowed from her nipples, milk Samuel should have. Tender breasts throbbed pain. This was so unnatural! So wrong!

"What does he look like?"

"Did you give him a name?" Wide-eyed girls begged to find hope in her answers, to make sense of things.

She wouldn't tell what awaited them at the hospital. Girls with fragile spirits needed something to cling to. Like a baby. "He's got chubby arms and legs, the bluest eyes . . ." *And dark skin.* "I named him Samuel." She squeezed the words past a throat tight from recalling those nurses' nasty comments.

"Was that the father's name?" Carla glowed, perhaps envisioning her strapping young farmer—the one who deserted her. Sylvia shoved away an image of Cliff. Why did men love so much, leave so fast?

"No, it's not his father's name," she snapped, then longed to soften the nasty tone. Sweet Carla, who never said a harsh word, would soon pay an awful price for her sin. She scooted close to let her shoulder graze Carla's. "I like the name Samuel. It's in the Bible."

"The Bible?" Carla flopped back, her elbow digging into Sylvia's still-sore belly. "Why in the world did you name him after someone in the *Bible?*"

To appease a God furious with my sin. To dedicate my son to a life of purity, hoping he will avoid my mistake. She rubbed sweaty palms, not wanting to be the dorm's laughingstock. "Because I like the way it sounds," she finally managed, hoping God wouldn't strike her dead for lying.

◆ ◆ ◆

"Psst! Sylvia!" Someone clapped her on the shoulder. "Get up!"

Her head bobbed to attention. Hazy objects materialized into pews and prayer books and created a yearning nothing could fill, except Samuel. While waiting for procession, flickering altar candles had lulled her to sleep and into a daydream of the old times, when chapel meant a chance to rub her belly, to hum to him, to love him. Now he was in the nursery; she was here. And the Latin mass Father intoned was just a stupid dead language.

"Didn't mean to startle you, dear." Aggie's breath tickled her ear. "Sister Carline and I need to see you after chapel."

She labored to nod. Three sleepless nights, two doctor visits, and the time had arrived. A final sign-off meeting, if what she'd heard was true, and she'd stand before the gates of living hell: life without Samuel. Unless she could convince them otherwise.

Tears blurred the chapel into gold and red and brown. She slid to the floor, rested her knees on the prayer bench, and gripped the smooth leather surface. "Please, Lord, don't let them take him away from me," she prayed. She tensed her muscles to trap the words inside. "Please." She begged with every ounce of strength. "I'll do whatever You want. Just let me keep him."

"Sylvia." It was Aggie, more insistent now. "We need to talk. Now."

She stumbled to her feet and exited the chapel with the other girls, who veered to the stairs and thumped to their rooms. She would give anything to go with them and avoid this final meeting.

Sister tried to link arms with her, but she let her arm hang limp in passive resistance. They walked past the nursery, toward the office. Short of shoving Aggie away, bursting into the nursery, and grabbing her son, what could she do? Three restless nights had led to the same answer. She had nowhere to take him, nothing to give him. Except herself. It was enough for her. Not enough for the nuns. She had no answer to the question that terrorized her, day and night: *Was it enough for Samuel?*

They entered the office. Sister Carline and Mrs. Stanz sat. Waiting.

Sylvia beelined to the chair where she had sat that first day, when Sister Carline had consoled her, but it offered no solace, for Mrs. Stanz's presence cannibalized the peace. She'd never liked Mrs. Stanz. Now she hated her.

"Hello, Sylvia." Mrs. Stanz sat near the window in a satiny green wingback. Satisfaction added a triumphant sheen to her rouged face.

Sylvia wedged her hands between her knees to keep them from shaking. Again she considered bolting with Samuel, then discarded the idea when her mind's stuck record played: Nowhere to go. No way to feed him.

Sister Carline motioned Agnes into a chair. Sylvia kneaded her knuckles in desperation. Oh, that Aggie would be an ally in the war to keep her son!

"We know why we are here." Out came Sister Carline's pince-nez. She took a file from Mrs. Stanz—the file surely outlining Sylvia's unfitness as a mother—and flipped it open.

Every rustle of paper stabbed Sylvia. To survive, she imagined downy skin, tiny lips. But her breasts swelled and throbbed in a mysterious mix of ecstasy and pain and forced her to her feet. She would do something. Say something. Now. "You may know why we're here, but I don't." She strode to Sister Carline's desk. Slapped her palm on the folder. "You have reduced my son and me to scribbles. That is all you care about."

Sister Carline's face turned white, except for circles of pink. She fixed blazing eyes on Sylvia, whose hands became slick with sweat. *What do they see? Rebellion? Selfishness, as Mrs. Stanz insists?* "I mean, no one's really explained it to me," she stammered.

"You must be out of your mind!" Exasperation laced Mrs. Stanz's high-pitched voice. "I clocked in ten sessions telling you how it is out there."

"It doesn't have to be this way." Sylvia whirled toward her. Why couldn't they understand? "He's my son, don't you see? When I held him in that cab and he looked at me"—her hands moved to her bosom as she imagined his dewy smell—"I could tell he loves me, too. That he needs me. I'm his mother. The only one he'll ever have."

A harrumph came from the chair near the window. "How many times do we have to go over this? A girl in *your* . . . position can't give him anything. That, combined with his . . . features, would severely limit his ability to be something in this world."

"I don't care about his dark skin! He's beautiful." Her teeth ground together from the urgency of her words. "And he's mine."

Mrs. Stanz hissed, "How could you have relations with a Negro?"

"My son's father wasn't a Negro. His skin's as white as yours."

Now purple-faced, Mrs. Stanz gulped air. Worked her mouth. For once, no words emerged. Sylvia fought an urge to mirror the same smirk she'd endured from Mrs. Stanz.

Sister Carline's ancient eyes flashed. She waved her arm.

"Sit," she demanded. "Now."

The holy indignation of the Home director dimmed Sylvia's resolve. She rubbed her hands, hoping to reignite a fire that would enable her to fight them. Another glare from Sister Carline slumped Sylvia back into her chair. Sister had always been, always would be, in charge.

"Since the father is not involved, nothing is gained from talk of his heritage. The child is a different matter. He has been baptized into the Holy Catholic Church."

The words rekindled Sylvia's flame. So God and the church had accepted her baby in spite of her sin. Another fire sparked. Why couldn't *she* have witnessed his baptism? After all, she'd dedicated him to God by naming him Samuel. She gripped chair arms until her fingers ached and locked her gaze on Sister Carline. Could they not offer more than a document? A speech? She—and Samuel—craved love. Compassion. Forgiveness. They could live here. Together.

"As his spiritual guardians," Sister continued, the file in her hand now, "we feel it best that he be permanently placed in an institution run by the Diocese of St. Paul."

Her heart stood still and then raced to rescue her—rescue him. "You mean an orphanage?" She conjured up the raggedy clothes, the sooty face of Oliver Twist. How could a place like that do better than she could? She was his mother!

A cry came from Sister Aggie. She turned to Sylvia, reached over and grasped her hands. "Have you not felt our love here, child? It will be the same for your precious Samuel!" Tears glittered Aggie's eyes. "He will be raised in the ways of the church, in the name of the Father and the Son and the Holy Ghost." She let go of Sylvia, crossed herself.

"You see, it's the best thing." Mrs. Stanz leaned back, her arms stacked like logs in a woodpile, so sure, so solid. So lacking in love, Sylvia ached to slap her.

"Don't doubt for an instant that we will care for him." It was Sister Carline now, each taking their turn to slay her under the guise of "what is best for your child." How could they be so sure what was best when she, *the mother of that child*, was not?

Ever so slowly, a paper edged toward her until it was close enough for her to read.

Termination of Parental Rights

I, the undersigned _____, have hereby abandoned my child to the church.

Sylvia's field of vision darkened until all she saw was the word *abandoned*. The black letters wrapped around her throat and squeezed. She leapt to her feet, snatched up the horrid sheet, flung it at Sister. "I am *not* abandoning him," she shouted. "You are *taking* him! I want him. I . . ." The room whirled, faster, faster. Her knees buckled. Her voice weakened to moans, then sobs. Her eyes closed, only to let a wild abstract of images invade. Leaping flames. A screaming infant. Empty hands.

"Now, now, dear." Sister Aggie managed to seat her, then knelt by her and stroked her hair. "It'll be okay. I'm here. I won't let anything happen to either of you."

Loving caresses and the silky words loosed the stranglehold about her neck. She noted Aggie's tear-filled eyes. The burden of sleepless nights, restless days, dimmed the flame that had enabled her to resist them. She was barely out of high school, in spite of all that had happened. The sisters were women of God. Wise. Holy.

Talking ceased. The heat register droned to fill the void. Aggie dangled a handkerchief. Urged Sylvia to take it. Her every cell pleaded exhaustion. Surrender. Her head ducked. A dark fog floated, dense enough to mute memories of his cries, his face . . .

"Let's get this done so both of you can move forward," Aggie said. "We have a plan for you, Sylvia." Again the paper inched toward her. This time there was a pen.

Sniffing back sobs, she read each word. Oh, for one minute with Mimi's lawyer, who understood the emotion behind words! But an esteemed Southern gentleman would never side with an unwed mother against the Catholic Church. She raised her head until her gaze fell on Sister Carline's rosary. Would Samuel be safe with those who had dedicated their lives to God's service, just as she had dedicated him to God? Would they keep him pure? Holy?

The heater blasted. Threatened to suffocate. Mrs. Stanz sighed.

Sweat dripped from Sylvia's brow, mingled with her tears, and pooled on the paper. Her fist opened. Closed. Like her, incapacitated by the horrific predicament.

"Sylvia, dear . . ." It was Sister Carline, her voice a mother's gentle chide.

She picked up the pen. Flicked her gaze to the first paragraph.

Abandoned my child. Abandoned my child.

"I won't sign it." The words came out dull and hollow. "Not like that." She pointed to the awful words.

"Are you off your rocker?"

"Now, Jane . . ."

"Well, I never heard of giving a hussy like this her say." Mrs. Stanz's face puckered into a dried prune. "We have provided room and board, medical care—"

"Sylvia, what is it that upsets you? Show us." Aggie stood, as did Sister Carline, and moved to Sylvia's side. The two nuns, one heavyset, one slender, bowed their heads, clasped their hands, as if beseeching God Himself to intervene. Furrowed brows, glistening eyes, spoke of their love for her, and that was the awful conflict. They loved her but could not abide her sin. Like God. Deep sobs racked her body; she did not try to squelch them. She had to surrender to good. To God.

"Dear, whatever is wrong? Show us." Sister Carline repeated Aggie's words. "We will do something about it."

They would? Sylvia felt her eyes widen. She struggled to say the right thing, but nothing came out. All she could do was point at the paper.

"It is a legal document, dear, nothing less, nothing more," Sister Carline said.

Of course they didn't understand. But then no one had, at least for a long time.

"I don't like it, either," Aggie finally said, flint in her tone.

Sylvia stiffened. Now she had an ally against that horrid word? She rose. "You don't?"

"What on earth has gotten into you?" Mrs. Stanz started toward the desk. Then she froze, as if unsure where she should stand.

"I do not blame you, Sylvia. Not one bit. But if we modify it . . ."

Mrs. Stanz's gasps broke Aggie's usual melodic pace.

". . . you have made a record for all posterity." She fanned her hands, her voice fluttery and poetic. "Your words will attest to how you really feel."

Sylvia sank back into her chair. Sweat glued her dress to the seat. If she did this Aggie's way, her true feelings would be preserved. She would compromise control of her child for the wording on a document. The paper fluttered in her trembling hands as she reread the heinous phrase "abandoned my child." Hateful words. She pursed her lips. Gripped the pen. She had to change it so they would know how this adoption had robbed her body of its lifeblood. Of love.

"Change it," Aggie encouraged. "Make it say what you want."

"Just so you sign it," came the awful raspy voice.

She tasted bile, longed to spit it at Mrs. Stanz. Instead she raised her head, let her gaze rest on three shiny faces. *They're as nervous as me, maybe even more so.* She unscrewed the pen cap, bent over.

Abandoned my child to . . .

Her teeth clenched. She gripped the pen and blacked out the nasty words. The heat register roared as she begged the right phrase to come. She opened her mind. Her heart. Began printing carefully.

I lovingly entrust my child to the church, the nuns, and to God.

Her achy eyes roved the page, found the blank line, and signed her name. As she dated it, the idea seized her to write Sheba and Sheila next to Sylvia. Before she could do so, the pen, the paper, and the pad were whipped away, leaving her alone with three women and the memory of her one pitiful acknowledgment of the most beautiful baby in the world. *Perhaps, if God wills it, Samuel will one day find this paper. And know how much I love him.*

◆

Samuel rose from the couch, sweating in the unusually sultry island night. He swabbed his forehead. It wasn't Hawaiian heat that had him worked up. It was the truth. He'd wanted to hate her; now he loved her. Should he tell her that he'd never gotten to see what she'd written? Of course not . . . unless she asked. Maybe not then.

"I'm sorry," she whispered as he opened the door, took a deep breath, stared outside. "I wish I would've—could've given you more."

Honolulu city lights winked to entice with cozy bars, all-night cafés. He turned his back on the view. "You gave me all you could then. I told you what the Bible meant to me. And you're giving me as much as you can now."

She shivered, as if his words overwhelmed her. "I did my best, Son. Then. And I'll do my best now as well."

He brought her a glass of water, sat next to her, watched as she drank, and then listened as she continued her story.

Chapter 27

Symphony No. 2, Adagio

Snow. More snow. Enough to smother the world. Through the basement window, Sylvia watched black boots sink into snow and then emerge. Boots just like these had taken Samuel two days ago. Despite the girls' gum smacking and laughter and a competitive rubber of bridge, cold seeped into Sylvia and threatened to freeze her to death.

"Sylv, it's your play. Sylv?"

Sylvia fanned her cards but saw a beautiful baby instead of jacks and queens and kings. What had her partner bid?

"Come on, now. It's one heart, pass, one spade. What's got ahold of you?"

Only Carla remained silent, chewing on gum. With her delivery date near, reality was surely smothering her.

"One heart, pass, *one spade!* Jeepers, Sylv, are you a dope?"

Cards slipped from Sylvia's hands. Scattered over the table. "I pass." She nodded at newcomer Sadie, who had only been allowed to kibitz. Until now. "Hey, Sadie," she snapped. "It's all yours. I'm done."

"What's with her?"

Sylvia fled the smoking room. Her sanity dangled by the slenderest thread. She had to get away from those who hadn't yet experienced giving up their baby.

"Sylvia, wait."

The familiar swish of Aggie's habit got louder.

Sylvia paused to catch her breath and steeled herself to face Aggie. Since she'd signed that paper, a veil other than the one Sister wore separated them.

"We must talk." Urgency swelled the voice that had encouraged, soothed, loved . . . then coaxed her to give away her baby.

"Yes?" Out of respect, Sylvia slowed, turned, waited.

"I need to talk to you. In private." Sister fumbled through the folds of her fabric and withdrew a key. After glances down the hall, she unlocked a linen room, stepped inside. Sylvia followed.

The smell of soap, mothballs, and bleach slammed Sylvia with memories of sterile white walls, an empty hospital bed. She cupped her hand over her nose, sure of one thing: this meeting would birth change.

Sister stood near metal shelves stacked high with blankets and sheets. *More sterile and cold white. Everywhere. Smothering me with its purity.*

"Sit down, Sylvia." Sister pointed to a metal chair.

Sylvia complied. What choice did she have?

Sister knelt by her side. Half-moons darkened the skin under her eyes. Sylvia shivered. If the change had upset Sister, surely it was bad.

"It's all settled. Just as we'd hoped." Her habit rustled as Sister handed over a letter.

As they'd hoped? A good change? "What has been settled?" Were these the special plans the sisters had for her? A job? Assignment? Hard work, a purpose, surely would melt the loneliness that had made her sluggish, disinterested; barely alive.

"You will leave here. Immediately. And don't tell anyone where you are going."

The words hovered like mist. Leave? Where would she go? Not back to Mimi's! When she clutched Aggie's sleeve, the letter fluttered unopened to the floor. "Don't make me. Please!" With prayers and rosaries, the nuns could keep her pure. Here she would be safe. She could change. Change was hard. Change took time.

"This is difficult for me as well." Spidery lines webbed Aggie's mouth. "We have prayed long and hard for you." She plucked the letter off the floor, thrust it at Sylvia. "We believe it is God's will that you start anew."

God's will: the words Mimi had said when she sent her away. "How do y'all know God's will?" Bitterness laced her words.

Aggie pointed to the letter. "Open it. There's a train ticket, directions to a woman's house. And not just any woman. A woman of God."

"A nun?"

Tinkling laughter rose from Aggie. "Nuns aren't the only women of God. There's money for a cab and food. Until you meet Miz W, that is. She will help you find a job, provide you a place to live." A steady gaze worked to assure her. "God will be there, Sylvia."

"Where? Where am I going?"

"The Windy City. Chicago. What they're calling the new city of jazz."

Sylvia struggled to focus on the cursive letterhead of the Catholic Home. Chicago? A new place . . . a huge place. *Whatever are they doing to me?*

"This is best for you, Sylvia. We are convinced of it."

Sweat from Sylvia's palms dampened the envelope. She dropped it in her lap. Again, others deciding what was best for her. Again she had no choice. But could it hurt to leave this place where she'd signed her baby over to the church? Could it hurt to shed everything she had kept here? Even the shawl that she'd wrapped around herself on sleepless nights—Carla had admired it. She could leave it for Carla. For the first time since the drugstore debacle, Sylvia envisioned walking out of the Home and starting anew. She picked up the envelope. Peeked inside. Saw a wad of bills. "I can't take this from y'all. Besides, didn't you take a vow of poverty? I mean . . ." She stammered, her face hot from embarrassment. What a nosy question! Where Sister got her money was no business of hers!

"It is true that I am poor in material possessions." Aggie's face took on a solemn cast. "But my brother does not have the same problem."

"You asked him to give you money?"

Aggie edged toward the door. "We have a complicated relationship. But he loves me and thinks his dollars give me a better life." Her eyes misted. "A better life. Ironically, that is the same thing God—and I—want for him."

"But I have no means to pay you back. No means of support, no kin to help. I—"

"We are your family, Sylvia. It is what we are meant to do."

Sylvia stared at her future, neatly contained in a soggy white envelope. Again, family was sending her away. But this felt different. She bowed her head. *Dear Lord, let this be different!*

"It's all settled. No one knows except us nuns. And Miz W, whom Sister Carline befriended years ago. It would be best if you kept it quiet, Sylvia. We cannot arrange things for every girl. Sylvia?"

As if through a fog, she heard Sister's melodic voice. With effort, Sylvia raised her head. Nodded.

Sister tiptoed to the door, signaled for Sylvia to follow. "I'll call a cab in the morning. Tonight you can pack up everything. Including the name Sylvia." She smiled past tearstained eyes. "You're free to be Sheila again. Or Sheba, if you'd like. If I remember, that was your given name."

Her throat constricted. Sheila? Sheila hadn't had—and lost—a baby. And Sheba had disappeared years ago. Could she shed a name that reminded her of so much pain, so much love? A dizzying image of Samuel's eyes collapsed her against a wall. It did not matter what her name was, so long as her heart sang his memory. She blinked. His memory . . . Perhaps there would be a way for him to know how she loved him, to know what she hoped for him. Samuel, one dedicated to God, deserved to know. She stepped toward Aggie. Clutched the letter. "Could you do one thing for me? One last thing?"

Aggie's eyebrows raised. The question flitted about the white room.

"What is it?" Aggie finally asked.

"Would you see that he gets my Bible?" She rushed forward, gripped Aggie's wrist. "Please, Aggie. Please. It's the only thing left I have to offer him. Except my prayers."

◆

Sleep, dear God. Let me go back to sleep. She did, and then roused enough to peek out the window at a glistening winter white landscape, as she'd done every time a raucous passenger or chatty porter had jolted her from painless slumber. *In my sleep, I can pretend I kept him. Then I wake up, and it's all a dream. A lie.*

Along the track, snowdrifts smothered all but fence posts and muffled every noise save train wheels pummeling straight, sure tracks. Her breath puffed to blur the window view and provide a perfect backdrop for that image to reappear . . .

Little Samuel's cocoa skin, blue eyes. Despite her thick wool coat, wool socks, and the well-heated coach car, she shivered.

She'd tried to escape with the *Chicago Tribune*, which an efficient porter had laid in her lap. She'd scanned front-page news of tensions over a Russian-Korean alliance, then flipped to the Local section. *Suspected Mob Hit Found in River* sent her reeling to the comics, which she'd always read to Camille. Their favorite, Prince Valiant, was nowhere to be found. She'd refolded the paper and set it aside. Nothing erased Samuel's image. Nothing at all.

She twisted in her seat until her back had turned to that dreadful frozen landscape. Even with her hands knotted, her eyes squeezed shut, she saw his perfect little face. "God, please," she whispered, "let me sleep. Sleep." *And dream of holding him again.*

A mournful whistle answered, as if the train knew her pain and responded in its own ironsides way. *Clickety clack, clickety clack.* The train's lullaby conquered her thoughts. *Clickety clack.* Her eyes drooped and closed.

◆ ◆ ◆

Something—someone—shook her shoulder. She startled to an upright position and stared into the soft eyes of a porter.

"Lil' miss, you 'bout the only one left." A starched jacket sleeve brushed against her cheek. "And yo' people done waitin' out dere."

"My people?" A lone widow wouldn't constitute "her people." Who stood out there in the Chicago cold, waiting for her?

"Sho' nuff. They been axing 'bout you, pesterin' de daylights outta everyone."

She grabbed her small bag, dug past a tube of lipstick, found the letter holding her future. Jittery hands unfolded the paper. Reread it for an umpteenth time.

Upon your arrival, Winnie Hildebrand will meet you at the check-in counter for the Short Line. If she stands on her tiptoes, she might reach your shoulder! May the Lord—

The porter grabbed her trunk and last bag. "You'se things be waiting right out dere." He pointed out her window. "By you'se folks."

Humming a jazzy tune, he headed down the aisle, leaving her with shaky hands and a sinking sensation. Apparently meeting at the Short Line counter was off. What if she peeked out the window at a snarling old bulldog of a woman who would rip her and her sinful ways to bits?

She stepped aside to allow an elderly lady with a sable hat and coat to pass by. The woman soon disappeared toward the exit but left the unmistakable scent of roses. The dreadful garden scene rolled in, so strong, she longed to cover her ears to shut out Mimi's *snip* of the vulnerable stems. Breathing hard, she set down her bag, pulled out her compact, dusted shiny cheeks, applied lipstick, and worked up the nerve to glance out the window. Miz W could not be as bad as Mimi. Her arms tingling with a strange mix of dread and anticipation, she hurried to the exit.

Three girls waved like they'd spotted a long-lost sister. Wool caps topped their heads; coats and scarves wrapped their bodies. "Welcome to Moody," they announced, with singsong voices. "We're the Three Musketeers!"

Three Musketeers? She hesitated to step off the train, sure they awaited another, and glanced around, then was drawn back to toothy smiles. Innocent, nice girls. Unsoiled.

"Hi, Sheila!" They bobbed up and down. The tallest girl beckoned with a gloved hand.

"Get on down, little miss," boomed the porter. "We got a dozen cars to clean 'fore the sun go down. 'Sides, it's five below out dere. You lettin' in cold air."

Cold. Cold. Always cold.

"Sheila! C'mon!"

With a last glance at the unfamiliar trio, backdropped by the cavernous depot she remembered from before, she grabbed her satchel, her purse, and stepped off the train.

Men carrying briefcases streamed past. One bumped into her, tipped his hat, and broke into a run. Others dashed and darted like maddened ants. Her pulse hammered. It sure wasn't lonely here in the daytime.

"Hey, Sheila!" A petite blonde wearing a green woolen coat stepped forward and gripped her hand. "I'm Margaret," she boomed over the crackling loud-speaker, the roaring engines, the occasional whistle, the passengers' cries. "This is Mildred."

"For goodness' sakes, Megs." Mildred scrunched up a freckled pug nose. "Call me Millie. *Puh-lease.*" She gave Sheila an easy grin. "That's Miriam."

A dark-haired girl pushed owlish glasses against her nose as she nodded.

"N-nice to meet you," stammered Sheila. Aggie had said nothing about teen-aged girls. "But I thought Mrs. Watson was—"

"Mrs. Watson? She'll tan your hide if you call her that."

"Yeah, Sheila. Get that straight right now. It's Miz W."

"She asked us to meet ya."

"Miz W gets what Miz W wants."

"Are you her daughters?"

The girls poked each other, then threw back their heads and roared.

"You might say so. We're part of the Moody family."

"Moody? What's Moody?"

"Moody Bible Institute. Our school. Where Miz W works. You will, too, if she has her way. Miz W gets what Miz W wants."

Cold seeped into Sheila. Miz W sounded an awful lot like Mimi.

◆

"Sure you don't want a soda?" asked Millie.

A malted milk machine whirred. A chrome counter gleamed. The Sweet Shop's soda jerks and garish wallpaper sparked Quarter drugstore memories. But tabletop Bibles, men dressed in suits, their heads bowed in prayer, testified to a different kind of joint.

"Another burger? More fries?"

As they cajoled Sheila into stuffing herself, a cheerful waitress refilled glasses, dazzled her with smiles. Everyone smiled. That would change if they discovered her past. "No, thanks," she managed.

"Miz W will have our hides if we don't treat ya right."

"You've treated me to so much." She patted her belly. "I was starved." She bit her lip, shocked she'd said that. The attention of these kind young ladies had loosed her vow to have perfect manners and reveal nothing of herself. On the train, she'd envisioned several scenarios, but none had included chatting with Bible students as if they were pals.

Before they'd left Union Station, Megs had arranged for a porter to deliver Sheila's bags and taught her to dodge the sludge sprayed by vehicles clogging downtown. To hail a cab, Millie had twitched that freckled nose, pulled off her glove, stuck fingers in her mouth, and shrilled an ear-buzzing whistle. Sheila had giggled. jeepers, they *were* fun!

During the bumpy cab ride, they had prayed for her and pointed out landmarks visible through a grimy sky and dusky light. She'd gasped to see the Palmolive Building, a Gothic wonder announcing Chicago was a city to be reckoned with. Grimy snow did not dim the flame lit by the warm welcome. And still no questions about her past . . .

Miriam tugged at Sheila's sleeve. "Hey, wanna come to my Bible study tonight?"

Sheila did not need a holy reminder of what she had done. Besides, she wanted to meet the mysterious Miz W. Was she an instructor? Stenographer?

Millie clapped Miriam on the shoulder. "Can't ya see? We've worn her down."

As if eager to agree, Miriam nodded. "You had a rough trip, didn't you?"

You don't know how rough. Sheila nodded. It was so much easier than explaining things.

"I've gotta scram, too." Megs rose, pulled her coat from a pile of wool and gabardine and tweed, and bundled up tight.

Millie leaned over the table. "What's your hurry? Did I tell you—?"

Chatters and whirrs drowned out Millie's voice. Sheila pushed back her chair, suddenly overwhelmed. She had acclimated to the Home's rhythms. Here everything was different . . .

The girls shushed. Their foreheads creased, as if they were attuned to her every thought. "Are you okay, Sheila?"

She hesitated. "I just wondered, will Miz W be here soon?"

Millie scanned the room. "Just a sec." When she jumped to her feet, she knocked her handbag off her chair.

Sheila retrieved it, noticing gouges in low-grade leather. In spite of the girls' impeccable grooming, she had sensed by the cut of their clothes, their pooling of money for her meal, that these girls did not sit in the lap of luxury. Perhaps they would accept a girl like her. Especially with the support of someone powerful, like Miz W.

"Hey, Sheila! Over here!"

Sheila moved toward Millie's distinctive voice. There, in the rear doorway, stood her gangly new friend, towering over a woman whose smile dimpled a plump, round face. A starched, white apron stretched over an ample belly.

"Sheila, meet Miz W."

A cook's cap bobbed as Miz W shuffled forward on feet that bulged out of work shoes. "Dear child, welcome to Moody." She trilled like the exotic birds that had occasionally dipped into Sheila's old courtyard, dazzled with their song, then spread wings and soared to some exotic land. Chicago?

Stammering, Sheila held out her hand. So the great Miz W was a cook.

"That's not the Moody way." Chubby arms pulled Sheila into the smell of cooking oil, garlic, and onions, one that carried Sheila back to Camille and her kitchen. Tears—surely the onions—burned her eyes.

Miz W finally pulled from the embrace. "I'm almost finished here. Millie, find some boys to get Sheila's things." She stood on her tiptoes to plant a kiss on Sheila's cheek. "God willing, we'll soon get you settled in."

She nodded, her soul warmed by familiar smells . . . familiar hugs. A jolly, affectionate cook? Like Camille. Definitely not like Mimi.

Chapter 28

Sonata Pathetique, Adagio Cantabile

With Miz W holding her arm and guiding her across LaSalle Street, Sheila only slipped once. A miracle, considering the patchwork of ice and pavement.

The boys drafted by Millie lugged Sheila's trunk like dock workers, yet natty coats and leather boots clothed them with Moody dignity. She looked back at the Sweet Shop lights, remembering the warmth that had conquered her arrival jitters. Gone were the students' chatter, the blenders' whirrs. Back was her familiar anxious heartbeat. She'd sloshed across only one street, yet was far removed from those girls' genuine smiles.

Smoke poured from flat-top roofs. Dimly lit apartments touched shoulders. There ended the resemblance to living things. In the Quarter's poorest neighborhoods, bougainvillea and trumpet vines layered vibrancy over decay. St. Paul boasted evergreens that caught snow and wore it like a fur coat. Bundled-up passersby were the only visible life on this Chicago street. She shuddered. Her new home.

Sewage stench rose from a steaming grate as she picked her way onto a snow-clotted sidewalk. A black cat leapt from behind a hydrant, then vanished with a screech that chilled her blood. These boys would protect them. Wouldn't they?

Someone moaned. A door slammed. Someone cursed.

Sheila froze, her boot inches from a curb. But Miz W lugged her forward until the two of them stood ten paces from crumbling stairs. A bare lightbulb illuminated a blistered front door. Bulging burlap sacks cluttered a tiny entryway.

Miz W bent, as if to move the largest sack. "Aye, Captain. A bit early, ain't it?"

The sacks rustled. Swollen eyes glared from a face thick with whiskers and soot.

"Move it over, Captain." Puffs of breath blossomed into white-silver clouds. "How's else to get my new boarder in?"

A wobbly rail kept Sheila upright. A *man*, not sacks, slumped against the door of Miz W's home. *Her* home, a row house not a hundred paces from Moody's arch. To think she'd once lived on Esplanade, one of New Orleans' grandest streets . . .

"Now, now, Captain. I won't have you scaring my new boarder. And you won't get that nice piece of cake I saved for you lest you move your carcass outta the way."

The man cackled. A boozy smell rose from a filthy army shirt. Her soldier—Cliff—flashed like a meteor into her mind. How had life after the war treated him?

As Miz W fussed over the captain, Sheila shook off memories. Straightened her shoulders. To help an old friend, Miz W had opened her home to a girl of dubious repute. Despite its shabby exterior, Miz W likely waged war against dirt. A smile cracked Sheila's frozen mouth. She'd be a cooperative boarder. Make Miz W happy. What Miz W wants, Miz W gets.

◆

"Whew." Miz W shut out the cold and the wind and the rosy-cheeked young men who had piled Sheila's things into a partitioned-off area. "How about some tea? Or would you prefer cocoa?" Five steps carried her landlady into a kitchen no bigger than a closet, with its waist-high refrigerator, tiny two-stool bar, two-burner stove, and crate-sized cupboard. But a cross-stitched proverb on the wall, a Bible on the chipped tile counter, lent warmth that money could not buy.

"No, ma'am. You've already done too much." Heat rose from her cheeks. Miz W had arranged for her to be met, had hung a privacy curtain in the small denlike space adjacent to the kitchen to create a bedroom. Just for her. Sister had been right. There were saints besides nuns.

"Pshaw. It was nothing. And don't you be feeling awkward around me." Still wearing her coat, Miz W smoothed a comforter over a nubby couch, plumped throw pillows, and pulled books and magazines off a mammoth cloth-draped table that swallowed most of the space in the tiny room. "Years ago, I cooked at the Home. That's where I met Carline. Believe me, we were thick as thieves."

Sheila tensed. Likely Miz W knew everything about her.

Crinkly eyes radiated warmth. "I know where you've been, dear Sheila. You've nothing to be ashamed about."

"But—but why didn't they tell me you had once worked there?"

"Why? Why? Why?" came out like a dove's coo. "Don't you be asking too many questions. We'll work through things day by day, ya hear?" She plopped a stack of magazines into Sheila's hands. "Enough questions. Sit down. Settle in. I'll be back in a jiffy."

Sheila gripped the magazines. "Wha-where are you going?"

"Gotta get Captain his vittles. We don't want the ship to sink, now do we?" A widemouthed chuckle revealed yellowing teeth. "He's an old sailor who can't find his land feet." Her attention turned to a clock hung on the wall closest to the door. "Then there's grease traps to empty. A floor coated with flour and crumbs." She clucked a time or two. "Don't worry about this old woman. It won't be but for a bit."

"I'll go with you," Sheila cried. Wrinkled cheeks and veined hands testified that Miz W pushed seventy. At least. Too old to go it alone with the captain and Old Man Winter.

"No, dear. You've had enough to deal with as it is. Besides, it's only three hundred steps to the Sweet Shop." Her eyes twinkled. "Believe me, I've counted 'em."

The periwinkle eyes held such intensity, Sheila wondered what motivated a woman to scrub pots and boil potatoes past retirement age. She bit her tongue. *This is not the time for questions.*

"Just sit a spell," Miz W continued. "Make yourself at home." Boots clunked toward the door. "Latch up behind me, dear. Just in case."

Just in case. Did bums slump in every stoop, or just this one? When the door clicked shut, she rushed forward, drew back the sash of the room's one window, and watched Miz W bob to the corner. Admiration kept her nose pressed against the chilly pane until Miz W disappeared into the warmth and light of the Sweet Shop. Miz W was part of the Moody family, something she'd tasted today but hadn't been able to savor and digest. At least not yet . . .

Outside, something shattered—a bottle hurled from a passing car?—and added to the steady stream of honking and cursing that split the night. She fought an urge to pace the tiny den. For good or bad, the Home had shut out contact with the real world. Outside this door lurked evils she had only read about in newspapers. She remembered Miz W's admonition, hurried to the door, latched a brass chain, clicked a dead bolt. Yet cold seeped through window cracks and chilled her spine. Keep busy; that was the thing. Unpack, read the pamphlets about Moody's Colored Pick-up and Child Evangelism Fellowship. Get off to a good start.

From the bowels of the building, a furnace shuddered. Air from a heat register fluttered the tasseled cloth of that curious table, exposing thick legs and a bench.

Her breath caught. A dizzying lightness shoved aside worry. Could it be? A tremor shook her, as it had when she had first put her lips to Papa's clarinet. She fell to her knees, gripped the edge of the tablecloth as if it were a costly lace veil, pulled it back.

Etudes and waltzes and ditties rose from her soul. The cloth covered a piano, and not just any piano! She slid onto the bench. A gleaming Victorian upright demanded to have its music released. She had to obey. There was no other choice.

Fingertips pressed the familiar ebony and ivory and set off Bs. C-sharp. D-sharp—the D-sharp had slipped a quarter tone flat. She drew back her hand, then tentatively tested a chord. A-flat major, deep like the whistle of a tug on the mighty Mississippi. Her fingers fluttered. This piano had carried her home!

Haydn and Beethoven appeared from nowhere and whispered into her ear. She let her fingers roam the keys. Maman, luscious French words rolling off her tongue, came next. Then Papa. The Quarter musicians, late as usual, kissed their mouthpieces and coaxed sultry tunes from lazy horns. Papa tapped his feet, whistling every octave, just for fun. The noisy Quarter erupted, waifs banging trash lids and shy-eyed Negroes humming along. Home!

Warmed fingers flew, desperate to capture everything. Her feet joined, first tapping, nice and polite, then tromping compliant pedals. Her throat picked up a minor chord that made it all whole. Drums beat a wild, exotic cadence, handed down by slaves. *Louder*, they beat, *all the way up de ole Mississippi, chile. All the way—*

"Sheila!"

Her spine jerked upright. Palms slapped the piano; keys answered by growling mightily. She bounded off the bench. What on earth had she done?

The door had opened, but the chain held fast and allowed a finger's width of freezing air into the room. Sheila shook her head in disbelief. She'd undraped a piano, locked her landlady out of her own home. Talk about bad first impressions!

"Yoo-hoo, dear!"

"I'm so sorry." Her fingers fumbled with the latch, finally unfastened it.

Snow frosted Miz W's dated coat and blue scarf. As she stomped into the room, glistening crystals kissed the floor and melted. "I figured you'd drift off." Miz W unbuttoned her coat. Hung it on a hook. "Until I heard the music. Then I *knew* you'd drifted off. To a place I never dreamed you could go."

"I'm so sorry," Sheila repeated. "I came in here to read, and . . ." She wrung her hands as Miz W removed her boots, set them by the door, and padded toward the piano.

Slowly, oh, so agonizingly slowly, her landlady creaked, groaned, rustled, to face her. "Come here, Sheila."

Sheila winced. What else should a snooper expect?

A crooked finger pointed to the bench. "Sit down."

Her head bowed with regret, Sheila complied. Why had she let the piano seduce her?

"Play."

Flummoxed by Miz W's stern tone, she tickled the keys. Warmth seeped back into fingers reconnecting with friends. A valve opened in her heart to flood her limbs. She conceived sounds and birthed them with a long-pent-up joy.

Something rattled, creaked, scraped, but she paid it no mind as her fingers strained to capture wild Chicago street sounds that demanded to be involved. She pressed the pedals, her legs frantic to be a part of the creation.

Her arm brushed against something firm yet soft. It was Miz W's sleeve.

Notes that she had not claimed answered her, and she answered back. Singing, crying, laughing—

"We'd better stop, dear."

Not now! Let me finish. Let me—

Someone gently shook her.

Sheila jerked her hands from their home. Life going dormant. For now.

Miz W, her face afire, pointed to the ceiling and then put a finger to her lips.

Sheila curled her feet about the legs of the bench, put her hand on her racing heart. What had happened?

Something thumped against the ceiling. Again. Again. "Wha-what is it?" Sheila whispered.

"It's the neighbors. And it *is* late, dear." Swollen hands found Sheila's achy fingers and held them tight. "Thank you, child." A tear rolled down Miz W's cheek.

Lovely notes rang in Sheila's heart. "Oh no, ma'am," burst from her. "I should thank you. I never should have . . ." She bowed her head, embarrassed.

"Never should have what? Returned my music? Music I've neglected since John died?" A great sigh shook Miz W's bosom. "And what did I do? I shrouded my old friend and pretended it had died, too. Didn't even dust this one Depression survivor." The blue eyes clouded. "Lord, forgive me, but I've withheld one of His most precious gifts. And you have returned it." Miz W groaned her way off the bench. Replaced the cloth. Once again the treasure was hidden, but Sheila prayed that it would be uncovered, again and again and again.

Chapter 29

On the Sunny Side of the Street

*A*nother *piece of paper that may change everything.* Sheila held her future in her hands, read the first few lines of it, and set it on Miz W's kitchen table. What *was* her name? Address? What should she put on this application?

The piano beckoned, as it did whenever uncertainty rattled her nerves. Her fingers found the gap in the worn hymnal. Hungry eyes absorbed quarter and half and whole notes, notes that nourished each cell of her body. Nourishment that would give her the strength to do this next hard thing . . . in years of hard things.

Her eyes closed. Her fingers caressed the keys that she'd grown intimate with in just two days. She pressed down the una corda pedal. It wouldn't do to fuel the simmering pilot light that was their upstairs neighbor, Mr. Polaski.

"Amazing grace," Sheila whispered, flattening her hands so that only the pads of her fingers touched the keys. "How sweet the sound. That saved a wretch like me . . ." The music took over, letting her gaze—and her imagination—flit about the room. The water stain on the ceiling became a graceful monarch, its wings spread to fly, fly, fly . . .

Thud. Stomp. A voice cut through beams and plaster to deliver a message both muffled and threatening.

Limp fingers found refuge in her lap, but her eyes flew to the song lyrics, which had told her what to do about the application. She lifted her chin, returned to the table, and picked up the pen, ready to do what she needed to do.

Name: _____. Moody Bible Institute would employ ordinary Sheila over exotic Sheba, mysterious Sylvia. She pressed down firmly. Wrote *Sheila Allen,* using the last name the Home had given her. Keeping secret her New Orleans past. *Address: 823 LaSalle Avenue, #106, Chicago, Illinois.*

Her careful print told nothing of what this tiny apartment meant to her. The piano. Indescribable. Dented appliances that had in just two days produced mouthwatering strudel, savory sausages, tart sauerkraut. Her stomach rumbled at the thought of a honey bun Miz W had carefully wrapped in foil and set aside for her to devour. As soon as she completed her application.

Home of Mrs. Winnie Hildebrand, longtime employee of Moody Bible Institute.

Careful not to lie, she answered the next question, the next. She'd scrubbed floors—at the Home. Dusted, mopped, washed and dried dishes—at the Home. Hope spurred her to flip the page. The bandwagon that was Miz W was so sure this was right. Sheila had jumped on board, a cheer on her lips. She turned the final page, exhilarated that only one and a half lines remained in this first step of the rest of her life.

In the space below, please give your personal Christian testimony, outlining how your life reflects Institute standards.

Her hand went to her forehead. She set the paper down, picked it up, reread the words, then jammed the cap on the pen and slammed it down. She could not answer this question truthfully and satisfy the standards Moody demanded from its employees, even one who would but wipe sticky remains of sodas and sundaes from Sweet Shop tables and take orders from the godly students who devoured, in equal measure, Scripture and food. Her appetite and hope vanished. She rose from the chair, flew to her bed, buried her head in her pillow, and cried.

◆ ◆ ◆

"Five minutes, dear!"

I've been in church for years. So why am I nervous? On this cloudless Sabbath, she adjusted her skirt and smoothed a quilt over her cot but failed to smooth fidgety thoughts. Moody students and Miz W had rained manna on her. Surely they wouldn't worship at an unforgiving place.

She pattered to her dressing table, grabbed her hairbrush, and vented tension on a cowlick born after Samuel's delivery. She put on her best hat and looked in the mirror. A girl with sad eyes and a dull complexion stared back. Her brush clattered onto the hardwood floor. Her body grieved the loss of Samuel, just like her heart, soul, and mind. Even the thought of her new job, thanks to Miz W's help with that last question, failed to revive her spirit.

"Aren't you open to God? Seeking His will, Sheila?" Miz W had asked. Three days ago, the answer she'd printed on the form had been yes. This morning? She wasn't so sure.

"We need to scoot!"

Sheila lifted her head, giving the girl in the mirror a brittle, forced smile.

"Don't forget your new Bible, dear!" came from the other side of the partition.

She pulled out Miz W's gift: the Bible she often held, seldom read. *Vengeance is mine; I will repay . . . Every man will be put to death for his own sins.* Though this was a different Bible than Honey's, with its crinkly new pages and purple ribbon bookmark, when she searched its pages, the same words leapt up and condemned her. Bold, black words, telling her things she already knew. Look at Maman's life. Her life. Bible in hand, she pulled back the curtain and smiled for Miz W, hiding the knowledge that the doors to this church—and God's kingdom—were as good as closed to her.

Nearly smothered by the crowd's dressy hats, wool coats, and polished shoes, Sheila edged closer to her landlady. Sunday morning at the corner of Clark and North was a Mardi Gras parade, religious-style. No riotous music, costumes, or revelers. Just hundreds of chattering voices and springy steps. Side glances noted bright eyes and rosy cheeks . . . brought on by fierce lake wind, biting cold, or something else? Hope glimmered. She craned her neck, eager to see what all the hullabaloo was about.

"This way, dear." Miz W guided her past a broad-shouldered man who had blocked their view. Sheila got her first look at Moody Church. It was a cathedral! Chills coursed through her in spite of a muffler, hat, and layers of clothes. She gripped Miz W.

Glistening snowflakes clung to pink brick columns. Classic arches proclaimed entrance to four Gothic-style doors. Diamonds patterned with gold brought her attention to a circular emblem: *The D. L. Moody Memorial Church and Sunday School.*

Church folk scurried up the steps and into the building as she gaped at the church's enormity. She'd snatched snippets of knowledge about "D. L." from the awed voices of students and Miz W's ramblings about "the good old days," when bums from Skid Row and Bronzeville tenement dwellers underwent the process of "being saved." Sheila had heard that kind of talk at Mimi's church. Here in Chicago, it sounded different, and not just because of the clipped Midwest accent. Staring at this structure devoted to God, she pondered the state of her own soul. Had God opened a door to salvation for her through such a place as this?

"Now, dear." Miz W patted Sheila's shoulder. "It overwhelmed me the first time, too."

"I don't belong here," Sheila stammered, then bit her lip. How dared she put Miz W in an awkward position?

"You're wrong." The wrinkled old face tilted, catching glints of sunrays. Though Miz W barely reached Sheila's shoulder, she radiated power. "You should've known D. L." She gestured toward the building. "He'd tell you that God built this. For the poor. The rich." She guided Sheila up well-salted steps. "He was quite a character."

"A character?" Characters hung out in parks. In bars. Not in church.

"He took the kids sledding on his birthday. Handed tracts to panhandlers till the day he received his promotion."

"His promotion?"

"Into heaven."

Such strange words. Strange folk. Even—especially—her Miz W.

They walked into a spacious entryway filled with the same bundled-up people as she'd bumped into outside. Now they smiled as if God Himself had greeted them. Would God greet her in His house, or would she be partitioned from Him because of her sin-stained life?

"Good morning." An usher handed them programs. "God bless." He led them under a shimmering, massive chandelier, down a carpeted aisle.

They wedged into a crowded pew. Miz W removed her mittens and stuck them in her coat pocket. Sheila did the same and opened the program, her eyes drawn to the bottom of the first page: *Ever Welcome to This House of God Are Strangers and the Poor. —Dwight L. Moody*

The words pulled at the armor guarding Sheila's vulnerable places. She again clutched Miz W's sleeve, overwhelmed, not just by the crowd, but by those words. A deep hunger told her *she* was poor . . . and a stranger.

"What is it, dear?" Miz W whispered.

Before she could answer, glorious sounds shook the walls and echoed in terrible, beautiful thunder. An organist was exploring the heights, the depths of the magnificent room! That, and the light reflected off the chandeliers, loosed

Sheila's hard places. She ducked her head to hide tears, then realized Miz W would understand and returned her gaze to the organ.

"It's God's music for strangers. The poor." Miz W smiled as if Sheila were kin. "For you. And for me."

◆

"Rescue the perishing, care for the dying." Sheila mouthed the words to the hymn as she craned her neck past feathered hats and padded shoulders.

"Jesus is merciful, Jesus will save." The choir director led the congregation in yet another stanza. Passion—and warmth—infused the voices around her. Sheila's reserve continued to melt.

"Won't you come? If He is calling you, don't let another moment go by." The reverend mopped his brow yet his gaze never wavered from the crowd.

Sheila ducked her head into the hymnal. Though she was one of hundreds in this grand auditorium, that gaze could seek her out. Find her. She could not risk it. Not now.

A veined hand rested on her arm. Miz W seemed to understand how she felt. She tightened her hold on the hymnal. With Miz W's help, perhaps she could soften, yet avoid a complete meltdown.

"Still He is waiting." Haltingly at first, Sheila joined in the singing of Fanny Crosby's hymn.

The organ boomed approval. The piano trilled delight. The instruments, the choir voices, the pastor's pleading, mingled into a symphony of song. She glanced up. Had the lustrous chandeliers brightened in homage to Jesus' power?

"I can't bear it, Jesus! I can't bear it!"

Murmurs shuddered through the auditorium. Heads swiveled. Yet the choir sang on. The pastor continued his call.

"I *can't* keep quiet, don't you see? They won't let me!"

Hairs bristled on Sheila's neck. What had happened? As the crowd's whispers grew into nervous chatter, the anguished voice pulled Sheila's gaze to the balcony.

A brown-haired man in a coat and tie gripped the shoulders of a thin, raggedy individual. The two seemed to be wrestling.

"No! No! You can't help! I'm gonna end it all."

The desperate tone clawed at her nerves. Something awful was happening . . . in church!

"He's about to jump!" A voice boomed over the crowd's buzz. "Stop him!"

Others scrambled to the side of the well-dressed man, who had restrained the other individual. A poor man. Definitely poor. A stranger, too? Other worshippers guided both men away from the rail. She dropped her gaze to the floor, afraid she would cry at the slump in the poor man's shoulders, the bent of his balding head.

Finally the rustles and murmurs quieted. Sheila stared at the hymnal's notes, but her spirit remained with that soul in the balcony. Though she wasn't dressed like him, though suicidal thoughts had not plagued her, she too teetered near a spiritual abyss. That man was her kin. Only she and God knew it.

"Thank you, choir. Thank you. And now, heavenly Father, let us . . ." The reverend closed what Sheila assumed was a most unusual Moody service. She bowed her head but cut her gaze to the balcony and scanned the crowd. Her eyes stopped on the back row by the exit. There he sat . . . with the first man who had grabbed him. The rescuer had draped his arm about the spare shoulders of her kin, who had buried his head in his hands, as if he hoped to shield himself from stares like hers. Or was he desperate to hide from the despair within? She longed to join him, to whisper words of hope. Dreadful thoughts wormed their way into Sheila's consciousness. *I don't have hope. Not really.*

"In the name of the Father, the Son, and the Holy Ghost, Amen."

The choir stood, as did the congregants. "The Lord bless you and keep you." Jubilant song swelled the auditorium. The very walls seemed to tremble from the knowledge that something extraordinary had occurred. Sheila sensed it but could not grab hold of its meaning.

She accepted Miz W's hug, though its warmth missed the depths of her spirit. As they gathered their things and bundled to face the blistering wind, she felt the depth of despair born from the knowledge of her kinship with that desperate man.

She nodded to friendly faces, even smiled prettily when Miz W "showed her off" to friends. No matter how hard she tried, she couldn't mute the frantic cries of that poor man in the balcony. Only God knew that she was right there with him, even though her feet were firmly planted on the expensive terrazzo of the ground floor of what was surely Chicago's most beautiful church.

Chapter 30

Victory in Jesus

H ey, Sheila!"
"Great to see ya, kid!"

"You, too." Sheila rubbed her arms, disgusted at pricks of jealousy. Moody students like Millie and Megs wore on their faces the peace another life offered, a life she yearned for but had not found.

"How's Miz W?"

"Great. She's in the back." Sheila pulled out an order pad. *Stick to business. Quit thinking you, you, you.* "What will it be, y'all—I mean, you guys?"

As she turned in the order, talk turned to the Four Horsemen, three Moody professors and a strange older student, reputedly an army general, who feasted on theology in a corner booth, their burgers and malts untouched. *So holy, they don't take time to eat.* Eager to stem comparisons to the Moody elite, Sheila glanced out the window.

Vehicles clogged the streets. People cluttered the sidewalks. Some weaved through the crowd, ragged clothes scant defense against an unexpected April freeze. Others, bundled in luxurious furs, strode with purpose. A well-dressed woman carried an infant wrapped in blankets. Dark curls poked out of a knitted cap.

A mad desire to rush out and snatch the boy from his mother's arms consumed her. She leaned over the counter and scrubbed with a vengeance but could not scour the image of Samuel's blue eyes, his café au lait skin. Was she mad to have such yearnings? Tears burned in her eyes. *Oh, that I could hold him . . . that I could touch him!* Again the counter was attacked with her pent-up, unattainable desire. *I might as well dream of getting in Moody. Studying music . . .*

Bells tinkled. Icy wind—and more patrons—whooshed inside.

Heads turned as two men strode by. The younger, with a typical Moody flat-top, guided the shorter, older man toward a back table.

Sheila followed, eager to get her mind off that infant's face. And her Samuel.

"Back here, Joe. That way we can talk." With an air of confidence, the younger man unfurled a scarf and peeled off a double-breasted coat, then helped Joe out of a threadbare peacoat. An empty chair became the hanger for their coats, a shelf for a Bible.

Joe sank into his seat. His head drooped to meet stained lapels. He pulled off a plaid cap to reveal a balding pate, slicked-down strands of blond hair.

The men looked vaguely familiar. Three months of waitressing here at Moody's hangout had introduced her to students and faculty. Joe wasn't in the Moody family; she'd bet a day's tips on it. So he'd entered the Sweet Shop as a guest of this other man. A student? Faculty? Not a regular, or she'd recognize him. She brushed off her apron. She'd make them welcome. Get her thoughts off herself. With purpose, she walked to their table.

"I'm so glad you called." The younger man pulled off leather gloves and jabbed them into his coat pocket. "It's gotta be tough out there." A smile complemented a well-chiseled nose and prominent cheekbones.

This one'll have 'em all swooning.

She steeled herself to feel nothing for the young man, despite his firm jaw and earnest eyes. Bustling near, she pulled a pencil from behind her ear. Grabbed her order pad. *Stick to business.*

"I just ain't cut out for it." Joe coughed, swiped his mouth with a grubby hand.

"None of us are." The younger man's hand covered Joe's tobacco-stained claws. "That's why we need Him." He gazed at Joe with such compassion, Sheila longed to slide into the vacant seat and hear what he had to say.

"That's why He kept you from jumping," the young man continued.

Jumping? Her breath escaped in a whistle; she longed to clap her hand over her mouth, but then she'd drop her pad and pencil and look even more foolish. So Joe had been the man in the balcony who was poor . . . a stranger? In that way, like her.

As the men were deep in conversation, she scurried to an adjacent table, crowded with five students clamoring for menus. She took orders for sundaes with extra nuts and cherries but managed to appraise the young man, the handsome man, who had saved Joe from jumping off the balcony. All the students she'd met had slurped dozens of malts this far into the semester. With his baby face good looks, surely he wasn't old enough to be a pastor. Though she knew better than to be attracted by him, she noted his thick eyelashes and steepled hands. If the pulpit called, he had certainly mastered the intensity needed to preach. She would gladly listen.

"Hey! Come 'ere!"

It was Millie, yanking her back to reality. She wiped off her hands—and her sudden infatuation—to check on her friend.

"What's new?" continued Millie who, along with Megs, played with studying.

"Just the usual." Sheila tried to infuse enthusiasm in her voice. "Work. Helping Miz W with her men." Six days a week, she and Miz W closed down the shop and then cooked pots of stew for vets who could hardly pull their heads out of a bottle long enough to eat. Around eleven, they got on their knees to pray before collapsing into bed. At sunup Miz W fired up the stove and she and Sheila baked bread before their shifts at the Sweet Shop.

Church and piano-playing brought joy to the Sabbath. With the radio's "Sunday Serenade" and Miz W's leftovers, the tiny apartment nourished both her body and soul . . . except when the baby in the upstairs flat cried at dawn. When a rosy-faced toddler smiled in church. When a woman passed the Sweet Shop holding a darling little one. In other words, all the time.

"There's a Glee Club concert next week. If you could get the evening off . . ."

Sheila smiled at dear Megs, whose camaraderie brightened her spirits. The Three Musketeers truly cared about her, even though she was just a waitress and only had this job because of Miz W. How would they act if they really knew where she had been and what she had done?

"Thanks, but I can't. Not this week." She bit back what she really wanted to say: *No matter how hard you try, I can't be one of y'all.* Desperate to change the subject and satisfy her curiosity, she leaned close. "Aren't those the guys from the balcony incident?" She nodded toward the back booth.

Millie rolled her eyes. "Edward Franklin, head in the clouds as usual."

"Cut it out, Millie. You're just jealous that he's not holding *your* hand." The two friends pretended to pout, then broke into laughter.

"I wouldn't want him even if he were interested."

"*I'm* surprised he deigns to be seen in here. All he cares about is Greek and Latin. Books so complicated, you can't even read their titles."

"You two, shush!" cried Megs. "He *saved* that man, you know. And I don't mean just his life. Edward Franklin's the real deal."

"How could he *not* be, his daddy bein' such a big-time preacher?"

"I got a list a mile long of preacher's kids not actin' like they ever set foot in a church," Millie said. "Much less witnessing, D. L. Moody–style."

Megs's eyes got big. "Did I tell you that Johnny Ames got caught—?"

"You want a knuckle sandwich?" Millie giggled, but her brows knit together.

Moody girls avoided gossip, and usually Sheila was grateful. Not now. She wanted "the scoop" on Edward Franklin. With Millie fending off juicy tidbits, she'd best be quiet.

Her friends chattered on, giving her the perfect chance to sneak another look at the back table, where the Bible had been opened. Heads nodded. Hands waved. "Amens" had been said, a lesson begun. Butterflies soared dizzyingly in her stomach. She straightened her apron. Those lips might be parched after so much praying. He *must* need a soda.

"See y'all." She nodded to her friends and took leave.

The girls stopped their chatter long enough to wave and blow kisses.

As she bustled toward the back table, she again pulled out her pad, her pencil, tucked curls behind her ears.

Joe's weathered countenance and bloodshot eyes flickered a look her way before fastening on Edward. "'Tis not," he insisted.

"'Tis so." Edward grabbed the Bible, ducked his head over its pages.

"Hello." She shifted her weight to combat a jittery step.

"Uh, Ed." Something like a laugh softened Joe's gravelly voice. "I think this young lady's tryin' to take your order."

As if she'd interrupted an altar call, a frown flitted across Edward's face, then vanished. Should *she* vanish? Or take his order? She fiddled with her pencil and made her decision. *Do your job, Sheila. He's just another customer.*

"Could I get you to pray for me?" she blurted out and then reddened. Her eyes fell onto the pages of the opened Bible. She kept them there, away from that handsome face, which had probably twisted in a smirk. *James. Chapter 1.* She would look it up later.

Joe coughed and wheezed and laughed. "Oh, he'd be happy to pray for you, miss. I gotta warn you, though, he means business."

"God means business," came out of Edward with such intensity, Sheila lifted her chin and looked him full in the face. "And so do I," he added, as he met her gaze. "But all this business makes me thirsty." He leaned back, nodded. "Two chocolate malts." He pretended to punch Joe in the arm when the older man protested that he was full. "Don't listen to him," Edward continued. "Just bring 'em on."

Sheila nodded and whirled toward the counter, ready to breathe again, ready to get away from so much . . . goodness. So much good-*looking*-ness.

"And Miss?"

She paused. What a voice!

"When you return, bring on those prayer requests, too."

◆ ◆ ◆

Home. Piano. Just what I need after another long shift. In six months, Chicago had claimed her as its own. When the weather—and schedules—allowed, the Four Musketeers would stroll the lakefront and let the autumn breeze tangle their hair. The bums no longer scared her; she understood them better than they would ever know.

She ducked under her curtain and changed into pajamas. Chicago was home.

From the dresser, her Bible beckoned; she accepted the call. Words that had once struck fear now offered promise. The Psalms. The Book of Ruth. James. She moved forward. A letter perched atop her Bible. Eyeing it with suspicion, she stepped closer. Embossed letters rose from the creamy envelope. She squinted.

Gabet, Toulong, and Steiner. Another glance confirmed the familiar French Quarter address. Spots danced in her field of vision; she leaned against the dresser and gulped air. What was Mimi's lawyer up to? What was *Mimi* up to?

"God, help me," she prayed through rattling teeth. She opened the letter and extracted two sheets.

> September 15, 1947
> Mademoiselle Alexander:
>
> It is with regret that I inform you of the death of your grandmother, Clara Alexander, who passed away September 1, 1947. Just before she died, Mrs. Alexander directed me to revise her Last Will and Testament. Though the document is quite lengthy, she wished that you, Sheila Alexander, be primary beneficiary, notwithstanding small bequests to Camille Wilson and James Lee for their faithful service.
>
> There is an irrevocable addendum to said Last Will and Testament: that you, Sheila Alexander, return to the State of Louisiana and preside as the Chairman of the Board of Directors of Alexander & Company, Cotton Merchants.

As executor of your grandmother's estate, I look forward
to discussing this matter with you in person. Of course the
estate will provide for every conceivable expense that you will
incur en route to New Orleans.
Very truly yours,
Emile "Jack" Toulong

She doubled over, then staggered into the parlor and fell onto her bench. The
piano took a pounding as never before. She mixed stanzas of jazz and hymns
into a discordant dirge born of grief and resentment of Mimi's last legacy. Mr.
Polaski banged and stomped his disapproval, but she ignored him. Gradually
the ebony and ivory took her grief and left a cold, determined irritation at whoever had disclosed her whereabouts. At Mimi, for her last attempt to seize control. Irritation at a family legacy of which she wanted no part. This time, Mimi
would not succeed. She would make her own decisions, live her own life. So
help her God.

◆

September 30, 1947
Dear Mr. Jack:
Thank you ever so much for contacting me regarding my
late grandmother's will. However, I am set on remaining in
Chicago with my new family. My preference would be that
you sell the cotton business. It has caused much pain and
suffering over the years.
As you are aware, I am uneducated in the ways of
barristers and businessmen. For that reason, I will leave the
technicalities of disposing of my grandmother's estate up
to you. However, if I do have any say in the matter, I would
like a portion of the proceeds to establish an endowment
for street musicians and any current residents of Birdie's, an
establishment with which my mother and father were familiar.
Please divide the remainder of the money between
Camille Wilson and James Lee, who were my real guardians
during the years after my mother and father passed. If

possible, please keep that request confidential and just lead
them to believe that Mimi provided them with the money.
They certainly earned it.

Forgive me for calling you Jack. That is how I like to think
of you.

Very truly yours,
Sheila Allen

◆ ◆ ◆

The Sweet Shop had the usual knot of chatty students, somber professors,
and the Four Horsemen, engaged in their usual lively debate. But today Miz W,
rag in hand, hairnet tight over her curls, stood near the soda counter. Sheila
checked her watch, sure she was early. Miz W wasn't in the kitchen. Despite the
Indian summer day, she shivered. Something was wrong.

"Hi, dear." Her landlady gulped.

"Wha-what is it?"

"There's a gentleman to see you. A Mr.—same name on the letter I set in
your room a couple weeks back." She ever so slightly tilted her head. "Been there
since noon."

Two hours? She glanced toward the back booth—where Edward usually sat.
Sure enough, it was Jack—Mr. Toulong, a newspaper spread on the table, a
half-eaten doughnut on a plate. She grabbed her order pad, turned to Miz W.
"But my shift . . ."

"Got it covered." Miz W squeezed her hand. "Don't you worry, I'm praying
for you." The scent of violets eased Sheila's jitters . . . but not her racing mind.

"Thanks." Sheila approached the back table. A New Orleans attorney had
journeyed to Chicago, just to see her. This could not be a good thing.

"Mr. Toulong—"

"It's Jack, remember?" His smile was so warm, the cigar smell that clung to
his clothes so inviting, her fear was flung off like a scarf.

"Hello, Jack." She held out her hand and noticed his empty cup. "More coffee?"

"Sheila, please sit down. Between the train porters and your landlady—yes,
I know about that, Sheila—I've drunk enough coffee to sink the Titanic all over
again."

She laughed, in the nervous way of an unexpected encounter. Fussed with
her hem, her hair, a chipped nail.

"I'm sure you're wondering what brought me all the way up north."

That and another thing. "How . . . did you find me?"

"We attorneys have our ways."

Sheila battled a grimace. Of course. Money. "I see." She would not be rude to this man, who was just doing his job.

"This is a hard thing for me, Sheila." He paused until she looked into his eyes, which were not as bright as she remembered. "And probably not being done quite by the letter of the law." His finger ringed the cup rim. "You see, dear Sheila, I come here today not as your lawyer but as your friend."

All the way up north. Just for her. "Thank you, Jack," she whispered. She exhaled as she studied his bald pate, his well-tailored suit. When had she last seen him? A holiday reception at his firm—how many years had it been? Three?

"About that letter you sent—"

"I know it's not—"

He held up his hand, adorned with a class ring. From the arch of his brows, she could tell Emile Toulong was not used to being interrupted.

"I understand how you feel—felt—about your *grand-mère*. We lawyers know much more than what's in our musty books." A sallow cast had aged the aristocratic face. "Not to mention, our office was a revolving door for her, she changed her will so often."

"How—how did she die?" Sheila managed.

"Heart attack. At home. Alone. The maid, Camille, found her." He continued to peer into her face, as if years of court appearances had taught him how to gauge reactions before asking the next question. "She wasn't a happy woman, as you well know." He sighed, again traced the cup rim. "But you could grant her last wish." His voice gained momentum, smooth and rich as divinity. A professional's voice. "In her own way, she loved you, Sheila. Loved your father. That money is yours. That *company* is yours. Do you realize how hard it was for her to hand it over to a mere girl? One without—"

"Social standing? Reputation?" She failed to keep an edge out of her voice.

"Hers was a hard life, Sheila. Bitterness trails loneliness and betrayal."

"Much of it her own doing." She gnawed her lip, sorry to say such unkind things to such a kind man. "I'm sorry, Jack. Please understand that this has nothing to do with her and everything to do with me." She glanced about, taking in the rosy cheeks, the serene brows, of the Moody crowd, the Bibles stacked on tables. "God's Sword, sheathed and ready to be used." It was her pastor's words, coming back, at just the right time, helping her to understand what she was doing. She straightened her back, crossed her ankles. "I'm . . . happy here. Or at least at peace. This is where I am meant to be."

The lawyer studied her. He reached into his pocket, pulled out a cigar, sniffed it, carefully put it away. "Are you sure? Are you unequivocally sure? About the bequests to musicians? To Birdie's? To Camille and James?"

She grinned. Now he was the nervous one. "I am, Jack."

"Well, if you're sure, I've got a long trip ahead. And work to do."

"The City of New Orleans." A catch made her voice whispery. *The city I may never see again.*

"I'll miss you, Sheila."

She nodded, trying . . . failing . . . to formulate words to express how she felt. So she *had* had another friend in New Orleans, one not fully appreciated. One she wasn't ready to let go of quite yet. "Could I get you a malt? The chocolate's swell." She struggled to keep memories from cracking her voice.

"That would be nice, dear girl." He took her hand, cupped it with his own, as Papa used to do. "That would be so very, very nice."

◆ ◆ ◆

Sheila nestled in the Moody pew. So many people, like Mimi's old church. Such a grand building, like Mimi's old church. Yet warmth permeated the Classical façade and buffered the cold November wind. Sheila took in the miracle of God: for nearly a year, she'd had a job at Moody, a life with Miz W. She'd even bought new clothes, set aside a bit of money for her future. *Future.* At first she had been living for the next Sweet Shop shift, the next church service. Now a Midwest future seemed probable, not just possible.

Two men stepped onto the platform fronting the choir. Sheila recognized one as an elder. The other man looked to be in his thirties or early forties. Wavy brown hair swept away from a broad forehead, a soul-searching gaze. A gray suit coat hung off a spare frame. She found her Bible, whose words had sprung to life for her when Dr. Tozer led the fall meeting. Since then, she soaked up truth, desperate to make *their* God her God.

The elder approached the podium. Adjusted the microphone. "It's my privilege to introduce the president of Northwestern Schools, an outstanding evangelist who recently followed God's call to the city of Los Angeles and, with the help of the Holy Spirit, led thousands to Christ. Please give a warm Moody welcome to Dr. Billy Graham."

Murmurs rippled the auditorium. After the elder adjusted the microphone for Dr. Graham's height, Dr. Graham moved forward. "Dear friends, I'm delighted to be here with y'all, but I've got to say, I could do without this cold." He gave an exaggerated shiver, eyes sparkling like ice crystals dazzled by a ray of sun. His soft but intense Southern drawl electrified Sheila. Buzzes rose from the packed auditorium. She wasn't the only one so moved.

Dr. Graham joked a bit as the congregation settled in. Then he gripped the podium, as if gathering strength. "Let us pray." Steel had infused his words. "Dear Lord, make Your Presence known to those gathered here today."

Sheila squeezed her eyes tight and willed the words to pierce her skin, if that was what it took to find Him. For without His presence, she was lost. And she was so tired of wandering, of wondering, how to find her way home.

As Dr. Graham transitioned from "Amen" into a sermon of lost sheep, hurting souls, she darted glances at fellow worshippers. The magnetic voice had silenced the usual coughs and rustles of coats. Once she was sure Dr. Graham was staring right at her. Unable to face one who spoke God's word, she let her hands fall into her lap and studied her nails. Guilt marked her, and she was tired of that. No, not tired. She was sick to death of it all.

"You see, dear friends, it is not your sins the Father sees when you cast your trespasses on His only begotten Son. No matter what you have done, no matter where you have been, Jesus will take on your burdens. Jesus can wash you white as snow."

He preached hope to one as stained as her? Tears gathered until the earnest, pleading face blurred. The hum of a new song rose from deep inside and began to drown out Dr. Graham's Southern syllables. If he truly preached truth, Jesus offered a way to the righteous God. Jesus offered a refuge from her past. Jesus offered a safety that even these hallowed church walls did not possess.

Her head bowed. Tears plopped onto her Bible.

Miz W took her hand and leaned close, her wiry hair brushing Sheila's collar. "Now, now, dear. Let it out." They drew stares of nearby worshippers, but Sheila didn't care. For months, she'd been stirred to a new understanding of God. Not just a stern Father that punished wayward children. Not just a selective Spirit, only for the pious. Not just a sad Jesus, disappointed at sin. Love permeated this mysterious triune God. She'd seen it in Moody students' smiling faces. She'd felt it in Miz W's warm hugs. All of them loved in the name of Jesus, who first loved them and sheltered them in His merciful arms. Jesus could free her from her past. Her present. Free her for her future. But she had to open her heart to Him before He could snatch her from the throes of sin.

"In the name of our precious Savior Jesus, amen." Dr. Graham raised his head and stared straight at her. "Won't you come? Come to Jesus now?"

Elders rose from the front row and turned to face the crowd. Hymn pages and satin robes rustled as the choir stood united. At the thought of what she must do, ice water shot through her veins, but she managed to rise. Could she make it down the aisle without collapsing?

"Softly and tenderly," the choir sang. "Come home," she whispered, amazed at how God had ordained this experience. Home, just what she had yearned for. Not South. Midwest. Not even Miz W's. For a final confirmation, her eyes fell on the three men standing near the altar, especially the one who had delivered God's message. She took a deep breath and leaned close to Miz W. "I'm going forward," she whispered. Urgency cut off any more words.

"Praise God!" Miz W exclaimed, enveloping Sheila in a hug. "That's wonderful!" She lowered her voice when someone nearby cleared their throat. "Should I go with you?"

Sheila shook her head. Like her other journeys, she had to start this one on her own.

"Calling, Oh, sinner, come home."

Organ chords swelled into a glorious musical amen, one she had never dared even to dream. Every fiber of her being cried *so be it* as she rushed to meet the One who would save her from her sins. Protect her from herself. As fast as her stiff new boots could carry her, she was coming home.

Chapter 31

Nocturne, Op. 9, No. 2

W hat a friend we have in Jesus. All our griefs and pains to bear." If the piano had been her friend before, now it was her soul mate. Her gratitude to God infused her playing with a tonal quality she'd never possessed. She stroked each key with just the right touch. Her foot learned just the pressure needed to mute sad minor keys, explode jubilant A and C majors.

Since her baptism, she'd memorized a passel of hymns and had tucked away old jazz tunes like last year's coat. What little time she had needed to be spent in praise. In thanks.

"Sheila, dear?" Bringing the smell of mothballs with her, Miz W bustled into the room. Her body had been squeezed into a worsted pink suit. "Are you about done?" Her eyes danced as she hummed the chorus of Scriven's hymn. Joy was infectious!

"It's only ten thirty, Miz W." When she hushed the piano, robin chirps filtered into the flat. And wasn't it glorious? When the Musketeers had hiked to the lake yesterday, daffodils and lilies played peekaboo from patches of green and enlivened their dreary concrete world. Chicago was about to undergo a transformation. Like she had.

Miz W cleared her throat several times, as she always did when some crazy idea was about to pop out. One of her schemes had Sheila joining a Moody choral group. She'd quietly demurred, changed the subject. Then Miz W suggested Sheila help in the nursery. Before and after the services, she cooed with babies, read stories to toddlers, as if they were her Samuel. She ticked off time. Two months ago, he had celebrated his first birthday.

"There's a meeting today before the service. About a children's choir."

Whew. "That's wonderful!" whooshed from Sheila. "Are you helping out?" she asked, eager to focus on something besides *him*.

Old eyes jitterbugged. "No, Sheila. *You* are."

*   ◆   *

She'd argued till her throat got hoarse as they slogged through slush to Moody's side entrance. It had been downright rude for Miz W to volunteer her without having the courtesy to ask.

"It's just until Easter. Anyone could do that."

Then why don't *they?* She swallowed sassiness. If God wanted this, she'd forge ahead. Besides, it was only a month until Easter.

Bible clutched to her chest, she followed Miz W into the empty sanctuary. Golden light cast by the Tiffany chandeliers, the pews' lemony scent, smoothed her frayed edges.

A yelp came from the choir loft. She lifted her head. Grimaced.

Children bounced from one step to the next. A harried-looking woman darted among them, her outstretched hands grasping for fluttering coattails, puffy skirts. Keen acoustics amplified squeals. This was a choir? Only if God wrought a miracle.

"You must be Sheila." The woman quit chasing children long enough to offer her hand. "I'm Kay, the choir director. Our goal is to perform for the Easter service. In fact, the music has been mimeographed—Stop it, Johnny! Right now!" She swooped upon a boy whose hand had tangled in the sash of a little girl's dress.

Giggles erupted from all the children except for the little girl, who sank onto the bottom altar step, buried her face in her hands, and wailed loud enough to send children scuttling up the aisle. Sheila suppressed her own wail.

"I cannot handle this alone." Kay massaged her temples, which surely ached. "Would you help out?" Her eyes widened, like a treat-seeking child's. "It's only until Easter."

"So I heard," Sheila managed.

The girl with the untied sash continued to wail at glass-shattering levels. Sheila hurried to her. "It's all right." She put her arms around shaking crinoline shoulders.

"No, it's not!" the little girl sobbed. "He ruined my new dress."

Sheila arched her eyebrows. *"Ooh-la-la!* Could I tie it in a French bow?" She infused the mysteries of Maman's Paris in her voice.

Sniffles miraculously ceased. "A . . . French bow? What's that?"

Sheila patted a mop of auburn hair. "It's a very special bow for very special girls named—what *is* your name, dear?"

Wet lashes fluttered to reveal curious eyes. "Betsy. What's *your* name?"

"I'm Miss Sheila. I'll tie your bow when you line up. Over here." She pointed toward the piano. "You can be first, you know."

As if she'd used a megaphone, children rushed back to the altar.

"I wanna be first!"

"No, me."

Sheila scanned faces that were smudged with—surely it wasn't mud?

"All right, children." A stiff-backed Kay stepped forward. "Let me introduce Miss Sheila, my coteacher . . . and accompanist for our piece."

"Gee whiz! A real piano!" Wrinkled shirttails escaped buttoned slacks as boys hopped about. Ponytails loosened as girls twirled. Sheila grabbed the arm of a girl teetering on the edge of a step and pulled her to safety.

"Can I play it?"

"No, me!"

"Tell you what." Sheila glanced at Kay, hoping for a nod of confirmation. The woman's glazed eyes prompted Sheila to again take control. "Line up right behind me. Quietly." She waved them behind Betsy, who beamed her good fortune at being first.

"All right. That's good," Sheila finally said when the last grumble had faded. She tiptoed to the piano, glanced back.

A dozen heads bobbed, toes arched . . . a perfect mimicry of her every move. She shivered with excitement. How dared she doubt God's hand in this? "If you'll be very quiet," she managed, despite the lump in her throat, "each of you may play three notes."

"Bravo!" echoed through the cavernous room.

A glance across rows of pews revealed only Miz W. She panned the balcony. Saw a brown-haired man. Her mouth went dry. Wasn't that the voice of Edward Franklin? With his head bowed, she couldn't be sure, but her heart fluttered all the same.

". . . my turn. Teacher . . ." Betsy tugged her skirt.

"Sorry." She scooted Betsy forward on the bench. Arched plump fingers. Fought an urge to again glance at the balcony—but lost. It *was* Edward.

One, two notes sounded. Betsy dangled her hands over the keys, teasing the others.

"Hurry!"

"I'll never get my turn."

Pushing away thoughts of why Edward Franklin was monitoring choir practice, Sheila tut-tutted, her hands on her hips as if she'd done this kind of thing for years. "Not another word. You won't get your turn until Betsy gets hers. And you"—she turned to Betsy—"finish up."

A little boy with a dimpled chin slid onto the bench and ran his hand across the keyboard. "Gee," he beamed. "I never heard such a purty sound."

"It's just the beginning!" Sheila grabbed the music and doled out copies. "Read the words, then sing them—quietly. Soon you'll have memorized the whole thing!" She whirled to help the next child onto the bench, the next. Heart strings vibrated as chubby, thin, long, short fingers found keys. Or was it that young man in the balcony causing the commotion within? The former, she hoped, but she feared that it was the latter.

◆

His head was stuck so far in that dad-blamed Greek book, the strange letters might rub off on his nose. As she bussed her last tables and stashed tips in her pocket, she tried to ignore the pulse battering her temples. How dared she set her heart on Edward Franklin who, like a Moody education, was unattainable? With her past, being a child of God was a miracle. That was enough.

She grabbed a rag, glad to focus on work, even if it was the late shift and her feet ached. She picked a table close to the Four Horsemen and moved the rag in circles, listening in on their conversation about the rapture as she cleaned.

"Sheila, time to go home," Maurice, the shift manager, called from the counter as he pointed to his watch. "Now scoot."

Relieved that he'd noticed the late hour, Sheila peeked at that back table. Deserted. She rubbed her jaw, and stared at the empty seat. A familiar book lay on the table. Her breath caught. Edward had left his Bible!

Urgency energized legs achy from her long shift. As knotted apron strings thumped her back, she grabbed the Bible and trotted out the Sweet Shop's jingling door. Cold rain pattered her cheeks. She hugged Edward's friend so it wouldn't get wet.

Twenty paces in front of her, an umbrella shielded Edward, who approached the hallowed arch entrance to Moody Institute. Another world. She had to catch him out here, before he reentered his sanctuary.

She ignored protocol, lunged forward, stuck her arm under his umbrella, and tapped his shoulder.

"Wha—" He wheeled, slinging water in smooth arcs. She froze under the intensity of the ten shades of gray in his eyes. She couldn't, wouldn't look away. He was so handsome, so good. Those clear, calm eyes testified about *him* the few times he wasn't testifying about Christ.

"I'm . . . sorry." She clung to the Bible as if it were a life preserver. And she *was* drowning. "You . . . you left this in there."

"How careless of me." When he took the Bible, his fingers brushed her wrist.

Heat surged at her pulse points. Brush fires ignited and telegraphed wild notions. Did romantic interest add that silvery flicker to those gray eyes? Or was he startled at being accosted by a soaking-wet waitress?

"This is no place to talk."

She tried to nod and wipe her face. The cutest freckles dotted his nose.

As if walking in the rain were normal, he took her arm, led her toward the arch. The umbrella tilted away from their heads, useless. Like her interest in a preacher.

Still, she leaned into him, her every fiber exulting in the pure electric joy of being close to a man. This man. It had been so long since she'd been held or touched or . . . kissed.

"Uh, miss." A blush spread across that nose. "Let's go in here. Dry off."

The rain let up enough for her to read the words etched into the great arch. *Moody Bible Institute. AD 1938. The foundation of God standeth sure. Jesus Christ Himself being the chief cornerstone.*

So certain. So somber. She did not belong here, in this sanctuary for the holy. Her throat went dry. She removed his hand from her arm. "I can't go in there," she mumbled. "I need to get home." She studied his spattered brown Oxfords. "See you around."

He touched her shoulder.

Did he see, could he sense, her misbehaving heart? She demanded her feet to trot across the street and home, but not a muscle moved. Just that heart, which beat unmercifully.

"You're good with the children." His hand seared her starched cotton uniform.

"The children?" Raindrops dripped into her eyes. Blurred her vision. But that was nothing compared to the way his comment rattled her brain.

"The ones at church. Best Easter program they've had in years."

"You saw me?" she managed. *Really saw that side of me?*

"It was Easter Sunday. How could I not?"

"But you're always so busy praying up there in the balcony . . ."

"So you saw me, too." With a flick of his thumb, the umbrella slapped shut, spattering both of them. Not that it mattered; they were already soaked. He laughed, loosing her mouth, her heart, her soul.

"How could I not?" she answered, daring to add a flirtatious tone.

They laughed. She wiped her eyes to drink in that pleasant, rain-splashed face. He offered his arm, and she accepted it.

They passed under the arch, out of the rain, and made their way to the library. Except for a smattering of patrons seated near the streetside windows, they had the place to themselves. Yet that didn't stop her from being awed to silence by the plank-and-pedestal tables, the card catalogues, the shelves and shelves of texts written by great theologians.

He pulled out a chair for her and carefully folded his coat over the back of the adjacent chair before sitting in it. "I don't understand. Why did you think you couldn't come here?"

The cavernous library took on the hollow echo of a cave; fortunately, no stern-eyed librarians shushed them.

Where would she start with why she did not belong here? Esplanade? Mississippi? The Home? She shook her head, unable to answer.

"Miss . . . I don't even know your name."

"No one does. That's why I don't belong here," she blurted, then glanced at the vacant help station, distant bowed heads, relieved no one seemed to hear her outburst.

"Well . . ." He scooted his chair so close, his shoes grazed her soaking Keds. "You're Miz W's tenant; like her daughter, from what I hear. Half the guys in the Sweet Shop are sweet on you, from what I see. You got baptized a few months ago—"

"You saw that?"

"How could I not? Now you are directing the children's choir. Doing quite well, as I said." His shirt sleeve grazed her shoulder, setting off more cursed, blessed sparks. His scent enveloped her. He smelled like . . . freshly cut grass. She let her eyes close. Relaxed until his shoulder bore the weight of her shoulder. She could get used to this.

"I'd like to see more of you."

She gulped for air. For an answer. "I'm not a student here," she finally managed.

"I know."

Her mouth opened, then clamped shut. The man had been studying more than Greek.

He took her hand. Looked into her eyes. "There is one thing I need to know before I can ask Miz W if it's all right."

She scooted away. This would never work. He would ask about her family. Her friends. A man with a future in the pulpit had to be sure. Safe. She let go of his hand, gripped her chair arms, tensed her calves. She needed to leave. Now. "What do you need to know?" she croaked, against her better judgment.

"Your name. I need to know your name."

Images of Maman, of Papa appeared darkly, as reflected in an antique mirror. So did another image, of a little girl who thought she could save the world. In the span it took to raise her head and study his gray, searching eyes, she nearly introduced that little girl, nearly began to pour out her sordid story. A glance at shelves bearing the weight of so many books about holiness and righteousness silenced the words perched on the tip of her tongue. She could not take him to New Orleans and that Mississippi beach. Most of all, she could not take him to St. Paul.

"My name is Sheila." Queasiness rocked her stomach but she refused to be swayed. "Sheila Allen." She dared not look at him for fear he would discern the lie on this their first true encounter. But it was not a lie, just a half truth. She *was* Sheila Allen.

He covered her hand with his. "Sheila Allen?"

She nodded.

"If it's okay with Miz W, would you have dinner with me?"

Chapter 32

Honolulu City Lights

She would chew slowly. Smile between sips of water. Endure fall-leaf-dry handshakes. For Edward, somehow, some way, she would survive her first dinner with Dr. and Mrs. Franklin. But would she be considered suitable marriage material for their only son? The instincts she'd honed for nearly twenty years said no.

"The weather's been amazing, hasn't it?" Edward had labored to infuse gaiety, even donned a polka-dot bow tie more apt for a clown. Yet conversation had stuttered and wheezed. Sheila balled up her napkin. Squeezed hard. She didn't belong here with the proper, righteous Franklins.

"Why, yes, Edward, it has." Mrs. Franklin had her son's fine brow. Silvery hair had been smoothed into a twist. A linen suit, gold watch, and pearl necklace mirrored her simple yet elegant Prairie-style home. A haven from the world, with its gaudy promises and lure of sin. A world Sheila knew too well. If Mrs. Franklin knew her past, Sheila'd be shown the door, perhaps not right this minute, but certainly before her romance with Edward blossomed further.

"Quite nice." Though Reverend Franklin kept eyes uncannily like Edward's fixed on her, he seemed to be floating, like the heavenly host, in a loftier dimension.

Sheila curled her toes, smoothed her soggy napkin, desperate to reach that higher plane. Nothing happened.

"Sheila and I took advantage of it and drove out to Riverview." A mission-style ceiling lamp set a glow to Edward's face. She loved him, forward and backward. Inside and out. He loved her, she was sure of it. But he didn't really *know*

260

her, even after a year of courtship. One year, and this was her first visit with his parents. That said it all.

"Riverview?" Mrs. Franklin swiveled her head, revealing a Patrician profile that included a disdainful gaze. Now fixed on her son.

Poor Edward. What would this do to him?

The Reverend jerked back to the lowly realms of this world. His chiseled nostrils flared. With their raised eyebrows, he and his wife telegraphed code across the table. An SOS about her invasion.

"Surely you can't mean the *amusement* park." The Reverend's fork clinked against time-tested mahogany.

"Where those . . . ladies were arrested?"

Questions buzzed.

Edward flinched, as if a dart had pierced his flesh. Like it had hers. But she was used to it. Edward was not.

Questions intensified and threatened to obliterate her beloved's voice. She angled her fork across her plate, like Maman had taught her. She would not allow attacks on the man who shared the gospel with beatniks and hobos, who escorted her about Moody as if she were a queen and not a soda jerk with a secret past. *They will not do this to Edward. Let them do it to me.*

Her napkin plopped by her plate. "Riverview was my idea. I begged him to take me." She shrugged, lifted her chin, like she was the newly crowned Riverview Ice Queen. "Finally he gave in."

Black stares signaled full-scale war.

She sighed, low and long. "It so reminded me of home. Especially the roller coaster. What do they call it? The Jetstream. Wild and high, till you are sure to fly."

A strangling sound came from the Reverend. He raised a glass, gulped water.

"Where did you say your people were from?" came from Edward's mother, who gripped the table with such intensity, the veins in her hands forked like branches.

"N'Awlins." Sheila drawled so long, so low, the words dripped with jazz and spice and mystery and decadence. Things she had known . . . once.

"And what did your father do?" Disdain hardened Dresden features. Right in front of her eyes, Edward's mother became unyielding stone.

Dissolute. Gambler. An evil wind sought out cracks and seeped nasty words into Sheila's consciousness. They funneled and struck. She leapt to her feet. Flew to the hall. Wrenched open the front door. Gulped silence. Let the still, cool air salve her open wounds.

The door slammed. Footsteps clomped near. Familiar arms encircled her, as did that lovely fresh-cut-grass scent. "I'm so sorry," he whispered in her ear.

"It's no use," she said, though her heart banged disagreement.

He gripped her chin. Turned it until she was forced to meet his gaze. "I love you, Sheila. That's all that matters."

"But your parents . . ."

"Will come around in time." His husky voice hammered at her defenses. And wasn't she desperate to embrace an ally! Especially such a good, handsome man?

"They won't," she managed, her voice squeaky. Weak. Wanting to believe him.

"They will." He found her hand. Squeezed hard.

Pain skittered up her arms. Finding exposed nerves.

"Edward, I've made a mistake. Something they—and you—will never accept."

His lips found hers. Kissed her as never before. "Is that a mistake?" He kissed her again. "Is that?" he managed, in between breaths.

Every cell in her body sizzled. She drew back, studied the silver glints in his fine gray eyes. Edward knew passion? To keep from falling, she melted against him. Closed her eyes. Returned his kiss. Let herself be consumed by that delicious burning flame.

He pulled away from her. Seized her gaze with those irresistible eyes. Probed until she shivered. "It doesn't matter, Sheila. The past is buried and gone."

"Edward, there are things you need to know—"

"Stop it, Sheila. Now." Edward pressed two fingers over her lips. Two fingers, that was all it took to silence words that would describe Sheba and Sheila and Sylvia. Words that would confess a past that no one but Jack knew. And the paper he'd sent her explained that attorney/client privilege bound him to keep her secret.

"Are you sure, Edward?"

"I'm sure. The past is over, Sheila. Gone." He kissed her hand. Kissed her lips. Kissed her neck.

When he pulled away, she swayed, dazed.

"All that matters is the future. Mine. Yours. Ours."

She thought of Jack's last letter, explaining Uncle's and Aunt's vow to never again speak to her, after what she'd done with Mimi's money. Her family, up in smoke, dead, or indifferent to her whereabouts. She thought of dear Samuel and what might have been. With Edward, she had a chance to live. To love. To serve God in a way that would please Him. And keep her safe.

◆

"So you married him and lived happily ever after." Jet lag, or perhaps worry, clouded Samuel's eyes. No wonder; it was two in the morning, Central Standard Time, though Hawaii was an ocean away from anything central.

She walked to the open window, let the sea breeze ripple her hair. The restless surf dredged up memories. The Franklins' reluctant blessing, the congregation's lukewarm acceptance, Edward's insistence that jazz not be played in their home. The thousand little irritations of a safe, sterile marriage. "I have had a good life," she told him . . . and herself.

"But did you love him?" her son demanded, his tone harsh.

Guilt made her face him. It wasn't fair for Samuel to think badly of Edward, who'd given her a home, a name, a mission. He'd been good to her. "I did—do love him. It's just he doesn't really know who I am. How can he love a woman he doesn't know?"

Someone knocked on the door. Sheila startled. Ever since the men had come for Papa so many years ago, she'd never liked unexpected visitors.

"We may be heading out sooner than we thought." Samuel hopped off the couch. Opened the door.

A man with a dimpled chin tried to smile as he entered the room. He wore a wrinkled but expensive suit, a red, white, and blue striped tie. Shadowing him was that familiar gray serge suit, those stiff collars and cuffs she'd starched and ironed countless times. Her Edward, out of place here in Hawaii.

Her heart pounded, furious as the surf. She'd loved, honored, and obeyed this man for eighteen years. He'd been her life since . . . she gave away her son. Maternal pride swelled her bosom. She crossed her arms, stared at bleary eyes. Whiskered cheeks. The reek of sweat and—liquor? Had Edward been drinking? Prickles skittered her arms. Who was this man standing two feet in front of her?

"Sheila." No slur in the word. No, it was brittle and hard.

"What—what are you doing here, Edward? How did you find me?"

"The general, Sheila. *My* friend." Edward inclined his head toward the young man. "This is John Berger. General Douglas's assistant."

So the Old Horseman hadn't kept quiet. So much for Moody loyalty. "Hello, Mr.

Berger." She shook a limp hand and, despite the betrayal, tried to smile for the sake of poor John, tossed unknowingly into shark-infested marital waters.

Then she stepped to Samuel, took his elbow, and guided him toward the men. "This is my son, Samuel Allen."

Samuel, his spine military stiff, held out his hand to Mr. Berger, who shook it. Extended it to Edward, who ignored it.

She ground her teeth to keep from shouting. How dared he ignore the best part of her? "Why are you here, Edward? Samuel and I have things under control."

Samuel squeezed her arm. "Mother—"

"I'll bet you have." Edward's eyes pierced her and then skewered Samuel. "No telling what line you've fed her to go along with your cockamamie scheme."

"He's fed me nothing, Edward. And it wasn't his idea." She stepped so close, she could smell Edward's sour breath. She swallowed hard. Winced. It was so unlike him to be unkempt. But then his wife had never before skipped the mainland.

"Sheila, you mean to tell me you arranged this preposterous scheme?"

She tapped her head. "I do have a brain in there. Though it hasn't been used much, most of the parts seem to be working." She glanced at Samuel. "Finally."

Edward's face reddened. Berger's paled. She was sorry—no, she wasn't. She leaned against her son, determined to stand by him.

Edward cleared his throat, smoothed his lapels. Touched gray temples.

She smiled bitterly. Wasn't he a master of transition? From pulpit to ballroom. From boardroom to classroom. Edward hadn't flown here to throw a temper tantrum. Edward had control now. Or so he thought.

"Samuel, it's a shame we had to meet under . . . such conditions." Edward moved forward until his shiny wing tips fronted Samuel's sandals. "I'm sure you understand why I can't let my wife—your, um, birth mother—accompany you to a third world country." He motioned John forward. "Mr. Berger here will do all he can to get your . . . friend out of Bangkok. His boss, a pal of mine, will make calls, contacts, whatever we can do to help."

Betrayal stung. Why had that Old Horseman done it? How many cups of tea had she served him? But it wasn't just the Horseman's betrayal that stung, it was Edward's refusal to see, really see, Samuel. Sheila lifted her chin. "Mali's not Samuel's *friend*, she's his fiancée!"

"Now, Sheila . . ." It was the tone he'd used when she begged to work at the shelter, begged to counsel that young pregnant girl, begged to take clarinet lessons. Her stomach churned. She was sick to death of placating tones. She stepped forward, her fists clenched. No matter what happened, she—and her son—wouldn't be placated.

"Edward." Her calm shocked her. It was Papa's confidence, after all these years. Maman's soft but sure notes. "I'm going with him. I've never asked anything from you. Don't deny me this." She stepped close, longing to find refuge in Edward's arms.

Not a chance.

Edward fixed her with a glassy, impersonal stare. The only signs that Edward was a man, not a statue, were beads of dripping sweat and that breath. She gripped him by his lapels, longing for him to know that Samuel was as much a part of her as he was. Knowledge of her mutinous thoughts made her bury her head into his shirt. She would give up everything—including Edward—for her Samuel.

"What has gotten into you?" He stepped backward, distancing himself.

She studied him, wanting to see love after years of devotion. A flinty stare, flared nostrils, was all she got.

"Do you realize what could come of this?" His eyes flicked to her face, then shifted to hone in on another target. Her son.

She darted gazes between the two men in her life. Felt her body crack along a fault line. *Her* fault; this whole mess. Still, someone would remain standing. And it would be Samuel if she had any say.

Samuel's unblinking blues locked on her as if she were the only person in the world.

Heat rose from her heart. Burned into the room. Shut out poor John's stammers. It was the lazy heat of a day on the veranda. Bees zigzagged, dizzy from the nectar of a thousand long-throated flowers. Maman fanned herself as she read aloud. Pipe smoke wreathed Papa, whose feet tapped the rhythm of his latest composition. Though she was in Hawaii, with one look, her son had brought her the sultry wonder of a New Orleans summer day. But that was just the start . . .

Cicadas droned with the chorus. Love, love, love, they sang, transporting her to Chicago. A blissful three-year courtship. Her marriage bed. Strolls by Lake Michigan, Edward holding her tight. Deep kisses by the monkey cage at Lincoln Park Zoo. A nearly perfect marriage. To a woman he didn't know. But he could know her. She moved to Edward, threw her arms about his waist. With God, it was possible. "Come with us!" She battled a screech of excitement. "They'd never stop *you*, a man of the cloth. We'll get her out! We'll—"

His fingers dug into her wrists, the sudden pressure dizzying.

"Are you out of your mind? I can't let you go through with this . . . this charade."

Something grazed her shoulder. She inhaled a clean soap smell, a hint of salt and ocean breezes. Samuel flanked her. A wall. A fortress.

"He's right, Mother."

The words slammed into her ears. She had played a tune called *safe* for years, and she was done with it. Neither of them could stop her. She jerked away from Edward, spun to face Samuel. "No, he's not."

Samuel's slender fingers, so like Papa's, touched her again. "It's no place for women. We talked about that before."

Women. Like your Mali, Son. She tried to conjure up an image of a dark-eyed, dark-haired beauty, but memory—or the Spirit?—presented her with a pale-faced prostitute, lying on her deathbed. Mali's fate, if they didn't intervene? The images would not let go. *If he loves her, so do I. And that means we will help her.*

"That's right. It's no place for Mali, either." She backed up and turned, both men in her line of vision so she could hammer them with resolve. "I'm going with you, Son." Music, soul music—God's music, she was sure of it—began to play. "We won't leave until we get her out."

Something like hate reddened Edward's face "If you do this . . ." he growled.

"What?" she yelled. "What will you do? Divorce me? Arrest me? Headline the papers with our nasty mess?" She noted how gray hairs had mottled the fine Franklin eyebrows. Aged him. She heard poor John's strangled sound. Right now, she didn't care. "It would reach Chicago, you know. It would be big in all the church circles."

A bluish hue touched Edward's lips. He lifted his hand, as if to strike her.

"So you're going to slap me around." Emboldened by a peace that trumped logic, she stood tall. Looked Edward in the eyes. "A man of the cloth, reduced to this." Adrenaline flooded her body. She took a breath. She couldn't let anger incinerate her. She had to rely on the Spirit. On truth. After all these years, she, of all people, would rely on truth.

"Well, what do you want me to do?" he snapped.

Despite his illogical comment—her Edward, illogical?—she longed to do whatever it took to convince Edward of her love. But she couldn't, not with Mali waiting. Dying, trick by awful trick. "There's only one thing you can do for me. For us." Though she'd softened her tone, she linked her arm with Samuel's and stepped away from Edward, whose open mouth exposed perfect teeth. Of course he was shocked. He'd flown all the way to Hawaii to find her, and had met someone quite different than Sheila, the subservient pastor's wife.

The door banged open. In strode Private Daniels, oblivious to the room's tension. "Captain Allen, everything's ready, sir."

Samuel joined Daniels at the door. The two whispered acronyms informing that plans had been made, orders signed, yet she could not tear her gaze from Edward. What she saw roiled her stomach. Hadn't she stabbed him for years with her lies? Her vision swam. *God, why must I choose between my husband and my son?*

"What was the thing you wanted me to do, Sheila?" Edward edged nearer. Emotions sparked those silvery glints in his eyes.

Her heart punished her rib cage, telling her how much she loved him. But he would not stop her from this thing she had prayed about. Shed tears and sweat about. Believed, with every fiber in her, God had willed her to do.

She breathed deep. "Pray, Edward." She exhaled. "Pray for Samuel. For Mali. For me."

◆ ◆ ◆

On the runway a C-130 roared to life, fueled by the Old Horseman's command. Strange that he'd given them a ticket to ride to Thailand despite blabbing her scheme to Edward. Typical top brass, Samuel had grunted. It was enough to scramble her brain. Was God orchestrating this thing, or was her desperate attempt to make up for her past ruining her future? Samuel was her future. But Mali? Was it God's will that a Thai prostitute be added to their family tree?

As a loadmaster and pilot darted in and out of the unwieldy aircraft, Samuel grinned. "So what do you think, Mother?"

"It looks like a giant pregnant guppy." She infused her voice with gaiety. A quaver betrayed her. "Except it's gray. And has a flag painted on its tail."

Samuel laughed, so easy, so free, she willed away misgivings about flying, about Mali, about Bangkok's seedy underbelly. She basked in the knowledge that she was content to die in a Southeast Asian country, if God willed it. And hadn't God answered her prayer to see her son again? Hadn't God shown her, with knowledge that penetrated to the core of her soul, that Samuel loved her back?

The loadmaster stood at the rear of the aircraft and motioned them aboard. Samuel helped her up the ramp and into the C-130's bowels, which were blanketed with gray insulation. A mysterious vapor oozed from the aircraft walls.

She took the stick of gum Samuel offered, put it in her mouth, and rolled the foil wrapper into a tiny silver ball. She'd entered another world. Strapped-down engine parts, code-stenciled crates, and two rows of inward-facing seats cluttered the narrow space. Overwhelmed, she flattened her spine against a support beam and waited for Samuel to tell her, a mindless woman who might as well be going to the moon, what to do.

"Are you okay?" Concern crinkled his eyes.

She nodded, chomping on the gum so she wouldn't cry. Funny how her peace vacillated with each rumble of this unwieldy thing.

An open door let in sun rays that beamed an aureole about her son. "Pretty loud, huh?" he mouthed and pointed to his ears.

She shrugged, intent on not being a burden. After all, she had insisted on coming along. The last thing he needed was a maternal yoke on his shoulders.

"Good thing you finished that story last night," he shouted over the engine roar.

"But I haven't heard any of yours." *Or Mali's.*

He leaned close, cupped his ear.

"I haven't heard your story," she shouted.

Laughter dimpled his cheeks. "Don't think it'll happen in here."

Steam continued to ooze from the ceiling, creating a netherworld. She, who had built her life around following rules, shattered it all when she set foot on this thing. Actually, when she had met him at Etienne's. What price would she pay for this new attitude of *carpe diem? But it isn't really new.* She thought of Maman, Papa, her slave roots . . . Sheba. *It's just been dormant.*

Samuel pointed to the plane's ceiling. "It's just the AC, Mother. Otherwise we'd freeze, swelter—or both." He patted her shoulder. "You're a long way from the South, from Chicago—a new adventure, huh?"

She could only smile at this son who'd discovered that boisterous little girl in a week . . . and think of the husband who hadn't done so in eighteen years.

"It'll go faster than you think." About the time he strapped down their bags, the aircraft wobbled forward like a wasp drunk on nectar. "Only a few hours to Kadena."

Kadena? Weren't they heading straight to Bangkok? What she *didn't* know could fill this thing. She hunkered down on the ledge they called a seat, her limbs stiff, her lips tight, as if God had sent her into a combat zone. Bangkok might prove to be just that.

As the aircraft vibrated off the ground, she bowed her head and raised prayers to the heavens. "Father, it's in Your hands. And so are we."

Chapter 33

River of Kings

W e'll grab a bite, then head to Pattaya."
A noncom, whatever that was, had met them at the terminal and driven them into the heart of Bangkok. At a tin-roof shed, Samuel exchanged dollars for *bahts* but held back wads of American green, the currency favored by those in illicit trade, or so Samuel said. *So Samuel said.* She bit her lip, trying to batten down doubts the bumpy flight had jarred loose about this scheme. Samuel wouldn't be the first man snared by feminine wiles. Was she risking her health, her marriage, her money, to line the pockets of a greedy girl? She nearly tripped.

"Careful, Mother." Though Samuel tightened his grip on her arm, she struggled to find the rhythms thrummed on the street. Cars, rickshaws, and miniature trucks had been converted into buses and stuffed with people. Shimmering canals cut through a concrete jungle and bore long-tails, sloops, and cruisers—boats the Mississippi and Lake Michigan rarely saw. Peasants, businessmen, and hookers thronged the sidewalks. Street vendors in pajama-like trousers dipped ladles into steam tables filled with delectable-looking dishes. She'd come a long way from Chicago.

"Pad thai, please," Samuel said.

Aromas of basil, mint, ginger, cilantro, turmeric, and lemongrass swirled with body-sapping heat to create hunger like she'd never experienced. The vendor's mysterious eyes were nearly hidden by a coned hat. Queasiness joined hunger pangs. What mysteries must be uncovered to find Mali?

"Two *baht?*" A gap-toothed grin creased the vendor's face.

Samuel raised two fingers. "Two *baht* too high. For two *baht*, two *pad thai kung.* Two apples." He paid, handed her chopsticks and a steaming bowl. "Ah, back to Bangkok. Where everything is a bargain."

Even young, innocent girls? She quashed doubts by concentrating on succulent shrimp and noodles drowning in a dark, oily liquid. Fragrant. Foreign.

Mangy dogs with running sores zigzagged the crowd. With bulging eyes and panting tongues, they desperately sought the food whose smells seemed to have driven them mad. Oh, it was a mad world! Was *she* mad to have come here?

"Not exactly a picnic table nearby, is there?" he asked.

She laughed shallowly, as did he. "But we're not here for a picnic."

He nudged her through the crowd until they both leaned against a storefront plastered with movie posters of voluptuous starlets sheathed in silky gowns and holding swords. She kept eating but struggled to focus on her food when the Orient passed in front of her eyes, stepped on her foot, jostled her hand. Thousands of people, among them, women in tight skirts that flaunted shapely legs. A cloud of musk and sandalwood tinged the air with aphrodisiacal allure. No wonder men flocked here looking for girls. Mali—the woman they'd crossed oceans to find—was one of them. She glanced at her son. Did Mali wear such clothes and shoot come-ons to everything in pants?

Bong, bong . . . She caught a rhythmic tympanic beat that echoed through cries, laughs, and a foreign tongue. "What's that sound?" she asked her son.

"The temple gong."

She savored the exotic tone but kept tracking the girls. "How do they allow . . ."

"Prostitution?" He shrugged. "It's partly the culture. Partly our fault for dropping a million love-starved soldiers into an agrarian economy." His wave encompassed the bustling sidewalks. "These are peaceful people. But they're desperate for food, especially up north. Dirty cops prostitute themselves by protecting the brothels, and the government looks the other way." He took a bite. "It's a thriving enterprise. Millions would starve if they closed up shop."

Oily sauce pooled in her stomach. Her grandmother had done the same to save Maman. Were things really so different over here?

◆ ◆ ◆

"The Oriental Pattaya. Step on it." Samuel fanned dollar bills close enough to the cabbie to ensure a leaden foot. It was always about money. Power.

Rice fields and *klongs,* banana and palm trees ringed houses on stilts and were juxtaposed with rickety structures that proclaimed, "Fix Cars," "Meet Johnny Walker." Countless signs taking advantage of the forty-four consonant, twenty-eight vowel language. Mali's language. Had he mastered it well enough to pull off this scheme?

Their taxi streamed through the outskirts of Bangkok and clamored with *tuk-tuks* and rickshaws and *baht* buses and bicycles for asphalt. Oddly, the cacophony of sounds soothed his frazzled nerves.

As they barreled toward Mali, vehicle traffic thinned, but not the pedestrian kind. Men in blue shirts and trousers carried their stoves—and livelihoods—on shoulder poles. A traveling monk, ditching the traditional saffron garb for a dull brown robe, slumped toward Bangkok. His eyebrows and head had been shaved, as custom dictated. For his mother's sake, Samuel wished he could explain the incongruities: Peaceful Buddhists; violent warlords. Modesty; prostitution. His own dear Mali, so pure, yet earning bread by lying on her back. But he didn't understand it himself.

Mali. Desire shot through him as he envisioned her curvy body under a silky sheath. To tangle his hands in her hair, touch her petal-soft cheeks, bring the light of hope to her dark eyes, rip her from that devil who imprisoned her with a threat to empty her family's rice bowls. So help him, he would release her from that pit reeking of incense and pull her from the gaze of that Buddha statue . . .

"It *is* beautiful." Childlike, his mother stared out the window. The awe in her voice confirmed seduction by the swaying palms and gulf's emerald waters. He'd certainly been seduced by this land and its people. If he married Mali, as he planned, he'd find a way to preserve her traditions yet free her from a culture that allowed her enslavement and abuse.

"Parts of it are beautiful, yes," he agreed. She hadn't seen the addiction and venereal diseases that seeped into fertile topsoil and poisoned the sweet-smelling flowers that wooed the tourists, the GIs—wooed all of them.

Her fine straight nose twitched, doelike eyes widened, and confirmed what he'd known through a half-dozen sleepless nights. His mother was too naïve, too innocent in the ways of the hooker scene, to risk taking her to Butterball's. He'd go solo, pay Butterball for Mali's bar fine, hopefully for the last time. Then they'd hightail it to the embassy, where his mother would pull out her letters from General Douglas and the financial documents showing her plan to sponsor Mali. If that Horseman had the power his mother thought he did, Mali's visa should be stamped, they'd book a flight back to the States, and live happily ever after. He closed his eyes, envisioned Mali wearing a wedding gown, and snapped to when the cabbie veered around an oxcart. *Get a grip, Bub. One step at a time.*

"You'll stay at the hotel."

She drew back, as if he'd slapped her.

The cabbie, driving with one hand, fiddling to no avail with a vent and the radio with the other hand, seemed to be ignoring them.

Samuel telegraphed a look to his mother. "The Oriental Pattaya," he said, both for Mother's and the cabbie's benefit. "Best digs in Thailand." He shrilled his voice like an eager tourist but again eyed the cabbie. Smiles hid souls hungry for money, power, and bent on betrayal. Things that would slay them. He hoped his mother understood that. "We'll unpack. Take a nap." He gave his mother a phony smile. "Then we'll celebrate. See the town."

"*Farang* want girl?" The rearview mirror caught the light of greed in dark eyes. Samuel grimaced. They knew more English than they let on. It was good that he'd been cautious.

"*Farang* no want girl." Disgust coarsened his voice. *Farang* did want girl, but not like this man thought. He resisted grabbing the cabbie by the scruff of his neck to show what he thought of the brothels. That wouldn't help Mali. He clamped his jaw shut and tried to let the peaceful scenery tame his wrath. It would take a miracle—and a soldier under control—to rescue his girl.

The cabbie pulled to the curb. Samuel shoved a fistful of dollars at the cabbie.

"*Farang* want *ganja*? Budweiser?" The man grinned again.

"*Farang* wants you to shut up, get our bags, and leave." He talked in the polite way Thais loved.

"Aye-aye, number-one soldier." The cabbie gave a brief *wai*, but a mocking smile showed English was definitely his second language. And told Samuel that they needed to scram. Fast.

If his mother heard the exchange, she didn't let on. The way her head swiveled, she'd been romanced by the stepping-stones that cut through the hotel's terraced garden of betel nut and cocoa palms, breadfruit and mango trees, banana plants and one ancient banyan. He took her arm and pulled her up a gradated slope, past uniformed gardeners who stepped soundlessly among the plants, hoses in their hands; up, up, up through an Eden perfumed by jasmine. Water tinkled into stair-step lily ponds and decreased the odds they'd be heard. The *swish, swish, brrrr* of sprinklers would mute their voices as well. They had to talk about this one more time. Out here in the open seemed best.

"They're so beautiful!" His mother plucked a jasmine bloom and tucked it behind her ear. Her arms spread as if to hug the magnificent garden . . . the magnificent country.

Her naïveté tightened his jaw, but he willed it away. Let her savor the wonders of Thailand. After all, she lived in the drab Midwest.

"Mali . . . it means jasmine." *And every second we waste, she's wilting, wilting . . .*

"I'm sorry." As if she'd noticed his urgency, she yanked the flower from her ear, flung it into a gurgling pond. "Here I am thinking about a flower when . . ."

"No." He found her hand, hoped a quick squeeze showed his gratitude for all she understood, all she had done . . . and was going to do. "It's okay."

They'd covered the basics as they'd waited for the transport, but he'd go over it again, just in case. Life as a pastor's wife hadn't prepared her for this. Then he remembered Sheba, the girl who'd taken on the mob, who'd hidden her past from the great Edward Franklin. She might be better suited for this than *he* was.

"We'll enter the lobby together. I'll register, of course. You admire the flowers, sniff the patchouli. Stay in the background. That's the way it's done."

She nodded.

"I'll give you the keys. Then I'll leave. They'll figure I'm getting booze or another . . . girl, both of which I'll do. Go to the room and wait. And hang onto that phone number."

A twig snapped. Samuel whipped around. A watering hose slipped from the hands of a gardener, who *wai*-ed in the usual way. Under the camouflage of a peaked hat, had his ears pricked, eyes darted?

Samuel pressed his lips together to telegraph his message: leave us *farangs* alone.

"*Kor tod.*"

Only after the man distanced himself did he respond, "*Mai pen rai.*"

"Can't be too careful," he whispered to his mother. "Warlords and police sleep in the same bed here. They've got eyes and ears all over. Most everyone is on the take. Or wish they were."

"Just like Chicago." She tried to laugh, but it quickly died.

"I'll get Mali. Bring her to the room. They won't think a thing about it." He prayed that wasn't a lie.

Her eyes widened. Her skin paled. "You mean . . ."

He cleared his throat. Nodded. So she just now understood the charade. Doubt again crept in about her being here. He shoved it away. *It's too late, Bub. Move forward, or this'll never work.*

They approached a marbled lobby of gleaming windows and steel beams. Worlds from the tawdry hotels and bars that flashed neon come-ons—*Girls, Boys, Girls and Boys*—day and night. Offering much. Taking more. He leaned close to his mother. "If I'm not back in two hours, take a cab to the embassy."

She nodded, still pale, as they crossed the line of no return.

"Good afternoon." A squadron of hotel employees greeted them. "Welcome." Samuel managed a tight smile. Received more nods. More *wais*. More masked Thais.

"You got the number? Address?" he mumbled while stepping to a counter.

Nodding, his mother moved toward a gargantuan vase of lilies and orchids that spread perfumed allure. Had it all intoxicated her? His soldier's sense told him she'd kept her senses. Understood. For now, it had to be enough.

◆ ◆ ◆

"Welcome to Pattaya! Most beautiful part of Thailand." The minute Samuel left the hotel, a bellman swooped her way. His starched shirt and black bow tie matched the dress of employees who crisscrossed the lobby with fluid, silent steps. Like everyone here, he'd glued on a smile. She did the same.

"May I show madam to her room?" The lift of his chin, his lean physique, reflected precision yet grace. A rare combination in men.

"Certainly."

They were a beautiful people, these Thais, with thick black hair, dark almond eyes. But it was the language of bowed heads, curved arms, clasped hands that mesmerized her. What claimed their hearts? Their souls?

He put his palms together, templed his fingers in front of his nose, and nodded. Her bags in hand, he ushered her into an elevator. A heavy-lidded gaze mirrored what she'd seen since their arrival: discipline and a reverence that transcended the bustling chaos of this hungry city. Did the Thai derive tranquility from the framed pictures of the King that graced the shop windows, the cabbie's dashboard, and this elegant lobby? Or was it the Buddha statues, prominent in those same places, apparently revered by all?

If only she'd had time to ask Edward about nirvana, karma, and the wrinkled, chubby Buddha figure plastered on posters, calendars, even napkins. Her mind swirled with fatigue, questions, and doubt. Had she angered God by setting foot in the land of a lesser god? Of course Buddha wasn't a god at all, but just a man who claimed to find his own way to heaven.

The elevator chimed. Its doors opened. The bellman bowed. Sheila stepped onto plush carpet, checked her face in a pagoda-style gilt mirror. Twenty-four hours had wreaked havoc on her touch-and-go complexion, her stubborn curls . . . her resolve. She'd freshen up and get on her knees before God. She—and her son—needed help.

A giggle rose from the hall. Another.

"Come on, you slant-eyed—" American curses shattered the calm.

Sheila tore about the corner. Had East and West collided? From the sound of things, it wasn't pretty.

A girl-child clawed at the arms of a man twice her size. Tank top straps had slipped off her shoulders and exposed bruises. "Gigi no can make boom-boom!" She flung her head about. An elaborate flower clip thudded onto the carpet. Thick lustrous hair cascaded and met the waistband of a red miniskirt.

"Gigi'll make boom-boom or whatever I say for five hundred *baht*, you miserable little whore."

Blood roared in Sheila's ears. How she hated the sound of that word.

A room door opened. Closed. Another door opened. Closed. A synchronized performance by disinterested patrons. But Sheila wasn't disinterested. She shed propriety, stalked forward. No girl should be treated like this. "Leave her alone! Right this instant."

The man lumbered close. A peace sign on a silver chain nested in a hairy chest and over a potbelly. A bristling GI haircut framed a swollen face and Jell-O jowls. Her fists doubled. How dared he abuse a mere teenager?

The girl darted into a room and reappeared carrying a shoulder bag and high heels. She performed the elaborate Thai bow and tiptoed past Sheila and the bellman, who spat raspy words at her.

The GI made an obscene gesture, directed at Sheila. "What do you think you're doin'?"

Making a scene, the last thing we need. She bowed her head, brought her hands together. Would the self-effacing Thai gesture work for her? "Sorry," she mumbled. "Not sure what got into me." She made a point to study the design of the creamy white carpet.

"Look, old lady," the man snarled. "I don't know who you think you are, but you got no right messin' with things over here."

Like you do? She shifted her stare to the velvety wallpaper, determined to continue the act. For Samuel. Mali.

A beige lizard slithered up the wall and disappeared into a crack. She suppressed a scream. Americans weren't the only creepy-crawly things over here.

"It's all karma to them, don't you see?" Her feigned humility seemingly doused the soldier's temper. "If she don't make nice-nice with us, she'll come back as a louse, leper, or another call girl. Only ugly and fat." He scratched himself and slammed the door.

What she didn't know about Thai protocol could ruin their chances here. She swallowed hard, turned to the bellman, and broadcast a thin smile. These were graceful, beautiful people, and she was a foreigner who needed a crash course in Thai 101.

The bellman stopped at room 509. Waited. Again she gave him her smile, and it was returned, or at least lips parted to show crooked teeth. But something glittered diamond-hard in those eyes that her Western mind couldn't penetrate. What a fool she'd been to think peeks into an Oriental kaleidoscope would show her the soul of this land! If she didn't handle things carefully, she, her Samuel, and his Mali might end up bleeding all over the lovely carpet in this lovely hotel in lovely Pattaya.

◆ ◆ ◆

Samuel climbed in the taxi. "Take me to the seaside cabana." Memories of Mali's silky skin and wind-chime voice spiked his command with urgency. Soon he'd see her. Touch her. He dug for his wallet. At Butterball's, he'd cough up more cash. Mali was worth every dollar.

The driver slammed on the brakes, sat on the horn, and cursed an ambling peasant.

Samuel pretended to study a stretch of aqua sea almost too stunning to be real. It was all too stunning to be real. As scores of GIs infected with the clap, addicted to *ganja* could attest, it was too real to be stunning.

"You want girl?" A different cabbie asked the same blankety-blank question.

He shook his head, keeping an eye out for the thatched hut near the peninsula where the *mama san* Butterball spent her days sprawling in a beach chair, sipping rice liquor, chucking fried grasshoppers into her mouth . . . and selling women to men. To get to Mali, he'd have to cajole this woman who'd risen from dancer to bar girl to guardian of the brothel. Butterball, who'd just as soon slap one of the girls as look at them. She hadn't become the brothel keeper's right hand because of a charming personality or curvy figure. It was her dollar sign eyes, her uncanny knack for keeping those eyes fixed everywhere . . . and nowhere. He'd have to be careful here. He grabbed his paper bag and leapt from the taxi.

As the cabbie sailed away, gulls rasped. Bare-chested soldiers in khaki shorts frolicked in the waves with girls in *sarongs* and bikini tops. These men, already in debt to the War, would pay a price for their fun. Those girls would pay a price, too. Like his Mali. He strode by the cabana, surprised at vacant barstools. Of course, it was only eleven; most of the girls slept until noon.

"Hey, *farang*." Butterball's pudgy face peeked from behind the smudged newsprint of a *Thai Rath*. She lay sprawled on a beach chair. "Long time, no see."

His gut tightened over this game. "Hey," he managed. Sweaty palms *wai*-ed. "I came for number-one girl." He fished an apple from the bag. "Your favorite. I remembered." Butterball, named by a GI who'd drunkenly toasted her on Thanksgiving Day, had one weakness: greed. And she adored apples, one of the few delicacies imported—and thus pricey—in this country of luscious fruits. An apple gave him something to dangle, like a fat worm. He held out the street vendor's plumpest variety.

The old head bobbed as the sea breeze rearranged her hair into a mullet. "*Farang* want new girl?" She grabbed the apple, leaned back, and bit into it. With maddening slowness, she munched, then finally added, "Zoomies say this new girl is number-one girl."

Waves of nausea hit Samuel's gut. So the airmen had a new favorite? Well, he didn't, and Butterball knew it. Hadn't he used the code "number-one girl" to get Mali time after stinking time? Something had changed. And not for the better. He strolled to the bar, paid for a beer. Pretending to enjoy the stuff, he took a swig, wiped his mouth. Every move he made was being dissected and analyzed. "*Farang* doesn't want new girl." The words twisted in his mouth, but he gritted his teeth, forced them past his tongue. "*Farang* likes clean girls, no diseases. Like Mali."

Butterball's eyes narrowed until they disappeared in her shriveled-up face. "Drought got us all worried. Danger of fire. Time for *farang* to be careful."

Samuel clenched his teeth, tasted sand and salt, smelled his own spicy-hot breath. Butterball was either trying to warn him or weaving a web to trap him. His neck hair bristled. It was time to get his girl. Cut the bull. "Where is she?" He stepped closer.

"*Farang* ask hard question. Too hard for poor *mama san* with sick child."

He swallowed to get rid of the bitter taste. *Sick child—what a joke.*

Two girls sauntered close, flashing the pick-up sign. The wind snapped their short skirts. Always on the make. The take. Like Butterball. He withdrew a wad of bills. Money, the language understood when doublespeak failed, would grease his way. To get Mali out might take every cent he had. It would be worth it.

A huge grin was his reward. Butterball snatched the bills from his hand. "Mali in new place. Better place. Bar fine guaranteed by Khun Sa."

Knives plunged into Samuel. Nothing could be worse. Even tourists had been warned about the warlord who'd built an empire of brothels and sex shops and bars, protected by private police as well as public officers on the take. Khun Sa dammed up millions—maybe billions—of *baht* and let them gush onto the government, the locals, with enough frequency to keep eyes averted from his illegal schemes. He'd even set up clinics for infected girls. If Mali was in the clutches of Khun Sa, they both were in trouble. He moistened his lips. "Um, where is that 'new place'?" Would Butterball notice the hoarseness in his voice?

"Top secret?"

"Top secret," he hissed. Butterball always protected her own weathered hide. But he couldn't blame her.

Butterball smiled and held out her palm. After he again filled it, she gave him the address. "Many thanks," she beamed. "Butterball make nice-nice for *farang*." She stuffed the money into cleavage produced by a low-cut top and a push-up bra. "*Farang*? We friends now?" she asked, in a childlike voice.

"Friends," he muttered. With friends like Butterball—he whirled about, sick to death of the games. *God, help me find her and then get her away from him.*

"Farang!"

A lightning-struck tone whirled him about. What had gone wrong now?

"Take back." Butterball held crumpled bills in her palm. "It bring bad karma." Something like fear had crept onto her face.

Tightness drained from Samuel's chest. Well, well. As the Thai would say, Butterball had released a captured turtle. It was God's miracle, pulling compassion out from under that leathery shell. He hurried toward the "barbershop," praying nonstop for God's help. If Mali had been tagged as the number-one girl of a warlord, he'd need more than one miracle to get her out.

Chapter 34

Rhythm of Crisis

*B*eautiful . . . *but still a cage.* A low-slung teak bed monopolized the tiny room. A tasseled Chinese rug splashed color on a wood floor. More teak gleamed from a wardrobe set on the short wall. Light poured into the room and set fire to the brass light fixture and gold enameled end table. Yet vertical windows, barred like a prison, set Sheila to pacing.

Her echoing footfalls sent tremors up her legs. Trapped in a gilded cage, how could she help her son? Years rolled away as she paced, paced. Samuel, rocked by someone else, fed by someone else. Samuel. Samuel. Samuel!

"Oh, God!" She fell to her knees, the familiar helplessness returning with other nasty friends: fear and insecurity. "I've never been able to help him. I thought I could now, but I was just fooling myself." Her fingers raked silk pile. "Please, God. Save him and this girl he thinks he loves."

Yea, though I walk through the valley of the shadow of death, I will fear no evil.

Old English script from Honey's tattered Bible emerged on the slate of her mind. Tears filled her eyes. Somehow she saw the pages as if it lay on the floor next to her. And it soothed her.

God is our refuge and strength, a very present help in trouble.

"Yes, God. My refuge. My help." Ageless words. Timely words. Supernaturally shown to this preacher's wife who never could seem to quote Scripture verbatim.

She sang the verse to God. It was ecstasy, to be grounded in truth as danger loomed near. She sang, prayed, and vowed to continue that cycle as she awaited what God had in store for them all.

• ◆ •

He grazed a shoulder, clipped a hip, but the hordes that drooped along the muggy Pattaya sidewalks didn't bother a glance. Why should they? GIs roved this City of Angels in search of just the right angel. As if a one-night stand could heal the battle scars on their bodies and souls. Well, he had an angel. But she was leaving this city before another man laid a hand on her.

At an intersection crowded with venders, taxis, and an elephant, he veered right, shaking his head. Only in Thailand would a street-walking elephant not get a double take. Mali's predicament didn't erase the good times here. Her giggles when he tripped on manhole covers. Her soft hand just so on his arm. Strolls through luscious gardens. Drives through fertile countryside. As heat rose in him, he quashed an urge to sprint. *Act natural, Bub. Slow-time, good-time GI.*

Wedged between the usual three-tiered inns was a tired concrete building. A sign, *Barbershop*, in English and Thai, hung over an uneven doorframe. He remembered Butterball's whispery, "Barbershop." Pushed open the door. *Ready or not, here I come.*

Light flooded the dark room; he rested his hand on the wall until he could see, then shut the door. His muscles tensed, he stepped forward, craned his neck.

A bar stretched across the back wall of a room that reeked of cheap incense. Portraits of Thai kings hung over rattan chairs. On an end table, a bronzed Buddha sat cross-legged. Of course there were no signs of barber chairs or the musky smell of the hair oil Thai men so loved. He'd stumbled into . . . not a barbershop, but a front for something darker than Cong-plagued jungles. Evil. He could smell it. Feel it.

"Good afternoon." From a side door, a stocky man with a shaved head entered the room. He wore a flowered polyester shirt, baggy pants, and had a girl tattooed on his forearm. Chinese, Samuel decided, surveying the fleshy cheeks, single eyelids, rounded chin less common in Thai. A barely perceptible *wai*. If stereotypes rang true, Chinese in this kind of place signaled corruption. Money. Lots of it.

He shifted about, affecting the behavior of a war-sick GI certain the madonna-face he'd met on his last R&R was a ticket to karma. He walked to the bar and drummed his fingers on it, sending a *jingjok* scurrying up the wall. It wasn't hard to play nervous. "I'm looking for a girl."

The man dipped his hand into his jacket, pulled out a jade cigarette holder, and lit the cigarette with a Zippo lighter. "Why you think I have girl?"

Don't betray Butterball. You promised her "top secret." "A mama san down at the beach said this was a first-class place. I've worked with her before," he added, when the man's eyes disappeared into folds of skin.

"Which one?"

Samuel slapped the bar, hoping to give the message he was eager. Insensitive. "I don't know, man. They all look the same."

"Ah." Did he imagine it, or did the man's shoulders relax? "Mama san friend have no suitable girl?"

The man's command of English confirmed Samuel's suspicions. This was no ordinary *mangda*; surely he'd found *Khun Sa's* eyes and ears. "She did." Though adrenaline rushed through him and he itched to check his watch, instinct said no. "But I want the one I had before." Yawning, he slid onto a stool. "Mawi, Mali, something like that. Great buns. Like Miss Universe, you know?" *Forgive me, God.*

"Ah, Mali." Catlike eyes tried to penetrate his soul. *If only I weren't black,* Samuel thought. Asians despised brothers, who thought things in *America* were bad . . .

"We have others." The man snapped thick fingers.

A girl in lacy bra and tights swayed through a side door. She grabbed hold of a structural beam and wrapped herself around it. Samuel swallowed disgust for the girl and pole act and clenched his fists, desperate to keep from slamming them against something. *Cool it, Bub! Your future—and Mali's—depend on it.*

"I prefer Miss Universe." He found his wallet. Laid a C-note on the bar. Money spoke this goon's language, he'd bet another hundred on it. "Here's her bar fine. All weekend."

"Weekend? More for weekend." Greedy eyes gleamed. "Mali very special girl, but for two more C-notes, she's yours."

Don't salivate here. Be careful. He settled onto the stool. Forced furrows into his brows. "I don't know, man." He forced a glance at the writhing girl, who, from the looks of her blank face, knew little English, knew less about come-hither seduction. Did Mali have to do this? "I'll go one more. But that's it." *Right.*

The goon let out a sigh. "Okay." He shook his head as if he had given away the crown jewels. Though he didn't know it, he had. "Koy Yai is reasonable man." He stubbed out his cigarette in a seashell, clapped his hands. "*Wing.*"

The girl bowed and left the room, as did Koy Yai.

Samuel let out a breath, pretended to scratch his leg, checked his watch. In a place that reeked of evil, he couldn't let up quite yet.

Footfalls sounded from the opposite side of the room. He turned his head, wiped his brow. He didn't have to try to play the role of lovesick GI.

A bamboo and bead curtain rippled, was parted by those chubby hands. Koy Yai bowed, stepped aside, swept his arm toward . . . the most beautiful girl in the world.

She wore a cream-colored shirt unbuttoned to show the simple gold chain he'd bought her. A silk sarong was slashed to show well-formed calves. Shiny black hair fell to her waist. Manicured toes peeked from rhinestone sandals. Almond eyes found his. Locked him up hopelessly and then threw away the key.

He swallowed a lump the size of Thailand. She was so beautiful, so pure, in spite of all she'd had to do. "Ma-li." He mispronounced her name to continue the sham. "Long time, no see."

"Hello, Closs Man." The mask over her emotions slipped to reveal glistening eyes, a faint blush.

Closs man. She'd asked about his cross and then lost interest when he spoke of the true God who died for sins. Hard enough to explain to one fluent in English. Only God could teach her . . .

Koy Yai folded his arms like the nearby Buddha statue and eyed him in a knowing way. Samuel's ears started ringing. Could that statue, or this man, unearth secrets? He clapped his palm over the cross nestled against his chest. Neither Buddha nor this *mangda* trumped God's will. If *a-soon*, that strange mix of karma and evil spirits, existed, God would extinguish it.

"We'll be together all weekend, Ma-li. Grab some clothes." He smoothed his pants, moved close. "Remember our beach?" He smiled overbig and gave her a sloppy hug. Inhaled a heady new scent. Expensive. He cringed. Sighed. *It's not her fault*, he reminded himself. *She'd have to take Khun Sa's gifts. And act glad to have them.*

With a *wai*, Mali disappeared. So did his heart.

Koy Yai found a bucket, set it on the bar. "Have a drink?"

No doubt centipede wine. Sealing the deal, like the Asians loved to do. "Sure." He sat down, made small talk, fought a tremor in his hand. Surely she remembered his vow to get her out. If all went well, in twenty-four hours, she'd be kissing Thailand good-bye.

◆ ◆ ◆

My girl. He managed to hold Mali's bag and pull her close. They beelined past GIs, bombed and staggering, in mid afternoon. Some slobbered on girls; some periscoped the streets for an easy target. Well, he had his girl now and wouldn't let go.

At a street corner, she turned to him, belted his waist with her arms, rested her head against him. She was such a tiny, vulnerable thing, used and abused by men's twisted notions of a good time. "Sam-wel," she kept whispering. "You came back."

"I came back. Like I promised." He touched her cheek, felt his pulse quicken at the feel of her skin, the smell of—that warlord's gift of perfume. He grimaced and shoved away thoughts of Mali being anywhere but here. Now.

Heads bobbed up and down the street. GIs. Girls. Tourists with beach bags. A crowd offered anonymity, yet the thug who controlled the district—and Mali—had eyes and ears on alert for changes. Anomalies. He spotted no police, but their khaki uniforms, with insignia and tag stripes, blended seamlessly with those of GIs. And GIs were everywhere.

He kissed her on the nose. "You're leaving. With me."

Her head swiveled. "You no understand," she hissed. "Khun Sa sees all things."

He took her arm, led her across the street. "We're getting you out. Taking you to America." He planted his forefinger in his chest. "My home. Your home. Our home."

"America . . ." She leaned forward. A hazy look clouded sparkling eyes. Was it fear of change, or had she changed her mind? The former, he prayed, with all his might.

A mob of GIs and their dates weaved close. One girl doubled over in laughter, her hair spilling to graze her skirt hem. A sweet-sour rice wine smell tickled his nose, a smell Mali surely learned from her addict father, a smell she surely endured from her clients. He looked into her eyes, desperate to see her soul's desires. Did she really want him, and America, which to her might only mean, despite all he'd tried to tell her, "the War" and drunken GIs' gropes and prods? He kept moving, his hand on the small of her back, his eyes darting from her to the crowd. Near a hectic taxi stand, he paused, took her hand. He had to make things clear. Now.

"I love you." He drew her near. Cupped her face in his hands. "I want to marry you. Mali, I want you to be my wife."

Her eyes filled with tears. Something he hadn't often seen. Doubt threatened to rob him of speech. "Unless . . . unless you've changed your mind—unless you don't want—"

Her arms went about his neck; despite her petite size, he stumbled, nearly fell from the explosion of his senses. "Mali want Closs Man—Samuel. But Ma-li's fate—"

"Forget 'fate.'" He caressed her cheek. "It's a lie to keep you in chains." He fought an impulse to sweep her up and carry her to a cab. "But I won't force you. It's your choice." He nodded at the GIs. The girls. "No more bang-bang. No more Khun Sa."

"Mali . . . *plod pai?* Free?" She tasted the word, as if a new spice teased her palate.

"Free." He drank in the curve of her brows, her glowing face. Most of all her nod yes.

He hailed a cab. Made a liquor stop on the way to the hotel to continue appearance of a tryst. In the back of a stale-smelling, ancient Toyota, he gave his bride-to-be a slow, deep kiss.

When they neared the hotel, Samuel leaned close to the cabbie. "Wait ten minutes, big tip." He patted the man's shoulder, careful not to touch his head, a big no-no over here. Three of us gonna party down." As if she dug it, Mali added tinkling laughter to his guffaw.

They sashayed through the lobby. Samuel punched the elevator button. Drummed a Stones song on Mali's shoulder for effect. A Texas-sized wave at the hotel staff closed the act every local had codified . . . and many despised as obnoxious. Intrusive. *Another GI, tramping through Thailand with big Western feet.*

He and Mali entered the elevator. The wine bottle became a microphone as he sang about satisfaction. But what he wanted was for Mali—for them all—to be free.

◆ ◆ ◆

"Mother, this is Mali."

They're safe. Sheila let her hands fall to her sides and smiled.

Somehow Mali bowed without wrinkling her silky wraparound skirt. She clasped her hands, brought them to her forehead. A madonna—except for the low-cut blouse. Sheila longed to pull her up, protest such obeisance. Would that show disrespect? She did what she'd always done when in doubt—smiled and kept quiet.

"Solly. Mali too much trouble." Tears pooled in luminous brown eyes.

"No, no." Compassion propelled Sheila forward, though her throat tightened. Was spiriting this girl from her country wrong? For all of them?

Samuel pulled Mali close, wiped her tears with his fingertips. "It's not your fault, darling. Don't cry."

Mali nodded. Sheila nodded. Yet the collision of two cultures gnawed at her insides. What was she supposed to say?

Samuel released Mali. Unscrewed the wine, dumped it down the sink. Turned on the faucet. "Call the embassy." Sheila had to strain to hear him over the gushing water. "Phone's safer up here than in the lobby. Though there's no guarantee."

There sure isn't. Sheila found the note, though she'd etched the number in her brain. Despite doubts, she'd do her part to let embassy personnel know to expect them. With God's help, they'd soon be on American soil, even if they were still in Thailand.

• ◆ •

Samuel grimaced as they exited the hotel. No more cabbie, who'd scrammed, despite a sure fare. It's possible he'd sensed trouble.

"Would you like taxi?" A valet approached from the bellman's stand.

Samuel made sure to grin like a fool. "*Patpong.* Our next adventure." They set down their bags. "We might stay awhile. You know . . ." *Farangs* wouldn't normally leave Pattaya's action, but if he slobbered on about the scene in Bangkok, it would set off an alarm.

The valet darted too long of a glance backward—or Samuel's nerves had gone haywire. He didn't know which.

A cab pulled up. The valet stepped to the driver's window and punctuated conversation with waves and head shakes. Samuel's jaw tightened. Three *farangs* shouldn't merit all this. He tapped that stupid Stones tune on his knee to calm down. Until a problem materialized, he'd shelf worry until later. At least his mother had gotten through to a secretary, who'd promised to inform the ambassador. The guards. *If we can just get there . . .*

"Where to?" the cabbie asked after the valet left.

"Bangkok." He ushered the women into the back seat, climbed in next to the cabbie.

"Chinatown? *Patpong?*"

"Lumpini Park." *Close enough to the embassy.* He tried to stretch his legs in the front seat of the Cracker Jack box–sized car, rested his arm on the seat back. "Hanging loose." Two hours to Wireless Road, US soil. His pulse raced, thinking about it. "Say, Sheila." Phony flippancy shrilled his voice. "You ready to rock?"

"Sure." His mother's squeaky voice testified otherwise, but the cabbie wouldn't know how she normally talked . . . unless he understood the language of fear.

"Big night. Gotta show off the bright lights. Ya know what I mean?" The phony leer fell flat; neither Mother nor Mali summoned energy to play wild woman. Poor Mali, really a country girl, was bound to be trembling. His mother surely cringed in disgust. If this was the price for Mali's freedom, he'd gladly pay. And more.

Motorcycles, *tuk-tuks*, and cars due junkyard burial clotted the road. Tin-roofed businesses lined both sides of the freeway. Then a patchwork quilt of rice paddies and canals introduced the Thailand few tourists met. Farmers working their fields, sitting under stilt houses. Oxen roaming the field. Children dancing through puddles. Samuel exhaled. An idyllic life. Like the one he longed to share with Mali.

The cabbie veered onto a side road.

Adrenaline telegraphed an SOS down his arms. They shouldn't have left the highway. He shook the cabbie's arm. "*Tham arai?*"

The cabbie mumbled those darn vowels. He didn't understand a single one.

He looked over his shoulder. Found Mali's eyes. "What did he say?"

Mali nibbled on her bottom lip. "Toyota need fill-up."

"No pay." Samuel siphoned anger into his voice, acting the tightwad tourist, ticked at locals for gouging him. He glanced at the cabbie.

The friendly Thai smile had turned to stone. The Buddha ornament looped about the rearview mirror sounded like a metronome as they bumped down a potholed road. Tick. Tock. Tick. No. It sounded like a time bomb.

It's all wrong. Samuel scanned the countryside for landmarks, grateful that drives with Mali had introduced him to Pattaya's back roads. Grateful that Mali could translate enough Thai to partner in this thing. A quality cabbie would keep his tank topped off, his car on the main highway. A plan fomented as he pretended to ooh and aah over a water buffalo. Better to go it out in the open, with the influence his ID and gun could buy, than be trapped in here. But how could he get the women out of this jail on wheels?

They stopped at the confluence of a canal, street, and footpath. He whipped about to face the cabbie. "Drop us off." He reached over and rattled his door handle. Swiveled to see the women. "Get out," he hissed at them. "Now!"

Something cold and hard poked his left side. A gun? Every fiber in his body was on fire. "Hands on dash," the cabbie ordered. "Womens, don't move, or I shoot!"

Samuel nodded and slowly raised his hands. Despite his precautions, Khun Sa's eyes and ears had found them.

"No!" screeched his mother.

"Quiet or he die!"

Sobs escaped Mali.

"*E nang karree!*" Curses, aimed at Mali, threatened to explode his gut. His teeth clenched. *My piece could silence him forever. But not with his piece poking my side.*

Something clicked. An irritating buzz filled the car.

"*Narong, dai Mali, farangs laew. Klai wat kao.*"

While the cabbie jabbered, Samuel dared a look. The cabbie held a walkie-talkie in his left hand, clinched the gun with his right hand. Samuel studied the man's posture, his expression. No doubt about it; this jerk would blow him away. And never think twice.

The walkie-talkie hissed and squawked. Samuel lassoed the itch to smash it—and the cabbie—to smithereens. *Go slow, Bub.* He masked disgust with a blank expression. *This ain't the end. Remember Hue City. They said we wouldn't leave that hellhole except in a body bag. God had another plan.*

The cabbie cursed and then banged the walkie-talkie against the steering wheel.

Samuel bowed his head. *Lord, may I fear no evil man. Lead us to safety. Comfort me, with rod and staff, if need be. Or the barrel of a gun.*

Chapter 35

Mystery

The countryside passed. Mali and his mother squirmed in the back seat. The cabbie interrupted the engine drone by occasionally screaming, "No move!"

Though Samuel longed to console the women, the tremble of the gun poking his side nixed that idea. The cabbie was majorly stressed, inexperienced, or both. Not good.

The cab's brakes squealed. Samuel raised his head but kept his palms cemented to the dash.

Doors slammed. Feet crunched against gravel. His palms pooled sweat.

His door opened. *"Ai, farang.* Out." Peripheral vision showed a shadowy form.

"It'll be okay," Samuel whispered to the women, and prayed he was right.

Someone yanked him from the car.

"E nang farree!"

Spots danced across his vision as someone continued to curse Mali. He forced air into flaming lungs. If he didn't cool it, he'd get 'em all beaten. Or worse.

Three men in Thai police uniforms waved guns. Stripped him of his piece. Whirled him around, jabbed a pistol in his face.

He raised his hands in surrender, darted his eyes, battled pinpoint vision. Forced himself to breathe nice and slow but let his mind race. When had they been sniffed out? Butterball's? The "barbershop"? The hotel? In the warlord's district, anything was possible. Likely, he'd never know. *And it really doesn't matter. The question that does matter: What do I do now?*

A man wearing a black T-shirt, linen pants, and black boots sauntered past the cops like he was royalty. Jet black hair fell about a pretty-boy face. He wore a gold watch, gaudy rings, and an amulet cloth necklace set in gold.

A bitter taste filled Samuel's mouth. *Meet the worst of East and West.*

"Good afternoon," the man said, in impeccable English.

Khun Sa. Samuel nodded. He'd met Khun Sa's eyes and ears. Here was the rest of the creep.

"But you're not here to talk about the weather, are you . . . Khun Sa?"

"Always talk about weather in Thailand." Not one muscle twitched on Khun Sa's face. "Humid for you. Dry for me. Strange combination."

"Yes, strange. Many strange things." Samuel tensed his fists, which ached to shatter that movie-star smile, that teasing reference to Samuel's sweat and the warlord's cool. Who wouldn't be cool, with his resources? Samuel fought the urge to grind his teeth. Sighed in a battle to slow adrenaline rush. Thais never cut to the chase. They might as well set up a tea table while the ambassador waited, the plane waited, his and Mali's life waited.

"A GI and his mother. Strange bedfellows for a Thai whore."

Muscles in his fist screamed to be released. Probably what Khun Sa wanted. Well, he wouldn't play. He'd borrow an Eastern tactic: avoid the question. Slather on praise. "You speak very good English."

"A thousand thanks." Another bow. "Yet you did not answer my question, Captain Allen."

Curses. To know his rank, this viper had connections with top-stripe Thais. Or a chameleon had infested the US barracks. Either way, they were in a pit.

Khun Sa pulled out a lighter and a pack of smokes and offered one to Samuel, who refused and stepped away from the smoke. From evil, which radiated from the man. A prayer flitted through Samuel's mind. *But I will trust in the Lord and fear no one.*

"Have you heard of me?" Khun Sa dragged on his cigarette. His chest puffed up to show an ego the size of this country. Well, he'd humor the creep.

"Pattaya's warlord." Samuel pasted on a smile, swiveled to check on the women, who were still in the back seat. At least they weren't being strip-searched or beaten, things rarely done to females, especially *farangs*. But this situation screamed unusual.

Khun Sa swaggered forward. "I prefer to be known as—how do you say it? Entrepreneur?"

Samuel ground his heel into gravel. How long would this take? He envisioned the embassy, closing early on Friday. "Not the word I'd use. Selling women isn't my idea of good business practice."

Khun Sa chuckled. "Come now, Mr. Allen. Even Buddha admits the future is impenetrable. I think of my enterprises as insurance against a shifting economy."

While smoke curled about Khun Sa's head, Samuel scanned the scene. These goons had found a Thai-scape untouched by humanity, except for the occasional peasant plodding along the road shoulder. Peasants would never butt heads with police . . . or a warlord. He tapped his shoe. Best play along, learn the rules. Thank God for his army ties, which could be wild cards if the enemy held all the trumps. Wild cards until the brass found out he'd been placed on mandatory leave and shouldn't even be over here.

"Enough talk of business." Khun Sa tossed down a still-lit cigarette. Ground it with the heel of his boot. "What game are you playing with Mali?"

So we both know it's a game. He rolled his eyes. *Pretend we're two men, telling it like it is.* "A night on the town. Sex. Laughs. You know. You're making millions on it."

"Mother and *e nang karree?*" Khun Sa spat on the ground. "You are a spy, *farang.*"

Samuel shrugged. Breathed easier. Better a spy than a thief of number-one girl.

The police muttered, rustled about, practically pawing the dirt to pounce on him.

Khun Sa clapped his hands. "Mali. *Maa nee!*"

A soldier helped Mali from the car. Samuel smelled her perfume. Redoubled his vow to help her escape this life.

Khun Sa stepped close to Mali, gripped her jaw, and turned it toward him. "*Sa wat.*" Kissed her loudly on the lips. "Long time no see."

Samuel boiled, seeing the slime touch Mali. Five minutes alone, and he'd squeeze the life out of him.

As if smelling his fury, the officers circled about Mali and their boss, who pulled out a handkerchief and dabbed his face. It gave Samuel time to glance at his mother, pale but calm, in the back seat. Showing the stuff she was made of.

Khun Sa pointed to Mali's bag. "Are you taking a trip?"

"He pay fine," Mali managed, her words feathery. "Pay for fun in sun."

"Bar fine?" Khun Sa pointed at the heaviest cop. "Open it."

The officer grabbed the bag and pulled out a sarong. Sandals. A black dress. A Buddha statue. A bundle of . . . letters. *His* letters.

Samuel's hands twitched to snatch them from view. He'd been careful to speak in ambiguities, but who knew, exactly, what that base translator had written?

"A Buddha for the weekend?" Khun Sa stepped close, punished Mali with fiery eyes and a thin-lipped sneer. "And love letters? You think I am a fool?"

Mali templed her hands near her head. "Great Buddha protects *khohn nuu* from *farang*. Great Buddha—"

"You lie." A slap slashed the thick air.

Mali's hand flew to her cheek. "Please." She dropped to her knees. "Let them go bye-bye. Mali come with you." Her face bore the flush-red brand of Khun Sa.

Fire spurted into Samuel. Mali wouldn't pay for his decision. He sprang forward. Grabbed Khun Sa by the temples. Pressed hard. Honed in on Khun Sa's throat.

Screams pierced the air. Hands clawed him, but he saw only the face of his love. His first . . . and forever . . . love.

A fist slammed into him. Another slam sent him reeling.

His knees sagged. He still saw Mali, only in slow motion. Though he battled to stay near her, he began to descend into a tunnel. Falling, falling . . .

◆

Sheila leaned against the front seat, her hands opening and closing as men zeroed in on Samuel and beat him until he was limp. *God, don't let them do this!* Her gaze clung to his bleeding face, his Marine uniform, and his closed eyes. She bit back a sob.

Men dragged him to a car. Shoved him inside. More doors slammed. The car peeled from the clearing. Disappeared. Her son, stolen away. Again.

Despite buzzing in her ears and numb limbs, Sheila pressed her palms together. Bowed her head. "God," she cried, "I beg You, help us. Deliver him from evil, O God." She repeated the words until warmth flowed to her limbs.

Mali was shoved back into the car. Guttural sounds gushed from Mali's trembling lips.

Sheila startled upright, then threw her arms around Mali. The dear poor child, facing such horrors without the one true God . . .

Walkie-talkie static buzzed through Mali's cries. Footsteps crunched against gravel. Someone yanked open their car door.

A stream of words fouled the air, though Sheila comprehended little. Khun Sa leaned into the car, grabbed Mali's arm, and again yanked her out.

Sheila's heart bludgeoned her chest. For Samuel's sake, she would stop this. She twisted her way out of the car. Wedged between Mali and the warlord. Bear-hugged Mali. "Leave her alone!" she shouted.

Khun Sa shoved Sheila away, grabbed a fistful of Mali's hair, and whirled her about.

Sheila lunged. Grasped air.

The man slapped Mali. Punched her in the stomach.

"Khun Sa, *proad! Ya!*" Mali cried as she crumpled to the ground.

Sheila's fury cascaded in waves. "Leave her alone!" Saliva spewed from her, but she didn't care. Let him hit *her*. She could take it. She knelt to embrace Mali.

Khun Sa edged closer. Blood vessels bulged in his neck.

An insane urge to spit at him seized Sheila. Instead she hugged the broken heap that was Mali. "It's all right," she whispered, hoping Mali would understand.

"Is it, now, Mrs.—shall we call you Franklin or Allen?"

Sheila fought shock waves. Though Samuel had warned her about the warlord's influence, she never imagined he'd know her name. To keep her hands from shaking, she massaged Mali's back. *God, step in here, tell me what to say. I have no clue.*

"Answer me, *farang!*" The cultured tone had melted.

She tightened her grip on Mali. Struggled to contain gasps. Were they coming from her? From Mali? From both of them?

Be not afraid of their faces: for I am with thee to deliver thee.

More weapons from Scripture, at just the right time. Sheila raised her head and met Khun Sa's gaze. "My name is of no concern. However, if you'd take us to the U.S. Embassy, we can clear up this misunderstanding."

An officer shuffled toward Khun Sa. Whispered into his diamond-studded ear.

A frown puffed Khun Sa's face. Grunts mingled with kicked-up dust.

The officer stepped back, took great interest in the ground. Sheila didn't budge. This warlord wielded power. *But he doesn't control You, Lord.*

Mali arched her back, as if she sensed change. Hair fell over her face and curtained her view. And that might be a good thing.

"It's okay, Mali. Okay." Sheila prayed that she was right.

In the time it had taken to glance at Mali, Khun Sa had masked his emotions. He nodded and smiled that ghastly smile. "We will accede to Madame's wishes."

What? Her ears buzzed. Her throat tightened. She replayed the words to make sure she'd heard correctly.

"Madame, if you will follow Sergeant Chon."

She tightened her hold on Mali. Of course. They'd dump her and leave Mali to this man's twisted sickness. Maybe let Samuel off, too. She breathed easier, thinking that. But they'd come here with one mission: to rescue Mali. God willing, they wouldn't leave without Samuel's girl.

"I will stay with her." Sheila tilted her head toward Mali.

"You don't know what you're saying."

Sheila took in the haughty curved brow, leering eyes. Hadn't she seen power, obsession, and perversion in the minds of Westerners? He'd shown her nothing new.

There is no new thing under the sun. Underlined passages again responded to her SOS. "I think I do, Khun Sa." She spat out his name. Pulled Mali close. "With the help of my God, I'm willing to face it."

Glittering eyes met her gaze. "Very well. Take them away, Sergeant. To the teak house."

Sheila and Mali were ushered into the police car. Another trip, this time without her son.

"God," she prayed, "may Your will be done." She gulped air. "Lord, may I rest in Your peace."

When she looked up, there was Khun Sa, crouched down so he could see into the police car. He fixed her with a puzzled expression. She sat straight. Decided to take a chance.

"Please set us free." She spoke with precision, as if she'd been handed a script and was merely reading it. "Let us go. We will do you no wrong."

Light blazed from Khun Sa's eyes. Straight teeth bared in a wolfish grin. "Chaos is inherent in all compounded things. You have been that agent of compound." Foreign words streamed from his mouth. "But I shall strive on with diligence," he finally said, in perfect English. "Do what must be done." He put his palms together, bowed, shut their door, hurried into another vehicle, and disappeared in clouds of dust.

◆

They swerved through hazy rice fields. Sheila banged against Mali's shoulder yet kept her eyes peeled for landmarks. She had to get her bearings. Stay calm.

Peasants squatted about a fire. Sleek children zigzagged through occasional clumps of banana trees. She patted Mali, hoping to soften shell-shocked eyes. She'd tried to memorize the turns they'd taken, the landmarks—a stilt house, a shimmering canal—but her mind jumbled with Thailand's wonders, unfortunately unfolding from the back seat of a corrupt cop's car. "Lo, I am with you always." She whispered the words the Spirit revealed. "Always."

They veered onto a rutted road that scoured the car's undercarriage. Reedy grasses scraped against their windows. Aqua and black butterflies soared skyward, wanting no part in the actions of men. She longed to soar with them, Mali by her side.

As the car slowed, a man dressed like a monk approached on the road's shoulder. Surely he'd help them . . . she pressed her face against the window, tried to make eye contact, but he seemed to be contemplating the grass blades his bare feet trampled. She sighed, settled in her seat. If she jumped out, that would leave Mali alone. Not an option.

Another stilted house came into view. Hens chased chicks and were shooed by a bent woman whose gray hair wound about her head. When she smiled, she showed pink gums and tongue and pitch-black teeth.

Mali began to tremble and covered her eyes with her hands.

The Spirit's comforting words caught in Sheila's throat as a black mist moved in. Was this the teak house Khun Sa had referred to? Was this their prison? Why did it scare Mali so? "What is it?" she asked.

The girl shook her head. Was it that she couldn't translate, or had fear captured her voice?

They were led up rickety steps into a room furnished with throw cushions and an Asian-style divan. Geometric rugs covered a burnished wood floor. A Buddha statue peered from a high shelf. Another trinket, a ceramic princess, winked, plastic leis wreathing her neck. Urns with cupped handles fronted a horizontal slatted window. An aesthetically pleasing room. So why had a black mantle shrouded Sheila's soul the minute she'd stepped in here?

The burly policeman led Mali into a side room, from whence Khun Sa emerged.

A chill seeped into the house despite the balmy air. Sheila clasped her hands to keep them from shaking. *Yea, though I walk through the valley of the shadow of death, I will fear no evil: for thou art with me; thy rod and thy staff they comfort me.* Sheila crossed her arms. She was not alone. Had never been alone.

"Sit down, Madame." Khun Sa lit a cigarette, sat on the divan.

Sheila lowered herself onto one of the throw cushions, tucked her legs underneath her body. She'd rather curl up next to a cobra than sit by Khun Sa.

Smoke curliqued to the ceiling. "So you don't care for my company."

"Why are you holding us against our will?"

He stretched out his legs, tapped his heels against wood. "Did you not hear Mali declare that she preferred to remain with me? She is my 'number-one girl,' after all."

She knotted hands that itched to slap him. "Neither of us prefers to stay here."

"What lies have poisoned my girl?" He clicked his tongue, shook his head.

"None. Now please let us go."

"Mali will remain here. You are free to leave at any time."

She thought of Samuel's soft eyes and caring ways. "I won't go without her."

Khun Sa jabbed his cigarette into what looked like a priceless jade bowl. "Then you will both stay here, with the ghosts that haunt this place. Learn firsthand how those who disobey Khun Sa must suffer for the truth."

"We are not spies."

In response, Khun Sa snapped his fingers. Their driver cop and another man sprung forward, pulled her to her feet, handcuffed her wrists, bound her feet with rope, then shoved her down, this time onto the divan.

Her father had been shoved around by thugs and hadn't buckled. She'd reflect his spirit, in her own way. "I am not a spy," she hissed. "So why are you treating me like one?"

A shrill laugh chilled the room. "Are not we all spies? Are not we all a result of what we have thought? Have you and your son not conspired against me?"

She tried to speak but found she had no reply. If Mali was indeed his "number-one girl," they had conspired by taking her. Now the three of them would pay the price . . . unless someone intervened.

"When you see things my way, I will let you go. Alone, of course. Until then"—with a twist of his lips, Khun Sa bared his teeth and gave a hideous grin—"enjoy the Teak House."

Sheila sank into the cushions, her cuffed hands digging into her back. Cold chills racked her body. When had she last stared evil in the face? That New Orleans voodoo woman. Evil had terrified her then; evil terrified her now. She bent her head. Begged the Lord to help her.

Fragments of Scripture worked as a salve to her achy body. She succumbed to exhaustion and drifted into sleep.

Chapter 36

Purple Haze

He opened his eyes. Found himself in the back seat of a bouncing car, staring at the back of cops' heads. His mind revved.

From a spate of mongrelized Thai he snatched the words "bar girl," "dishonor," something about "next step." He struggled to sit up, realized they'd handcuffed him. He bent far enough forward to see bare, shackled feet. Every muscle in him tensed, quadrupling the pain. Needles stabbed his skull. His muscles screamed for relief. Here he was, a Marine—trained and tested yet impotent to help Mali and his mother. His head dropped. "God, keep them safe," he whispered.

Questions drifted in and out of a mushy brain; he struggled to seize them and formulate a plan. He opened his mouth. "Where . . ." Cotton coated his tongue. As his sanity spiraled like a crazy top, he clenched his teeth. Swallowed hard. Pulled from his mind's lockbox details he could use to ID Khun Sa and his men. Deep breaths infused confidence. He'd deal with this like he'd dealt with that raid. That ambush. If he knew anything about the Thai, they'd avoid a head-on with U.S. brass. With God's help, he would make sense of this.

"Take me to the base," he finally mumbled, with all the authority of a limp rag.

Howls split his head in two and drilled deep the stupidity of his request. If they acquiesced, he'd claim police brutality. They'd claim he'd abandoned protocol. Squeezing his eyes shut eased the pain, helped him think. So did pressing his forehead against the window. There had to be an answer. Would Uncle Sam work for him or against him? He feared the latter.

GIs had dragged bar girls into back rooms and beaten them instead of the Vietcong who'd killed their buddies. Combat-crazed men had stuffed *ganja* in their rifle barrels and inhaled the weed until they passed out, their guns conking them in the legs.

He longed to rub his aching forehead, but the cuffs prevented him. If instincts rang true, these goons would dump him in the seediest part of town and let his story blend into the tales of a thousand Bangkok nights. They'd be rid of him yet wouldn't have to worry about his claims reaching anyone with enough stripes to butt-kick Thai police chiefs.

He gritted his teeth. Eventually someone from the base would vouch for him. Hogbody. Deacon. Taylor. First he had to get out of here. "Could you take me to Club Victory?" he asked khaki shirt backs, shiny hair.

No answer.

Maybe he'd thought the words instead of spoken them. "Club Victory?" Like cheap alarm clocks, his ears buzzed and clanged pain into his brain. Spent, he fell against the seat back. Did the earlier pummeling cause this . . . or had they drugged him?

"Club Vic-to-ry?" The passenger-seat cop eyed the driver. Shrugged. Thai flowed like water, Samuel doing his best to translate. "Drugs," "later," was all he could comprehend. He lowered his head. Forceps gripped his skull. He willed every fiber to be still. Took shallow breaths to keep his rib cage from crushing his insides. Summoned reserve strength. Knew he'd need it.

The car swerved. Brakes squealed. He banged into the front seat and then collapsed onto the floorboard, like a bug on its back. His eyes closed. "God, give me wisdom. Strength. Peace."

The back door opened. Samuel tried to get up but couldn't move.

"Club Vic-to-ry it is," laughed one of the cops.

A smooth gray cloth smothered his face. Samuel shook his head, banged it against the seat. Bucked. Twisted.

The cloth blocked out light. Breath. He fought a fruity smell. Surely they wouldn't go to this . . . much . . . Troubles ebbed, as did throbs and jabs at his head. He was floating now, in a river of apple wine. Letting the lazy, luscious sensations take him away.

◆

Spiders and scorpions crisscrossed teak walls. Sheila, so frightened of creepy-crawlies, welcomed creatures more human than Khun Sa, who sauntered in and out, having his way with Mali, from the sounds that seeped under the door of that nearby room. Thank God Samuel wasn't here to be tortured by what had occurred and might continue to occur if she didn't do something soon.

Hoop-hoop! Exotic bird whistles pierced the air, saying, "Good morning, you fool! You fool!" The caged-in feeling, sultry heat, and handcuffs pressed in, making it hard to breathe. And it was so hard to think . . .

She stretched her neck. Tried to prepare for a new day. To help Mali, she had to stay alert. Fight the fogged-brain feeling that worsened after they fed her. She cast a look at the black-toothed housekeeper, warden, cook, who sat cross-legged on the floor and chewed a stubby wad of leaves, then spat into a tin can. *She's doctoring the soup.* Though her lip quivered with anger, she leaned against the divan, which had become her prison, except for guard-escorted outhouse visits, and massaged her fingers, desperate to hatch a scheme freeing Mali from her more heinous prison. She ignored her growling stomach. Vowed to not eat until they were free. She'd subsist on the Word, whispered by the Spirit. By prayer. It would be enough.

The old woman began to hum in a toneless, throaty way that threatened to erase the verses. Sheila clung to what was left of her mind. *Though you walk through the valley of death . . .*

The door creaked. Sheila raised her head, expecting Khun Sa. The thought gnawed away at her appetite and strengthened her resolve. With God's help, she would get through this.

A tall, gaunt man with a shaved head bowed and entered the room.

She struggled to rise, but could not. Movement birthed waves of nausea. She opened her mouth, unable to contain the beginnings of a sob.

The man shook his head, brought his finger to his lips.

The old woman rose, bowed in an elaborate way, and left. Remnants of her chewed-up leaves attracted antlike insects that moved in on their next meal. Predators everywhere. *Oh, God . . .*

Fighting a shudder, she studied the man's angular cheekbones and ivory skin. Was he here to prey on Mali . . . or her?

"*Yai.*" The man spoke a foreign tongue in reverent, hushed tones.

The woman waddled away. Dishes clanged from what she assumed was a kitchen. Was it safe to be alone with this man?

"I am sorry your visit has not been pleasant."

To hear such a cultured man besides Khun Sa speak her language strangely comforted her. She met a gaze that seemed to hold wisdom, seemed to know suffering. She noted shaved eyebrows. Blinked. That man who'd trod the lonely road . . . "Aren't you the monk I saw?"

"I do not know what you have seen, madam. I only know what exists."

She digested the strange words while studying the man who seemed to possess the calm of Edward as he prayed. Yes, she had seen him on the road, she was sure of it. But he'd shed his robes, slipped sandals on his feet. She pictured Edward in his custom-made suit and polished wing tips. Totally different men. Totally different faiths. Would a Buddhist monk—if that was even true—help her escape? She sat as straight as she could, though she trembled from a desire to open this man's heart, this man's soul to their plight. Mali's life, her life, Samuel's life, might depend on it.

"You speak English well." She scrambled to say something, anything, to garner sympathy.

"My father is a high official."

"In Bangkok?"

"He has been there, too."

"But not now?"

"He is everywhere."

She dug her fingernails into her tender palms. His double-talk was maddening. Could he help Mali? Samuel? She gathered her resolve, darted a look toward the room the old woman had entered, heard sizzles and bangs. A wok? She spoke quickly and softly. "We're being held here, against our will. Won't you help us?"

He glanced past her, as if something out the window captured his attention. "It is your destiny." Like a bit actor, he intoned the words. "We live in an illusion—"

She arched her back and turned, hoping he could see her cuffed hands. "Is this an illusion? Being chained like a dog?" Spent, she licked dry lips.

"Some would say you were a dog, in another life," he said, and then turned to leave.

Despite his flippancy, his drooped shoulders, the furrowed brow she'd glimpsed before he'd spun about spoke of turmoil in a spirit used to peace and tranquility. *God, help me get through to him.*

"My husband's a minister," she whispered. "A man of God. He preaches peace and love. 'Blessed are the poor in spirit, for theirs is the kingdom of heaven.'"

Did he pause for the briefest second?

"'Blessed are they that mourn, for they shall be comforted,'" she continued.

"'Blessed are the meek, for they shall inherit the earth. Blessed are they which do hunger and thirst after righteousness, for they shall be filled. Blessed are the . . .'"

His hand on the knob, he turned, bowed—affirmation or decorum?—and left.

"'. . . merciful, for they shall obtain mercy,'" she said, her audience now the feasting cluster of insects.

Later the housekeeper walked in, a steaming bowl of soup in her hands. A guard unlocked her cuffs. Sheila rubbed reddened, achy wrists. The woman nodded and smiled, as if she understood everything . . . or nothing.

Sheila bowed her head and begged God to give her a sound mind in the face of the monk's words and the housekeeper's everything's-rosy smiles. The words she had earlier spoken became her prayer, and lent a supernatural glow to her inner being. "'Blessed are the pure in heart, for they shall see God.'" Sheila set down the bowl. "God as my witness, I'll pray this until I believe it. Or until You let them kill me." She took a deep breath. "'Blessed are the poor in spirit . . .'"

◆

The lyrics to "Purple Haze" coaxed Samuel's head from a tabletop. He stretched out his hands, amazed at the reds and blues that strobes pulsated onto his fingers. It was right to be here. The core of humanity, the essences needed to solve world peace, had been condensed and packed into this room.

Women floated by. Some bent over and shared with him their mounded breasts. He smiled at them, smiled at the GIs at other tables, with even more lovely girls in their laps.

A pouty-lipped woman took his hand. He rose to his feet, would've sailed to the ceiling if she had not stopped him. She pressed her body into his, fingered the material of his shirt. Desire crescendoed and detonated what remained of his sanity. He wanted this girl more than anything he'd ever wanted in his life.

Drums echoed the beating in his heart, his groin. He put his hand on the smooth, round buttocks, tried to move with the girl, but his legs were crumbling . . .

The music bade another girl, then another to join him and the pouty one. They somehow propped him up, led him into another room. Beads that the girls wore about their necks clinked as he tried to embrace them all. Love oozed from every pore of his body. He had managed to capture love in a glimmering gemstone, turn it over, and examine every facet of it. Love had never been ex-amined like this before!

Long lovely Thai vowels spoke a lovely, lovely, love language that rolled off his tongue. Every fiber in his body cried out. He had never imagined such love existed. He loved this room. Loved the music cascading through his veins. He ached with love for all of them. Especially the girl with the pouty lips. So like . . .

Through a fog, yet another girl called to him. He squinted until he could see her perfect almond eyes, a tiny mole near her ear. With a tremulous voice, she begged him to stop. Why would she argue against love? To reassure the girl, he reached toward her, but the pouty girl grabbed his hands, pinned them to his sides.

Someone thrust another pill into his mouth. Forced him to swallow. Pushed him back onto the bed, where pain and pleasure swirled into an ecstasy of sensation.

Waves of pleasure ebbed, pain flowed. Ebbed. Flowed. His eyelids drooped, though he fought to stay awake. The room darkened. The great love began to fade. He had climbed the pinnacle of love. Now he was coming down.

◆

Another sunrise blared through the window. Yet the housekeeper kept chewing, chewing, that red-green wad, then spitting it into a bowl . . . or the floor, where those insects circled as if it were a chuck wagon. Though Sheila wouldn't eat, she hoped mealtime approached. At least they'd uncuff her so she could spill soup on herself and dump the noodles under the cushions . . . where she'd stashed one chopstick. Thankfully, the housekeeper hadn't noticed. Too busy chewing.

Another man walked into the room.

Sheila held her breath.

"You, *farang*." A wolfish grin stretched the man's face. Greasy hair hung about his ears. "Me want."

Sheila's skin crawled. To get as far away from the man as possible, she curled into the sofa. Was it her turn to be abused? "The Lord is my shepherd," she whispered.

Leering eyes took over the man's face as he stepped nearer. "Me want *farang*." He held out his arms. About his wrist was tied a string, from which dangled a key.

Desperate, Sheila craned her neck to see past the man to the front door—the only way out, as far as she knew. Dared she take her chances with the guard posted outside? Or *was* this the guard, bored and angry? Whoever he was, he had the key to her freedom. And she would get it.

The man sat next to her. The odor of booze and an unwashed body wrenched her stomach. She stifled a scream. "I . . . I have money. Dollars. Just unshackle me."

He shrugged, as if he didn't understand.

"No handcuffs." She cut her eyes to the bag. "And I'll give you *baht*. Dollars. In there."

A guttural laugh chilled her soul. He wasn't interested in money.

The man shoved her down. The handcuffs bit into her back. Her head jerked; with the same reflex, something inside her snapped. She ground her teeth together, done with reasoning, with bribes. Rape spoke a universal language—of violence and power. And she'd speak it right back.

She twisted about until her fingers reached into the grimy space between the divan cushions. Every muscle screamed as she stretched, stretched . . . and felt the smooth ivory chopstick. First she'd cajole him to free her, then stab him in the eye.

She drew up her knees. Tried to shove him away. "Hey!" Though it gagged her, she summoned a smile. "Let me go. Then we'll have fun."

He hovered over her. A gleam entered dark eyes. Then he fell on her, clawed at her clothes.

Desperate to do something, anything, her fingers tweezed the chopstick.

The man began to groan.

"No, no, no," she whispered, to drown out his voice. She closed her eyes, gripping the smooth ivory with all the strength she could summon in bound hands riddled with needle-stabbing pain, slick with sweat. She eased the chopstick from the crack in the cushions . . .

"*Aug pai, ai sat!*"

She quaked all over. Turned her head. It was Khun Sa. A savior? She gagged at the thought.

Her attacker struggled to his feet and staggered away, cutting a swath around Khun Sa.

Her breath escaped. The chopstick's ivory smoothness caressed the tips of her fingers, yet needles of pain continued to stab her hands . . . and her sanity. While she was being attacked, the old lady sat not five yards away, chewing her cud. As she'd gripped the chopstick, murder gripped her mind with such intensity, her head ached. She shook all over. Was she in prison . . . or an asylum?

"So sorry." A white cotton shirt and silky pants emphasized Khun Sa's leanness. He wore the usual necklace.

Khun Sa's tone snapped her back to reality. Oh, if she could only rip off his semblance of civility and expose raw evil. Yet as villainous as he was, he'd saved her from what Mali endured. She relived the touch, the smells, of the man as she let the chopstick fall into its hiding place. Would she spread *her* legs to escape? *Kill?*

Yes.

Though she was the daughter of a prostitute, she'd allowed legalism to shelter her and had the gall to judge women like Mali. She'd wielded Christian dos and don'ts under the refuge of Edward's ministry rather than Christ's solid rock. She'd smothered love with rules, and then blamed Edward when he did the same. The past exploded in Technicolor as she traced every step toward safety, smugness, death. She bowed her head. *Lord, forgive me. May I do this Your way. Even if it means death to Sheila . . . to Sheba . . . to Sylvia . . . to all of me.*

When she could again breathe, she raised her head.

Khun Sa adjusted a gold ID bracelet. "As you see, things are complicated here."

His cat-and-mouse tone lit a match to her simmering pilot light and vaporized fear. "My husband is a man of repute." She maintained a matter-of-fact tone. "He will notify the authorities. You can't keep us here forever."

"To find you, they must dive for a pearl in the ocean. Nonetheless *you* are free to go. Just say the word."

"How about my son?"

"Safe in the hands of the authorities."

Choosing to believe him gave her energy to point to the bedroom. "Let Mali go. You could have anyone." Her mouth snapped shut. Had she said those words?

Handsome features hardened like stone. "I paid for her. She is my property."

She swallowed repulsion. "Perhaps you would let me take her place."

The mask collapsed. Khun Sa's mouth gaped. Eyes darted about, as if desperate for an escape route. For a split second, a startled boy stood before her. Then the eyes regained their glint. The lips tightened. When the spine straightened, Khun Sa the warlord had returned. "You?" he spat. "No. It is she who must pay. I took care of her bar fine. Gave her the best clothes. What does she do? Betray me with a mixed-breed *farang*."

So racism knew the Thai language. Another universal behavior. "Why don't you just discard her?"

"I don't understand."

"Find someone more suitable to your standards."

"Mali must pay for her choice." He stalked toward her room. "It is her fate."

"And it is my fate to stay here with her."

"In that case, I will not keep you bound. The guard will take those off." He gestured toward her hands, her feet.

Sheila felt her lips curl. Surely not the one who tried—

"Do not worry. That one will not touch you again. The new guard, and your own mind, will be prison enough." He opened the door to Mali's room. "Now I must see my number-one girl." He slammed the door behind him.

A creaking sound drew Sheila's attention to the front door, which had opened to reveal the strange man . . . the monk.

Chapter 37

Sinner Saved by Grace

"Just what I need, Allen. A complaint from RTA." Bald-headed Colonel Engle picked up a file, slapped it onto his desk. "We're laying their women, strip-mining their resources, usurping their land, and you can't keep your pants on." Red eyes scoured Samuel's face. "Not to mention, you're supposed to be on leave, according to UCM—"

Engle's rant enflamed skin that itched from head to toe. Every joint ached. Fever racked his bones. Malaria? Images blinked like strobe lights. Where had he been? Samuel fidgeted in his chair. What had he done to land him in this steam room of an office? The colonel's, no less. Wasn't he supposed to be finding someone?

"According to this report"—the colonel dug through stacks of folders, put on wire-rimmed glasses—"you assaulted a police officer, trashed a bar. And that's page one of a twenty-four-hour rampage."

Images coalesced, as did memories of Mali, his mother, and a pretty-boy Thai who for some reason he wanted to skin alive. Yeah. That warlord . . . Khun Sa. But where did gorgeous girls fit in? He rubbed his head, asking his brain questions. Pain replied.

The door opened. A man entered, saluted the colonel, and nodded at Samuel.

"At ease, Private," the colonel grumbled. "What can you confirm?"

"Captain Allen at Club Victory from 2100 till at least 2300."

"Uh-huh." The bald head gleamed as the colonel buried his face in the report.

"The manager called RTA when Allen refused to pay bar girls after . . . receiving their services."

Images of a pouty face wrenched Samuel's stomach. Vomit threatened to spew. Surely he hadn't committed such . . . acts. Surely this was a horrible nightmare. "God," he whispered.

With a nasally voice, the private continued to report. "He left the club before the officers arrived. We found him passed out by a barbershop this morning."

Samuel quit listening and hugged his strangely twitching arms, desperate to still them. He'd prided himself on purity, lording that over his mother, a love-starved teenager who'd made one lousy mistake. He gripped his chest as if to halt seepage of lifeblood. Blood polluted by sin. What had he done? What had he become?

"Captain? Captain!" Curses flew from the colonel's mouth.

"Yes, sir. Sorry, sir."

"I thought you'd want to join this chat. Since it's about you. And your future." The colonel leaned forward. "Here's the deal. Cut the crap. Give it to me, low down and dirty. You hear? No bleached clean version."

This would take an ocean of bleach. But he'd never been one to lie, the one accolade still hanging on his moral Wall of Honor. He'd come clean and enlist the support of his superior in the search for his mother and Mali. "My mother and I came here—"

"Your *mother*?" Expletives erupted again. "Why would you bring her here?"

"To help get my fiancée out of Bangkok."

An openmouthed, red-faced stare told Samuel that he was either about to be tossed in the brig or that he'd finally succeeded in shocking the man into silence.

"I met her on R&R and promised that I'd come back for her," he continued.

"What a pretty story! For a thousand *baht*, she'll be standing on a bar stool, waving Old Glory and wearing flowers in her hair."

The disdain that laced his superior's voice tightened Samuel's jaw. "The trip over here was arranged by . . . a general, sir."

Bushy eyebrows rose. "And I'm Nixon's brother." The colonel pounded his desk. "Tell it like it is, man. Now!"

Sweat trickled from Samuel's pores. He battled nausea. Again he tried to sit tall as he pieced together images floating in his brain. "We took a taxi to Pattaya. Found Mal—my fiancée." He swabbed his brow with a damp palm. "Got stopped by a warlord—"

"Who says he was a warlord?"

"M-Mali." *And Butterball, but no way I'm going there.*

"The prostitute—your *fiancée*—says he's a warlord?" More curses. "Go on."

"Next thing I knew, I was wearing handcuffs. I think they drugged me, knocked me out, and drugged me again." The weight of what happened pressed in; he quivered uncontrollably.

"Holy—" Again the colonel swore. "Get the man something."

The private returned with a bottle of Coke. Samuel gulped down the lukewarm drink and nodded gratefully. "Thank you, sir."

"Uh-huh. Now continue."

"Next thing I remember, I was at a club. I . . . ended up with the girls, like the report stated. Though it seemed surreal. A dream." He cut a look at his boss, hoping he bought the explanation for his immorality. "They gave me a pill—"

The colonel slapped a freckled hand on his desk. "*Yaa baa.* Laced with heroin, no doubt."

Samuel closed his eyes. So Khun Sa had messed him up. Tried to kill him? He shook all over; whether from drugs or rage, he didn't know. "I need—excuse me. Sir, I need your help."

"My help? You're facing charges. And we can't get involved in a little—"

Samuel managed to stand though pain knifed his body. "It's not little, sir. It concerns my mother. My future wife." *If she'll have me after I tell her what happened.*

The colonel dug at his neck, slumped back in his chair. "This is what happens when East and West collide. There's just no avoiding it."

Samuel's muscles craved movement, yet jellied limbs wouldn't move. He slumped against the wall, summoned strength. That creep was holding captive both of the women in his life. Something had to be done. "Sir—"

"Tell you what, Captain." The colonel scooped up papers, shoved them into a folder. "We'll work with the locals, see if they'll cook the books. Get rid of this." He fanned the report. "As for this other thing, you're on your own. Uncle Sam can't get involved with . . . bar girls, girlfriends, or whatever you want to call them."

◆

A knock interrupted the men. The door began to creak open.

"Private, what did I tell you?" shouted the colonel. "No interruptions!"

The private, who'd been standing by Samuel, was shoved aside as three men stalked into the room. One wore khakis, a white Oxford shirt—Samuel's jaw went slack. *It can't be . . .* He straightened his spine. Unless he'd lost every aching marble in his head, Edward Franklin stood before him. He locked eyes with steely grays. Felt his mouth work in an attempt to verbalize this mess. Remained speechless.

Next to Edward stood the suit they'd met in Hawaii. Behind the suit stood—Samuel cocked his head. "Holy . . ." he whispered before he caught himself.

Though only the man's shoulders and head were visible, Samuel had seen enough stars. Enough stripes. Framing the door was a four-star general with snowy hair, a square jaw, a hawklike nose, and flinty blue eyes. Tanned, leathery skin and an aristocratic bearing placed him anywhere from seventy on up. Samuel's elbow banged the wall when he tried to salute. What was going on? This had to be a dream.

"Excuse me, sir," wheezed the colonel, his clueless eyes apparently stuck on Edward. "PR's in the other building."

"I don't need PR." Crankiness hardened the voice heard by hundreds of church members. And his mother, Edward's wife. "I need Colonel Engle."

The colonel sighed. "What you need is the receptionist. Sir."

The general eased past Edward. "Colonel Engle, I'm retired General Roy Douglas. I think we can forego the receptionist. Sir."

Papers flew as the colonel leapt to his feet and saluted. The private's skin blotched like a teenager's. Samuel held his salute and tried to stand tall, though every ounce of energy, every ounce of brainpower, had been sucked from him.

"You're dismissed, private."

The private skittered out the door. Papers rustled in his wake.

Two general-sized stomps, and the door shut. Two more stomps, and massive palms slammed on the colonel's desk. Again papers shook, as did Samuel. "We need an office."

Is this the Horseman? Samuel stared at a general-sized strip of beef jerky, dressed in khaki. *Mother didn't prepare me for this . . .*

"With an outside line," continued the general. "Secured."

Samuel nodded wildly, as if he were the one getting blasted instead of the colonel.

"Your lip needs to be zipped on this, Colonel." Not a muscle seemed to move on the general, yet power radiated from every inch of his body. History-book images of Patton, of MacArthur flitted across Samuel's mind.

The colonel rubbed his glasses against his shirt as if sight had failed him, put them back on, punched an intercom, and parroted the general's requests to a shrill-voiced female.

With a pivot, the general's eagle eyes froze Samuel in place. "At ease, Captain."

Samuel tried to pull from his cockeyed salute. Somehow his arms tangled, then his feet. He thunked to the floor. Stared at spit-clean combat boots with rubber soles.

A hand swooped down. Yanked him to his feet. Set him in a chair.

Samuel's jaw went slack. The general's ramrod spine had barely moved to pick him up off the floor. *If this man's on our side, praise God. If not . . .*

"Sorry . . . sorry . . ." The marbles had clanked from his brain and slipped into his mouth.

Eyebrows disappeared under a cap bill decorated with those four gold stars. "Good grief, soldier. What's got into you?"

"*Yaa baa,*" came from the suddenly-all-smiles colonel. He handed a file to the general, who seemed to scan it, then thrust it toward the man wearing the suit.

The general turned to the colonel. "Thank you. That'll be all, sir. Appreciate your hospitality." Crisp salutes were exchanged. "We shouldn't be too long."

Hurried footsteps carried away the colonel, leaving Samuel with Edward, a general, and his assistant. Only combat training kept him from slumping back onto the floor. Would Edward be next to read the report of his sleaze?

Again an iron fist gripped him, this time in a handshake. "I haven't properly introduced myself, Captain Allen."

"Yes, sir," he said, and flinched. *Why jabber, fool? You haven't been asked a thing.*

"Officially, I'm General Douglas. Your mother knew me as one of Four Horsemen. The stubborn one." Something like a smile stretched his lips.

Samuel gripped the chair arms. So the old Horseman hadn't betrayed Mother. Or had he? The room seemed to spin. Spots of light haloed the general. Samuel lurched forward, would have fallen. Again the age-spotted hands came to the rescue. "Heavens, Son. Get some grub down you. A shower. That's an order."

"Yes, sir."

"We've got work to do. You couldn't help a flea in your present state. Much less sway an Ambassador."

◆

As soon as the man entered, the housekeeper scurried away, leaving Sheila to face yet another mask. Was this man a monk or wasn't he? Should he evoke fear? Gratitude? She clasped her hands. Bowed her head. She had pleaded for an angelic presence. Was this it? Whoever, *whatever* he was, to come and go as he did, he must have clout with the guard.

He glided across the room, pulling nary a creak from the wood floor, a hovering presence, all bones, yet somehow fluid. "I bring food for the poor in spirit," he said.

Had God etched those words on his heart, or was he a mocker? Sheila interlaced her fingers. Sat tall. She would trust him. What choice did she have? "I'm glad you have food, for I am hungry." She took in his sunken cheekbones, drooped mouth. He looked hungry as well.

A note was thrust into her hands.

1200 today. Fruit for the poor in spirit. Expect bountiful crop.

So he would help. Or was it a trap? Should she nod, thank him, or do nothing? While she was deciding, he grabbed the note, popped it into his mouth, and swallowed.

For the span it took him to reach the door, she questioned her sanity. Had the note been in her hand, or had she imagined the rough, pulpy texture, the bled-through-the-paper words? Had she even come to Thailand? Or was this all a bad dream?

The strange man opened the door. The free world's birdsong and insect chirps proved her sanity . . . didn't they? When the door closed, she pictured a second hand swooping, a minute hand creeping, toward 1200. Lord willing, food would be delivered. She and Mali would partake.

◆ ◆ ◆

Hot grub and a shower loosed *yaa baa*'s choke hold. Samuel put on borrowed clothes. Plopped onto some GI's bunk in the deserted barracks. Grabbed his shoes.

Pictures of girls and American flags had been tacked on pitted walls. Fatigue hats and skivvies ringed bedposts. A gritty life. Gritty men. He couldn't sit here and look at it for one more second. He cinched his belt. Khun Sa held Mali, his mother. It was time to act. Now.

Footfalls clattered. Edward stormed into the room, bringing squinty eyes and a tight mouth. Samuel gulped. Would he rather look at those posters . . . or this face?

"I'll get right to the point"—sweat beaded Edward's forehead as he folded thick arms—"and skip the I-told-you-so's. For now."

Samuel nodded, as he had when the general rasped commands. Edward also commanded an empire, though of a vastly different sort.

"The general called in an old friend, and I mean old." Edward glared like an infuriated spouse. Fitting. "A Thai general named Narong. Their alliance dates back to World War II. The Free Thai Movement." Jowls reddened. "He pulled every string and then some to take care of your mess."

Samuel rose, holding out his hands as if in a peace offering. He regretted involving his mother in this. To think, he'd once planned to blackmail them. "Sir—Reverend—"

"Spare the niceties," Edward snarled. "They're neither needed nor wanted." An inhale expanded the formidable chest. "Here's the plan. This time, *you* listen. As we speak, two generals are having tea—" The word seemed to choke him up. Edward cleared his throat, then continued with the same intensity. "Yes, tea! While my wife endures Lord knows what."

Samuel bristled. *And my Mali.*

"It's part of the game. A game, while my wife . . ." Edward clenched his fists.

Samuel again extended his hand. "I know how you feel, sir."

Hands gripped his shoulders. Shook him. "You don't know anything, you little—"

Grenades exploded in Samuel's brain. "Little what?" He jabbed a finger at Edward. "Go ahead. Say it. I've heard it all. At the orphanage. In school. Nam. Here." Spit showered the air. Good. The man needed a bath. This self-righteous prig had no business judging him when his mother hadn't. He swallowed. Mother. Mali. Man, he was way outta line. Off track. He wiped his face. Prayed, then met slate eyes. "This isn't getting us anywhere. You may not buy this, but I want her out every bit as much as you do." Strange calm captured his tone. "She is my mother, whether you like it or not. I love her. She loves me."

"You listen here—"

"No, you listen. Sheila told me how you saved that man in that balcony . . . heck, you've saved hundreds. Maybe thousands." He took a breath, willed away tears. "I'm just trying to save one, sold into whoredom by her father." Now he was the one crossing his arms. "Her *father*. At age fourteen. A year older than Mother when her world fell apart. Same thing my grandmother—Sheila's mother—had to endure. Have you even bothered to learn about that?"

A dozen emotions flitted across Edward's face, as did hues of pink, red, and gray. From somewhere in the distance, a superior barked orders, soldiers droned responses. A bird twittered. Yet Samuel had no more words. *God, please help me. I can't do this—I can't do anything—alone. Just pray. To You.*

Edward opened his mouth. Closed it. The great pastor, also at a loss for words.

"As I was saying . . ." finally wheezed from him, "two generals, if the good Lord allows it, are on our side. I don't know one of them, but I do know the other, and so does God." The once-fluid voice started and stopped, like a hay-wire engine. "We met when I was a student at Moody, where he traded *The Art of War* for *Systematic Theology*." Edward rubbed his forehead. "Roy's got friends in everything from pagodas to the White House. I pray to God they answer when he knocks—"

"Me, too," whispered Samuel.

"—but even before they answer, we'll be there. I've got a plan, Captain. Insurance, just in case. To save your Mali. My Sheila." His face hardened, then took on a soft cast. "Our Sheila." Edward lumbered a step closer. "Are you in?" he growled.

Samuel surveyed a face that expressed the strangest mix of grief, joy, and peace, then honed in on battleship gray eyes, a determined jaw . . . a hint of a smile. Samuel glimpsed a changed man. And when that changed man extended his hand, with all the strength he could muster, Samuel shook it. And nodded.

Chapter 38

Khank Kow Kin Khluay

A shriek reverberated through smoky fog. Ice-cold fingers gripped her shoulders. Sheila struggled to discern reality from nightmare even as she slogged through a flooded rice field.

Someone—something—whirled her about. It had a huge belly and horrid pinhole eyes. Bells tolled as she wrestled and writhed. *God, save me! In the name of Jesus—*

Slippery fingers burned her flesh. Another creature evanesced like an amoeba. It had glowing red intestines that contracted and expanded, as if taking ghastly breaths. As she watched in horror, her lifeblood began to drain out from her fingertips. A pus-yellow tide that reeked of crude oil seeped closer, closer, infecting her skin, penetrating her pores. She kicked, scoured her arms. *In the name of Jesus, let me be!*

Cackles crescendoed and faded.

Darkness fell. Silence.

She shuddered. Opened her eyes. Ran her hand along the divan fabric. Breathing spurted. She inhaled a greasy turpentine smell. *God, what is real? What is not?* She raised her head.

There stood Khun Sa, looming over her like the remnants of those dream-beings. His eyes absorbed the heat of the sun, whose rays splattered yellows across the room. His knuckles gripped the handle of a large metal can. Gasoline.

With abandon Sheila's eyes roved the room. *Not another fire, Lord!* Breath accelerated; her heart raced to catch up. All the while the old woman sat chewing, chewing. In a room bursting with light, blue-black midnight blazed in the old woman's eyes.

A caldron bubbled. Boiled. She wasn't the crazy one here. She straightened. This man—this house—had no power over God. Despite that horrid dream—it was a dream—it was time to act like she believed Him.

"*Farang* sleep the morning away. Sorry I must disrupt your slumber."

She stretched her lips into a masked smile. Like his. "Whiffs of gas will do that."

"It is your last chance, *farang*. Action must be taken."

Had the fruit bearer forced "action"? Or was it Samuel and his army connections? She gauged pouty cheeks, tight lips. Khun Sa's unhappiness was good news. She wobbled to her feet. Leveled him with a gaze. "You have no control over me, Khun Sa. I will not leave Mali. Do you understand?"

Rage twisted the handsome features so that he looked like one of her nightmare creatures. "No one can stop me. Not *thep*. Not *Ai Narong*." He shook the can. Gas sloshed sickeningly and matched the roiling in Sheila's belly. The Thai words meant nothing. But the smell, the menacing shake of the can, translated perfectly. He meant to start a fire.

"*Ying tee dieow dai nok sorng dtua.*"

Sheila's hands fisted. She itched to shake him! "A gentleman such as yourself would surely translate for a guest in his home," she managed.

"You want translation? I will fire one shot and get two birds." His laugh slithered down her spine. "How do *farangs* say it? Kill two birds with . . . one fire. Khun Sa must repay those who betray him. Besides, it is your karma."

Her mind whirring, Sheila stared at unbridled hate. *The heart is deceitful above all things, and desperately wicked. Who can know it?* As she twisted hands still achy from the earlier handcuffing, an unseen Actor whispered asides. *Nor was a hair of their heads singed.* Was God promising protection like He provided for those Old Testament faithfuls thrown into the fire?

"So you do plan to kill her." *And me.*

"Enough talk." Khun Sa whirled. Clapped his hands. "*Kao ma!*"

Two men dressed like peasants stormed into the room. The old woman scuttled out the door. All Sheila could do was listen to the Spirit whisper Scripture, and wait.

"*Mat mun,*" Khun Sa barked. "*Wie gop ai Mali.*"

They grabbed her, led her into the room that held Mali, and shut the door. A click informed that the door had been locked. At the same time, a curtain to the past parted to show another time, another place: a scared girl named Sheba. A strange smile settled on Sheila's lips. This fire might destroy her body, but it would not destroy her life, safe in the hands of the Unseen Actor, Director, Producer. She could, she *would*, trust Him with that life.

◆

Edward stopped before double glass doors. Faced Samuel. "You sure about going in on this?"

Samuel nodded. "It's a win-win. If Douglas comes through, they'll be on our heels with the backup. If not . . ." *I'm a Marine.* He dropped his head to avoid seeing Edward's pasty skin, thick middle. He shoved open the door. Edward would be fine in the jeep that Hogbody had "borrowed" for them. He couldn't worry about Edward now; the women came first.

"What about your career?" Edward asked.

What about my career? I'm busted. Just because the Horseman will save my mother doesn't mean he'll trump the colonel for me. Samuel battled an image of a nasty letter of reprimand flopping into his permanent record, then shoved away thoughts of possible court martial, the brig. *That's for later. When the women are safe.* "Forget my career. What about Sheila?" he answered. "Mali?"

Though Edward grunted, a hint of a smile crossed his face. They shook hands and walked outside. *Emergencies make strange bedfellows.*

"Beautiful day, huh?" Edward rolled his shoulders and smoothed into their act.

"Perfect." Samuel, prayed that would prove true. His eyes skittered to the parking lot. There they were, just like Edward had said. He squinted, grateful for the cover of aviator shades. Metallic, impenetrable, keeping perceptive Thai soldiers from peering into his soul.

Two topless jeeps idled in the visitor spaces. Four Thai—and four mounted rifles—waited in each vehicle. If his eyes were working, the drivers palmed walkie talkies. Adrenaline shot into high gear. Edward had been right on; more than theology filled that skull.

With their free hands, the drivers drummed steering wheels, ready to roll at Narong's command, according to Edward. But if God willed, they'd reach the women first.

General Na-rong. He mind-played the name, intent on nailing the pronunciation of the man caricatured in Thai newspapers. The man revered by many, despised by many, fortunately not military. Samuel tightened his jaw. Thank God Thai troops idolized the man who'd labored behind the slippery Eastern curtain to negotiate neutrality during World War II. The man who once used Western ties to save the Thais would now use Eastern ties to save *farang*.

With GI precision, he pivoted to face Edward. Barely nodded. Edward *wai-ed*, as they'd planned. The Thais would note Edward's every crook and bend and wonder why Samuel merited such obeisance from an older, distinguished-looking man.

He crisply saluted Edward and began his strides to destiny. *Clomp, clomp.* He forced iron into his limbs, his neck, and his chin. Body language spoke volumes; he needed a *Gunsmoke* walk to pull this off. Two feet from the first jeep, he stopped. Folded his arms. "Where?" He made sure to weight his voice with granite.

Not an eyebrow moved on the Thai masks.

"Where is he?" he shouted, moving only his mouth. "Get it out, man!"

The Thais eyed each other. Muttered. *"Arai wai?"* was all he understood.

He ripped off his shades. Stepped close enough to the first jeep's driver to note a scar under his eye. "Is that all you can do, sit there and mumble *arai wai?* I need Khun Sa's last known address, and I need it now!"

The man clicked on his walkie-talkie. Held it to his mouth.

"What, you can't speak English?" Samuel waved his arms like a lunatic. "Fine! Then give me that." Samuel held out his hand. "I'll tell Narong how you follow orders. You'll be in World War III when Narong is through with you." His eyes burning from sweat, Samuel leaned closer to the jeep. To the men. "Or have you forgotten what Narong did to his detractors in World War II?"

Thai language streamed from the jeep, which creaked from the jostling of bodies and gave Samuel time to whisper a prayer.

The walkie-talkie clicked. Was set down. "You want teak house address?" the driver finally asked.

Teak house. So they were at a teak house. "Yesterday," he snapped. Edward was a genius.

The man scrambled for a pen and paper. Samuel bit back a curse. All those loopy letters. He couldn't read a one, but they didn't need to know that. "No time for paper!" He pounded his fist on the hood of the jeep. "Just spit it out, man! Or I tell Narong."

The driver turned his head. Fixed his eyes on some distant point. "Turnoff one mile from South Pattaya Beach. Gravel road through rice field."

As he nodded, Samuel envisioned the corner where they'd intersected with Khun Sa. Right by the beach exit. With that recollection, the soldier's directions, and a general knowledge of the area, he could find that teak house. *Lord, let them be there,* he prayed. *And let me find them in time.*

A jeep chugged up next to him. Hogbody jumped out. Despite a sunburn, never had his old bunkmate looked so good. "You better get this thing back in one piece." The Texan's scowl belied his soft drawl. They shook hands. "Speaking of pieces, they're in there. Locked and loaded. Now I'm outta here. Don't wanna be anywhere close to your hide when this comes down."

After a nod of thanks, Samuel jumped into the jeep, U-turned out of the lot, and headed toward the gate, stopping only to pick up a very red, very sweaty Edward.

• ◆ •

A new prison. But they can't imprison my soul. A cot piled with blankets and pushed against a back wall had become Sheila's—and Mali's—holding cell. Clothes littered the floor. The room reeked of incense. Candles, statues, a garland of red bows and carnations adorned a dresser. Pretty things in a room where ugly things had been done.

Her hands and feet bound, Mali lay in a huddle near Sheila's feet. Bruised cheekbones and a black eye confirmed what had been done to her. "It's okay, Mali," Sheila said, longing to put her arms around Mali and share the Word until Mali stood firm and tall and bowed to none save the Savior. First they needed to get out of here.

She hurried forward and bent by Mali. "I'm going to untie you." Sheila looked into Mali's vacant eyes and tried to coax expression from them. "Set you free."

Mali shook her head. "Mali no free. Khun Sa my fate."

"No." Sheila shook her head. "He is not your fate." Achy fingers scrambled to untie bindings about Mali's ankles. She played tug of war with the cord, only managing to fray a single cottony thread. "Father God," she whispered, forcing calm into her tone. "Our lives are in Your hands. You are our rock and our salvation."

A breeze slapped wooden blinds against the wall and brought an oily smell into the room. A smell that had spanned an ocean and over twenty years to find her again.

Sheila gagged and doubled over. Saliva roped from her mouth. *God, is this Your will? Must I endure every crackle, spark, and flame as I did before?*

A dreadful moan rose from Mali.

Though the hair on her neck prickled to remember fire's language, Sheila redoubled her efforts to free Mali. "God, be my Deliverer," she whispered as she battled Mali's restraints.

Sounds seeped under the door and seemed to singe the hairs on her arms. Her mouth went dry. Fire, her old enemy, crept closer . . .

"It's okay, Mali." She raised her voice, desperate to drown out the crackle, the snap she knew so well. She closed her eyes, glad that the orange and yellow demons had yet to find her. *But Lord, if You don't do something, they will. Lord—*

The door opened. Tendrils of smoke—and the monk—slipped into the room. He brought his palms together. Bowed. "I bring fruit."

Dry heaves shook Sheila. "Fruit," she managed as she stood and staggered forward. "You came," she kept saying, louder and louder, doing her best to smother the nasty enemy's sounds.

As if she did not exist, the monk floated past her and knelt by Mali, whose face was pale, her eyes wide and empty.

The monk flicked his wrists, which hovered about Mali's hands.

Bindings thudded to the floor.

Another flick, near Mali's feet. More restraints were loosed. Yet Mali did not move. Neither did the monk.

Sheila tried to see past the placid brow, the dreamy gaze. How had he managed to free Mali so quickly? Who was he, beneath the expressionless Thai mask? She did not understand . . . "We—Mali—thank—" She coughed as smoke made its presence known and compelled her to grab hold of Mali and tug her toward the door.

"That is not the way."

Crackles and snaps confirmed his answer. He stood by the window, raising the slatted blinds.

Sun rays haloed his face. "You must go. Now." He motioned Sheila forward.

Sheila nodded. Gripped Mali by the shoulders.

"This time there is a ladder for you, Sheba."

She reeled, in shock. Wobbly knees threatened to buckle. She had not heard right. This man could not know of the balcony. Her past. Her real name.

"You must go." Power infused feathery words. "Your son awaits."

Samuel. She snapped out of a near swoon. "Where is he?"

"He must pass through his own fire. It is his fate." Dark eyes settled on her and cleared her mind. He had freed them. She must trust him . . . or die by fire.

She nodded mutely and led Mali to the window.

"First you climb down. I will help your friend."

She peered into the eyes, needing reassurance. Had Khun Sa yet found a way to triumph? Was this fruit bearer rotten to the core? "She . . . is not well," Sheila protested, though wafting smoke built a case against staying here another moment. Could she trust this man with the woman Samuel loved?

"Blessed are the poor in spirit, for theirs is the kingdom of heaven."

"Blessed are those who mourn," she whispered, "for they will be comforted." As if on a breeze, she drifted to the window, let the words permeate her soul.

Scriptures escaped chattering teeth. Sheila gripped the sill, extended her foot out the window, and rested it on the top rung of the ladder that this man must have provided. She thrust out her other foot and slowly flattened it on a rung. Stretched to find another rung. Pivoted. Grabbed the ladder sides.

"Mali?" Her eyes riveted to the window. "Mali?"

Soothing sounds cut through the smoke, though Sheila could not comprehend the words. "Mali? I'm here," she cried. Surely the man had not tricked her!

The precious pale face appeared at the window. Mali extended one leg, then the other.

"Mali, come. I'm right in front of you," Sheila said, then worked her way down, her eyes never leaving the heel of Mali's foot.

When Mali stepped on the last rung, Sheila pulled her into an embrace, then clasped her hand and half pulled, half dragged her away from the house. God willing, she would not stay to greet the imps of yellow and orange. God willing, she would never see them again.

Chapter 39

Introduction

*M*ove! *Move!* Samuel veered around a water buffalo that had edged off the shoulder and into traffic. The smell of salt, manure, and exhaust slapped his face. He gripped the steering wheel. Every joint in his body ached, but still he prayed, "God. Keep them safe."

Edward, covered with dust, white-knuckled the dash brace and doorframe. Surely praying, though Samuel heard no words. Samuel peeled his eyes for the exit. Found it. Left the highway.

Pavement transitioned to gravel, then rutted mud. Many ruts, in an area where few owned vehicles. Khun Sa's men, fouling the idyllic landscape? He accelerated. When the road detoured into a rice paddy, he followed.

Squawking birds fluttered from shiny puddles. Slush sprayed across the windshield, creating a brown rainbow against a dazzle of blue and green. Samuel swallowed grit.

As the jeep bludgeoned the mud, terraces smoothed into flatland. Samuel let up on the gas, scanned the lush fields. Spotted cumulus puffs of white, gray—a vertical column of smoke. Not clouds. Someone had set a fire. He stomped on the pedal. The wheels spun, then dug in. They lurched forward, Samuel zigzagging tree limbs, stacks of cleared bamboo, an animal carcass. His throat tightened. He could smell the smoke, smell death. *God, don't let it be too late!*

Flames leapt from a rooftop. He searched the horizon for cover. Spotted a lone banyan twenty yards to the east and slammed on the brakes. Pushed open his door. Yanked an M-16 from the rack. Jammed a .45 into the waistband of his pants. Turned to Edward. "You stay here."

"No," boomed from the passenger's seat. "We're in this together."

Samuel gripped Edward's arm. "Exactly. You wait here." He gestured toward the gun rack. "With our friends. They're loaded and ready," he added, assuming Edward had never used a gun. Probably never held a gun. *There's always a first time . . .* "Watch for jeeps. Narong's men." An image of Khun Sa's rat brigade flashed. Samuel's chest tightened. Edward wouldn't know good cops from bad cops. Neither did he. Only God could help them. Hadn't that always been the case? "If you hear a gunshot, follow it."

A frown flitted across Edward's face. Finally he nodded.

Samuel leapt from the jeep.

"I'll be praying," rang in his ears, along with the whooshing of blood. The sun at his back, he paused, his ears pricked for sound, then heel-toed, rotating forward, grateful for soft, soundless earth and stands of palm trees.

Smoke streamed tears from his eyes as he crept closer, closer to a crackling, leaping conflagration. If the women hadn't escaped, they were ashes.

A bush rustled. He froze. Pricked his ears for a squeak, a breath. Any sign of life. Heard more rustles near a footpath. Padded closer, closer.

Sniffle. Rustle.

He panned the area. Eased onto all fours. Crawled through standing water toward a bamboo cluster—and a flash of pink. Lantom flowers . . . or something else? He fought tunnel vision. Crept closer . . . saw a patch of flesh—an arm? "Who goes there?" he hissed, his trigger finger tensed.

Bamboo stalks parted. His field of vision narrowed as his mother . . . his Mali . . . staggered toward him. With every step, beads of muddy water splashed onto a backdrop of green, brown. His heart threatened to explode as he leapt to his feet. He check-pointed his rear, then advanced, desperate to touch Mali's hair, kiss her lips, hold her and never let her go. *Thank You, God. They're—alive!*

Five yards—he seemed to be sloshing through cement.

"Sam-wel!" Hers was the voice of an angel.

"Son! The fruit . . . the monk found you!"

A chill ran up his spine. What was his mother talking about? *God, surely this didn't break her.*

He heard a click.

Samuel's world whirled. He spun. Took a knee to the ground. Stared into the soulless eyes of Khun Sa, who was aiming a pistol slightly to Samuel's left. He shuddered. Fought vertigo. No doubt Mali was in Khun Sa's sights. Samuel dropped his weapon. Heard it thud onto the soft damp ground.

"*Nee sua pa jorakeh.* You have escaped a tiger, only to be eaten by a crocodile."

Mali's cries raked his skin. He clamped down emotions. Forced calm into his limbs. "So now you are a crocodile. And a kidnapper."

Dark eyes glittered. "You call me a kidnapper? She is my property."

"She's not property, you idiot, she's a woman. A woman you've used and abused. She doesn't want you, and you know that, so . . . what? You throw a fit? Burn something down?" He pointed at the house.

Khun Sa tightened his grip on his gun. "Freeze!"

"Or what, pretty boy? You gonna kill us? I've called in the troops, you know."

"Troops won't come for you," Khun Sa said, yet his brow wrinkled. "You're just another problem American GI."

"But they will come for me," came from behind him. It was his mother, her voice hollow, as if her ordeal had burned out fear. "I will tell them you tried to kill us."

"That was your choice, madam," Khun Sa snarled, then hissed, "Mali, come here! Now!"

Her head bowed, Mali padded past; it took every ounce of willpower not to pull her into his arms. If he did, the man who'd apparently tried to incinerate them would surely pull the trigger and wipe them out. Still, he could do something. "Be still, Mali."

Mali teetered and stopped, her bare feet sinking into mud.

"*Ma ha gu!*" Khun Sa pointed his gun at Mali. "Now!"

"Go ahead, coward! Pointing that at a woman." Samuel wiped his mouth.

"Oho! What's that I see at your waist?"

"A handgun. Just part of my uniform."

Khun Sa grinned. "Part of mine, too."

"Yeah, along with your silky shirt, your pretty-boy pants." Samuel spat. Advanced a step. "Why don't you settle it like a man? *Luk pu chai.* You and me, buddy. No guns. Just your fists." He doubled his fists. "My fists."

Samuel caught a blur of white in his peripheral vision. His pulse quickened, his ears pricked. He'd heard no jeep rumbles, no gears grinding. *Lord, let it somehow, some way, be the troops. Not a nosy local.* He forced breaths.

Khun Sa hesitated. "I would not want women subjected to your destruction."

"Why not?" Samuel leered. "You've subjected them to everything else." He stepped closer. "Come on," he taunted. "Come on." He raised his voice, desperate to distract Khun Sa, now that he could see clearly just who was creeping forward. "Fight like a man."

That would be a waste of time. Useless. It is all useless." Khun Sa planted his feet in a shooter's stance.

Footsteps thudded. Khun Sa pivoted.

As Samuel flew to Mali, Edward, gripping the butt of an M-16 like a sledgehammer, slammed it into Khun Sa, who staggered, then fell to the ground.

Edward. *Thank God he didn't listen . . .*

◆ ◆ ◆

As Sheila rushed to Edward, she tripped and fell to her knees. She raised her head, brushed back the tears that impeded her view of Edward. Precious Edward.

Mud and dust tie-dyed his clothes with shades of brown. Gray hair had flattened against his skull. He jogged toward her, his jowls shaking, his eyes bleary, his breath coming in spurts. Her Edward, here in Thailand, with a gun. Had he ever touched a gun? What in heaven's name was happening?

Her limbs trembled, released from the throes of death, so she just sat there in the mud, waiting. He had come for her, in ways beyond her wildest dreams.

"Sheila . . ." Hoarseness captured his voice. He pulled her to her feet. Kissed her hair, her neck, as if oblivious to what three days in hell had done to her appearance. *God, what had she done to him?*

She pulled out of his embrace long enough to find his eyes. "My dear," she whispered, "what have I put you through?"

He crushed into her as if he feared she'd vanish. She closed her eyes. "Edward, I'm so sorry." His shirt muffled her cries, absorbed her tears. She loved this man, needed this man. Why hadn't she helped him come to terms with her past? She'd basked in his safety, his rules, and then resented him when he couldn't adjust to a bombshell of a secret. Could he forgive her?

"Sheila, it's been torture"—he kissed her brow, her eyelids—"without you." Gone was the fluid preacher voice. "Every minute. Every hour."

She had done this to him. "Edward, can you forgive me? I'm so, so sorry."

"No, I'm the sorry one." He lifted her chin, studied her face. "I've neglected you for years. Forgotten how to love you. What a fool I was, letting you come here alone."

She stopped blubbering. Stared into his eyes. "But I wasn't alone. The Spirit, the Comforter whispered Scriptures. And a fruit bearer, a monk . . . Edward, did you arrange for him to rescue us?"

Edward shifted about. His eyes flickered across her face, as if he were trying to make sense out of her words. She couldn't blame him. The incident had seemed surreal. Supernatural. But it wasn't. That monk had led them from the fire!

"How did you find us, Edward?" Her voice shook. She needed to understand.

Whatever had bothered Edward seemed to evaporate like the strange mists in this country. She'd asked a question he could answer. Explanation of the monk would have to wait.

He stroked her hair. Smiled. "As soon as you left Honolulu, I was on the phone. Thank God your Old Horseman came through."

"The General?" Her spirits soared to meet the Thai blue sky. She hadn't been betrayed, she'd been saved!

When he nodded, they broke into crazy laughter, then cried. Despite all of her attempts to play it safe, God had devised the wildest plan for the wildest situation. As she kissed Edward, she scrutinized every wrinkle on his face . . . and rejoiced at the idealistic sparkle that had lain dormant in those fine gray eyes. She glanced at Samuel, at Mali. A dark cloud descended. "What about him, Edward? My *son*?" She nodded toward Samuel and Mali, entwined as one. Whispered, "What about *them*?"

"We'll get through this, Sheila," he finally said. "With me at your side. At his side. Mali, too. It won't be easy, but we'll do it together."

She raised her head. "What about the church? Your plans?"

"You . . . are my wife." The brashness that had boomed from the pulpit for a decade now battled hesitancy . . . and won. Thank God. She needed confidence. Control. She needed Edward.

"He is your son," Edward continued. "If God works out the rest of it, so be it. If not, so be that. Amen."

Fresh tears streamed from her eyes. *God, You've given me the son I never had, the husband I had all along.*

The grinding sound of vehicles joined the whisperings of Edward, of Samuel. "Who—who is it?" She could not withstand another shock.

"The army." Edward kissed her nose. "Don't worry, Sheila. They're on our side."

◆

It's a grand old flag. Patriotic tunes flowed through Sheila as the red, white, and blue rippled in the breeze, spreading warmth matched only by the presence of Edward. An entourage of Thai and American soldiers had escorted them from Pattaya to the massive U.S. embassy here at Wireless Road. As they entered the building, she brushed at her soiled clothes. *As if that'll help.* She'd longed to freshen up, but her belongings were in ashes. Besides, Edward—and Samuel, who hadn't let go of Mali—insisted they finalize paperwork as soon as possible and leave for home. Suddenly dizzy, Sheila leaned against Edward. To think that the two of them had faced off, bitter rivals, less than a week ago. *Only You, God . . .*

They clattered through long halls. Were guided into a massive office dominated by an ornate carved desk and a half-dozen cushioned chairs.

Light flooded the room via multipaned windows. She craved light, after such darkness.

A tall, thin man rose from a seat behind the desk, though Sheila saw little of his features because of the dazzling brightness. But she knew from the nameplate on the desk that the ambassador to Thailand, the key to Mali's future, stood before them.

"Reverend and Mrs. Franklin, Captain Allen, Miss Wattana, we've been expecting you. Please, make yourselves comfortable."

Samuel guided Mali into a chair; Edward did the same for her. Sheila managed a shaky smile. Would the ambassador help Mali? Miss Wattana?

When her eyes adjusted, she saw five men standing near the ambassador's desk. One of the men appeared to be a highly decorated Thai soldier, who was flanked by three Thai. The other two wore American uniforms. One, all bone and sinew, lit up a familiar craggy face with a smile. The Old Horseman lumbered forward to take her hand.

Years fell away as tears flooded her sight. She was back at the Sweet Shop, bringing him tea, wondering why God would call such a man to the ministry. Now she saw that the general's experiences, his clout, enabled him to be used of God. To think she had doubted his intentions. "General," she cried, "how can I ever thank you?"

He patted her shoulder. "No, Sheila. It's me that's indebted to you, both of you." Two strides, and he clapped Edward on the back with such force, Edward winced. "The foundation's kept me young. Alive. At my age, that's saying something."

"General . . ."

"To you, Sheila, it's Fred." He gave her a rare chuckle. "Or the Old Horseman."

An image of the monk flashed into her mind. Surely one of the general's men. "Fred, you saved our lives."

"It was a joint operation, like the best of maneuvers." He pivoted and bowed to a stocky man with a short neck and dark skin. "Sheila, Ed, Captain, Miss Wattana, I want you to meet my old friend, General Narong."

Samuel and the other soldier saluted. Not sure what to do, Sheila stood. Mali leapt to her feet.

When Edward nodded, so did Sheila. But Mali, weeping, fell to her knees, bowed, and brought her hands to her forehead.

General Narong, waving a cigarette held between stout fingers, addressed Mali in crisp Thai. Slowly, she rose and moved to stand beside Sheila, who, with Edward, stepped forward.

Edward thanked General Narong, giving Sheila time to study the man's tinted glasses. Another Thai that was mysterious. Inscrutable. Was the monk one of his men? The longer Sheila studied the powerfully built man, the more convinced she became. General Narong, or one of his soldiers, had served up the "fruit bearer."

General Narong nodded toward Sheila and Edward. "Is this the family you speak of?"

Again the Horseman grinned. "My spiritual family."

"Ah. I am happy for you, friend." The grizzled old soldiers gripped forearms, stared into each others' eyes, and locked gazes as if for them time careened backward.

Finally General Narong pivoted to face Sheila and Edward. "Then you are my family as well."

"I can't thank you enough," burst from Sheila. "Your man saved us."

For an instant, the Thai mask disappeared. Muscles twitched on General Narong's powerful face. "My man?"

"The monk," Sheila whispered.

The general turned to the Thai soldiers. "*Pra Arai?*"

The men shook their heads. By the time the general faced Sheila, his face held a placid grin. "It is your blessing," he murmured.

Sheila matched his smile, though she noted the staccato whispers and narrowed glances of General Narong's soldiers. She'd done something wrong, said something wrong. It had to do with the fruit bearer. Again she needed a course in Thai 101. Or a lesson in international protocol. Until then, she'd better keep quiet.

The ambassador cleared his throat. Returned to his desk. On cue, the soldiers, including her Samuel, sat down. So did Edward, Mali, and Sheila, whose legs had begun to wobble, whose smile had begun to slacken. So much had changed, in such a short time. She longed for stability. Routine. She needed to go home.

"We regret the . . . unfortunate circumstances you've faced." The ambassador spoke in a businesslike tone, as if others awaited his time. "To rectify this, we have cleared Miss Wattana for issuance of a permanent visa. After the requisite physical, which is scheduled for tomorrow, her file will be complete."

Samuel rustled about. "What about the financial verification? The presentation of a marriage license? I was told—"

"Everything has been taken care of, Captain Allen."

"How? When?" her son asked.

"So many questions from your young soldier," came from General Narong.

"It is the younger generation," sighed the Horseman. "But for this one day, we will spoil them, no?"

"They are only children for so long." The generals exchanged secret smiles.

Sheila took in the ruggedly handsome faces, the rows of ribbons and medals, the vastly different physiques, both radiating power. Perhaps she would hear these men's stories one day. Perhaps she would tell hers as well.

The ambassador pushed a file across his desk. "Here are the papers, Captain Allen. Both yours and those of Miss Wattana."

Samuel stumbled to his feet, picked up the folders, and sat back down.

"General Douglas has signed as financial sponsor for Miss Wattana. As such—"

No longer listening, Sheila gripped Edward's hand to keep from sliding onto the floor. To think that the Horseman would do such a thing for Mali! For Samuel! For her!

"That leaves only the question of betrothal."

Despite the curved chair arm between them, Samuel drew Mali close.

"As I understand it, Reverend Franklin, you have found an expatriate here in Thailand authorized to perform a legal and binding civil marriage ceremony."

"I have." Edward boomed. "He will do so after tomorrow's physical."

Sheila buried her face in her hands and let tears of joy fall unimpeded. Another surprise . . . from Edward. She did not deserve this, did not deserve any of this. That was the point. God's grace could not be earned. And who understood His mysterious ways?

Papers were signed. Men saluted, then left. Sheila leaned against her husband and let the sunbeams that streamed through the ambassador's windows hit her full in the face. She thought of the things she had done, the things she had failed to do, and the things she needed to do. *With this man at my side, with You in my heart, Lord, I can be whoever You want me to be.*

• ◆ •

"Captain Allen!" The colonel's nasally voice echoed off the lavish imported tile of the embassy hall.

It was just a matter of time. Samuel gripped his file, touched Mali's arm, gestured toward his mother and Edward. "Could you wait here? It should only take a second." *Right.*

He pivoted and saluted his superior, waiting for cursing to slam into his ears. Mali could leave. Did anything else really matter?

"Looks like the brass and the bass pulled you outta the muck."

Samuel stared down at his paperwork. Surely he didn't mean that they'd overlook his unauthorized trip to Thailand.

"Don't tell me you don't know."

Keep quiet. Don't set him off in front of your family.

"Okay. Play dumb," the colonel hissed. "I'd run you through a blender for your little countryside amble in a truck full of weapons, but apparently I don't have a say, so go ahead with those 'I dos' and get outta here."

A hot tide rose. If he didn't get sleep, food, he might say something he'd regret later.

"Too bad we don't all have a 'spiritual family' to clean up our piles of—"

"Can I be of further assistance? Sir?"

The colonel's face reddened.

Samuel glanced at Mali, pale, unkempt, and ashen. His mother, pale, unkempt, and ashen. "Request permission to leave. Sir."

"I'll give you permission to leave, all right. Come your next leave, don't show your sorry face here, or I'll kick you all the way to Saigon."

Samuel saluted. "I promise, sir, not to return to Thailand." *In uniform.*

Doctor Gradus ad Parnassum

Is Edward there?"

"Yes, of course. One moment." Sheila twirled the telephone cord around her finger. What a difference six months made! Not even Thelma aggravated her now.

As she returned to the kitchen and her newspaper-reading husband, she breathed in the scent of freshly mown grass. September meant open windows, cool breezes. Things she loved about Chicago. She lightened her step, threw her arms about her husband, nibbled on his ear. "It's Thelma," she whispered, after a kiss or two. Another thing she loved about Chicago: men like her Edward.

Groans and rustles of the *Tribune* preceded steps to the study. "Yes, Thelma," she heard him say as she went to the stove, refilled his cup.

He never used to linger over coffee. Now Fridays were morning wonders . . . and afternoon delights.

She tiptoed to his desk, set the cup on a coaster.

Be right there, he mouthed at her, his eyebrows headed for the ceiling. "Uh-huh. It is a concern, Thelma. But Deacon Sites can handle it. As I told you when we got back from Thailand, I'm taking Fridays off." He tapped his fingers, fiddled with his pen.

Sheila suppressed a giggle. Thelma had better be careful, or she might be demoted.

She sashayed back to her kitchen table, nice and cozy with three placemats now. In nine months, she would add another. For Samuel, who would complete his final tour of duty in Vietnam and join Mali in the guest bedroom until they found a place of their own.

For the pure luxury of it, Sheila poured herself another cup of coffee and laced it with thick cream. Maman always said—

Coffee sloshed onto the floor when Edward pulled her into a hug.

"Oops! That's what I get for being romantic."

Sheila giggled. "It's okay. The last thing I want you to do is stop."

He took the cup from her and set it on the table.

"Happy birthday, darling."

She puffed her lips, pretended to pout. "I thought we weren't celebrating until tonight."

"Etienne's," they both said, laughing. Edward now knew everything.

"This time, make the reservation for the Franklins," she continued. Good thing she could joke about it. Good thing *he* could joke about it.

"Speaking of your name, there's a little something else," he said, when they quit laughing. "Just from me."

"Now, Edward. You promised, with the unexpected expenses we incurred on the trip. Helping Mali get settled . . ."

"It's nothing big." He went to the knickknack drawer, pulled out an envelope, and handed it to her.

To: My Precious Wife

She ran her finger along a gold seal, uncertain what this could be. Surprises scared her. And he knew that now.

"Go on. Read it."

She might as well, as she could read nothing in his face. She unfolded the paper.

> My Darling,
> You've added music to my life since the day I first saw you waiting tables in the Sweet Shop. I loved you even before I heard your remarkable story. Contrary to what you feared—and I gave you reason for fear—knowing about your past has only grown that love. May God—and you—forgive me for trying to smother your bold, jazzy spirit.

"Oh, Edward." She had to wipe her eyes to see him.

"There's something else. You didn't see it, I guess."

She dug in the envelope. Found a small rectangle . . . a ticket? She squinted. What in the world?

This coupon is good for one year of clarinet lessons at Chicago Conservatory School of Music. Just call the number listed below. Edward.

P.S. You're registered as Sheba Franklin.

She pulled him close, kissed him, let him lead her to the bedroom. Somehow Thailand had released, not just Mali, but a transport carrier full of legalism and secrets and pretense. Could she really be Sheba? Allow her African-American legacy to shine on the world? Play the rhythms that had been gifted to her from her parents, from the South? Venture back to New Orleans, Edward at her side? Could she allow Sylvia to testify for the sake of girls who crept into makeshift doctor's offices to have their child vacuumed from their body? Could she keep those parts of Sheila that had been disciplined on things pure, right, lovely, and noble?

She pondered the strange things God had shown her, the strange things He hadn't shown her—like who truly had delivered fruit—and whispered a prayer. On her forty-first birthday, Sheba had been reborn. Now that she was going to be a grandmother, it wasn't a moment too late.

Author's Note

On July 8, 2007, I was sipping my morning caffeine fix, my head buried as usual in the *Chicago Tribune*. There was Gail Rosenblum's article based on the story of Sandy Sperrazza and her daughter. Coffee sloshed all over the table . . . and I didn't care. What would it be like to give up your firstborn? How would it feel to meet that baby twenty years later? Though I skimmed the sports and business sections, my heart remained with that unwed teenaged mother in 1960s America.

Later I Googled Sandy, a nationally known adoption advocate, and left a message on her answering machine. A cautious Sandy checked me out and then let memories pour over the phone line. *The Rhythm of Secrets* had been born.

I fictionalized Sandy's story but still drew upon her sojourn in a St. Paul Catholic home for unwed mothers. My protagonist, Sheila, predates Sandy by over a decade. As a tribute to Sandy, Sheila was named "Sylvia" while at the Home, the name given to Sandy during her stay.

One thing I regrettably could not alter in my novel involves the use of the "N" word. Though warned that some readers would for that reason "ban" the book, and though I've been criticized over my use of the word in *What the Bayou Saw*, I stand by my decision to show the history of bigotry in all its ugliness and let literature continue its age-old action as a catalyst to change hearts. Healing and restoration follow only when an honest and frank appraisal of wrongdoing takes place. In an attempt to receive wise counsel on this issue, as in *Bayou*, I consulted many friends and colleagues who have lived with Deep South prejudice. The responses? Unequivocal yeses. Does it pain me to have to use such a word? Of course. But it would pain me more to deny the daily indignities inflicted on people of color during the story's era—injuries, unfortunately, still inflicted today. I did limit the word's use to one scene, where a maid questions the authority of her employer. To omit the word entirely would not portray with any accuracy the racial climate in New Orleans during the 1940s.

From the plethora of research materials accumulated to write *The Rhythm of Secrets*, I particularly want to recognize: *New Orleans in the Thirties* and *New Orleans in the Forties* (Widmer), *Dream of a Thousand Lives: A Sojourn in Thailand* (Connelly), *Child Prostitution in Thailand* (Sorajjakool), *Those Other People* (O'Donnell), *The French Quarter* (Asbury), *Memoirs of a Bangkok Warrior* (Barrett), *Call Him George* (Stuart), and *The Girls Who Went Away: The Hidden History of Women Who Surrendered Children for Adoption in the Decades Before Roe v. Wade* (Fessler).

Dr. Michael White, accomplished New Orleans musician, provided not only an astonishing oral history of jazz music but got a copy of his CD *Dancing in the Sky* into my hands . . . and hopefully into the subtext of this story. I could not have integrated music into the book without the help of musician/teachers Sally Pullen and David Hirst.

I had a ball selecting the music literature, with the help of Sally and David. YouTube links to performances of the pieces are posted on my Web site, www.pattilacy.com. (Regrettably, I had to substitute alternates for the Thai selections as the specific arrangements were not available.) Be inspired, as I was, by the history embodied in the music.

It is my prayer that *Secrets* will make you laugh, cry, think, and most of all, praise the One who, by His sacrifice on the cross, offers the only way to true identity as a child of the Living God. Thank You, Jesus.

Book Discussion Group Questions

1. The book opens with Sheila Franklin, a pastor's wife, getting a mysterious phone call. Has your life been transformed in one second? Share such a time.

2. As in Patti's first two novels, *The Rhythm of Secrets* employs a frame device that links the past and present. Do you like to see two stories unfold at once or do you prefer a more linear approach?

3. The book's settings are instrumental in our heroine's metamorphosis. Discuss things you learned about WWII French Quarter, postwar St. Paul, Moody Bible Institute in Chicago, and the red light districts of Vietnam-era Thailand. In what ways does the heroine change as a result of her setting? Discuss ways your environment influences who you are.

4. How does our heroine Sheila exhibit growth as the story unfolds? How about Edward? Samuel?

5. Patti has threaded "music literature" into the pages of this novel. Discuss ways that music becomes a character in the book.

6. Starting with her first experience at Mimi's New Orleans church, trace Sheila's faith journey. How has your walk with Christ been similar? Different?

7. How has societal treatment of unwed mothers changed since the era when Sheila was sent to the Home in St. Paul? Is it different inside and outside the church?

8. The device of a fire is used during two pivotal scenes in the book to "transform" our main character. Discuss similarities and differences between the two life-changing trials through which Sheba/Sheila walked.

9. A mysterious man confronts Sheila at the teak house. Discuss his role. Do you like the open-ended approach to this character's involvement? Why or why not?

10. Two Vietnam veterans shared their experiences with Patti as she constructed Samuel. Time-travel back to the turbulent '60s. Did this novel evoke feelings or memories of that period?

11. How do the nuns, Miz W, and the Moody girls influence Sheila?

12. Discuss Sheila's conversion experience.

13. Patti drew from real-life incidents—Sandy Sperrazza's memories of her time at a Home, Billy Graham's preaching during Moody's Founder's Week, a gentleman who did attempt to jump from Moody's balcony. Did these scenes seem realistic to you, or did you find even truth hard to believe?

14. Discuss the "so-what" of this novel, the takeaway value, and the themes.